T0128032

# Dark
# Imaginings

## Also by Eric B. Olsen

### Fiction

The Seattle Changes
Death in the Dentist's Chair
Proximal to Murder
Death's Head
If I Should Wake Before I Die

### Non-Fiction

The Intellectual American: Essays
The Films of Jon Garcia: 2009-2013
The Death of Education

# Dark Imaginings

A Novel By
## Eric B. Olsen

authorHOUSE®

*AuthorHouse™*
*1663 Liberty Drive*
*Bloomington, IN 47403*
*www.authorhouse.com*
*Phone: 1 (800) 839-8640*

*Published by AuthorHouse 05/02/2018*

*ISBN: 978-1-5462-3604-7 (sc)*
*ISBN: 978-1-5462-3603-0 (e)*

*Print information available on the last page.*

For my mother,
Karon Lynn Fountain Olsen

# Introduction

Though *Dark Imaginings* was my third novel, it was actually the second novel I began writing. I had started my would-be career as an author by writing horror short stories, all of which are collected in *If I Should Wake Before I Die*, and I had always wanted to return to the genre and write a horror novel. So after taking a few months to edit and prepare my first novel, the medical thriller *Death's Head,* for submission, I finally started in on *Dark Imaginings* and worked on it for about six months. But the failure of my first novel to gain any traction among editors and agents led me to put the book aside and change directions. Because my primary goal at the time was to become a published author I decided to make a serious attempt at writing series murder mysteries with *Proximal to Murder.* It was only while that book was being edited and prepared to submit that I finally returned to finish my horror novel.

I must have already written the bulk of the novel at that point, as I was able to complete the final work on *Dark Imaginings* just a few months after *Proximal to Murder* was finished. But it's clear to me from looking at the content now that I also must have spent a considerable amount of time reworking the ending later by adding in the love interest in an attempt to improve the last third of the book. The one memory I have of beginning the novel that remains vivid to this day is telling my friend Patrick about the story. He laughed and said, "Writers always write about other writers." I'm not sure how prevalent it is in mainstream fiction, but horror writers are certainly drawn to writing about themselves. Stephen King's *The Dark Half, Misery*, and "Secret Window, Secret Garden" spring immediately to mind, as does Peter Straub's *Blue Rose* trilogy that revolves around writer Tim Underhill.

I suppose writers of the supernatural are predisposed to connect the inspirational nature of their work with something otherworldly. One of my favorite anecdotes of Stephen King's is when he saw what was purported to be H.P. Lovecraft's pillow in a pawnshop window and he had the idea of writing a story about a writer who bought it and, after sleeping on it, began to experience in his dreams what Lovecraft wrote about in his stories. The thought was too terrifying even for King to consider writing. The idea for my novel probably began with the fairly clichéd notion of a copycat killer who wanted to make an author's stories come true, but actually occurred in the supernatural realm. Though the King novels mentioned above no doubt loomed large in terms of inspiration, it's difficult for me to recall precisely where the original idea came from after all these years. In truth, the novel is something of a lost book for me.

*Dark Imaginings* was the first novel that I finished on my own. A large portion of it had been edited by my wife at the time, but we separated somewhere near the end of writing the manuscript. So in addition to divorce and dating and finding a new place to live, that's probably the reason that I didn't even begin writing my next novel for another nine months after this one was finished. The editing process was not something I was used to doing alone. In addition, reworking the ending must have occupied a good portion of my time as well. But the thing is, I can't remember ever submitting it to an agent or editor once I finally had a polished copy. My best recollection is that once I was completely finished with the manuscript I still believed my best hope for being published was continuing on with my dental mystery series.

The most fascinating thing for me in looking back at the novel now, is how closely it mirrored my life at the time: trying to be a writer, the breakup of my marriage, meeting someone new, and even having two sons years later. Nearly everything, with the exception of the supernatural elements, was drawn from life. Most of the names used in the story are variations on the names of people I grew up with or who were working with me in my job at the bookstore. The character of Don Holman was based on one of my dad's best friends, and the Rainier Tower where he works was chosen because of its memorable appearance in *The Changeling* with George C. Scott. Something else I discovered in reading the manuscript was another one of my ubiquitous references to Steven Spielberg's *Jaws*, with the boat that Giles charters at the end of the story named for Robert Shaw. At times it feels almost painfully intimate to read, and yet no one else could possibly understand all of those associations. Which is the way it should be.

Another aspect of my writing that really stood out for me on editing the manuscript was my clear intention to create a completely interconnected fictional world in all of my novels. Not only does Daniel Lasky from the first two novels turn up, but so does Janet Raymond. And, of course, both Paige and Giles Barrett would appear in my next book, *Death in the Dentist's Chair*. The detectives Dalton and Haggerty were characters that had appeared—along with Lasky—in the horror novel *Blood Hunt* that Patrick and I had tried to write together. And finally, Camilo Serafin, who has a small cameo in this book, appears in a major role in my last mystery novel, *The Seattle Changes*.

This is also the first appearance of my fictionalized hometown, Hallowell, Washington, the mirror image of Hoquiam, Washington, but located on the southern side of Grays Harbor rather than the north. The name of the town was actually an incredibly obscure homage to Stephen King. I can remember being fascinated that King had chosen the name Castle Rock for the fictional Maine town that much of his early work revolved around, because there was a Castle Rock in Washington State, a few miles north of the Columbia River in the southern part of the state. I wanted to choose the name of a town in Maine for my fictional Washington world, but I also wanted the homage to be pointed. Looking up the name Castle Rock in the atlas I could see that there were dozens of towns and places with that name in the country. What I wanted to do was choose a place name in Maine that wasn't used anywhere else in the U.S. Hallowell also had the benefit of beginning with the same letter as my hometown and contained the same number of syllables.

I remember reading about King fans who would pore over his novels to figure out where the settings in Castle Rock were in their actual locations around Maine. My thought was, when I hit it big and became a published author that my own fans would one day figure out the connection between Hallowell and Stephen King. Clearly, that didn't happen. Interestingly, after finishing the second book in my dental mystery series, I had plans to revisit Hallowell and set an entire novel there. The book was another work of horror called *Screaming Room Only*, a Lovecraftian tale about a haunted movie theater, inspired by King's "The Library Policeman." That book featured a female protagonist and was fully outlined, but I only made it a few chapters in before I decided to put my literary aspirations on hold to become a teacher.

The title of this novel was one that I had come up with on my own, but later I took a look through *Books In Print*—the physical books, back before the Internet—and discovered that there was already one other book titled *Dark Imaginings*. It was a collection of fantasy stories written by Robert H. Boyer from 1978. I remember tracking down a copy of the book at one point though I never actually read it, as I was never a big fan of fantasy fiction. Ultimately the book was obscure enough that I didn't feel there would be any problem in using that title, and since there hasn't been another book published with that title since, I feel even better about it now.

One of the questions I've had on revising all the previous works in this series is whether or not to update the settings. That wasn't an issue on this book because of the two different timelines, where the second part of the book takes place twenty years after the first. At the time I had to imagine what the future might be like and try to make some predictions in regard to technology that turned out to be well off the mark. Although I do remember Patrick enjoying the fact that in the second half of the book I have a character driving around a Geo Metro, a car that had only recently begun production the year I finished the manuscript. Since the car is now defunct I was tempted to change it, but instead I find that it speaks to the economic circumstances of the character and his care and skill in keeping a car like that running. Twenty-five years later, of course, it's the second half of the book that is set in the present. Updating that part of the story was fairly delightful because I didn't have to guess about anything, and now that section of the book is a lot more accurate because of it.

Of all the books in the series I have probably enjoyed revising this one the most because I was so unfamiliar with it after all these year. Overall, I'm very happy with the results. If there's a major flaw it's something I didn't really consider at the time it was written, and only became apparent to me after watching, of all things, the film *Be Cool*, the sequel to *Get Shorty*. Both of those films are about finding undiscovered talent, but they could not be more different in their outcomes. *Get Shorty* revolves around an unproduced screenplay called *Mr. Lovejoy*. Everyone in the film says how great it is and the audience is able to suspend its disbelief fairly easily because they obviously can't read it. But *Be Cool* is a film about music, and the audience can hear the talented female singer for themselves. With shows like *The Voice* and *American Idol* on television viewers have heard hundreds of girls over the years who can do the same thing. So when everyone in that film gushes about how great she is—while the audience can hear that she's just like everyone else—it doesn't work.

The sections of my novel that are purportedly the stories that Giles Barrett writes were never really intended to represent the actual stories themselves—which was why I never italicized them the way that conceit would normally be done in print. Instead, they are supposed to be the visions that he has that in turn provide the inspiration for the stories he actually does write—stories that are obviously much better than the scenes I present in the book. But there's no way for the reader to know that and so their natural assumption is going to be that those vignettes in my novel are supposed to represent the great works of horror fiction that Giles is so well known for. And in the same way, that doesn't work either.

Another bit of credulity straining comes with the turnaround time for Giles' stories when they appear in print in the horror magazines he writes for. It can typically take a year or more for a story to be published, as magazines generally work well ahead into the future when it comes to fiction. My only thought at the time was that his popularity would have induced editors to simply make space in their newest issue, something that happens to Stephen King on a regular basis. But in the interest of compressing time it was also something that I felt I needed to do, especially since the plot hinges on that particular aspect of the author's work.

Despite my best efforts, the novel proceeds at a fairly leisurely pace, which seems to be the case with all of my novels. While I've always professed an affinity for plotting, it's clear that my real emphasis back then was on character. Except for the end of each half of the novel, all of the real horrors happen offstage. I think what I was trying to do was follow something Stephen King once wrote to explain H.P. Lovecraft's writing style—that the reader will always imagine something more horrible than the writer can ever write. And in that sense, the horrific scenes of terror that a writer slaves over will usually produce something like relief in the reader rather than the desired effect of outright terror, because the reader was actually imagining something far more horrifying.

Unlike the other novels in the series, this book has no additional short work at the end. The reason is twofold. First, all of my other short horror fiction has already been collected in *If I Should Wake Before I Die*; and second, this is the longest of my novels and so I felt it was able to stand alone. While I haven't read a horror novel in twenty years, and have no idea what the modern trends are, I still stand by this work as something I would enjoy reading myself—however out of step it may be with current sensibilities. In the end, that was the real reason I started writing fiction in the first place, to tell stories that I would enjoy reading, with the hope that others would enjoy them as well—a hope I also have for readers of *Dark Imaginings*.

Eric B. Olsen
March 14, 2018

# PART ONE

# It's Always Darkest Before the Dawn

Present fears
Are less than horrible imaginings.

—William Shakespeare
*Macbeth*

# Chapter One

. . . Leather boots echoed softly on the pavement of the sidewalk. The city at night was quiet. Street lamps flooded the way, but Doug Boyd walked through the yellow pools of light oblivious to everything. He was on his way to make a sale.

Doug walked everywhere these days, or rode the bus when he could cough up the fare. The heels of his boots had worn down on the outside edge from his slightly pigeon-toed gait, but he was oblivious to that as well. He hadn't driven since his nineteenth birthday when he plowed into that black dude. He still couldn't remember anything from that night except that he'd been drunk, stoned out of his mind, and had his license revoked. Oh, and that he killed the guy. So, now he walked.

Doug's hair was light brown, long and stringy, and he wore several earrings on each ear—an array of studs, dangling crosses and death's heads. His hands were thrust deep into the pockets of black leather pants that had seen better days. In his right hand he could feel the last five bucks he had to his name, and with his left he alternately caressed his Zippo lighter, warm from his own body heat, and scratched his balls.

The pulls on the zippers that crisscrossed Doug's scuffed black leather jacket jangled like spurs with his every step. One pocket held a hard-pack of Camel straights with two left inside. Another held slips of paper that he used as I.D. when he needed it. In yet another was a switchblade that he had probably killed a kid with—he hadn't stayed around long enough to find out that time. But the real treasure was in his inside breast pocket, nestled up against the Iron Maiden T-shirt he was wearing: two plastic baggies, each with an ounce of gooey bud rolled up inside. Two longshoremen, regular customers, were waiting to meet him at a tavern where they routinely did business. After the sale he could finally afford to eat.

Doug was walking north through the southern end of town, and the domed stadium nearby was dark. Too bad. Lots of sports fans liked to smoke a little reefer after the game. And since they usually didn't have a clue how much to pay for it, he could make a bundle and still keep a quarter for himself.

He continued on toward downtown where the action was, turning corners and cutting through alleys. He could walk through here at night because the downtown district wasn't predominantly black, just your basic junkies, whores and punks, nothing a white boy from Spokane couldn't handle.

But when Doug rounded another corner he stopped, and no one could blame him either. She was long-legged and big-bosomed, with tight clothes, high heels and lots of makeup. Gorgeous, but not the kind of girl you took home to meet the folks, not without a deposit anyway.

"What's shaking?" he said.

"Hey, baby, you wanna party?" she asked, in a voice that sounded so much like every other whore's he thought they must all take lessons from the same teacher.

"Sure. How about a blowjob?"

"What's in it for me?" she said, her voice suddenly slipping from cloying and seductive to throaty and street-wise.

"Five bucks."

She laughed and that made him smile. He said that to all the working girls. Most of them just got pissed off, but he liked it when they laughed. "I think you got the wrong girl, baby."

"What's your name?" he asked, finally walking up close to her.

"Pamela. What's yours?"

"Boyd."

They stood silently for a minute, looking each other over. Her hair was red, but she didn't have one of those freckly faces. No, she was straight from the pages of *Playboy* or *Penthouse.* Her nipples were hard beneath the thin white tube top she was wearing. "You cold?" he asked, almost interested in her answer.

"I'm all right. You got anything else to offer me besides that stupid grin on your face?"

Doug kept smiling. "I got some nice dope. We could smoke it back at your place."

She laughed again. "And where would that be?"

"Wherever you want it to be."

She motioned with her head toward the alley and winked at Doug. "C'mon over here," she said. "Show me what you got."

He followed her into the alley, his eyes fixated on the swing of her ass. When she turned to him it was dark, and he didn't notice the slivers of white resting on her lower lip.

She was leaning back against a dirty brick wall, the smell of garbage wafting from the open Dumpsters surrounding them. She pulled him toward her and latched onto his mouth, her tongue probing deep inside. Doug pushed his erection against her belly and cupped a breast in his hand while she ran her hand up the back of his neck, entwining her fingers in his hair.

When she jerked his head back, Doug found himself staring into her eyes. They were black and cold and he began to shiver. They were deep and endless and he wanted nothing more that to crawl inside them, curl up into a ball and die. With all of his strength he forced his eyes to snap shut. He had felt his will draining from his body before, but now he could feel it coming back.

He struggled for a moment to free himself from her grasp and then went for his knife. The moment it clicked open he felt his body being lifted off the ground and slammed into the wall on the other side of the alley. The knife clattered away from him and he slumped to the ground, but he would not open his eyes. He *could* not open his eyes; if he looked into hers again he might not

Eric B. Olsen

be able to resist this time. He tried to crawl away but she grabbed hold of his hair again and pinned him to the ground.

She had been foolish to throw him, but she couldn't control her anger any longer. The fact that he'd been able to close his eyes at all had shocked her so much that she hadn't been paying attention when he reached for his knife. And now here she was wrestling with him like a mugger. She felt the anger swell again. She could have crushed his head with one hand but she resisted, pinning him instead to the ground, her left hand planted firmly on his chest. If he wasn't going to look at her of his own free will then she would have to help him along.

The fingers of her right hand slowly mutated while he squirmed beneath her left. Her nails became razor sharp and she reached down, carefully slicing off one of his eyelids. He screamed as she did the same to his other eye, and even though blood washed down over his exposed eyeballs, she was able to look into his eyes and capture his mind with hers.

The screaming stopped a few moments later, and when she tilted his head back he offered his veins to her willingly. Blood flowed freely from the gash in his neck she had made with her teeth, and she fed unhurriedly, savoring the coppery-tasting liquid as it slipped down her throat.

But once her thirst had been slaked she was dismayed to find that he was still alive. She stood up next to him, looking at the tiny rivulets of blood running down his neck, and placed the spiked heel of her shoe over his left eye. When she pushed down a satisfied smile turned up the corners of her blood-drenched mouth as she heard the distinctive pop.

Slowly, she walked around his head and placed her heel over his right eye, this time feeling a warm jet of clear liquid splash against her leg. Finally, she straddled him, her heel poised over his forehead, and drove the spike into his brain. Finished now, she disappeared up the side of the building . . .

Don Holman smiled and nodded as he turned the last page

of the manuscript. He removed his glasses and set them on the desk in front of him as he pinched the bridge of his nose between his thumb and forefinger. "That was a nice story, Giles. I know a couple of magazines I can call right now. I should have a check for you in a few weeks.

Giles Barrett was standing at the large picture window in his agent's office, lost in thought, looking off at the blue-gray expanse of Puget Sound. Don's voice brought him back to the present but he didn't want to return just yet and studied the city of Seattle below him one last time, from the Kingdome in the south to the Space Needle in the north.

Finally, Giles pulled himself from the view and walked back to the couch at the left of Don's desk. "Thanks, Don," he said, still distracted, and sat down heavily.

"All right, what's on your mind? You've been pacing around here all morning."

Giles took the opportunity to lie back full on the couch, his legs stretched out and his arms behind his head, and the thought that talking to Don seemed more like analysis than business ran through his mind. "I've written enough short fiction, Don. I want to try my hand at a novel."

"Sounds good to me. I could play half a dozen publishing houses off against each other. With your reputation and popularity, the bidding could be very competitive."

A long silence ensued, and both men were reluctant to say what was on their minds: maybe Giles would never write a novel. He had begun seriously more times than he cared to remember, always starting out strong for a week, two tops, before sputtering out and, in despair, turning his first couple of chapters into another short story.

Then he would bring it to his agent at the Rainier Tower, one of Seattle's high-rise office buildings, and Don would tell him how great it was. Then Giles would go on to bemoan the fact that he still hadn't written a novel, and the whole thing would begin again.

"I'm serious this time, Don." But Giles said that every time, too. Strike analysis, this was more like theater than therapy.

Don nodded, his face taking on a look of genuine concern.

Giles sat back up. "I'm tired of being known as a short-story writer. There's no money in it. I want something more to show for myself than a bunch of stories in magazines that no one's ever heard of."

"Plenty of authors write short fiction—"

"Mainstream fiction, sure. By *my* stuff's never going to wind up in *The New Yorker* or *Harper's*."

Don was smiling now, a big-toothed grin that always put Giles at ease. He was a well-dressed man, who, at fifty-one, was sixteen years older than Giles. He had a high, intelligent forehead and deep set brown eyes, framed by a helmet of brown hair. Don represented about ten other Northwest authors—he certainly wasn't making a living off of Giles' work—as well as actors, painters, and musicians. But aside from being his agent, Don was also one of his best friends. "That's because you write horror, Giles. Lots of other horror writers started this way. Just look at—"

"Clive Barker. I know, I know."

"The comparison is more than justified. Barker published short fiction for years before he wrote his first novel. As soon as *Damnation Game* was published, that was it. Now he's Steven King's heir apparent.

"You write circles around those guys, Giles, and the public knows it. You've put more life into the old monsters than they ever had in the first place. Werewolves, vampires, mummies—they've all been so exploited over the years that none of the younger authors want to touch them for fear of being called derivative and unimaginative.

"The problem is the public still loves them. And you know how to do them justice. There's a reverence in your work that people can see, that they can feel when they read it. Why do you think a Giles Barrett story sells twice as many magazines as anyone else's?

"I think it's great you want to write a novel. Believe me, no one would be happier about it than I would. So why don't you take some time off and just do it? Instead of writing short fiction, write long."

Giles sighed. "It's not that easy, Don. Sometimes I think I don't have any control over what I write. I get ideas but they never last more than twenty pages."

Don was leaning back in the big leather chair behind his desk, legs crossed. "Okay. How about this? You're doing fine with the short stuff—you're getting top dollar for each story—so why sweat it? Seriously, Giles, I think you put too much pressure on yourself to produce. Every time you start a novel, it's like you want to finish it over the weekend. And when Monday comes and it's not done . . . so what?"

Giles was nodding, deep in thought. "I want to try again."

Don laughed, a hearty, endearing laugh.

"What?" asked Giles in mock irritation.

"Nothing. What do you have for me this time?"

Giles brought forth from his briefcase the outline that he had worked on the night before. The ideas had coalesced in his mind just as he was nodding off to sleep. He had immediately run down to his office, switched on the light, and spent two hours writing it out before turning in with satisfaction. Now he handed Don the sheaf of yellow legal paper and sat back, watching the reaction on his face as he read.

"It's better than anything in the genre," Don said as he straightened the sheets of paper and handed them back to Giles. "But then I say that every time I read one of your outlines."

"I'm going to do it this time, though," said Giles, bolstered by Don's comment.

"Excellent," said Don, pointing to Giles' manuscript on the desktop. "And in the meantime, I'll take care of this and get back to you."

The two men stood up, their discussion at an end, and walked to the door.

"I'm looking forward to reading the novel," Don said, pumping Giles' hand.

"Thanks, Don."

Down on the street the cool wind tousled Giles' hair. Even in May Seattle was cold. Giles buttoned his coat and walked briskly toward his car on the next block.

He was really going to do it this time; he could feel it. The elusive novel would finally become a reality. Giles had made a firm resolution last night that every minute at his computer would be spent on the novel. No distractions. A few months of concentrated effort and he would be on the best-seller list.

Giles clutched his briefcase to his chest and ran the last few yards to his car.

# Chapter Two

That afternoon Giles sat down at his computer and typed out eight pages of good, clean prose. As he went over it a second time, proofreading on the screen, he was almost giddy with excitement. The beginning was perfect. The atmosphere was dark and foreboding, and his characters, even at this early stage seemed exceptionally well thought out.

He had the outline propped up in front of him at the desk but he hadn't looked at it once. Giles could see the entire story in his mind like a parade viewed from the air. As he wrote, the story simply unfolded, snaking through his mind, and for the first time in years he was really excited about writing.

Behind his desk was a file drawer full of false starts and half finished ideas. He didn't know why he kept them; all they did was depress him. The years of incomplete projects looming behind him as he worked were a constant reminder of his self-imposed failure. But maybe it really *was* behind him now.

When he had first begun to write, in college, he believed that the most important thing for him to do was complete a project. There was no use launching into the Herculean task of a novel, so he began with short stories, and for the most part it was the right decision. The exhilaration he felt as he zipped the last page of a finished story out of his typewriter was better than sex—well, almost better. And it seemed to him that at last he had found a vocation.

He sold that first story to the college literary magazine.

Sort of. Payment came in the form of contributor copies. He sent dozens of them out to his friends and relatives and received some encouraging comments from the few people on campus who had actually read it, most notably the man who had made it all possible: Don Holman.

At the time Don was a comparative literature professor at the University of Washington, and Giles had happened upon his class in fulfilling requirements for his history major. The class was an overview of the horror tradition in literature beginning with Horace Walpole's *The Castle of Otranto* and ending with *The Case of Charles Dexter Ward* by H. P. Lovecraft. Giles had always loved horror movies, but there were never enough good ones. Don's class opened up a whole new world of fictional terrors that delighted and inspired him.

One day Don kept Giles after class. He said he was impressed with Giles' test essays and asked him if he had ever written fiction. Giles' answer was no, but he immediately went back to his apartment and began a story about an entity that returned every fifty years to a rural road in Chicago to kill someone.

He took those few rough pages to Don the next day but was disappointed in his subdued reaction. Don gave him some useful criticism, though, and over the next few weeks guided and encouraged him. By the end of the course he told Giles that he should submit the story to *The Quarterly.*

Once he became a published author it was one story after another, every one a study in horror and dark fantasy. By his senior year Giles had published no less than six stories in small-press magazines that specialized in horror fiction. Even with that success though, he couldn't seem to break into the professional magazines—the ones that paid money for stories.

The April prior to graduation, Giles was talking with Don in the HUB about his troubles and Don confided that years ago, after finishing graduate school, he had exhaustively sought to publish something of his own: his doctorial dissertation on the works of H.P. Lovecraft. He was just about to give up when a small press finally gave him the go-ahead. Don didn't make any money on the deal, but at least his book was in print. He told Giles that a few years later, the editor of the publishing house had quit to start up his own magazine called *Dark Imaginings.*

Don's one phone call to that editor was all it had taken to launch two careers. Before long Giles was being regularly published and receiving two to three hundred dollars a story. A year and a half later, on the strength of an outline and a strong recommendation by the editor of *Dark Imaginings*, Giles was offered a book contract. The Holman Agency, with Don as its sole associate, entered into negotiations with a New York publisher and garnered a five-thousand-dollar advance for Giles.

And that was when the trouble began. Thank God Giles hadn't spent the whole five grand. After six months of gazing blankly at the paper in his typewriter Giles had managed to write only twenty-five pages. He couldn't seem to find the right voice, the right atmosphere, the right words. Before he knew it the first two deadlines had gone by, and then the extension. Finally, the publisher asked for the money back. Giles sold his new car and borrowed another thousand from his mom and dad to pay back the advance. Eventually he repaid his folks, but his ego never recovered.

During the next six months Giles drank himself into oblivion. He more or less quit writing in order to barhop full time. At one point he even picked up his typewriter and hurled it through the window of his second-floor apartment in a drunken fit. The sidewalk below lay strewn with glass, broken keys, and black-and-red two-toned ribbon. Luckily, no one had been walking beneath the window at the time.

It seemed ironic to think about now, but it was one of those bars he was hopping to all the time that started him writing again. That was where he saw the man. He was dressed entirely in black sitting in a booth in the corner. It was dim in the bar and his face seemed to float above the table. He sat alone, steely-eyed and evil looking, neither smoking nor drinking, and seemed to be gazing intently at a group of women at another table.

It was eerie. Giles thought he looked like a vampire, and a

story began to take shape in his mind right there at his stool. He tossed the last of his money on the counter, not even finishing his drink, and wrote out a twenty-page story in longhand that night. Six months later, with Don as his agent, it was published in *Playboy* and Giles was a thousand dollars richer.

But in his heart of hearts, Giles knew that he really wanted to be a novelist. To his way of thinking that was what a successful author did: he wrote books. A smile came to his face now as he pushed himself away from his desk. He was finally at the end of a ten-year rut. He was going to write that novel.

Giles switched on his laser printer and checked the paper, then typed a few commands on the keyboard. While the printer was doing its thing, he walked upstairs to the kitchen and removed a cold Guinness from the fridge. It was celebration time. He fished in one of the drawers for an opener, pried off the lid, and took a long pull, letting the sweet aftertaste linger in his mouth until he heard the printer shut off. Then he took another sip and headed back down to his office.

Giles stretched out on the couch across from his desk with the hardcopy and began to read. He was only about halfway through when, above him, he heard Paige pull into the driveway. The garage door began its arduous grind open and the distinctive throb of the Peugeot's motor idled into the garage and then abruptly ceased.

He hopped off the couch and ran up the stairs, past the front door landing, and up into the living room. When Paige came in through the kitchen door, wearing an emerald green pantsuit that made her look drop-dead gorgeous, Giles was there to greet her with a kiss. She looked at the bottle in his hand and the grin on his face and set down her briefcase.

"Well, you're either drunk or celebrating. Which is it?"

The grin got bigger. "I'm writing a novel."

Paige had made a move to take off her coat but she stopped. Silence ensued.

"Don't worry," he said, his hand going up defensively. "I just had a good day."

Giles took the last couple of swigs from the bottle and set it on the counter next to the sink. He watched appreciatively as Paige slowly removed her suit jacket. She was five-eight in her heels with a smooth round face and a body to match. She looked incredibly sexy in the silk blouse she was wearing.

"So Don liked your story?"

He held out his hands. What's not to like?"

She smiled, then, the smile that had made him fall in love the first time he'd seen her. Moving to take her in his arms, they kissed passionately. This time when they finished he kept her pressed tight against him. Feeling her body through the sheer material of her blouse and slacks made him smile, then he let her slip away.

"How was your day?" he asked.

"Fine. I had to see a couple of Marcy's patients this afternoon because she wanted to leave early. She and Butch are going to the beach for the weekend."

"It's still going to be pretty cold out there, isn't it?"

"That's what I said, but she told me she wasn't planning on spending much time outside the hotel room."

They laughed together, a married laugh, shared humor that made him feel closer to her than he had ever felt with anyone else. He watched her body move as she walked easily around the counter. First she took a glass from the cupboard, followed by a bottle of Evian from the fridge. She poured the glass three-quarters full and replaced the bottle.

Then she picked up the glass, leaving her briefcase on the table and her coat hanging off the back of a chair, and began to walk out of the kitchen.

"I can't wait to get out of these clothes," she said, still walking.

Giles followed her as she took a sip of water. "Mind if I watch?" he asked.

She stopped in the hall and looked back at him, the corners of her mouth turned up in that smile. "I was kind of hoping you'd help."

*Eric B. Olsen*

\*     \*     \*

Paige Barrett luxuriated in the feeling of Giles' body snuggled up next to her, his hand running slowly across her bare stomach. She loved having sex with him, and though it was not as frenetic as it had been when they were dating—all of six months—it was infinitely better. For Paige, it was the reason a person got married. And though their lovemaking might have become somewhat predictable over the last ten years she didn't think that ecstasy could ever be monotonous.

She rolled up onto him and hugged him tightly, then looked into his eyes and kissed him on the mouth. "I'm hungry."

He smiled at her and said, "Great. I bought a new pasta I want to try tonight."

She rolled back off of him and watched as he padded naked into the bathroom. Then she propped herself up on a pillow and began to think. Was he really going to try another novel? The thought at once excited and terrified her.

He was such a passionate writer; sometimes it seemed he loved writing more than he loved her. When his work was going well and things were coming together, there was no one more pleasurable to be around. Conversely, when he felt blocked, he was more like one of the monsters in his stories.

It had been, what, two or three years since he'd started the last novel? Would the drinking start again if he couldn't finish this time? God, she hoped not. She didn't really know if Giles was an alcoholic or not; she wasn't sure he knew himself. He went through a six-pack of beer every couple of weeks and sometimes he had wine with dinner, but it never appeared as though it would be a struggle for him to stop. He didn't seem to crave it. And yet, when he couldn't write . . .

She remembered the last book he tried to write, about zombies roaming around a remote part of British Columbia. He almost tore his hair out once he'd reached the third chapter, and when he finally gave up he'd gone on a three-week bender. Every night she

16

had dreaded coming home from work. He was never abusive to her, though, just drunk, self-destructive, wallowing in self-pity.

She'd thought about leaving him then—not seriously considering it, just imagining what her life would be like without him. She'd thought about what it would be like to be on her own again, to be with someone else, to have sex with someone else. But in the end that's all they were: just thoughts. The only thing they had accomplished was to make her sad, so she put them out of her mind and decided to wait it out. Eventually, he snapped out of it.

She remembered the day, too. They had gone to the grocery store one Saturday morning, ostensibly to get food but she had a feeling it was to replenish his dwindling stock of beer. While they were there Giles had become obsessed with a woman who was pushing her child through the aisles in a shopping cart. The woman was very nondescript and Paige could no longer remember anything about her, except that Giles couldn't seem to take his eyes off her the entire time they were there. He didn't buy any booze that day, and as they were carrying the bags to the car he said to her, "I think I have an idea for a story." And that was it—back to the Giles she knew and loved.

The toilet flushed and Giles emerged from the bathroom, slipping on a pair of sweatpants and a flannel shirt that had been hanging over the back of a chair. "I'm going out to start dinner," he said. "Are you taking a shower?"

She nodded. She always took a shower after work.

"Okay," he said, walking over to the bed to kiss her. "See you in a little bit."

She watched him leave the room and listened for a while to the sound of pots and pans as he worked in the kitchen. Page was a little reluctant to leave the warmth of the bed but she pushed herself up anyway and walked into the bathroom. After starting the water she stretched languidly in front of the mirror.

Her blonde hair was cut short, to keep it out of her way when she worked. She liked how it framed her face, but she also liked the face it framed. The lines that had begun to creep up on her years ago were now firmly entrenched; she was thirty-eight and she looked it. And that was okay with her.

Paige had never been one to obsess about her figure or her looks. She wore little makeup, and sometimes not even that. It wasn't that she was militant about going against the tide of female expectations, it's just that she had a lot more important things to do than spend and hour in front of a mirror with a curling iron and a tube of lipstick every morning.

Looking down at her legs she smiled. The angle of the light exposed the fuzz that her blonde hair normally camouflaged, revealing that she hadn't shaved her legs in a while. Then she raised her arms and smiled at the stubble on her armpits too. Again, she wasn't making a statement, but during the winter what was the point? She wasn't going to be going sleeveless, and if she decided to wear a dress the next day she could always take care of it the night before.

Then she remembered back to an old boyfriend commenting on her apparent lack of "feminine hygiene" and her telling him flatly that if he didn't like hairy legs he should shave his own. That had been their last date. She certainly hadn't been offended at the time, and the whole thing amused her now. In the end it wasn't something she gave a lot of thought to, and apparently neither did Giles; if he had, they probably wouldn't be together today.

The mirror clouded up with steam and Paige stepped into the shower thinking about the first time they'd met. She was in her fourth year of dental school at the University of Washington, and working in the dental clinic there. God, he'd looked young; he still did. Even at thirty-five he could pass for someone ten years younger.

He had come in to get a filling and she'd taken very good care of him. His response to her attentiveness was positive and at one point, while she was making conversation, she asked him if he was still in school. Naturally, she had meant high school, but when he said that he had graduated from the UW the year before she was quite surprised, as well as interested. She copied down his phone number from the file, called him up that night, and by the next weekend they'd had their first date.

Six months later she had passed her state boards, was a full-fledged dentist, and was married to a writer. There were two other women in her graduating class with whom she had become good friends in dental school. The three of them had talked about working together after graduation and during their senior year they all took out hefty loans and leased some prime office space near the Elliott Bay Medical Center in the Magnolia District of Seattle.

Jeanette's dad, it turned out, was loaded and was able to give her the money interest-free. Paige didn't think Jeanette was a very good dentist, having a penchant for pushing crowns instead of trying to fix teeth. But the result of her lazy work was that she was able to see more patients than either Paige or Marcy. So as long as her patients didn't complain, and bottom-lines being what they were, there was precious little left to say on the matter.

Paige shut off the water and toweled quickly; she didn't want to be late for dinner. Giles prepared most of their meals, as well as doing most of the housework. She had never asked him to, but things had sort of evolved that way, and that left their evenings free to enjoy each other. Finished drying, she slipped on a robe and into some slippers and followed the smell of cooking food.

✦ ✦ ✦ ✦ ✦ ✦ ✦

A smile appeared on Paige's lips even before she had opened her eyes. It was Saturday. Oh, how she loved the weekends. No patients to see, no schedules to keep, no high-speed drill whining in her ear all day long. God, it was glorious.

Her memories of the night before, the delicious dinner Giles had made, the incredible sex—they always made love more when he was writing—faded into the smell of fresh coffee and the faint clacking of keys on a computer. Giles was always up early on Saturday and Sunday mornings, writing until noon, sometimes later. Afterward, they would go out for a late breakfast in the University District, and then off to haunt the used bookstores in the area.

Paige sat up and stretched. Giles had laid the morning paper at the foot of the bed for her and she reached out and pulled it to her. A look at the clock told her it was eight-thirty; another half-hour and he would be bringing in a hot cup of coffee for her. After she was through with the paper Paige would stay in bed, deeply engrossed in one of the half-dozen novels she was reading simultaneously. Weekend mornings while Giles was writing was the only time she had for pleasure reading and she relished it. At noon he would be back up here and they would shower together and spend the rest of the day bumming around.

The Barrett's split-level home was located in Shoreline, just north of Seattle below the Snohomish County line. In the upper section of the house, in addition to the two bedrooms, were the kitchen and the living-dining room area. Downstairs in the lower level were the laundry room, library, and Giles' office. Saturday morning Giles was busily hammering away at his computer. At his elbow was a steaming cup of coffee that would probably be tepid before he got around to taking another sip.

That was the way it had always been. Giles only worked half-days on the weekends so that he could spend the rest of the day with Page, but he usually got more work done then than he did on the weekdays. Today was no exception. He had finished up the first chapter of the novel and was a good ways into the second. Next week things would slow down to a normal pace, the excitement of the new project having worn off, and he would wade into the more tedious task of rewrites and adjustments to the outline. But for now he was happy to let his newfound inspiration run rampant.

A few minutes before nine he finished the paragraph he was working on and walked upstairs to the kitchen to warm up his coffee. He was wearing a pair of black sweat pants and a faded gray sweatshirt with "Miskatonic University" emblazoned across the front. The tile was cold as Giles stepped onto the floor with his bare feet and he warmed one foot on the top of the other as he stood at the sink.

He dumped his cold coffee down the drain and poured himself

a fresh cup, then leaned back against the counter and looked out the kitchen window as he took a sip. It was raining, in typical Northwest fashion, somewhere between a drizzle and a downpour. He tipped the mug to his lips again and took another sip.

They had bought this house as soon as they were married and really had no desire to move anywhere else. It was open and well lit, and even though it had plenty of windows they had decided to add a couple more when they moved in. They paid through the nose for heating during the winter, but the extra light was well worth it. The house had grown with them through the years and had come to be almost a third party in their relationship.

He and Paige didn't do much socializing, preferring each other's company. They also kept their other obligations to a bare minimum. Giles hadn't decided to get married so that he and his wife could be off doing separate things when they weren't working. That was one of the reasons he was glad Paige was a dentist instead of an MD. She worked regular hours, Monday through Friday, dental emergencies tending to be a few and far between.

They had talked about children early on and decided to postpone indefinitely. Now it looked like indefinitely was going to turn into permanently. But Giles felt no remorse, and if Paige did she didn't show it. In a way, they were too greedy to share their lives with anyone else. They both had their careers, and they had each other. There just didn't seem to be room for anyone else, so it was probably for the best.

Giles opened up the cupboard and pulled out a white mug that said "Dentists Do It In Your Mouth." It was a gag gift that one of the other dentists she worked with had given her. Paige claimed to hate it, but Giles noticed that it always seemed to work its way into the dishwasher and then back up to the cupboard.

He sighed and smiled to himself. We have a good life, he thought, now that I have a book to write. Then he filled Paige's mug three-quarters full of steaming coffee and headed off for the bedroom.

# Chapter Three

It only took until Wednesday for the well to run dry. Sunday Giles had resisted the urge to rewrite the first chapter, but by Monday afternoon he had given in. Tuesday was wasted on reworking the beginning of Chapter Two and today he hadn't been able to pick it back up at all. It was happening again.

The vision of a solitary basketball player at the foul line came to his mind. There's no time left on the clock and his team is down by one point. All the other players have been corralled away from the key by the referee as he dribbles the ball. With each bounce the player's face becomes clearer: it's Giles himself. The bleachers are full of people stomping their feet and screaming at the top of their lungs. But beneath the shouts Giles can hear it, pulsing in his ears, the faint chant of, "Choke! Choke! Choke!" One last bounce of the ball. Then he pulls the ball to his chest, sweat beading off his face, bends his knees and tosses an air ball.

A buzzer sounded and Giles nearly jumped out of his chair; the clothes in the dryer were done. He stood and walked the few feet to the laundry room next to his office. All day long he had been doing things around the house—anything to avoid working on the novel—and this was the last of it. The house was spotless.

Giles had finished folding the clothes and was about to take them upstairs when he heard Paige pulling in. Gratefully, he stopped and exited his word-processing program and turned off the computer. Only thirty pages and he had hit the wall. Damn.

He met Paige as she came out of the kitchen. "Hi," she said, heading down the hall toward their bedroom. "How'd it go today?"

Giles followed her with an armload of laundry. "I got a lot of work done."

"That's terrific."

"Unfortunately, none of it was on the book."

"Well, if it's any consolation, the kitchen looks great."

"Thanks a lot," he said, feigning indignation as he plopped the clothes down on the bed.

Paige walked over to him and hugged him and then they kissed. "Are you going to be all right?"

"You mean, am I going to start drinking again?" She was about to deny it but he cut her off. "No. I think I've just been a little too hard on myself."

"I've been telling you that for years."

Giles chuckled and began to put the clothes away while Paige undressed. "Yeah, well, you know me. If I can't get it done in a weekend, I don't want to do it at all."

They finished at the same time and Giles watched Paige walk into the bathroom naked. Then he sat down on the bed at leaned back on the pillows as he heard her climb into the shower. He had closed his eyes and was letting the sound of the water lull him to sleep when the feeling came over him.

Giles opened his eyes and continued to lay on the bed for a minute, thinking it might pass, but it only continued to get stronger. He stood and walked to the dresser, searching for something to write with. Finding a stub of pencil, he jotted down a note on the back of a stray charge slip telling Paige that he had left and would be back as soon as he could. That was all he could really tell her because that was all he knew himself.

Giles took out a flannel-lined windbreaker from the hall closet and left through the front door, still in his sweats and tennis shoes. The feeling assaulted him again as he was heading for the garage, causing him to about-face and walk down the driveway toward the street. He checked the pocket of his coat and miraculously found three one-dollar bills folded up around a grocery receipt.

He would need them for fare. The feeling had been quite clear on that point; Giles would be riding the bus tonight.

When Paige stepped out of the shower she yelled for Giles but he didn't answer. He was probably in the kitchen making dinner, she thought, or hoped. Still dripping, she went into the bedroom draped in a towel and almost instantly her eyes were drawn to the slip of paper at the edge of the dresser. She read it and knew that it might be midnight before he came home again.

She sat down on the bed, not minding that the spread would get wet, letting the towel slide to the floor and her face fall into her hands. Paige wept. The sadness that had been creeping into her ever since Giles told her on Friday that he was working on a novel now came out in great sobs. It wasn't Giles' leaving that caused her tears, but because she was finally alone she could release her pent-up emotions.

The tears weren't from a lack of faith on her part; Paige would have given anything to have Giles finish a book. It went much deeper than that. She knew it was a bad thing to think, especially because of all he meant to her—he was a wonderful writer and she loved to read his stories—but she truly believed that he would never be able to write a novel.

She brushed strands of wet hair away from her face and went to her closet to put on a robe. The sadness was still there, but she had a handle on it now. She walked out into the kitchen and pulled open the refrigerator to count the beer bottles. He hadn't had any today. She saw tonight's dinner inside and shut the door; she wasn't hungry.

The newspaper was on the kitchen table and Paige took it with her back to the bedroom. She would read it and then try to get some sleep, knowing that it wouldn't be possible until she heard Giles come in the front door.

Giles felt as if he were being propelled down the street. Two blocks south of the house he took a left onto 145th and headed toward Aurora. When he crested the small hill and could see the streetlights, he broke into a run; he would be late if he didn't. He was a block away when he saw the familiar yellow and brown of the Metro bus as it pulled up to the stoplight. It sat idling noisily at the crosswalk. Giles quickened his pace. He was still half a block away when the bus pulled into the intersection and then out of sight. He was at once terrified that the bus would not stop and yet somehow confident that it would.

He rounded the corner to the beeping of a wheelchair being lowered to street level by the lift. Giles slowed and caught his breath, reaching the bus with time to spare. When the lift had retracted he stepped inside, stuffed a dollar in the fare box, and walked to the back of the bus.

It was still rush hour and the bus was fairly full. He found an empty seat on one of the benches that ran parallel beneath the side windows in the rear, and relaxed. Around him was a microcosm of the city. There were men and women in business suits, leather-clad teenagers, all races—Hispanics, Asians, blacks and whites—in everything from overcoats and galoshes to T-shirts and shorts.

The feeling was not as strong now, but it was still there in the pit of his stomach as he looked at each of the passengers. On the opposite side of the bus, directly in front of him, sat a teenage couple, nearly sexually indistinguishable in their Mohawks and black lipstick. To the left of them was a plump businessman in a light raincoat, his briefcase in his lap and a relaxed, easygoing look on his face.

Against the back end of the bus, to Giles' right, sat a black man in jeans and sweatshirt who had the most intense look of boredom on his face that Giles had ever seen. Next to him were two women: one was rather obese with white hair and a flowered dress that was straining at the seams; the other was Hispanic, with black hair and dark eyes. In her lap was a small child, a girl no more than a year old, and in the seat beside her was a small boy. The boy was three or four at most, happily swinging his legs out and banging his heels against the floorboard, and irritating the hell out of the man sitting next to Giles.

The man to his right was old and had a three-day growth of

gray hair on his chin. He was squirming in his seat and looked as if he were ready to strangle the kid who was banging his feet. On Giles' left were a couple of college students with backpacks in their laps; the boy had his head back, eyes closed and mouth open, sleeping, and the girl had a book splayed open, reading.

The feeling was still there, in his stomach, waiting. With stops every couple of blocks, red lights, and rush-hour traffic, a ten-mile bus trip in Seattle could easily take three hours. He had to hand it to the Metro drivers, though. Driving in town always left him tense and frustrated; he couldn't even imagine doing it in a bus.

During the next hour of the jerking, spasmodic bus ride, people came and went. With each new arrival and departure Giles studied them, and the feeling stayed the same. But now, somewhere east of Ballard, it was growing with a vengeance. Someone rang the bell-pull lighting up a square red sign by the driver that said STOP. A block later, the bus pulled up to the curb.

This was it. Giles could barely contain himself. He was watching the door, looking to see who was getting on, when he heard a grunt from behind him. It was the fat woman with white hair, hefting herself up on her stout legs. And then he knew.


. . . Gisele Kummer had one more transfer to make before she would be home. The German deli up at the Alderwood Mall was the only place she could get a decent loaf of black bread, and even though she had to take two different buses to get there, it was worth it. She just couldn't bring herself to bake anymore.

Back when Emil was still alive she had baked nearly every day. She had made breakfast for him in the mornings, cleaned the house and washed his clothes while he was at work, and always had his dinner waiting when he came home from the paper plant. Three years ago he'd died of emphysema.

It had started with a nagging cough, and even though he'd refused to quit smoking, she had never said a word. He was the head of the house and it was her job to take care of him until he died, just as it was his job to see that she was provided for when he was gone. After a particularly severe coughing attack, during which she had called an ambulance to rush him to the hospital, Emil had returned home with a bottle of oxygen. He would have to breathe pure oxygen through a thin tube beneath his nose for the rest of his life, the doctors said. They had been right.

He had retired only a few years before, and in addition to his pension they were both eligible for social security. It wasn't too much longer before Emil had become bedridden and dropped down to just over one hundred pounds. She would have to lift him out of bed in the morning and set him in the tub to bathe him. During the day, when he had to go to the bathroom, she would pick him up, carry him in, and set him on the pot.

She was taking him back to the bedroom one day when his head lolled over onto her bosom and a surprisingly large amount of saliva poured out of his mouth onto her blouse. After setting him back down on the bed, she walked over to the phone and called another ambulance. She sat calmly in the living room sipping a cup of coffee until they arrived.

He hadn't left her rich, of course, but he had been a good husband. Gisele had first met him in a Bellingham hotel where she was working as kitchen help, newly arrived from Germany in 1946. It was the only work that she could get. Emil, a second generation German, was making a delivery from an Alaskan fishing boat that had just put into port. Over the course of the next two years she saw him three more times. It was on the third time that he proposed and she said yes. A few years later, when Emil had found a job at a new paper plant that was opening in Seattle, they had moved.

Gisele stepped off the bus and sat on the covered bench to await her transfer. A man who had been sitting in the back had come off right behind her and stood just a few yards away. He was looking at her. In one of her beefy arms she cradled her bag of bread, and with the other she clutched her purse. She was a large woman, but there was no shame in that; she was German after all. Her mother and grandmother had been bigger.

The next bus came and she flashed the driver her green

transfer slip as she stepped on, walking to the back of the bus because the benches were easier to sit on than the small, forward-facing seats. The man who had been watching her had followed her onto the bus, and now he was walking back toward her. There were only a few other people onboard yet he chose to sit right across from her. Well, she was damned if she was going to let him intimidate her. She scowled at him and then turned her attention toward the front of the bus.

Gisele Kummer had come to her American Dream by way of Bergen-Belsen, a transfer camp located fifty kilometers east of Bremen. It was originally designed as a holding area where Jews coming from the West were placed until their transport to Auschwitz. Gisele was just out of school in 1942 with very few prospects for marriage, the war having taken most of the eligible men from the small town of Belsen. She had gone out to the camp to look for work, been asked to join the Wermacht as a formality and been assigned to the children's camp.

Until the end of the war her work had been fun, caring for and feeding the little children, getting them ready for their trip. But when the trains stopped going east and the Jews from the camps in Poland began flooding back into Belsen, things became chaotic. Commandant Kramer had been sent in from Auschwitz along with thousands of sick and starving prisoners. A typhus epidemic soon broke out, there was not enough food, and still more and more prisoners kept coming in.

By the spring of 1945 the food had simply run out. Hundreds of prisoners were starving to death every day, and what with the epidemic and the shortage of German labor the prisoners were told they would be fed according to how many bodies they could haul out to the burial pits each day. Of course they were not fed; she could not even feed her children and it made her sad when they began to die of starvation.

Finally, the British came. They took over the camp and, to her intense disbelief, they actually made Gisele and the other Germans move the dead bodies, forcing them at gunpoint to touch diseased and decaying carcasses. She had always wondered why they had gone to such lengths; the prisoners were dead already.

She had been beautiful back then, big-busted and shapely. Her hair was blonde and her lips red, and her tight uniform made her feel womanly. She'd had sex with several of the German officers, even married ones, but her flirtations with the British were only rebuffed. They humiliated her instead.

After her imprisonment, when they could find no evidence of her being involved in any "war crimes," she was released and, rather than stay in her guilt-ridden country, she immigrated to America.

At last the bus approached her neighborhood and Gisele reached around to pull the cord above the window. The man across from her was still staring. When the bus slowed to a stop she stood and walked to the front, thanking the driver as she stepped off. The door closed behind her as she turned left and began walking ahead of the bus, glad that she only had a few blocks to go before she would be home.

The bus began to pull away from the curb and then stopped suddenly. Gisele quickened her step. She heard the door open and close and then watched as the bus drove past her. She did not want to turn around. She heard the other set of footsteps behind her and knew who it must be.

Why was he following her? She had no money. Rape? She certainly wasn't beautiful anymore, though she still couldn't get over this society's definition of beauty: thin girls with no tits or shape of any kind. They reminded her more of the prisoners at Belsen than objects of desire.

She crossed the first intersection; one more to go. She risked a look back and confirmed that it was him. What in God's name could he want? She sped up again, walking as fast as her chubby legs would carry her.

The last intersection. Middle of the next block. She fished for her keys in her purse, feeling a layer of sweat form beneath her skin and the snug fabric of her dress. At last her house was in sight. She could hear him behind her, closer. He couldn't know where she lived, but if she broke out into a run at this point he would probably reach the front door before she did.

She held the key firmly in her hand, closing in on the front walk, and when she reached it she turned onto it and ran. The key slid home on the first try and, putting all her weight behind the door when she'd stepped inside, she slammed it shut. Gisele then locked the door and headed for the kitchen.

She was almost angry with herself for being afraid and, after she had set her bag on the counter, allowed herself a brief smile.

A loud boom at the door made her twist her head around in fright. Instantly, she picked the receiver up off the wall phone and dialed 911 just as the door boomed again. A recording answered and put her on hold, so she hung up. The door boomed a third time and she reached for a big kitchen knife over the breadbox just as she heard the front door breaking in. If the goddamn police won't take care of this, she thought, I'll do it myself.

She squeezed her large frame next to the kitchen door and held the knife high. She heard footsteps and the tinkle of glass as he broke something in the living room. But she had left the kitchen light on; she wanted him to come this way. It's going to be a bloody mess, she thought, because she didn't plan on stopping until the *Schweinhund* was dead.

As the man stepped into the kitchen Gisele stabbed at him with the knife. But before she knew what happened he had one hand around her wrist, the point of the blade halting inches from his chest, and his other around her throat. He squeezed her wrist but she wouldn't let go of the knife. When he squeezed her throat, she did. The knife clattered to the floor and she groped wildly with her free hand, her forgotten purse still swinging from her elbow.

She caught him in the face with her fingers and raked her nails across his cheek, but instead of flesh, a rubber mask came off in her hand and she froze. That face—it wasn't human, and yet she was sure she had seen it somewhere before. He wasn't a *Schwarze*, but his skin was brown, and his hair was the exact same color. It was as though he were made of clay, and yet his features were animated. His nostrils flared and muscles rippled beneath his forehead and she could see his brown teeth and tongue between lips of the same color.

He threw her to the floor and her hands went to her throat in spite of the pain in her body. A moment later he was on top of her, leaning in to her and staring with lifeless brown eyes, his clay-colored hair falling in his face. Then, from out of his collar fell a medallion, a gold Star of David suspended from a chain around his neck, and she knew.

The Golem was on top of her now and he reached for the knife, his other hand firmly around her throat. When he placed the knife underneath her dress between her legs she began to scream, but he didn't try to stop her. Her screams could never make up for the millions who had died in the gas chambers. He slit her dress open and then tore it off.

The rolls of flesh shook as she screamed and cried. He cut the material between the cups of her bra and her large, shapeless breasts spilled out. With a single yank, her underwear was torn from her hips.

He looked down at her naked body and felt nothing. She scratched and clawed at his face but he felt nothing physically, either. He was simply doing what he must do, what must be done. They all must die.

He pushed the knife into the folds of flesh above her snow-white pubic hair and ran the blade up to just beneath her ribs. Blood welled from the wound, spilling over onto the floor, running down between her legs, and up onto her chest. She was screaming louder now, her legs kicking against the floor, one shoe still on.

Then the Golem dropped the knife and pushed his free hand into the thick layer of yellow capillaried fat beneath her skin. More blood flowed as his fingers moved aside intestine, stomach and liver. When he reached the diaphragm he had to thrust his hand hard to puncture it. She had stopped screaming then, or had passed out. He worked his hand in further until he touched her beating heart, his fingers encircling it, feeling the muscle contracting rhythmically in his palm. He looked at her face and saw that her eyes were only half shut, pink tongue poking through her bared teeth, and then he squeezed her heart in his giant hand until it popped . . .

"Hey, buddy, this is the end of the line. You're gonna have to get off now."

Giles was suddenly awakened from his trance. He looked around and noticed that he was the only one on the bus. A glance at his watch told him that it was already nine-thirty, but the last thing he remembered was the woman getting off the bus.

He stood and walked to the front holding out another dollar.

"Can I pay another fare?" he asked the driver.

"This is the end of the line, buddy. I head back to the bus barn from here."

"Will you be going near Aurora by any chance? I'll be glad to pay you."

"I'm afraid it's gonna take a lot more than a buck. They can fine me a hundred if I get caught making an extra stop, and it looks like you're about ninety nine short."

The driver was a thin, sandy-haired man in his thirties, with the name Michael embroidered on a white patch on his Metro uniform. Giles fingered the remaining dollar in his pocket and gave the driver his best looks of desperation. "They won't hear about it from me."

The driver sighed. "Ah, what the hell. Keep your money. Just make sure you stay hunkered down in the seat behind me."

"Yeah, that's fine."

"In about ten minutes I'm gonna stop a block from Aurora and I won't have time for any long goodbyes. You got that?"

"Sure. Say, do you have a pencil or something?"

The driver wrinkled his nose at Giles and finally dug in his shirt pocket and handed him a ballpoint pen. "I need that back before you get off."

"No problem. Thank you."

As the bus pulled out Giles picked up a scrap of paper from the floor, brushed off the dirty design of a sneaker sole and began writing the first lines of his new story.

# Chapter Four

The alarm clock went off at six a.m. and Paige swung her arm over to hit the snooze button, gaining herself another ten minutes of wakeful sleep. Next to her she could hear Giles breathing heavily. He had come home around eleven and gone directly downstairs to work. She had no idea when he had come to bed but she had been able to nod off shortly after midnight.

Paige guessed that he was back to writing short stories, because his episodes—that was what she called them—were always followed by a flurry of productivity. It was his Muse, she thought. There was no other explanation for it, at least none that he had given her. She had asked him several times in the past what he did when he was gone. He had told her that it was nothing, that he would simply wander around aimlessly for a while. Sometimes he would get an idea for a story, and sometimes he wouldn't. Although she couldn't really remember a time when he'd come up empty, she was sure there must have been some. Eventually, she had stopped asking. She just hoped he was past the stage of grieving for the book and could continue to focus on his other work.

Paige's dreamy thoughts vanished as the alarm began to buzz again. She turned it off this time and committed herself to getting up.

When Giles hadn't moved by the time she was finished dressing, Paige felt too depressed to make coffee and decided to stop at Starbucks on her way to work.

\*     \*     \*

Giles didn't wake up until shortly after noon. For a moment he wasn't sure where he was until the memories of the night before came flooding back to him. He rubbed his face in his hands and yawned. Paige was gone. After hauling himself out of bed, he pulled on his sweats and plodded out to the kitchen to make the coffee.

As the machine gurgled the brown ambrosial liquid into the pot, Giles's thoughts turned to his writing. He had gone downstairs the night before with the slip of paper from the bus containing the notes he had written, and churned out thirty pages of rough draft. Whatever it was that had compelled him to write had evidently been sated.

Outside, patches of fast-moving clouds drifted beneath an otherwise blue sky. The warmth of the sun was tempered by gusty winds that could be seen in the limbs of the trees. When the coffee was done he poured himself a cup and walked downstairs to the library.

This was the one place in the world that could make Giles happy just by being there. Looking over his books and thinking of all the stories, people, and lives that were captured in their pages worked like a tonic on him. Thinking of the men and women who had labored to produce whole other worlds, or struggled to explain their own, inspired him. And God knew he could use a little of that inspiration now.

As he opened the door ten oak bookcases, each seven feet tall, lined the sides of the walls of what he and Paige had briefly considered turning into a guest room. The division was nearly fifty-fifty between non-fiction and fiction. On the left-hand wall as he entered were two cases devoted entirely to World War II studies, followed by a case of general history, American history and Northwest history. The last two cases were fairly diverse, with shelves containing books on law, medicine, the occult, political science, philosophy, and biographies.

Beneath the half-windows at the end of the room that looked

out onto the back yard were four smaller cases with books on film studies, fully half of those devoted to horror films. And against the right-hand wall were five cases of fiction.

In the first case were the classics—Giles' favorites being the complete works of Hemingway—along with mysteries, science fiction, espionage, and war fiction. There were plays and short-story collections, paperbacks and hardcovers in equal mix, and he had to admit that most of them had gone unread. Someday he hoped to get around to reading as many of his books as he could.

The middle three cases contained nothing but horror fiction. He had the standards: King, Barker, Strieber, Rice, Levin, and, a personal favorite of his, Peter Straub. He also had the classics, everything from Walpole and "Monk" Lewis to Stoker and Shelly to Lovecraft and Jackson. There were also a myriad of genre paperbacks that he had collected over the years, the good as well as the bad.

The last case was Paige's: fiction by Anne Tyler, John Irving and Larry McMurtry, as well as nearly everything by the science fiction author John Wyndham, and some non-fiction titles—none of which Giles had the desire to read.

In the middle of the room were two wing chairs, each with a matching ottoman, separated by a table with a reading lamp in the center. Giles walked around the room for a few minutes, thinking that he might like to read something, but then he walked back out again and into his office. He really needed to work. Next to his desk was a single oak bookcase containing a complete set of the Encyclopedia Britannica as well as all of his dictionaries, etymology books and English handbooks.

Giles sat in his chair and leaned back, not bothering to turn on his computer just yet. He needed time to think about this. He had written his thirty-second story last night; what bothered him was that it was the second time in only a few weeks that he had written under the influence of the . . . Christ, he thought, the only word he could think of was *possession.*

Considering he usually wrote only three or four stories a year as a result of the possession, Giles never really thought too much about it. But now . . . Would he continue at this pace? Would he be able to write on his own at all?

He shook off the thought and sat up to his computer. After turning it on and calling up the story, he sat back and looked at the first page as it glowed on the screen. Rough draft he had called it earlier. That was a laugh. Whenever he wrote a story in the throes of his possession he never had to change a word. He stared at it a few minutes more, then fired up the laser printer and printed it out.

When Giles was done leafing through the pages he looked up at the clock and saw that it was already one. He reached past his mug—half full of cold coffee—for the phone, and put in a call to his agent.

"What a coincidence," said Don, his boisterous voice spilling out of the receiver. "I was just about to call you. What did you need to talk to me about?"

"No," said Giles. "You first."

"Well, I got a call this morning from Catherine over at *Dark Imaginings* just about five minutes after I sold the vampire story . . . to a different magazine. Anyway, she's doing some sort of special issue and she wanted to know if you had a piece you'd like to contribute. I was just wondering if you might have something in the hopper you're working on, or maybe a date I could give her . . ."

"As a matter of fact, I finished up something last night that should work just fine."

"Are you serious?"

"Yep." Giles smiled. He wasn't known for being able to produce on demand, and in light of the finished product sitting on his desk Don's tactful approach with him seemed amusing.

"That's great. I'm going to call her as soon as I get off the phone with you."

"Do you want me to bring it over today?"

"No, I'll send over someone from the office to pick it up and fax it to her this afternoon. Will you be home?"

"The rest of the day."

"That's great. Well, I'm going to get on this thing and get it taken care of. If you need anything else just give me a call, okay?"

"Sure. I'll talk to you later, Don."

When they had both hung up Giles shook his head and smiled. Don hadn't even asked him what he had called about. Giles supposed it didn't really matter, though. Maybe for once he ought to try and work through his problems without Don to hold his hand.

He put the story in a Manila envelope, picked up his mug and then made the trek upstairs. At the landing he dropped off the envelope on the table by the front door and then continued on up into the kitchen.

He set his mug on the counter and grabbed the handle of the coffee pot, intending to refill it, but simply left it there. He was thinking of the novel. He had more than just run into a brick wall, with its connotation of somehow working around it. No, he knew that the novel was dead, stillborn, and nothing he could do would bring it back to life. Somewhere in the dark recesses of his broken heart he knew he would never write another word on it.

Giles released his grip on the coffee pot and hesitated only a moment before opening the fridge and pulling out a beer.

Oh, no, Paige thought as she reached into the refrigerator for the Evian. Two empty six-pack cartons sat chilling quietly on the bottom shelf. She pulled them out, folding and stuffing them into the recycle bin under the sink before pouring her water. Giles hadn't met her in the kitchen, which was a sure sign that things were going from bad to worse.

She tried not to panic, but it was difficult. She loved him with all her heart, but she didn't adapt well to change. For Paige, pleasure was the avoidance of pain, and one way to make sure that she could get the most pleasure out of her life was to always have things the way she liked them. Whether it was her favorite shampoo or toothpaste, or the restaurant they went to on the weekends, if it was always the same she knew she would never be disappointed.

Another way to achieve pleasure was to simply schedule pain out. With no obligations besides work, no bridge club, no tennis lessons, no church on Sunday, she could do whatever she wanted with her free time, which consisted mainly of being with Giles.

Paige didn't like things to intrude on, or interrupt, her daily routine. Like it or not, she made the money in this family and she felt some pressure in that knowledge. Mortgage payments, car payments, utilities, and credit cards were ultimately her responsibility. She did not begrudge Giles; the fact was simply there and as long as it was going to be, she preferred the rest of her life to run as smoothly as possible.

Most of the time it worked. When it didn't, ironically, it was usually because of Giles. He could be unpredictably moody, swinging between highs and lows so fast that she sometimes felt left behind. She knew that there was no malice in what he did but it had a profound effect on her all the same. It could happen anywhere, driving in the car, shopping at the grocery store, going out for dinner. He might speak to her angrily or glare at her, and though it was nothing but a momentary outburst for him, Paige found it difficult to recover as quickly as he did.

She took a deep breath, her chest hitching as she sighed. Damn it, she told herself, don't start crying now. She took another drink of water and noticed the red light flashing on the answering machine. For a second she wondered if Giles was gone, but of course his car was in the garage when she pulled in, though that wasn't always a guarantee. She walked over to the phone and pushed the message button.

"Hey, Giles . . ."

She recognized Don's voice immediately.

". . . looks like we got our wires crossed somewhere this afternoon. I sent someone over to pick that story up but there was no one home. Don't sweat it, though. I called Catherine back and gave her the good news. She's excited to read it. I just wanted to let you know. I'll call you tomorrow and we can get things sorted out then. Talk to you later."

The machine beeped, rewound the tape, and reset automatically. Paige pressed the save button so that Giles could listen to it later, finished her water and then walked out into the living room.

The coffee table in front of the couch was littered with empty beer bottles and the TV was on but the sound was muted. Giles was sprawled out on the sofa asleep. His mouth was open and a barely audible snore registered every time he inhaled. Paige didn't know what to do. If he was still drunk . . . She shook her head, not even wanting to think about that possibility, and turned for the bedroom. Maybe if he heard her in the shower he would wake up and sort things out before they had a chance to argue about it.

As the hot water steamed up the bathroom and she stripped out of her clothes, Paige felt herself on the verge of tears again. God, she hated that. There was nothing to cry about—not yet anyway—and here she was having to fight with herself not to. Her chest felt tight and the back of her throat burned as she stepped into the shower.

When Paige returned to the living room she was wearing only her bathrobe. Giles was sitting up on the couch, head in his hands.

"Hi," she said warily, trying to gauge his mood. When he didn't answer she ventured a question. "What's for dinner?"

"I give up," he said, looking up at her. There was no anger in his eyes, but there didn't have to be to let her know what was coming. "What are you making us?"

"Come on, Giles, don't do this. Not tonight."

"Pardon me. I didn't know there was a better night . . ."

She was scared now. "You know what I mean. Please, I don't want to fight—"

"Then leave me alone."

Paige stood silently, looking at her husband and feeling pained. If there was anything she could do right now to help him she would gladly do it. Why was he being so unreasonable? Why couldn't he—why wouldn't he confide in her? If he would only tell her what was bothering him . . . "What's wrong, Giles? Is it something about last night? Did something happen? Is it something I did?"

"Look, just leave me alone, okay?" He leaned back now, arms crossed on his chest, eyes staring blankly at the television.

"I just want to know why you're upset."

"I don't want to talk about it."

"Can't you see I'm worried about—"

"Jesus Christ," he said. He didn't shout it, but he didn't need to, as Paige flinched anyway. "If I want to listen to your scintillating conversation I'll ask for it. Until then, just leave . . . me . . . alone!" On the last part he finally raised his voice, and Paige was glad, because it broke the spell.

Her fear had turned to anger but it didn't stop the tears, and when she felt them come she let them. She almost couldn't believe what she was feeling. Along with the anger, sadness, and worry, was an emotion she never thought she would know. She had loved Giles more than she could love any man, giving everything of herself to him. But as she stood there looking at him she was almost more frightened by her own thoughts than she was about their fight. At that moment, the only thing Paige felt toward her husband was hatred.

# Chapter Five

June had been a dismal month. Fully seventeen of its thirty-one days recorded measurable rainfall. But that was standard, if not expected, in Seattle. People who lived in the Pacific Northwest realized that summer, for them, runs from July through September, and sometimes through October depending on the year. There was one sure indicator of the beginning of summer, and that year it looked as if it had come early, as there would apparently be sun for the Fourth of July.

But the weather wasn't the only thing that had been dismal the past month. For weeks now Giles felt as if he were caught between two halves of himself. He longed to get back to his desk and write, while at the same time loathing his office more than any place on earth.

His relationship with Paige hadn't been much better. They still spent their weekends together, dinners out, and a movie once in a while, and yet none of it seemed important to Giles. In desperation, he chose to read.

During the past month he had gone nowhere without a book, and was reading novels at the rate of three or four a week. Giles would go down to the University District in the morning, after Paige had left for work, stopping first at Bulldog News to check out the new horror magazines. Then, after buying at least one, he would head up to eat breakfast at one of the cafes that lined University Way—The Ave, as the students referred to it—and finally wind up at the University Book Store.

Returning home with his cache of reading materials, Giles would make a pot of coffee and sit in bed reading all day. As a result, things around the house had been severely neglected; the floors needed vacuuming, the kitchen was a mess, and a mountain of dirty clothes had piled up in the laundry room. Sometimes Paige did the housework when she came home, and sometimes she didn't. Giles simply kept on reading, during dinner, before bed, in the bathroom—if he could have read in the shower he would have.

Giles was sitting in bed one Thursday morning reading the latest issue of *The Grim Reader* when he remembered the newspaper. Paige was still asleep next to him and he snuck out of the bedroom and down to the front door. The front page of *The Post-Intelligencer* was festooned with red, white and blue bunting across the top to commemorate Independence Day. Giles picked the paper up off the mat, closed the door behind him and made his way into the kitchen to brew the morning's coffee.

While he waited, he continued thumbing through *The Grim Reader* he had brought with him. He had been amused to find out yesterday when he was shopping that it contained the story he had written about the female vampire. He'd already spent the check Don had sent him two weeks ago, and since he hadn't received his contributor copies yet he'd gone ahead and bought one.

Giles poured two mugs of coffee, wedged the paper and the magazine under one arm, and went back to the bedroom. Paige had evidently been roused by the smell and was propped up in bed waiting for him.

"Thank you," she said as he handed her one of the mugs.

In answer Giles held out the morning paper but she shook him off.

"No, go ahead. I'm just getting to a good part in my book."

Giles had noticed that Paige was also doing a lot more reading as of late, although she made no secret as to why. If he was going into self-imposed isolation, she'd told him, she would have to keep herself entertained until he was through. She didn't like it one bit—on that point she had been more than clear—but she said she was willing to wait for him.

Giles unfolded the thin paper and laid it out on the bed. He leafed through the pages one by one, scanning the print for headlines that sounded interesting. At the end of the business section there was a tiny article about restaurants that had recently been shut down by the health department. After verifying that they were not establishments he and Paige frequented, his eyes wandered up the Vital Statistics listed just above.

Something in the Deaths column suddenly caught his attention: Boyd, Douglas E. He must have made a noise after reading the name because Paige looked up from her book. "What?"

"Nothing," he said, and went back to the paper. He looked at the name again—the listings were all from the last week of June—then he reached over and picked up the magazine from the nightstand to confirm what he had already known. Doug Boyd was the name he had used in the story. God, what a weird coincidence, he thought.

Giles had often wondered about the names he made up in his fiction. There was no doubt that someone somewhere would have those very same names, but to find out that person had been living in Seattle—it seemed incredible. He made a mental note to check through the phone book on future stories to prevent it from happening again. Most of his characters tended to be on the despicable side, and he didn't want anyone suing him for libel.

When he had finished with the paper, Paige put down her book and pulled it over to read herself. One thing he was thankful for was that she hadn't let his horrible mood affect the way she treated him. She'd been very nice, even taking Friday off so that they could have a four-day weekend together. Now all they needed was something to do.


They hadn't showered together on the weekends since their fight last month, and today was no exception. But Paige had noticed a decided change for the better in Giles' behavior, he wasn't quite so compulsive in his reading, and they were talking more. As for sex . . . well, there was always room for improvement. At least he reached for books now, instead of the bottle.

Giles hadn't had a beer since the night she'd found him sleeping on the couch, or anything else alcoholic as far as she knew. He didn't seem to need it; he just needed something to take his mind off his novel. Be it reading or drinking, he didn't seem very picky; it just had to be something. Thank God for that, as Paige couldn't say the same for herself. So far she had been able to put up with an awful lot to get him through this, but she couldn't have said the same if he was still drinking.

When they had finished dressing they drove over to the U. District in Giles' Grand Prix convertible. It was bright and sunny by noon and Giles put the top down as they made their way east on 145th and then south down Roosevelt. Paige remembered how excited Giles had been to get the car, just like a kid in a candy store.

When Giles turned to her and asked "What?" she realized that she'd laughed out loud.

"Oh, I was just remembering the day you bought the Pontiac."

Now Giles laughed, his face seemingly shedding off weeks of frustration, and Paige thought she would melt with relief. "Yeah," he said. "But what about the two weeks after?" They laughed together this time. "Remember how I took you to work in the mornings and then drove back to bring you home every night?"

She nodded. "You were crazy about it."

"And crazy about you. Still am," he said, reaching over to take her hand in his. She squeezed it tightly and rubbed the hair on his bare arm. She could see him getting back to normal now, very definitely.

After breakfast they walked down to the used bookstore a couple of blocks away. A half-hour later Giles had a Hemingway biography and five or six novels picked out, and Paige had been lucky enough to run across a hardback copy of Wyndham's *The Chrysalids*. They were up at the counter paying for books when she realized she didn't want the day to end yet.

"Why don't we go over to Northgate?" she asked. It was one of the large shopping malls in Seattle and fairly close to where they lived. But Giles' face clouded up and she thought for a second that things might not be quite as much back to normal as she had hoped.

"No," he said. "I'd rather go to Southcenter. I've always wanted to go the Universal Studios store down there."

Paige put her arm around Giles and hugged him, and he did the same to her. They walked back to the car, and after they had put their books in the backseat of the Pontiac Giles held Paige close and kissed her deeply. Her stomach churned with emotion. It had been so long, just waiting for him. He had never let her try to help him; he'd had to do it on his own. And now he was being wonderful.

"I'm so sorry," he said, pulling his face away but still hugging her tightly. "I love you so much."

"That's okay. I love you, too. I'm just glad you're feeling better."

He smiled, wrapping his arms around her waist and lifting her off the ground. Then she wrapped her arms around his neck and kissed him again.

The sun and the open air felt good as they drove down Interstate 5 toward the south end of Seattle. The area had grown up incredibly fast over the past few years. The community just south of the city limits had recently been incorporated, naming their city after the major metropolitan airport it contained: Seatac. The name itself was an abbreviation of Seattle and Tacoma, the two largest cities the airport was located between.

East of the airport was the sprawling complex of buildings collectively known as Southcenter. Originally it had simply been the largest shopping mall in the state, but now, with the addition of dozens of stores and strip malls all clustered around, it had become a sort of shopping Mecca. One of the newest businesses to set up in the mall itself was a store owned by Universal Studios that sold all of the products available in California and Florida.

Giles still had the broken Bela Lugosi mug that he had picked up the last time they were in California, and Paige managed to convince him to buy a new one. Once they had left Universal and were passing through Nordstrom, Paige remembered that she didn't really have a pair of shorts that she liked. It appeared that summer was here at last, so she led Giles over to womenswear. She picked out three possible candidates and then Giles followed her brazenly into the dressing rooms.

Similarly, he had no compunction about bringing her into the men's dressing rooms when he was buying clothes. It made her a little nervous at times but she had to admit she liked it. Stripping in front of him with mirrors all around was very sensual.

"You know," she said teasing him. "Sometimes they have hidden cameras in these places to catch shoplifters."

"Well today's their lucky day then, isn't it?"

"What do you mean?"

"They get to see you with your clothes off."

Giles liked the first pair more than she did. They looked all right but Paige didn't like the way they fit. The second pair was better, and as she was taking them off, facing the mirror, she suddenly felt Giles' hands slip around her stomach. The shorts fell unceremoniously to the floor. As she stepped out of them, Paige looked in the mirror to see Giles, but he was too close behind her, hidden behind her reflection.

Paige's heart began to beat faster as she heard a couple of girls giggling a few stalls down and felt Giles, insistent, behind her. She had to admit that the thrill of the surroundings had increased the intensity of what she was feeling and so she decided to give in to him.

A few minutes later, legs quivering, skin thinly sheened with sweat, Giles began to giggle. "Don't," she whispered as loud as she dared.

She was afraid she might start laughing herself when at last he stopped and eased back away from her. She quickly pulled up her underwear and when she turned around they embraced for a long moment, then they kissed and she began to dress. Paige decided to buy the second pair of shorts, recognizing a good omen when she saw one. She was having a terrific day.

Waiting behind a woman at the cash register, Paige said, "Could you pay for this while I go to the bathroom?"

"Sure," said Giles, smiling at her and pecking her on the lips. "I'll meet you right here, okay?"

"Great."

Paige was only gone a minute, after cleaning up and running her fingers through her hair, but when she returned to the cash register Giles was gone.


. . . She felt, more than heard, the man come up behind her. "Find what you need, then?"

She turned to the gentleman and nodded politely as the girl put the receipt in the shopping bag. "Yes. Are we late?"

The gentleman looked at his watch. "No, but we'd better be off."

"Very well," she said and slipped her hand through the gentleman's arm as he offered it to her, allowing herself to be escorted from the store. The plane wasn't scheduled to leave for a couple of hours, but Collette Leavey had insisted on stopping at Nordstrom first to do a bit of last minute shopping before leaving for Stockholm. Dr. Leavey, technically, and her husband Christian were attending the Nobel Prize ceremonies where she— along with three other colleagues—was to be awarded the prize in medicine.

Outside the mall in the parking lot she slid behind the wheel of their gold Mercedes. Christian simply couldn't get used to driving on the "wrong" side of the road, and furthermore, couldn't stand the "ghastly" traffic in the States. Collette slipped off a white pump, started the car, and sped off toward Sea-Tac International Airport.

Since being offered the position of Chief of Neurosurgery at the Elliott Bay Medical Center in Seattle, her research had taken off at a surprising rate. It wasn't as if she'd ever performed brain surgery, but the position as head of neurology had already been filled. And since the hospital administrator, Mark White, owed her a favor, he had paved the way for her to get the neurosurgery spot. Two hundred thousand a year wasn't bad for working three days a week. The facilities were excellent and she had a full staff that did most of the work.

For her part, Dr. Collette Leavey preferred to stick to the theoretical side of medicine, her Nobel speaking for itself. She'd had one success after another since coming to Seattle, finding new drugs and new combinations of drugs to combat degenerative brain disorders. Papers had soon followed, along with extensive studies and experimentation. When the call finally came from Stockholm, she was not entirely surprised.

They pulled into the circular drive and Collette deftly maneuvered the Mercedes into the garage in the hub of the airport. After leaving the car in the hands of a valet, Christian took their two light bags and they walked together through the terminal to the information counter at Swedish Air Service. Christian handled the details and then they would be escorted to the SAS lounge to wait for their flight. While there was direct service from Seattle to Sweden she couldn't deny Christian a few days in London, so they would be stopping there first before flying into Arlanda Airport in Stockholm for the ceremonies—all first class, of course.

Dr. Christian Leavey—Ph. D. in biochemistry—as well as being Collette's husband, was one of her most ardent supporters. Collette had met him on sabbatical in England. He was quite British, quite rich, and quite smitten with her. Besides being an exquisite lover he was an even better theoretician, a quality not lost on Collette.

She'd led him on just enough to ensure he would propose before she was to leave England. Once he did, she was set for life. Collette was adamant that they live in the States, however, and Christian proved his love for her by moving to Seattle and becoming an American citizen. He would do anything for her and she wanted to make sure it would always be possible for him to do so.

To that end she had already begun her most recent experiment. In her purse was a vial containing the latest in her work on neuro-regeneration, and it would someday make the Nobel she was receiving the following week seem like an award for the invention of the Band-Aid. She had attained limited success with animals in the laboratory and was making more progress every day.

When the flight was announced they were ushered into first-class and took their seats. It would still be quite a wait as the business and coach sections filled up, and Collette occupied the time by going over her acceptance speech. The other three recipients were doctors from Chicago who had done the crucial work of verifying her test results in a study done there six years earlier.

She became aware of the plane moving out of the boarding gate, but didn't realize it was taxiing out to the runway until Christian grasped her hand.

"Love?"

She turned to him. "Are we taking off?"

He nodded, and she saw his forehead crinkle at what she knew must be the thought of a long flight without being able to smoke his pipe. She leaned over and kissed him on the cheek, then fastened her seatbelt.

Once they were airborne Christian ordered champagne and he toasted her success. Collette looked up into the face of her husband and knew that her love for him was only equaled by her love of science. She may not have been beautiful by society's standards, but wealth and power had made her beautiful, and she reveled in that particular beauty. Christian, on the other hand, was as handsome as they came, and though he was several years older than her she planned on having him around for a very long time.

They had only been in the air for an hour when the champagne had run its course. "I'm going to the bathroom," she said, drawing his attention from the Feynman book he was reading.

"Hurry back," he replied.

But when Collette reached the restroom it was occupied. Damn, she thought, and made her way through the business section back to coach. At least this plane had another bathroom, she thought, unlike that God-awful Concorde. It might be a faster way to get to where you were going, but the experience was closer to that of riding a bus than a luxury flight. Narrow-bodied, with two seats on each side of the aisle, and *one* bathroom—no thank you. Eventually she made her way to the restrooms at the rear of the plane.

After stepping inside Collette put down the seat, pulled a few paper towels from the dispenser, splashed them with water, and vigorously cleaned it. When she was finished she hitched up her skirt, squirmed out of her pantyhose and sat down. She was breathing through her mouth to avoid the smell, and fishing in her purse for her mirror when the plane began to shudder for several long seconds.

Collette froze as she felt the plane dropping, continuing to lose altitude even after it had stabilized. Then it began to shudder again, violently, and when the cold chemical liquid in the toilet sloshed up and splashed her naked cheeks she screamed. Even as the plane was falling from the sky she stood, wadding up a handful of toilet of paper and drying off her wet skin. Collette's stockings and panties were still around her knees when the plane began to dive and she was thrown against the door.

More liquid sloshed out of the toilet and ran beneath her feet. Her high heels slipped and she fell down hard, forcing another scream. The plane seemed to level out once more, but they were still dropping fast. The pressure on her ears was excruciating and she worked her jaw as she pulled herself up from the wet, stinking floor.

Collette held on to the sink to brace herself against the jarring motion of the plane. Finally, she was able to yard up her wet pantyhose. But when she realized that the contents of her purse were now strewn all over the floor and rolling through the green liquid, she went back down to her knees. Luckily, the vial and syringe were still tucked securely into the side pocket of the purse.

When she finally realized what must be happening she began to cry. Then without warning, she was thrown into the door like a rag doll as the plane hit the ground.

The noise was deafening. The jet shrieked and groaned under the strain of the crash landing and Collette screamed along with it. With one hand she covered her head as she was battered around the tiny compartment, the other hand desperately clutching the empty shell of her purse.

When everything finally came to a stop, the bathroom was tilted toward the door at a forty-five-degree angle. Collette was still sobbing. She smelled smoke. Then she reached up to release the handle and spilled out onto a dark, wet field. Rain was slanting down in the black night, and through it she could see a trail of burning debris hundreds of yards long. The tail section had broken off and, miraculously, she was alive.

At that moment her first and only thought was that she must find Christian. But when Collette stood, her right heel sank into the soft, uneven earth and she twisted her ankle and fell to the ground. She was in an agricultural field of some sort, and she was cold, deathly cold. Sobbing heavily, she tore the pumps from her feet and flung them into the night. She stood, tentatively, saw no other people around and limped toward the burning wreckage ahead.

It seemed as if she had walked forever before she saw the first people, but there was nothing she could do for them. Most were little more than charred lumps of burnt flesh and blood. Some were alive, screaming in torment. Arms, legs, torsos—the entire area was like a slaughterhouse—and the disgorged contents of wounded luggage lay strewn across the field among its human counterparts. Collette limped on.

Eventually she came upon a flaming section of plane that resembled the nose, and began searching for Christian. Black mud and soot streaked her dress, while tears and snot streaked her face. Her throat burned from the acrid smoke in the air, and from far away she heard the sound of sirens. Then she saw it: Christian's shoe.

She pulled on the exposed leg, dragging the body out from the flames. When she was far enough away that she could stand the heat, she rolled him over and screamed again. Christian was badly burnt. His face and hands were black, his hair reduced to singed and smoking stubble. The suit he was wearing had virtually melted to his body and still she threw herself upon him in a vain attempt to determine if he was still alive.

There was no pulse in his charred neck, and she backed away from him through the muddy soil and wept. The sirens were nearing, and when she regained her composure she was almost surprised to find the empty purse still in her hand.

Collette scrambled back to the dead body of her husband and stripped out the pouch on the inside of the purse. She removed the syringe, extracted about two cc's of the liquid in the vial, then threw the vial away. With a steady hand she inserted the needle just under Christian's jawline into his carotid artery and she injected the drug.

The syringe went the way of the vial as Collette straddled her husband's stomach and with both hands began to pump on his chest. As long as his brain hadn't hemorrhaged, the drug would be able to reach his brain. Then, and only then, would he have a chance.

In the lab she had only been concerned with the length of time that the dead animals—dogs and monkeys, mostly—remained alive after the injection. The test subjects had been immobilized with spinal injections to make them easier to work with, so it had been impossible to see their physical reactions. Collette had only been concerned with the reanimation of dead tissue and how long that reanimation could be sustained. She was pumping Christian's chest hard, thinking that she may have been a little too single-minded in her testing, when he suddenly opened his eyes.

Pain. Pure unadulterated pain. There had been the crash and then . . . nothing. Minute after minute of floating, rising, a destination yet unknown and then . . . unmerciful, unrelenting pain. It was a twisting, writhing agony, seemingly without end. His brain felt as if it would explode, his muscles and skin were aflame, and above him . . . his tormentor.

Christian gasped and sucked in a gulp of frigid air. He couldn't move yet, but the pain was sending bolts of electricity to every cell in his body. The thing was still hovering over him.

With every breath he grew stronger, but so did the pain. Flames lit up his lungs and fire raced through his blood, then the blackened stumps of his hands sprang open shooting new flares of pain back through his body.

His arms moved up and the thing began to go away. Then he reached out to it and his tormentor stopped. When it grabbed his hands he let out a tortured scream that he could not hear. The thing above him swam around in front of his eyes and he grabbed it by the neck, pulling close to his face and screaming again. His body was regaining strength, jolting him with agony until he was finally able to roll over with his tormentor beneath him.

When he squeezed the pain backed off, so he squeezed some more. Tissue broke beneath his fingers and hot liquid streamed out from the thing. He closed his eyes and squeezed even harder. Tendons snapped and muscles squirmed in his hands, threatening to escape, and he had to hold on even tighter, the circumference of his grip growing smaller and smaller until he finally felt something hard.

He tried and tried but the slender thing would not give anymore. So he shook it over and over, battering it against the soft ground until finally it broke off in his hands. When his eyes opened he saw the head rolling away. But now the pain was back. In front of him was the fire and he felt as if he were on fire and perhaps that was where he had come from and perhaps that was where he should return. So he stood, the pain pushing him onward, and ran back into the burning wall of flames . . .

# Chapter Six

As Paige came out of the store and stepped off the curb into the parking lot, she was suddenly afraid that the car wouldn't be there. She had seen the shorts she was going to buy lying on top of a rack of other clothes and, after a cursory look around, ran outside. The soft slapping of her tennis shoes against the hot asphalt kept her company as she raced up the seemingly endless rows of cars. When she reached the space where the car had been, the Pontiac was gone.

She wanted to panic. Fear and anger welled up inside, immobilizing her. Then she saw it. Paige had been in the wrong row. She took a step toward the car and began shaking, her chest heaving and her heart racing. She stopped for a moment and took a deep breath, and when she had regained her composure she ran to the car and climbed inside to wait for Giles.

A whole month, she thought, that was how long it had taken them. They had almost been back to normal and now he had gone and done it again. What was happening? He was keeping something from her; she knew that much. And it wasn't just these episodes. His writing had become almost a secret world, one that he only shared with Don. Was she jealous? Sure, and why not? They shared a life together; they shared a bed and all that that represented. And yet this thing was having a direct effect on their marriage but he wasn't sharing. She didn't like it one bit.

Paige sighed and reached over into the backseat for the books they had bought earlier in the day—a different lifetime ago it seemed now. She didn't feel like rereading the Wyndam book so she looked through Giles' novels, finally selecting something called *Dr. Orlock's Secret: A 1930s Horror Fantasy*. Images of Lugosi and Karloff, Fay Wray and Lionel Atwill sprang up in her mind and she opened it to the first page of text and began to read.

The afternoon sun was hot and Paige had taken off her shoes and socks, tucking her legs underneath her. She had a spare set of keys but decided to simply wait for Giles. How long, she didn't know; she was going to play things by ear since she had something to keep herself occupied.

The book was good, and though she had only been reading for a couple of hours, Paige was already a quarter of the way through it when she looked up and saw Giles standing beside the driver's door. He had a miserable look on his face as he silently opened the door and slipped inside.

Where have you been? What the hell's going on? Why are you doing this to us? There were a million questions she wanted answers to, demanded answers to. But by the time she found her voice the only thing she could ask was, "Are you all right?"

Giles nodded, still looking forward.

"Do you want to talk—"

He silenced her with a shake of his head.

Damn it, she thought, and closed her book, making her even angrier when she realized she'd lost her place. They sat there in an awkward tableau until Giles finally started up the car and backed out of the parking space.

Evidently they were back to square one. Three more days of this, she thought glumly, and that was when she really became upset. Paige kept her eyes averted from Giles as they drove home in silence. The tears had begun to flow because she was actually looking forward to going back to work on Monday.

Friday morning when Paige woke up she could see that Giles hadn't been to bed the night before. She looked at the alarm clock; it was already nine. She should have been smelling coffee and wasn't, but that was the least of her worries.

Lying awake in bed thinking, for the first time in her life Paige didn't know what she was going to do. Divorce? That was fine on TV, but in real life things moved a lot more slowly. They still hadn't talked, let alone tried to work things out. Their marriage wasn't at the crisis stage yet, just uncomfortable, although for Paige that was bad enough. No, it would still be a while before she thought of divorce as an option.

Giles had gone downstairs after they had come home yesterday, and that was the last she'd seen of him. It had always been a rule that she wouldn't disturb him while he was working, though rules didn't seem very important when their relationship was in jeopardy. Maybe she should get upset, she thought, scream at him and throw things. But that didn't seem likely to achieve anything except to create an even more insurmountable wall between them. Giles would just withdraw further, and perhaps it would push him back to drinking. With their last confrontation still vivid in her memory she had no desire to do that at all.

Paige felt herself wanting to cry again and she almost screamed with anger. She simply had to get a handle on her tear ducts or she was going to go out of her mind. She yawned and stretched, and then hauled herself out of bed. Throwing on her bathrobe, she walked down the hall to the kitchen, sticking her head into the living room to see if Giles was in there.

It was empty, but a rumpled blanket was lying on the cushions of the couch. She supposed he had slept there for whatever amount of time it had been. Giles had still been writing when she'd gone to bed at eleven. A terse note on the kitchen counter informed her that he wasn't home, and she wadded it up and threw it away before starting the coffee.

She still had her book to read, although at the rate she was going she would finish it by noon. Paige was sad that it had to end; she hadn't enjoyed a novel that much in a long time and it had gone a long way toward making yesterday tolerable. She waited in the kitchen, staring blankly into the sunny backyard, until the coffee had finished brewing. Then she poured herself a mug and walked back to the bedroom to finish her book.

The first thing she did was throw open the curtains, flooding half the room with light. Then she put some classical music on the small stereo Giles kept on his side of the bed and lost herself in reading. She was on her second cup of coffee when she heard the Pontiac pull into the garage. Paige was still lying in bed and she set her book down to wait. The kitchen door opened and she listened as Giles went right downstairs. She had expected as much, and that was why she was shocked when a few minutes later he suddenly appeared in the bedroom doorway.

"We have to talk."

He looked rumpled and unshaven and in one hand he held what looked like a newspaper and a magazine. Paige had a lump in her throat because she knew that she'd done the right thing by waiting for him to come to her. He was ready now.

She put her book away and set her coffee on the nightstand while Giles sat by her feet on the bed. He looked once at the paper and the magazine and then set them aside. "I think I'd better start at the beginning. There's something I've been keeping from you."

"I know."

Giles looked at her and frowned, then relaxed and nodded. "Yeah, I don't suppose I really tried very hard to keep it a secret. But it was never meant to be a secret in the first place. It just sort of evolved into something I didn't want to talk about."

"The . . . episodes?"

He nodded. "The first time it happened was before we met. It was right after the book deal fell through."

"I remember the time in the grocery store," Paige said.

"Right. Well, I'm not sure I knew what was happening to me then, but it seemed harmless enough. I would get this fixation on a total stranger and suddenly I knew everything about them . . . well, fictionally. I knew their past, where they lived, what kind of person they had been, everything. Then I would get an idea for a story about them and write it."

He shifted uneasily on the bed and rubbed his whiskered chin. "But even while that was going on, I was always aware of my surroundings. Whether I was in a bar, or the store, at least I knew where I was." Then he stopped.

"Is something different now?" Paige asked.

"Yeah. But it didn't happen all at once, and it wasn't anything I was really aware of until today. I don't know—this sounds so weird, but I think I'm possessed."

"Giles." She leaned forward and took his hand in hers. "What are you taking about?"

He turned and looked into her eyes and she could see how really tired he was. "I don't know where I am anymore. When this thing comes over me, it's like I pass out, and when I come to I'm somewhere else. That happened yesterday. One minute I'm standing in line at the cash register, and the next minute I'm out at the airport. I really can't remember anything in between, except that I have this kind of story in my head."

He pulled his hand away and stood up. Paige didn't know what to say. She hadn't expected anything like this. She'd read about psychological disorders where blacking out was one of the symptoms. Schizophrenia? God, she hoped not. "It's been happening a lot more lately," she said. It wasn't a question.

"Yeah," he said, pacing at the foot of the bed. "Before it was just . . . I don't know, some kind of quirk. I'd write a story about it and that would be that." Giles stopped and ran his hands through his hair. He looked distracted and confused.

Paige was sitting up ramrod straight in bed, making sure she understood every word Giles was saying.

"But now," he went on, "it's as though I *have* to write, like I don't have a say in the matter. It used to be that I lived in fear of the day when this possession would stop—that maybe I wouldn't be able to write anything good that didn't come to me in that way."

He hadn't been talking directly to her, but now Giles turned and locked his gaze on her. "I'd give anything to know it wasn't going to happen again. This thing scares the shit out of me."

"Oh, sweetheart." Paige threw off the covers and went to him. She was only wearing a short nightshirt and his hands were cold through the material on her back as he put his arms around her.

They held each other tightly for a long time before Giles pulled away.

"There's more," he said, releasing her. He took a few steps back and looked into her eyes again. "These stories I come up with? I have a bad feeling that maybe they aren't fiction."

If blood could freeze, Paige's did. She knew his work, and suddenly her lack of clothing made her feel naked and vulnerable. She wanted desperately to put something else on, but stopped herself. Paige didn't want Giles to think she didn't trust him. Besides, she was unclear as to what he meant. "What are you saying?"

"I'm not really sure, but I think I might know ahead of time that these people are going to die." Giles walked around to his side of the bed and grabbed the previous day's newspaper. He laid it out and flipped through it, then stopped and grabbed a magazine off of his nightstand.

"I wrote this story last spring," he said, opening it up and giving it to her.

Paige read the first few paragraphs. "Was this the time we were downtown looking for that service center to get the VCR fixed?"

Giles nodded. "Now, look at this."

He was pointing to a section of the paper headed DEATHS. The name above his finger was the same as in the story and relief suddenly flooded into her. Was that all this was about? "It just means that the name is the same. That's bound to happen once in a while."

"That's exactly what I thought yesterday when I read it." Giles sat down on the bed. He didn't seem very relieved. "Remember the story I wrote last month, and we got into that big fight the next day?"

". . . Is that a trick question?"

He smiled. For the first time that morning Giles looked like his old self. Then he hung his head down. "I'm sorry, Paige. I've been such an asshole."

She knelt in front of him and took his hands again. "Just keep being honest with me, sweetheart, and there isn't anything we won't be able to get through. So what about that story?"

He picked up the other magazine off the bed and handed it to Paige. "Don sold this one at about the same time as the vampire story."

It looked to Paige like some sort of anniversary issue of *Dark Imaginings*. She quickly checked the contents and then leafed through to Giles' story.

"I went into McDonald's for breakfast this morning," said Giles. He picked up the folded newspaper he had brought with him. "There was a copy of the *P-I* lying on the table I sat at, and when I was looking through it I found this."

The *Seattle Post-Intelligencer* was the city's morning newspaper and Giles was pointing to a listing in the Deaths column. "And this is for today?" she asked.

Giles nodded and stood back up, pacing the room. The name in the story was the same as the one in the obituary: Gisele Kummer.

"That makes two," he said.

"But you don't even know these people."

"I think I do. I think they might be the same people I saw, the actual people I wrote the stories about."

"That's impossible."

"Then how do you account for this?" He was pointing accusingly down at the papers and magazines on the bed and then Paige stood up.

She could see the frustration in his face, the strain, and she was well acquainted with the effect it was having on their marriage. "Just what is *this*, Giles? Two people with the same names that you used in your stories died. It's just a coincidence."

"But I really think they might be the people I saw when I was possessed."

She wished he'd stopped using that term. "Maybe, but you don't know that, do you?" Giles looked at her but didn't respond. "For all you know this Kummer woman could be anybody. She could have just been passing through town. For God's sake, Giles, it's only a name."

Giles took a breath. "All I know is that I wrote two stories and now the two people I wrote about have been killed?"

"Killed?" So now they were getting down to it. The relief came upon her so fast Paige almost laughed. "Where does it say that they were killed? Giles?"

He frowned, and she knew that he didn't have an answer to that one. "It doesn't, I guess."

"My God, you had me so scared."

She hugged him again and now she finally understood. For some crazy reason he felt responsible. Somehow the mere fact—make that coincidence—that these names popped up in the Deaths column had suddenly twisted her husband into a guilty knot. It was ludicrous, blackouts or not. There was simply no way that two anonymous people Giles happened to lay eyes on *once*, and then make up names for in a story, could possibly be the same two people with those same names.

For most artistic people imagination was supposed to be a good thing. Ironically, for Giles, it was the opposite. When he needed it to write, it was nowhere to be found. He needed the prompting of real people in natural situations to inspire him. But this? No, it was coincidence of the highest order—he could have seen or heard those names anywhere and just didn't remember it now. And yet he was sure that it was all his fault that they had happened to die.

Of course there was still the matter of his blacking out, but that seemed infinitely curable compared to his paranoid delusions of murder. As far as she was concerned he had stressed himself out over that damn book he was trying to write. It had been so long since the last time she had nearly forgotten what it was really like. Blissfully forgotten.

She held him at arm's length. "Giles, if these people had been murdered you would have read about them on the front page, not just on a listing in the Deaths column, right?"

He nodded.

"You could have seen those names anywhere, in the phonebook, you could have heard them picking up a pizza, at the grocery store, anywhere. But the fact that they died is just one big coincidence. And in the end it really doesn't matter how they died because that's *all* it is, okay?"

She looked deep into his brown eyes and he smiled again. And at that moment she wished she didn't have any clothes on at all. She wanted to climb into bed with him and forget this had ever happened. "You really think that's all it is?" he said.

"I'm positive. I think you're still punishing yourself over that book. That's bound to make you feel some strange things. But I don't think you're possessed, and I don't think that people are dying because they have the same names as characters in your stories."

"I love you," he said suddenly, surprisingly. Then he put his arms around her and held her again, his head bent down on her shoulder.

"I love you, too." She stroked his hair. "That's why I'm here. I just want you to be honest with me from now on, okay?" He looked up and nodded. "No more secrets?"

Giles shook his head. "No more."

When she felt his arms close tighter around her, suddenly Monday seemed much too near.

# Chapter Seven

The first thing Giles did when he woke up the next morning was go downstairs to his office to make a phone call. Before leaving the bedroom he had checked carefully to make sure that Paige was still asleep.

They hadn't talked any further yesterday about his discovery because he'd felt then that he'd sort of botched the job. He hadn't made things very clear to Paige because he hadn't been thinking very clearly himself. She was understandably skeptical when it came to the supernatural, and Giles supposed he was, too.

He had spoken of being possessed and it *was* frightening for him; he hadn't exaggerated on that point. But even with the blackouts, it was hard for him to believe that he really had any kind of psychic powers or precognition. No, the possession he was talking about, the visions of those two people he had named Boyd and Kummer, Giles truly believed, was one that somehow had been created in his own mind, a product of his own imagination.

For one thing, he had never felt afraid while it was happening, only afterward, realizing that he had completely lost control of himself. And while the feeling seemed to control him, it never felt as if it was coming from outside of himself. The possession, he felt, was coming from within. It seemed impossible, then, that there could be any supernatural force at work here.

So, what *was* going on? Giles had a theory. He simply had one hell of a time trying to write—which was business as usual—and watching other people worked like a drug in him. But his

Eric B. Olsen

very dependence on those people must have somehow altered his consciousness, allowing him to see how they were going to die. That was what really frightened Giles.

But even then, how could he have known their real names? There was no escaping the fact that two people actually named Boyd and Kummer had died. He wanted to believe, like Paige, that it was just a coincidence, but he couldn't. And he supposed he knew why. One thing that he hadn't pointed out to her had been the fact that the ages of the Boyd and Kummer in the newspaper were very close to the ages of the people he had seen.

And yet it seemed impossible that they could be the same people that he had seen and inspired him. In the end, that was going to be the key to finally figuring out exactly what *was* going on. Until he knew if they were, everything else was speculation. But how could he know for sure? Other than viewing the bodies or tracking down bereaved relatives to look through their photo albums, he didn't think he could. And that gave him an idea. He was reasonably sure that he knew someone who might be able to help him, and right now that was going to be the only thing that would set his mind at ease.

"Seattle Police Department," said the male voice on the other end of the phone.

"Hello, I'm trying to reach Daniel Lasky."

"One moment."

Five years ago when he and Paige had attended his ten-year high school reunion, Giles had been surprised to learn that one of his former classmates was now a Seattle cop. He hadn't talked much to Daniel that night, and wasn't even sure what to say to him now if he reached him. But Giles knew that he had to find out if Douglas Boyd and Gisele Kummer were the people he had seen and written about.

He felt like hell for keeping this a secret from Paige, especially after his promise to her. But at this point his sanity, or some semblance thereof, was of paramount importance. The uncertainty about what was happening had been gnawing away at him since yesterday morning. He had to know.

The man came back on the line. "What precinct was that?"

"I'm sorry. I don't know."

"Well, we have a Lieutenant Lasky working out of the Magnolia Precinct."

"That must be it."

Giles wrote down the number the man had given him and then hung up the phone. Lieutenant, he thought, and mentally whistled. Despite the confident, self-assured look of the man he had seen at the reunion, to Giles, Daniel Lasky would always be the rather geeky kid he had gone to high school with.

Unlike most of the kids from Giles' graduating class in the small town of Hallowell, Washington—H.H.S. class of 1980— Daniel hadn't gone through grade school and junior high with the rest of them. His family had moved to Hallowell in 1976 at the start of their freshman year. Even at that time, when the grooviness of the hippy era hadn't completely died out and the disco era had yet to begin, Daniel Lasky looked as though he had stepped straight out of the 1950s.

He wore peg-leg trousers—usually black or gray—replete with creases and cuffs, a thin leather belt, white socks, and black oxfords. His white button-down shirts were always short-sleeved and would only occasionally have a modest striped pattern to them. The skinny black tie had lasted a couple of months, and afterward he wore his shirts with the top button open, visualizing the crisp white T-shirt he always wore underneath.

Daniel used plenty of Brylcreme to keep his hair slicked back in a stylish pompadour—the only problem was that it hadn't been the style for two decades or more. He also wore glasses with big black rims, and sometimes complemented his look with a cardigan sweater, or a black trench coat if the weather was nasty—rubbers over the oxfords, naturally.

To Daniel's credit, Giles supposed, he had never worn a pocket protector. Rumors were rife, of course, as to why he looked that way—his mother picked out his clothes, he wanted to dress just like Dad, their family was too poor for anything other that Salvation Army castoffs—but nobody really knew, and for some strange reason that Giles never figured out, nobody had ever bothered to ask him. Throughout high school he had simply remained a fashion enigma.

Daniel played saxophone in the school band, had a few friends, was on the debate team, made average grades, and in all of Giles' dealings with him, he had been a very normal, likeable kid.

Now, of course, Daniel's hair was cut shorter and contained no trace of Brylcreme. Contact lenses and the prevailing style of clothing had made him appear no different from any of the other men at the reunion. None of that, however, could change the image that was indelibly etched in Giles' mind. To Giles, Daniel Lasky would always be the kid that time forgot.

But even with all of that, Giles had never really known Daniel. And now, as he looked at the number on the pad in front of him, he almost hesitated to call. It *was* Saturday, though, and there was a good chance that Daniel wouldn't even be at the precinct house. So Giles dialed, and was surprised when it was answered on the first ring.

"Lasky."

"Uh, hi, Daniel." They had always called him Daniel in high school, never Dan or Danny. "This is Giles Barrett . . . from Hallowell . . . we went to school together."

"Sure, what can I do for you, Giles?"

"Well, I uh . . . I'm not sure where to begin. I'm living in Seattle now. I don't know if you remembered."

"Uh huh. Still married?"

"Oh, yeah. I'm not sure if I told you before that I'm a writer."

"Right. I think you said something about that at the reunion. Sorry I haven't had a chance to read any of your books."

Giles smiled. "That's okay. But that's really what I wanted to talk to you about. I'm doing some research for a story I'm writing and was wondering if you might be able to help me out."

"If I can. What, like detective stuff?"

Not exactly, but now that Giles thought about it, that might be the way to go.

"Exactly. I've come up against this problem that I can't seem to get around and if you have a couple of minutes I thought you might be able to answer a few questions."

"I'll try."

"Great. I'm writing this story where a private detective is looking for these two missing persons."

Giles stopped. Okay, now what? Suddenly this didn't seem like such a great idea.

". . . Yeah?"

"Well . . . he's got their names and descriptions, but no pictures of the people. Then one day when he's reading through the newspaper he sees both of their names listed in the Deaths column—"

"And he has to figure out who killed them?"

Oh, Christ, Giles thought, and felt himself break out into a light sweat. This was not heading in the right direction at all.

"No, no, Daniel, that's not what I meant. It's just that, well, the names are the same, of course, but how could he *know* that it was actually the same people he's looking for and not just people with the same name?"

"Ah, I see. Well, the first thing to do would be to go and have a look-see down at the morgue."

"I thought of that, but my detective isn't licensed. He's an amateur sleuth, and I don't think he could just walk into the morgue and look at the bodies."

"Yeah, you're right." Daniel was silent for a moment, and Giles wished more than ever that he hadn't called.

"Hey, how about this?" Daniel said. "What if your detective has a cop friend? You know, like they do on TV, someone on the inside who can feed him information."

"Sure, that could work." Giles' mind was racing. "Thanks, Daniel."

"No problem."

"But that gives me another idea."

"Yeah?"

It was more than an idea. It was almost an epiphany. Giles

had planned on trying to find a way of indentifying Kummer and Boyd on his own. But if Daniel could be persuaded to do the dirty work for him, so much the better. Obviously Daniel hadn't read any of his work, so he could use that to his advantage.

"The reason I had this idea in the first place is that something like this has actually happened to me."

"Really?"

"Yeah. It all started with this book signing I had here in Seattle last year. A couple of days ago I was looking through the Deaths column and I'm almost sure that two of the people listed there were people I signed books for."

"Wow, that's bizarre."

"Yeah that's what I thought. The thing is, I feel like I should send a card or something to their families, except there's no way I can be positive it was them. I was just going to forget about it, but since you brought it up I was wondering if there might be some way you could find out if it was really them?"

"Hmm, I don't know. I mean, I'm really not sure where I would start. Do you have any reason to think that they were murdered?"

The questioned stopped Giles cold. He wanted to reply; he wanted to say something, but the words caught in his throat. He was sweating freely now.

"Jesus, no, Daniel," Giles said in a tone of humorous misunderstanding that was about as far as he could get from the way he actually felt. "I just thought you might have some way of finding out if they were the same people I had seen, that's all."

"I understand. But what you might not realize is that unless there's some evidence of a crime, and one of our units respond, the body wouldn't be at the morgue. Also, I don't know what the folks you saw look like. The only way you'd be able to identify them is from autopsy photos, and the only way we would have those is if it was a part of a murder investigation."

Giles wanted nothing more than to slam the receiver down and forget about this whole mess. But that wasn't possible, was it? Oh, no, because he had gone ahead and called his good buddy

Daniel. And now old Daniel the cop had his wind up—wind thoughtfully provided by his old pal Giles. The lie came easily.

"No, you're right. I don't know what I was thinking. I'm really sorry, Daniel, calling you up out of the blue like this for nothing—"

"Nah, that's okay," Daniel said, sounding totally unconvinced. "As I said before, I'm not sure what I can do, but why don't you give me those names anyway?" He waited but Giles didn't answer. "Giles?"

"Yeah, I had them right here on a slip of paper and now I can't find it."

Giles shuffled a few papers to complete the ruse, but of course the yellow Post-it note was right in the middle of his desk, fairly glowing like a homing beacon. He was torn between not wanting to give Daniel the names, and desperately wanting to know who Boyd and Kummer were.

After explaining the situation, there was no earthly reason for Daniel to ask him for the names. Maybe Giles was just being paranoid, though. Maybe Daniel didn't really mind doing him a favor. In the end, Giles' need to know won out and he gave Daniel their names and descriptions.

"Okay, Giles, I'll try to take a look into this when I get the chance. Can I get your phone number?"

Giles gave him that, too, and then they said their awkward goodbyes. Finally, Giles set the receiver in the cradle and leaned back in his chair. His body trembled from the chill of the drying perspiration beneath his sweatshirt. What had he done? Why had he even called Daniel? So what if they were the same people. How was that his responsibility? He hadn't known they were going to die. He certainly couldn't have prevented it. The whole thing suddenly seemed to Giles like a colossal waste of time.

One thing he had to make sure of was that he didn't take things out on Paige again. He had the feeling that if he did, he would risk losing her. It was nothing solid, nothing concrete, just a feeling.

He had always needed her, but he didn't think he had realized until just now, how much. What would happen to him without her? He didn't even want to think of that possibility. And yet, right on the tail of that recognition came the inexplicable yet overpowering lust for self-destruction.

All he wanted to do at that moment was drink himself into oblivion. He wanted to forget it all, to numb himself, and the most convenient way to do that was to curl up with a case of Guinness and die. He gripped the armrests tightly and closed his eyes. His mind was tired of thinking.

Finally, he sat up, pushed himself to a standing position on legs that had grown wobbly with fear, and walked upstairs.

When Giles entered the kitchen he went straight for the refrigerator, but instead of reaching for a beer he took out a white ceramic canister emblazoned with the green Starbucks logo and set in on the counter. Then he pulled over the coffee grinder, measured out two scoops of beans from the jar, and ground them to the coarse consistency he preferred.

Giles stood there for a moment, savoring the aroma of the freshly ground coffee and tried to think of nothing else. After putting away the beans he filled up the glass carafe with water, lifted up the flap in back of the white Krups machine and poured it in, replaced the carafe, and turned it on.

Giles sat at the kitchen table to wait while the coffee brewed. He was going to have to forget about Daniel Lasky for the time being; there was nothing more to be done about it. He would hear from him in a few days that he'd found nothing and that would be that.

For his own sake, however, Giles tried to put the whole affair in some kind of logical order. First, the people. He did not know them, had not known them previously. The time he had seen Douglas Boyd . . .

Giles shook his head. He was just going to assume, until he heard otherwise, that they were *not* the people who had died. Paige had a point. For all he knew Gisele Kummer might just as easily be an American-born, second generation German Jew. And Doug

Boyd—the man Giles had seen, anyway—was white; the man in the paper could very easily have been black.

The time he had seen "Doug Boyd," he had been with Paige. He'd even been driving, in complete control of himself. He hadn't had his first real blackout until he'd seen "Gisele Kummer" on the bus.

Second, the stories. They had been written well over a month apart and there didn't appear to be any connection between the two of them. They had been written without anyone's knowledge; Paige hadn't even seen them. He'd just cranked them out and sent them to Don. They had even appeared in different . . .

The magazines.

Giles placed his hands palm down on the cool surface of the kitchen table to keep them from shaking. The rich aroma of brewing coffee had filled the room and he suddenly felt lightheaded. The rush of relief and terror that gripped him was almost too much. The magazines. Of course. Why hadn't he seen it before?

Giles stood up and grabbed a mug off the rack next to the stove. He poured himself half a cup with an unsteady hand and sipped the dark steaming liquid. It felt good in his stomach, ironically, the first jolt of caffeine having the effect of calming him down, and he recognized it as an addictive reaction, a caffeine junkie getting his fix. Even if the drug was a stimulant, his system welcomed it by relaxing him.

He sat back down, his mind thinking clearly and calmly now. Each of the two deaths he had read about had come in conjunction with his buying the magazine the stories had appeared in. He had never connected it before because in his mind the stories were old news, written months ago, and the magazines themselves had seemed of no importance to him. But the public—they were seeing the stories for the first time when the magazines hit the newsstands.

He wasn't sure of the precise date that each of the magazines had become available to the public, but with Don's help it would be easy enough to find out. And Giles was willing to bet money that they had come out *prior* to the deaths of Boyd and Kummer—perhaps even as much as a week previous. It made perfect but horrible sense.

Except that you're supposed to be going on the assumption that they weren't the same people, he told himself—remember? But what if they were?

Suppose some sick, twisted psychopath was waiting for every horror magazine with a Giles Barrett story to come out, picking a person who looked just like the ones he described in the story, and killing them—

But that wasn't right.

Giles was startled by his own thought, and a slosh of coffee spilled over the side of his mug. He stood up and used the dishrag near the sink to wipe up the spill.

This person wasn't simply killing look-alikes, he was going by the very *names* Giles had used and killing them for that reason. And if that was the case, then Giles *was* involved. Worse yet, he might even be responsible. Innocent people, whose names he had simply overheard somewhere and had stashed in his subconscious, were being stalked by a psychopathic killer. But why?

With that sobering question still hanging unanswered in his mind, Giles refilled his coffee mug and walked downstairs, skirting his office and heading into the library.

He sat down in one of the wing chairs and looked around. Books towered over him on every side. A small pile of paperbacks lay on the floor near the fiction wall and Giles remembered they were the ones he had purchased on Thursday—minus one. Paige still had that one up in the bedroom. But that was only a minor distraction from the real reason he was down here. Straight ahead of him, next to the door, in three large red slipcases and sitting on a shelf by themselves, there were copies of the magazines in which Giles' stories had been published.

Worrying about it now was a futile exercise. After all, he didn't even know for sure about Boyd and Kummer. And there was no telling when his good buddy Daniel would be on the horn, if ever. But still, he couldn't help wondering. If it *was* true, how many other people had been killed? When had the killer started targeting his stories? When had it all begun? When were the police going to connect them? And then, of course, there was the 64-thousand-dollar question: when would they connect the murders to *him?*

Giles sighed deeply. There really was nothing he could do about his previous work. And then he had a brainstorm. He might not have control over the past, but he could sure as hell exert some control over the future. Even if, by some horrible coincidence, he was responsible for the deaths of Boyd and Kummer, he didn't have to be responsible for Collette Leavey.

Giles ran out of the library, leaving his coffee mug behind. He went into his office and looked through the Seattle phone book. He flipped into the white pages and looked through the L's, but there were no Leavey's. The directory skipped from Leaver to Leavitt. There were two Leavy's, but neither of their first names began with a C.

Giles sat back stumped for a moment, and then smiled. He picked up the phone and dialed information.

"What city, please?" It was a woman's voice.

"Seattle."

"Name?"

"Leavey, L-E-A-V-E-Y, Christian or Collette."

He heard the faint clacking of computer keys before the operator came back and said, "I'm sorry, sir, but that number is unlisted."

"Thank you very much," Giles said. Then he hung up and laughed out loud.

Giles turned on his computer and quickly called up his latest story. Changing the name was as simple as typing in the old one the first time, and replacing it with something new. His word processing program took care of the rest. But Giles went at this one simple change with more determination than he'd had since starting his aborted novel.

He settled at last on the name Eldritch, as a variation of Eldridge. It was a bit heavy-handed, symbolically, but he thought it fit rather well with the story. The more he looked at it, the more he liked it. A quick flip through the white pages and another call to information confirmed what he already knew: if anybody actually had that name, they didn't live in Seattle. He picked out Louise for the woman, and he thought Lionel sounded good for her husband.

That done, he changed the names and printed out the story when it suddenly occurred to him that just changing the names might not be enough. What if the killer—always assuming there was one—decided that the name wasn't that important after all? Would he simply decide to kill some other innocent woman using Giles' story as a blueprint?

He reread the last passage on the screen. It was one of the most visceral parts of the story, his trademark, but it would have to go. She couldn't die. He struggled for a while, trying to find the voice of the story and finally managed to make the changes to his satisfaction. After saving the text he reprinted the last few pages and stuffed all of them in a Manila envelope. He could give it to Don on Monday.

The story itself might not appear in print for several months, but the mere fact of taking that preventative measure, as irrelevant as it might turn out to be, did much to assuage his feelings of guilt.

When Giles finally leaned back in his chair, he noticed he didn't have his coffee cup. Then he remembered he had left it in the library. He glanced up at the clock against the wall as he was leaving the room and smiled. It was time to wake up Paige.

# Chapter Eight

Giles was up early Monday morning making coffee while Paige was in the shower. Coming clean with her on Saturday had definitely been the right thing to do and, as a result, he and Paige had spent most of Sunday in bed. By the time they had gone out for dinner Sunday night, Daniel Lasky was little more than a distant memory.

When he heard the shower turn off, Giles walked down the hall and through the bedroom and stuck his head into the adjoining bathroom. "Need a hand in there?"

"I prefer *both* of yours."

He could see Paige's naked form through the frosted glass of the shower doors, and when she slid one back to step out his heart began to race. She was magnificent. Giles pulled a towel off the rack and handed it to her, then slipped his arm around her waist and kissed her.

"Mmm, are you sure this is Monday?"

"Unfortunately," he said and held her close again. "I have to take that story you read last night over to Don this afternoon."

Giles had released her and was heading out of the room when Paige reached out and touched his arm. He stopped and looked back at her.

"Thank you for letting me read that, Giles. It means a lot to me that you're sharing your writing with me again."

He shook his head. "I'm just sorry that I ever stopped. I love you," he said and kissed her again. Then he walked back into the bedroom.

"Can you bring me some coffee?" he heard Paige yell as he reached the hall.

"On the way."

Paige's departure for work that morning was preceded by another long, passionate kiss and promises of what was to come that evening.

Giles went downstairs, mug in hand, a happy man. There had been no episodes yesterday and he supposed that was the real reason for his good mood. He and Paige had talked a little more—she had even read the last few stories he had neglected to show her—and bolstered with the changes he had made on behalf of Collette Leavey, he felt confident again. So confident, in fact, that he was going to try something he had never attempted before: resuming work on his novel.

In the past, once his work had gone into the file cabinet it was there for good. But now he pulled open the top drawer, brought forth the sheaf of papers that comprised the first chapter and a half, and began to read it at his desk. It was still as powerful as he had remembered. The real trick was going to be sustaining it. Slow and steady wins the race this time, he thought. No more trying to write three hundred pages over the weekend.

During their conversations the past couple of months, Don had been nice enough not to ask how the novel was going. It would be good to be able to bring up the subject himself. Giles took a deep breath and then turned on his computer.

"Let's rock and roll."

Three hours later Giles had Chapter Two finished. Thirty-five pages of first-draft text were done, and if he continued—calmly and collectedly—he should be able to finish the book by the end of the year.

He fired up the printer and then went upstairs to refill his mug. While he was up there he put in a call to Don and they set up a meeting for one o'clock, right after Don's lunch hour. Giles had just enough time to shower and drive into downtown Seattle.

"Things are looking up," he said to himself as he went back downstairs to shut off his computer equipment. "And it's about fucking time."

When Don turned over the last page of the story that Giles had titled "The Unscheduled Stop," he didn't look up right away. Instead, he stared at the top of his desk for a few moments, eyebrows furrowed, and then, finally, up at Giles.

"Go ahead. Give it to me straight."

"Don't get me wrong, Giles. This is good stuff. It's just that . . ."

"Yes?"

"Well, I'm a little concerned with this ending."

Giles chuckled at that. His mind had been on the book, and as to whether or not this story was any good he was completely indifferent. It would either be published, as is, or it would go into his file cabinet. There would be no negotiation.

But Giles didn't want to be that blatantly inflexible with Don, especially when his friendship had been so valuable to Giles. It wasn't worth damaging their relationship over a stupid story.

"What's so funny?"

Giles shook his head. "Nothing. What do you think is wrong with the ending?"

Don straightened up the papers and set them down again, face up. "Well, it's just that it doesn't seem to pack the punch that you usually deliver. Frankly, it seems a little timid."

That's exactly what it is, Giles thought. You can't put one over on the old English professor. "How do you think it should be instead?" He was notoriously thin-skinned when it came to his writing and he didn't invite criticism often. Don looked a bit nonplussed, but Giles urged him on anyway. "No, go ahead. I'd really like your opinion."

Now it was Don's turn to chuckle. "Okay, but just remember that you asked for it."

Giles nodded.

"I think the woman should die. You've got the ambulance and police coming way too soon. I think that if you held them off, and he killed her before he ran into the flames, it would be a lot more powerful."

"Hmm." Giles leaned back into the cushions of the couch and crossed his legs, as if he were giving serious consideration to Don's suggestion. Nevertheless, he was marginally interested in where this was gong. "How exactly do you think he should kill her?"

Don's jaw looked as if it were ready to drop, but he managed to hang on to some of his business like demeanor in spite of that. "Well, you've got him choking her—why not go all the way? What would make me think of Giles Barrett? If he squeezed her head off."

Giles burst out laughing at this and Don finally stood up and sat on the edge of his desk facing Giles.

"All right," Don said. "What's going on?"

"God, am I that predictable?"

"What are you talking about?"

Giles reached into his briefcase and brought forth two pages of manuscript—the original ending—and handed them to Don. He watched the look on Don's face slowly change from confusion to comprehension as he read.

"Why you son of a bitch," Don said, cutting loose with a hearty, boisterous laugh. "What are trying to do—test me? See if I'm still worthy of being your agent?"

"No, no, nothing like that. I changed it to what you read first."

"What the hell for? This is perfect?"

It was a good question, but Giles didn't feel like telling Don the truth. He'd been able to kick-start the novel and was itching to get back to it. Fortunately, Don had practically given him another way to go.

"You said it yourself. You guessed exactly what the original ending was. I don't want people doing that. I don't want everybody to always know how my stories are going to end."

"Hey, aren't you forgetting your audience? They're the ones who are going to be reading this. They expect certain things. In a way, they *want* to know what's going to happen, and they know that you'll give it to them."

"I suppose you're going to start calling me a hack writer next?"

Don held out his hands in front of him. "Hold on, don't go getting artistic on me. I happen to think you're a wonderful writer—"

"Thank you."

"And I'd like to think I had a little something to do with your modest success."

"Your contribution is gratefully acknowledged."

"But regardless of your talent, my job is to sell the stuff you write. And therefore, any comments I make in regard to your writing are strictly financial in nature. Now, if you don't want to talk about your audience, how about the people who buy your stories: the editors?

"You've got a helluva reputation, and one that I've had no small part in cultivating. Most stories have to wait around for months to get into an issue with space, but I can usually get yours into the upcoming issue, and get paid on acceptance rather than publication. It's not a bad deal. But that's all because you're a known quantity. Editors like to know what they're getting. They have advertisers to please and bills to pay, and in the case of fiction, a tough time getting subscribers. Editors don't like change."

"Yeah," said Giles morosely. "That's too bad, isn't it?"

Don chuckled again. "Welcome to the real world of publishing, my boy. Now," he said, walking back to his chair and picking up the story. "What do you want to do about this?"

"I don't know. I wouldn't want to be responsible for you losing clout with your editor pals, but I probably won't have many more stories for a while. At least not like I have the past couple of months. I've been doing some good work on the novel lately."

Don's eyes widened. "That's great. I was kind of wondering how that was coming along."

"Yeah, I'm trying not to get too hyped into a frenzy this time, and it seems to be paying off."

"That's one piece of fiction I would truly love to have the opportunity to sell."

Don knocked on the top of his desk with a knuckle and picked up the story again.

"Just give it a try," Giles said. "Maybe a smaller magazine would be interested. Go ahead and hang on to it for now. If you feel like selling it, fine. If you don't . . . it's up to you."

"Fair enough," said Don, and both men came to their feet. They shook hands and Don agreed to let him know if he sold the story, while Giles assured him he would keep him apprised on progress of the novel.

Giles was on the street and out in his Pontiac with plenty of time to spare before rush hour. He ran through the dial on his radio as he merged into traffic northbound on Aurora, stopping when he heard the familiar horn section. It was the Beatles, and Paul McCartney was singing about how he absolutely had to get someone into his life. The sun was out, the top was down, and Giles cranked up the music. A couple more hours on the computer and then watch out Paige; Giles was going to be feeling good tonight.

In three months Don Holman would be fifty-two, and even though he had plenty of money socked away, retirement was not something he could ever imagine for himself. He planned to be wheeling and dealing on his deathbed. All he needed was a phone.

Don lived on Bainbridge Island with his wife Sharon, and Monday through Friday he took the ferry across Puget Sound to Seattle and his office in the Rainier Tower. Twelve years ago he had started up his agency by working out of their tiny apartment in Ravenna in his spare time, talking with editors on the East Coast in the wee hours of the morning before heading off for the classes he taught at the University of Washington. He quickly found that he had a knack for salesmanship—along with an eye for talent—and before long business was booming.

In addition to Giles, whom he'd taught in college, he had been able to lure a couple of heavyweight Northwest mystery writers away from their agents by making better deals for them with a New York editor he had gone to graduate school with. Once the word was out that artists in the Seattle area could be represented by an agent they would be able to see in person, whenever they needed to, Don was finally able to leave his job at the University and go into business for himself.

He missed teaching, but he sure didn't miss the pay. Now he and Sharon owned a beautiful home on Bainbridge that overlooked Puget Sound, he had a luxurious office in a downtown Seattle high rise, and he and his wife took at least two trips to New York every year and globetrotted for a month every summer. For Don, life couldn't get much better.

Though its beginnings were inauspicious—a one-man operation working via an extra phone in the spare bedroom of his and Sharon's apartment—The Holman Agency now boasted three full-time agents: one for artists and photographers, and one for actors and models, while Don handled all of the writers himself. In addition, a receptionist took care of incoming calls and set up appointments, and each of the agents had his own part-time secretary.

As soon as Giles had left, Don called Diana Lund into his office. Diana worked for Don in the afternoons, after the calls to New York and the deal making of the morning were through.

He took a blue pencil from the University of Washington beer stein sitting on his desk and marked the section of Giles' story where he wanted the original ending to go. He still had the two extra pages Giles had given him. In the end, Giles had never expressly forbidden him from changing it, and to Don's way of thinking there was no reason not to. The story was simply better with the stronger ending. He had always believed that a writer's first instinct was the most inspired, the most honest, the most true. And besides, he knew exactly who he was going to sell it to.

The vast majority of Giles' out-and-out horror stories were easy enough to sell to the few commercial horror fiction magazines in existence. The problem was that they could only afford to pay around two or three hundred dollars. If Giles had a few books to his credit Don might be able to get him into *Playboy* again—and receive a couple thousand dollars for his trouble—but at the rate Giles was abandoning his novels that might never happen. That's why Don was so excited about the possibilities for this story.

The medical and scientific elements involved made it a sure bet that he could get it into the largest commercial science fiction magazine in the country, *The Science Fiction Digest.* He had recently met the editor, Dean Weston, at a fantasy & science fiction convention in San Francisco. With a little cajoling and a few promises, he could probably get him to pay fifteen hundred. That ought to soften the editorial blow to Giles' ego.

Don's cut was ten percent, and even though the standard rate was usually fifteen his contract with Giles stipulated that it would remain at ten as long as he stayed with the agency. Most agents didn't handle short fiction for clients at all because the pay was so low, and a hundred and fifty dollars certainly wasn't going to pay the rent on his office space. But then Don didn't represent Giles for the money.

The man was temperamental, thin-skinned, unmotivated, and sometimes depressing as hell. But Giles had a quality that guaranteed him representation by The Holman Agency for life: Don absolutely loved his writing. Maybe it was the fact that Don had "discovered" Giles in his comparative literature class, or maybe it was because they had become such good friends over the years. But the fact was there were a lot of other people out there who also liked Giles' stories, so Don felt he was in good company.

When Diana came into his office, Don handed her the story. "I want you to retype this last page where I've marked it." Then he handed her the two sheets of paper comprising the original ending. "When you get there I want you to add these two pages, from where it's marked to the ending, okay?"

"Sure thing."

"I'm going to type out a letter, and when you're through I

want you to fax the whole thing. I'll make the phone call tomorrow morning."

"Okay."

"Thanks, Diana."

"You bet."

Don was beaming as his secretary left the office, his mouth turned up in a big toothy smile. This was going to be a healthy payday for Giles, the biggest one in a long time. He couldn't wait to see the look on Giles' face.

# Chapter Nine

Giles was euphoric as he turned off of Aurora toward home. He had never been able to overcome his depression about writing quite like this before, and the potential in him that it hinted at was almost overwhelming.

But his confidence seemed to drain away the instant he saw it: a car parked in front of the house. There was also a man wearing a rumpled brown suit standing at the door. Giles recognized him when he turned around and suddenly his confidence completely vanished. It was Daniel Lasky. And he wasn't smiling.

Giles parked behind Daniel's car instead of pulling into the garage. He turned off the ignition and sat for a moment gripping the steering wheel. He did not want to get out. Finally, he took a deep breath and opened the door.

Daniel walked back down the large wooden front steps to meet him. Giles hadn't seen him in a couple of years, and it looked as though he had been sleeping in his suit since then. But he also wore a serious expression on his face and it was still a little unnerving for Giles to have a cop parked in front of his house, friend or no friend.

"Hello, Daniel. This is a real surprise."

He nodded. "Giles." And the two of them shook hands.

"What's going on?" Giles asked, as if he hadn't called him up two days before.

"Uh, would you mind if we went inside and talked for a few minutes?"

"No, that's fine."

Giles walked up the stairs and unlocked the door. He let Daniel go in ahead of him. "Just up the stairs and to the right," Giles said, and followed Daniel into the living room. "Can I get you a beer or something?"

"No, thanks, really. I just wanted to talk."

Giles took a seat in one of the chairs across from the couch. He was trying to act casual, but it was difficult with his heart hammering in his chest. "Is this about my phone call the other day?"

"Yeah, I'm afraid it is." Daniel hesitated before continuing and Giles didn't think he was going to like what came next. "How much do you know about Douglas Boyd and Gisele Kummer?"

Giles' chest tightened immediately. "Jesus, Daniel, is this an official visit?"

"No." Daniel shook his head. But his expression remained solemn. "I'm here on my own time, but I need to know the whole story about why you called me."

"What do you mean?"

Daniel shrugged. "I just need to know everything. Anything else you can tell me would be helpful."

"I still don't understand. Helpful for what?"

Daniel didn't answer.

"Seriously, Daniel, I told you all there is to know. The only reason I remembered their names at all is that I like to sign first and last names when I autograph." He hated lying, dreading the idea that Daniel already knew he'd never published a book. "To be honest, not that many people show up, so I usually have lots of time to talk to the ones who do. Then, when I saw their names in the paper, it kind of spooked me. That's the only reason I called you."

"What about the story?"

He knew. That's why he was here. He knew about the stories and now he was going to nail Giles with the evidence. The words stuck in Giles' throat. "What story?"

"When you called me, you said you were working on a story."

Oh Shit! Giles was going to need a Rolodex before long to keep track of all his lies. His palms were already sweaty, and now he could feel twin streams of perspiration trickle down his sides from his armpits. He only hoped that his face wouldn't give him away.

"Right, the story. Well, I haven't been working on it much lately. It seemed like such a unique situation when I discovered their names—that's what gave me the idea, actually. I thought I could figure something out when I came to that part where the detective has to verify that it's them, and when I couldn't, I thought I would call you.

Daniel leaned back on the couch and loosened his tie. Jesus, thought Giles, how long is he planning to stay? Then Giles stood up. "Uh, if you don't mind, I think I'll go ahead and get a beer for myself. You sure you don't want something?"

"No, really, I'm fine."

Giles walked into the kitchen and by the time he reached the refrigerator door his hands were shaking. Get a grip, Barrett, he told himself. He took hold of the door handle and tried to relax, but he couldn't. After taking a Guinness from the fridge—and fumbling off the cap on the edge of a cutting board because he couldn't find an opener—Giles took a long pull. A slow easy belch escaped his stomach and he felt a little better.

He took another gulp before walking back out to the living room and taking his seat in front of Daniel. Daniel looked much more relaxed now, arms across the back of the couch, coat unbuttoned, legs crossed, and it went a long way toward easing Giles' anxiety—that and the Guinness.

"I didn't mean to come down so hard on you, Giles—it's just that I had to know."

"That's all right. I want to help out as much as I can."

"Was that the only time you saw them, at this book signing?" Daniel wasn't taking notes and it made it much easier for Giles to answer.

"Yeah."

"And what bookstore was this at?"

Giles shook his head. "I don't have any idea. Like I said, this was a couple of years ago and I did a bunch of autograph parties around that time . . . I honestly don't remember."

Daniel was silent for a moment and Giles took a sip of his beer.

"I'll tell you why I asked," Daniel finally said, and for the first time he smiled. "If you though *you* were freaked out, that was nothing compared to what happened to me. I had some free time this morning and decided for the hell of it that I'd go down to the computer room and run those names you gave me. I didn't really think anything was going to turn up, but I'll be damned if they didn't *both* come up as ongoing investigations."

For the moment, Giles forgot about being afraid. "Are you serious?"

Daniel nodded. "Boyd's file was listed with headquarters downtown so I gave them all a call to find out why. It turns out he was found dead in an alley, definitely murdered, and as of this morning the case is still unsolved."

A knot like a rock formed instantly in Giles' stomach, and he set his beer back down instead of taking another sip. He thought he should say something, but couldn't think of what, and Daniel continued.

"The Kummer case was out of Ballard and I called them next. Want to take a guess why she was under investigation?"

"Murder?"

"Yeah. She was found dead in her kitchen. It was a real bloodbath. After that . . . your giving me those two names was such a coincidence. You can see why I was more than a little curious."

Giles' nod was almost unconscious. "You don't think they're connected in any way, do you?"

"No, it doesn't look like it. Completely different M.O.'s, different parts of town, one outside, one in the house, male, female." Daniel emitted something that was almost a chuckle. "No, right now you're the only thing that connects them, and I sure as hell didn't know what to make of that. Sorry I didn't call you first to let you know I was coming, but I really needed to sit down and talk to you face to face."

"That's okay. It's just so incredible. I certainly never imagined anything like that when I saw their names in the paper."

"Listen, Giles, even though they're not my investigations, I'd really appreciate it if you'd give me a call if you do remember anything else."

"Sure."

"Sorry about bothering you at home like this, but, well . . ."

"Hey, no problem, Daniel. I just hope you catch the guys who did it."

Daniel stood up and buttoned his coat. Giles stood quickly and walked toward the door. He had Daniel go down the stairs first and then let him out.

"If you do remember anything, go ahead and give me a call, Giles. Even if you don't think it's very important, it might be to us."

"Absolutely. I'll call you if I think of anything else."

"Okay."

Once Daniel had walked down the steps and out to his car, Giles shut the door and ran upstairs. He was surprised to find his beer bottle empty—he didn't remember finishing it—and as he listened to Daniel drive off he walked out to the kitchen for another.

When Paige came home Monday evening and saw Giles on the couch, she began to cry. Quietly, she turned off the TV, collected his beer bottles and took them into the kitchen, and then went to bed.

"Jesus, Don. I don't know what the hell I'm going to do."

Don leaned back in his chair trying to assess the story he'd just been told, while Giles paced his office like a caged animal. Don had been surprised to find Giles waiting outside his door when he came to work. He looked like shit, wearing a dirty sweatshirt and sweatpants, a five o'clock shadow, and obviously unwashed hair.

"What about that story you gave me yesterday?" Don had already faxed it out the day before, and Dean Weston had probably already read it this morning. Don hoped like hell Giles wasn't going to make him pull it.

"No, it should be fine. I called around all afternoon yesterday. There's no one named Louise Eldritch in King County. No one by that name, period, as far as I know." Giles was really tearing up the carpet pacing.

"Listen, Giles. Why don't you sit down for a minute so we can talk about this?"

Giles stopped pacing and looked out the window. "I'm scared, Don. I don't know what happened to those people, or why they were murdered, but somehow I'm responsible."

"Whoa, now. Let's not get carried away."

Giles turned away from the view and faced him. "Are you going to deny that I'm involved after what I just told you?"

"Easy, Giles, that's not what I meant. All I'm saying is that there's a big difference between being involved and being responsible. If you want my opinion, the police are full of crap. I think that cop was way off base coming to your house like that."

"He's a friend."

"Hmpf. With friends like that . . ."

Giles walked over to the couch and practically fell into it. Don was normally very protective of his morning work hours—they were reserved exclusively for phone calls to New York—but Giles had looked so panicked that he ushered him into his office right away. What Giles then proceeded to tell him, had Don alternately baffled and angry.

"It wasn't an official visit," said Giles. "I guess he was doing me a favor."

"Come on, the guy was harassing you. Thankfully you didn't tell him about the stories."

Giles put his head in his hands and Don decided to rein his anger in. "Giles," he said softly. "You were at home all last week—you told me so yourself. Now, if some psycho is killing people who happen to have the same names as the characters in your stories, it's not your fault. I'd even go so far as to argue that you're not involved.

"This guy could be obsessed with anyone's stories, Stephen King, Tom Clancy, Patricia Cornwell . . . Hell, he could have just as easily decided to kill people from Judith Krantz novels. It's not your fault."

Giles lifted his head and then sat back on the couch. "I realize that, Don, but the fact is they were *my* stories. *I* wrote them, not Judith Krantz. And how do you explain that both of these people lived right here in Seattle? Don't you see? How could I not have known about them? Jesus, you don't know what it's like to have a cop in your front room accusing you, and knowing he's right. I'm scared to write anything else."

"Hey, don't talk like that."

"It's true. I went downstairs this morning and just looking at my computer gave me the shakes."

Don didn't like where this was heading. "What about the novel?"

"What about it?"

"If this guy's as demented as we think he probably doesn't have the attention span to read novels. It sounds like he goes in for short stories. I'll bet he's so busy reading every horror magazine that comes out to find your stuff that he doesn't even know what's out in the bookstores."

"So what's your point?"

"Why not just work on the book? Nobody's going to get killed while you're writing a novel, right?"

"Yeah, like I'm really going to be able to stop thinking about this long enough to focus on a book." Giles was up again and pacing. "I don't know, Don, I just don't know what to do."

Don had never seen Giles this worked up. He'd been so confident the day before. Hell, he'd even solicited criticism, and today here he was talking about not writing at all. It was distressing. Don wanted to do something for Giles. He didn't want to just sit around telling him how everything was going to be fine. And then it came to him.

"Giles!" He blurted it out so loudly that Giles stopped in his tracks and turned to him. "What's the one thing that has you so upset?"

The incredulous look that Giles' face twisted into was almost frightening. "Are you serious?"

Don stood up and walked around the desk. "It was a rhetorical question." He took Giles by the arm and led him to the couch and sat him down. Then Don leaned against his desk and smiled. "I just thought of something. The real reason you're scared is that you don't know, positively, that the people you saw were the people who were killed, right?"

Giles looked puzzled and Don continued. "Look, the connection's only been established between your characters' *names* and these people who were murdered. The police did that for you, right?"

Giles nodded this time.

"Now, you say that you got the idea for the characters from people you actually saw, on the bus or wherever. But there still hasn't been any connection made between those people you saw and the ones who died. You knew the people who died had the same names as your characters, the only thing different now is that you know they were murdered.

"If I'm hearing you correctly, what you're really worried about is that the people you *saw* were the ones who were killed, *but you don't know that.*"

Giles looked a little more relaxed now. He seemed intent on Don's explanation and so Don continued. "If you could find out that the people you saw were still alive, that would absolve you of any responsibility, wouldn't it?"

"I already thought about that, but the only way for me to know would be to see the bodies. And it's too late for that now."

"Sure, maybe fore those two. But what about somebody you know? How about a new story where the person you write about is someone you see on a regular basis?"

"Jesus Christ, Don. Do you know what you're saying? And who do you suggest I single out for death?"

"Me."

There was silence in the room, but Don was smiling. The psycho-killer theory was interesting, but Don didn't put much faith in it. To his way of thinking the killings were coincidence, synchronicity if you wanted to attach some cosmic significance to it, but either way it was chance, pure and simple. If Giles wrote a story about him and had it published, when nothing happened it would prove that this thing was all in his head.

"No. I couldn't do that."

"Come on, what are you afraid of?"

"Besides the obvious?"

"Nothing's going to happen to *you.*"

For the first time that morning Giles was relaxed enough to grin. "But then I'll have to sell my stories myself."

"You'll save yourself ten percent"

Still grinning, Giles shook his head. "I really couldn't, Don. Not even for fifteen."

Don laughed. "Come on, I think it would be great. Have me be this mean and nasty agent who gets what's coming to him."

"Oh, so we're talking non-fiction now."

Don put his hand to his chest in mock pain and surprise. "I'm deeply hurt."

"Seriously Don, it's not what you think. I couldn't even if I wanted to. Writing stories—for me it's different. I can't just whip up something to order. I have to have . . . some kind of idea, inspiration, whatever you want to call it."

"Maybe I can help. We can come up with something together. I do know my way around the genre."

Giles sighed and sank back into the coach. Don stood and walked over to the picture window and looked out, thinking. The sky was a brilliant blue, and there was just enough of a wind to put white caps on the water of Elliott Bay. Down twenty stories below, the city was alive with cars and people, but behind the glass in Don's office there was only silence. He smiled.

Despite his protests, Don knew Giles wanted to do it. They both knew it would settle the matter once and for all. The only thing they needed now was an idea, something to give Giles' creativity a kick in the ass. The problem was Don had never been very good with ideas. He could recognize great fiction, but he really had no idea how to create it. The scariest thing he could think of sounded like a silly idea for a story.

When he was a small boy he had been afraid of pumpkins. Well, jack-o'-lanterns to be exact. It was something he had grown out of eventually, but even now he couldn't put his finger on exactly why they had frightened him. Maybe Giles could think up a reason.

"Listen, Giles, what do you think about—"

As Don turned away from the picture window, his eyes met Giles' and his words stopped dead. Giles was still sitting on the coach but his eyes were open wide and his jaw was hanging slack. He was staring so intently at Don that it was unnerving.

"Hey, Giles? You all right?" Don took a couple of steps and then stopped. Giles' eyes were tracking him. His heart was beating rapidly and for a moment he wasn't sure what to do. Giles was just sitting there. His arms were hanging limply beside him, and a thin strand of drool slowly inched down from his lower lip. He looked catatonic.

Don finally ran to his desk and grabbed the phone, acutely conscious of Giles' eyes burning into him. He was pounding out the digits of the security desk in the lobby when his hand froze. Suddenly Giles had spoken.

"I just don't think it's a good idea. That's all."

When Giles left Don's office it was a few minutes before ten. He had hoped that his talk with Don would help him decide what to do, and to some extent it had. But Don had begun to act strangely just before he left. And the idea about writing another story—that was positively ludicrous. Giles felt that while he might eventually be able to return to the novel at some point, any more stories were out of the question.

Even this early in the morning it was warm out. Giles pulled the Pontiac convertible out into traffic, and at the first red light he stripped off his sweatshirt. As he eased into traffic northbound on Aurora he thought again about what Don had said. He had been right about one thing, though. If Giles could be sure that the people he had actually seen were not the ones who had been killed, he would certainly feel a lot better.

He was glad he hadn't told Don about his possession, or trances, or whatever the hell they were. He hadn't had one since Collette Leavey, and she was no longer in danger of dying. There was a certain attraction to Don's offer to appear in a story, but Giles was certain if he had known about the trances he would never have suggested such a thing.

No, it was best for now just to play it safe. No more stories, no more calls to Daniel Lasky. Time to keep a low profile and hope the whole thing would blow over.

Giles parked in front of the house, grabbed his sweatshirt off the front seat and took the wooden steps to the front door two at a time. The house was dark and cool as he unlocked the door and stepped inside. He took a deep breath and walked up to the kitchen, dropping his shirt on the table.

Late morning sun was still streaming in through the windows, making patterns on the floor. He sat down and pulled off his sneakers, then stood up and walked to the fridge. The squares of light on the floor were warm under his feet. He pulled open the door and was about to reach for a beer when he saw the two empty six-pack cartons. Suddenly he remembered the night before. Giles shut the fridge and slumped back down in the kitchen chair. Paige hadn't been in bed when he woke up this morning, but to tell the truth he couldn't remember coming to bed the night before. Damn it, he thought, I did it again.

He hadn't had a chance to tell Paige about the visit from Daniel or anything. She had, no doubt, found him passed out on the couch. Jesus, why couldn't he remember? He looked at his watch. It was almost ten-thirty. She was probably with a patient, but he had to call her. He had to let her know he was sorry.

Giles stood and headed for the bedroom to use the phone in there, when he suddenly had the urge to go outside. As he opened the front door and stepped out onto the stairs he saw a white DHL delivery van pulling out of the driveway. Maybe that was what had drawn him out. He must have heard the vehicle subconsciously and that was why he'd looked outside.

Giles shook his head and went back into the house. When he shut the door he couldn't help noticing that it seemed awfully hot and stuffy. That's strange, he thought, and frowned. Hadn't it just been cool in here? And for the first time he noticed that he was drenched in sweat. His hair was matted to his forehead and he pushed it back. Not having showered this morning, he was also quite aromatic.

Immediately he walked up the stairs and went into the kitchen to open a window. But he stopped as soon as his feet hit the tile floor. Giles' heart was beating heavily in his chest. His sweatshirt was still on the table, one chair was pulled out, but something else was different: the squares of sunlight on the floor were gone. Before he even looked back up his throat began to tighten and perspiration began to flow again. The clock over the stove read three-thirty.

# PART
# TWO

# The Darkness Visible

People can die of mere imagination.

—Geoffrey Chaucer
*The Canterbury Tales*
"The Miller's Tale"

# Chapter Ten

Don Holman was working late in his office on Friday, October 31st. He was so busy that he didn't realize the significance of the date. The reason for his single mindedness was simple: in less than twelve hours he and Sharon would be hopping on a plane for Hawaii. He always had to work late the night before a vacation to get the office in shape before he left.

Don had already packed for the trip and had their golf clubs in the trunk of the car, and he was going to pick up Sharon at the ferry terminal the next morning. After that they would drive south of town to Sea-Tac International Airport, and then it was aloha, Seattle. Eight years ago, even though he had dragged his feet most of the way, Sharon had finally convinced him to plunk down some cash on a time-share condo north of Kaanapali, on the island of Maui. Don was afraid that being locked into a schedule every year would be a pain in the ass, but as it turned out—which it did more often than not—Sharon was right.

They had the condo for three weeks every November and were always back in time to have Thanksgiving dinner with her folks. But more than just being convenient, the condo had turned out to be a blessing: it seemed like every time October rolled around Don was itching to get out of town. He was planning on properly thanking his wife over the next few weeks. Tonight, however, he would be sleeping alone.

There were a myriad things to be done before he left town. Letters had to be drafted, his associates had to be briefed on various projects that were ongoing with his authors, and no matter how much he planned he could always count on one big disaster landing on his desk the night before he was supposed to leave on a trip. And this trip was no exception. As a result, Don had fallen into the habit of staying in a hotel the night before he and Sharon left on vacations.

The last ferry for Bainbridge didn't leave until 12:30, but after staying this late at work Don didn't want to do any driving at all. Nope, once he wrapped up things at the office he would walk the two blocks up to the Sheridan and crash as soon as his head hit the pillow. Then in the morning, after a wake-up call, a shower, and room service, he would pick up Sharon and the fun would begin.

It was nearing midnight, and Don was trying to remember if there was anything else he needed to do before closing up shop. The last thing he expected was to hear a knock on his door.

"What the—" he muttered, whirling around in his chair to look at the door. The only person he could think of who would be up here this late was a security guard. But the building didn't have security guards. They had one man down in the lobby, and that was it; he never left his desk. Or at least he wasn't supposed to.

"Who is it?" Don shouted.

The knock came again, louder, more insistent. He grabbed the phone and punched in the number for security. It rang but no one answered.

"Someone to see you, Mr. Holman," came a muffled voice from beyond the door, and Don slowly set the phone in its cradle.

It must be security, he thought; that was why no one had answered the phone downstairs. It must be damned important if someone had come here to see him in the middle of the night, and the guard at the desk was just making sure it wasn't some bozo trying to fake his way into my office. Good man. It was simple once he had thought it through.

Don stood and walked to the door, somewhat relieved but also a little apprehensive, wondering who it could be. He swung the door open, but there was only one man standing on the other side. He was wearing gray coveralls and brown work boots, and certainly didn't look like the guard downstairs.

"Who the hell are . . ." Don was confused until he looked into the man's face, and even after he recognized who it was he still couldn't figure out what was going on. But when he saw the jack-o'-lantern—three square teeth jutting out from its carved mouth, triangles cut out for eyes and nose, and candlelight flickering from inside its hollow shell—he knew.

The dark figure rushing along the sidewalk looked at his watch again and almost fainted; his wife was going to kill him. Camilo Serafin was heading up Fifth Avenue as fast as he could, a briefcase in one hand and the collar of his coat flipped up around his neck. He had only passed the bar a few months ago, and as a new associate lawyer with Chaney, Cushing and Lom he was putting in eighty-hour workweeks. The hours were killing him but it was worth it. Camilo's wife Marita, however, took an entirely different view.

She had spent eight long years putting him through school, and now was supposed to be the payoff; now they were supposed to be together, sharing their life, making babies. It wasn't fair, she said, that they made him spend more time away from her than he ever had when he was going to law school. Camilo tried in vain to explain it to her.

Because of his position with the firm they had a nice house, two cars, and the potential for a lot more. Marita always countered with the fact that they could have all the money in the world and it still wouldn't make up for the time she had to spend alone. She would make a good lawyer, he often thought. In the end, they compromised: the least he could do was come home for dinner, and if he had to go back to the office after that, he could.

But tonight Camilo had let the time get away from him. He hadn't called home and before he knew it, it was midnight. Parking for associates was free, the only catch was that the garage was five blocks away. Camilo was almost there, running as fast as he could past the Rainier Tower on his right, when he heard a noise.

He slowed up because the sound was so strange, a cross between the pop of a cork and a cymbal crash. It sounded close, but not really. It was almost as if it had come from above him. Camilo slowed to a walk and looked up just in time to be showered with glass. Before he had time to put his briefcase over his head and shake the shards from his hair, a body smashed to the ground directly in front of him.

Camilo was instantly splattered with blood and brains, and he looked down at his overcoat—the one Marita had bought him for his birthday—in disbelief. Only after he had regained his senses long enough to realize what had just happened, did he walk over to a nearby lamppost, lean his head over the curb and vomit.

Giles was working hard on the novel Saturday morning when the doorbell rang. The distraction was enough that he took time to quickly save the text and it suddenly rang again, so he trotted upstairs to answer it before it woke up Paige. There were two men standing on the front porch when he opened the door. They were both wearing black overcoats and serious expressions, and one of them held some papers, folded into thirds, in his hand.

"Are you Giles Barrett?" said the one with the papers.

Giles looked around, hoping to see Paige at the top of the stairs, but she wasn't there.

"Giles Barrett?" the man asked again, and Giles finally turned back.

"Yes," he said, and the other man grabbed him by the upper arm and pulled him out of the door. "What the fuck's going on?"

"We have a warrant for your arrest."

"Paige!" he yelled back into the open door.

"You're being charged with the murder of Donald C. Holman."

The news hit Giles like a sledgehammer and he almost collapsed going down the stairs. The man with the papers had to grab his free arm and together the two of them led him the rest of the way. Giles' throat had constricted to the point where he couldn't call out for Paige again. Don murdered? The thought was overwhelming. How could they possibly think he had done it?

Only now did he see that there were two cars in the front of the house, one of them a green-and-white King County Sheriff squad car with two uniformed officers standing next to it. The house was shielded from the neighbors by trees, but there was no way they could have missed this.

"You have the right to remain silent . . ."

The words were coming through a fog of emotion. How could Don be dead? There must have been a mistake.

". . . will be used against you . . ."

Don was going on vacation today, he and Sharon. They weren't even supposed to be in Seattle; they were going to Hawaii. He had talked with Don only last week.

". . . the right to an attorney . . ."

The door on the unmarked car was opened and he was guided toward it. Murder? Had they really said murder? What was going on?

". . . Do you understand theses rights as I have read them to you?"

They waited for an answer but Giles couldn't give them one. He had heard the words a thousand times on cop shows and movies, but never in real life. Was this real? Drops of water splashed his face, snapping him out of his trance. He looked up. It was beginning to rain.

"Mr. Barrett, do you understand your rights?"

"Yes," he blurted out, and instantly he wished he hadn't, because suddenly Paige came barreling out of the house.

"Get your hands off him, you son of a bitch!" she screamed, but Giles was pushed inside the unmarked car and the door was slammed shut.

It wasn't until he tried to sit up that he realized his hands were cuffed behind him. When he finally righted himself, he could see Paige coming toward the car. One of the uniformed officers tried to grab her but she twisted out of his grip. "Get your goddamn hands off me, and let him go!" The other officer caught her this time and she let loose with a string of profanity that, under ordinary circumstances, would have made Giles laugh.

As the car he was in pulled out of the drive, Giles noticed that his feet were still bare. They drove off, and in the background he could still hear Paige screaming.

The Saturday morning drive downtown was relatively devoid of traffic along Aurora, but there were plenty of traffic lights, and Giles had time to sober up along the way. The sky was a blanket of gray and occasional drops of rain dotted the windows where he sat. All he had on were his sweats and he was cold.

As far as he understood the situation, someone had killed Don, and evidently the police thought Giles had done it. Impossible. Giles felt twisted up inside, but it wasn't with fear; he hadn't done anything wrong. Most of the emotional strain he was feeling was over Don. He was also going to have to contact Paige somehow.

The car was driven up the exit ramp off Aurora, veering down Wall Street and then taking a left onto 2nd, into the heart of downtown Seattle. If he had looked, Giles probably could have seen the Rainier Tower, but he didn't want to. He hung his head down and didn't raise it until the car had stopped and the door was opened for him.

The car was in an alley. One of the plainclothes officers pulled him out and they stood in front of a door with a camera mounted above it to the right. The officer gave his name and was buzzed in. Giles stepped inside and was immediately confronted with two uniformed officers. The patches above their breast pockets read: King County Department of Corrections.

The four of them were in a small room about six feet square with glass on the two sides without doors. It felt to Giles as though they were in an aquarium. The cop announced that he was giving up custody and one of the corrections officers handed him a clipboard to sign while the other frisked Giles. When that was finished, the cuffs were taken off and given back to the cop before he left. The entire scene was being monitored by cameras and another corrections officer behind glass to Giles' right.

Next, the two officers led Giles through the door, down a small hallway, and into a large room that looked like the lobby of a bank. He was taken up to the counter where another officer took the clipboard, wrote down some information, and then began rattling off questions at Giles: name, address, birthdate, etc. And when that was finished he was taken across the room to a large holding cell containing maybe twenty other men.

Throughout the entire procedure Giles had remained relatively silent. Everything inside the facility was running according to plan. He was being processed. Once in the cell Giles found a place to sit and let his head fall into his hands.

He couldn't believe he'd been arrested. Even though he knew he was innocent, fear churned in his stomach. Somewhere above him a speaker called out a name in a dull monotone. One of the men stood and walked to the front of the cell where he was escorted out by one of the officers. It would be six hours before Giles heard his own name called.

When the car containing Giles had gone, and Paige had calmed down enough, the officer finally released her,

"Where are you taking him?" she demanded.

"Public Safety Building, ma'am."

"Where's that?"

"On James Street between 3rd and 4th. But you shouldn't go down there until someone calls."

Paige glared at him. "When I want your opinion, officer, I'll ask for it. Now get off my property!" She didn't wait for them to leave. She ran up the stairs into the house and slammed the front door. Then she headed immediately downstairs. Giles' computer screen was still glowing, and Paige almost broke down.

"You bastards," she muttered. "He was writing." She had no idea what he was working on, but she was damned if he was going to lose it. She quickly saved the text, but it had apparently already been done, then she shut down the computer. The closest thing they had to a lawyer was Don, and Paige looked through the papers on the shelves above Giles' desk until she found his address book.

She punched in the number for Don's Bainbridge home and waited, but there was no answer. What the hell was she going to do? They had an accountant, but a fat lot of good he was going to do them. She slammed down the phone. "Damn it."

Instantly she picked it back up and dialed the number to her office. A wave of relief swept over her when the receptionist answered. "Magnolia Dental Clinic. May I—"

"Connie! This is Dr. Barrett. Is Marcy with a patient?"

"Uh, I'm not sure."

"I need to talk to her right away."

"Okay, let me check."

Marcy liked to have a weekday off and usually worked until noon on Saturdays, then took Sunday and Monday off. Paige heard rustling on the other end of the phone, and then she heard Marcy's voice. "Paige?"

"Oh, Marcy, thank God you're there. Giles has been arrested."

"What for?"

"I don't know—they wouldn't tell me. Could you meet me at the police station? I don't know what I'm going to do."

"Sure. I have a couple more patients, but I can have Connie send them home. Where should I meet you?"

"Downtown. I can't remember the address. 3rd Avenue, I think. He said it was some public building."

"Okay, I'll find it. Are you all right?"

"I don't know. I'm just so goddamned mad. It was like the Gestapo coming in here or something—they just pulled him out of the house. Thank God I was already awake."

"Are you leaving right away?"

"Yeah, I just have to get dressed and then I'll be right there. Do you have a lawyer?"

"Sure. Do you want me to call him?"

"No. Not yet. As long as you're there with me, we can decide what to do together."

"Okay, I'll meet you there in a few minutes. If I'm late just wait for me on the street."

"Thank you, Marcy."

They said a quick goodbye and then Paige ran upstairs and into the bedroom. She shucked off the work clothes she had grabbed when she heard Giles yell, then stepped into a pair of jeans and pulled on a sweater. As she was slipping on her tennis shoes her hands trembled. She yanked the laces of her left shoe and tied it off quickly, but when she did the same to her right, one of the laces snapped. Her body jerked upward with the momentum, and she felt an intense pain in her stomach.

They were the only pair of tennis shoes she had. What was she going to wear now? The heat behind her eyes was pushing forward and she slipped her right shoe off and threw it with all her might across the bedroom.

"You son of a bitch!" It hit the top of her dresser with a crash, sending nearly everything on it to the floor. Then Paige slumped to the floor along with the thrown shoe and began to sob.

When Giles' name was called out he stood and walked to the door like all of the men he'd seen go before him. Watching through the glass, he was familiar with the process by now. At the counter he was asked more questions and his name was run through the computer for outstanding warrants. Then he was taken to an open room next to the counter for pictures and prints.

Giles was told to stand on a red line in front of a pole with hash marks indicating feet and inches. He turned to face the camera and a flash momentarily blinded him. Next he turned to his left and another flash went off.

When they had finished taking his mug shots he stepped forward to a desk for fingerprinting. The officer began, one by one, pressing each of his fingertips onto an ink pad and then rolling them onto a white card. He had to give three sets of prints with his individual fingers as well as two sets with all five together. In five minutes the whole process was finished and Giles was given a paper towel to wipe off his hands. The ink did not come off.

Finally, he was whisked away down another hallway and up to a nondescript wooden door. Giles was ushered inside and set down on a chair behind a wooden table with one empty chair on the opposite side. Then they left him alone and shut the door.

Giles stood as soon as the officer was gone and tried the door. It was locked. On the wall across from where he had been seated he saw his reflection in a large rectangular mirror, and suddenly Giles became self-conscious. It didn't take much imagination to figure out what that was for.

The room was twelve by twelve feet; all the other walls were a blank, dirty yellow. The wooden table was bolted to the floor, but the matching wooden chairs were free. Giles' bare feet were cold, as was the rest of him, and eventually he tired of pacing, threw the wad of paper towel on the table, and sat down.

He didn't have his watch on and had no idea how long he had waited; it could have been anywhere from fifteen minutes to an hour. His feet were dirty, his hands had ink on them; he was cold, hungry, and felt emotionally drained. Wasn't he supposed to get a phone call, or was that just a cop show fallacy? So far, everything else had been right on the money. He had to talk to Paige. She must be going crazy.

Eventually, the door opened. It was Daniel.

"Jesus, am I glad to see you," said Giles. "What the hell's going on?"

Daniel said nothing at first but tossed three plastic bags onto the table, each containing several sheets of typewritten paper.

"We found the stories, Giles."

# Chapter Eleven

The glare on the plastic from the single naked bulb overhead made it impossible to see what was in the bags, so Giles pulled them across the table in front of him. The first page in the top bag had the words "Street Walkers" typed in the center, and below that "by Giles Barrett." Giles recognized it at once as the story about Doug Boyd and the vampire.

He looked up. Daniel's expression was one of extreme disappointment. Giles was relieved. If Daniel had been supremely pissed off, things could be a whole lot worse. Giles pulled off the top bag and looked at the next story: "Retribution." That was the one about Gisele Kummer and the Golem.

The knot in Giles' stomach felt about the size of the basketball. He thought he'd been scared before, but that was nothing compared to what he felt now. His bowels felt loose and he had to pee. He felt as guilty as if he'd really killed them.

And he understood now, in a way he hadn't been able to before, that these people must have really died. The police had made the connection and thought he was responsible somehow. But that was the operative word: somehow. They must have been a little unsure about exactly what his involvement was. What other reason would there be to send in Giles' old high school chum to interrogate him? Daniel, however, was in no hurry, patiently waiting for him to finish, so Giles took a quick look at the last story.

"Trick or Threat," by Giles Barrett. Giles was puzzled. He'd never seen this before, and his eyes automatically scanned over the few lines of text visible on the first page. The story was about a literary agent named Alan Barlow, obviously based on Don.

He held up the bag. "What's this?"

"We found them in Holman's office, along with copies of all your other stories. They're not quite as accurate as the police reports, but they're just as detailed.

"No, no, I mean this last story. I've never seen it before. I never wrote this"

Daniel sighed and took the chair across the table from Giles. He looked weary. "Come on, Giles. Don't do this to yourself. It doesn't look very good."

"I mean it, Daniel. I never wrote this story."

At that he slammed his open hand on the table. "Goddamn it, Giles. Will you just stop it? It's too late for any more lies. We checked into your story on Kummer and Boyd, and guess who came out with egg on his face? Me. It turns out Giles Barrett doesn't have any books to sign."

Giles felt a blush creep up his neck. His lies had caught up with him, and that would make it a lot tougher for them to believe him now.

"Three people are dead, that we know of," said Daniel. "There are teams going over the rest of the stories right now. I didn't want it to happen this way, but they wanted you off the street."

Daniel sighed and rubbed the back of his neck as he leaned back in the chair. He was wearing a different suit since the last time Giles had seen him, but it still looked just as wrinkled. He was also sporting a days' worth of growth on his face, and his eyes looked bloodshot. "We're going to need a statement, Giles. We'll need to go through the murders one by one. Do you have a lawyer?"

Giles shook his head.

"Well, maybe you should think about getting one."

Suddenly the door whipped open, startling Giles. The two plainclothes officers who had arrested him stood in the doorway. "Lasky," one of them said, and Daniel stood up and walked over to them. They shut the door and once again Giles was alone. He could hear something like shouting going on outside the door but he couldn't make out anything specific.

When Daniel came back a few minutes later, he took the seat across the table from Giles again.

"Listen, Giles. I don't know what's going to happen from here on in. I may be part of the investigation, but it's looking like I might not. Get a lawyer."

Giles didn't like the sound of this. "I don't know any. Who should I get for something like this?"

"Damn it, Giles. What are you trying to do to me?"

"I need your help, Daniel."

"You lied to me."

That stopped the conversation dead in its tracks, but Giles was desperate. "I know, and I'm sorry about that. But I don't know who else to ask. I don't know who to trust. I called *you*, remember? Or none of this would have happened."

Daniel nodded, then took out a small notebook from the breast pocket of his coat and a pen from his shirt. His face was stoic. "I'm sorry, Giles. I'd like to help you, but I can't." He wrote something down. "From what we can tell so far, you've lied about everything." He quietly tore out the page, replacing his notebook and pen. "And when this thing comes to trial, I'm afraid I'll have to testify to that."

Daniel folded up the slip of paper and pushed it to the middle of the table. Giles suddenly became aware that from where Daniel was sitting—the one-way glass positioned directly behind him—no one could see what he had done.

Giles didn't react. "So, what happens now?"

"Do you want to answer some questions?"

Giles looked at the slip of paper; folded up tightly into a tiny square it looked like little more than a gum wrapper. He pushed his hands forward on the table, almost touching it, and said, "I think I'd better make a phone call first."

Daniel rubbed his red eyes and nodded. When he pushed his chair back to stand up, Giles simply picked up the paper and held it in his hand while Daniel walked away. The door opened before he reached it and one of the other cops whispered something to Daniel. Then he turned back to Giles.

"Let's go."

Giles was taken out of the interrogation room by a uniformed officer and led to the holding cell he'd been in earlier. There were a dozen men in the cell, none of whom Giles recognized from before. He stood for a moment against one wall of glass, and when the officer had gone he unfolded the slip of paper and read it.

*Janet Raymond.* That was all it said. She must be a lawyer, Giles thought, and wondered what he was going to do with the paper; there were no pockets in his sweats.

An hour later Giles heard his name called. He tore the paper into a few pieces and dropped them before he stepped up to the door. Two officers guided him down a hallway and into another large room. This one looked like a department store. Giles was given a towel, soap, toothbrush, toothpaste, comb, and shower shoes, then led to a green-tiled institutional restroom just off this main room. After finally being able to relieve himself he was told to strip down and shower.

It felt good under the hot water and Giles luxuriated in the hot spray until one of the guards stuck his head in and yelled, "Let's go." He hadn't soaped down, brushed his teeth, or anything, and he didn't care. He dried off and was about to dress when the guard told him to bring his clothes out with him.

Naked, Giles handed over his clothes and was given a pair of briefs, white socks and a t-shirt, red denim pants, a matching red pullover shirt, and a pair of tan canvas slip-on shoes. He dressed quickly in front of the guards. Next he was handed a gold blanket, two white sheets, and a thin foam bedroll. On these he placed his toiletries and waited while one of the guards made a phone call.

The guards wore stern looks and their orders were short, but Giles didn't feel as though they hated him. They were doing a job; it wasn't personal. They took him down a long hallway to what felt like the other end of the building and then they waited by an elevator. One of the men spoke to a camera mounted on the wall. "9th floor, west."

"On its way," a tinny voice answered through a speaker. Giles could hear the elevator descending.

As they waited, Giles looked around and was amazed at the facility. Every one of the ten-foot high walls, from the three-foot to seven-foot mark, was glass—bulletproof, he assumed. It looked thick and slightly yellowed, but Giles could see everywhere with perfect clarity. It was remarkable.

Every so often a small room housing a single guard and banks of monitors was visible. Everything was easily controlled because each guard could see everything that was going on from everywhere in the building. Escape—though Giles couldn't even imagine trying—seemed impossible.

When the elevator opened the three of them walked inside. The guards pressed no buttons but the doors closed automatically and they were whisked up to what Giles assumed must be the ninth floor.

They stepped off on what he further assumed was the west wing and headed down to the central hub of the floor, the same glass all around affording Giles a look at the housing floors. Each wing appeared to have several large common rooms spreading out before a command post like a fan.

At the central hub the two guards turned Giles over to two other guards then left. One of the new men began frisking Giles again while the other went through his sheets, blanket and bedroll.

After that, Giles was turned over to two more guards and taken into the west wing proper. Now he could see that there were five rooms on each of the two levels. The guard called to an officer at a glass-enclosed desk. "Tank B, felony."

The door to the lower level was opened and Giles was led down the stairs and onto the floor. The racket was unbelievable. Everywhere he could hear the sound of men talking and shouting over the blaring of television sets and radios. One particular chant that cut through the pungent air was, "New meat. New meat."

Giles hoped they weren't talking about him. But when he

looked over, one of his guards smiled at him. Giles had thought that things couldn't get any worse. Now he wasn't so sure.

Tank B, it turned out, was a large semi-circular area constructed of white concrete blocks, sectioned into four rooms. Each room held about twenty men, most of whom were lying on their bedrolls and staring blankly at the TV set suspended above the doorway. One of the guards cleared a space between reluctant prisoners and then turned back to Giles. "Set your stuff down and come with us."

Giles didn't ask why; he did as he was told. He followed the guards back the same way he'd come in. After another pat down at the central hub, he was taken into a long rectangular room that looked like every prison visiting room he'd ever seen in the movies. The long room had banks of sit-down phone booths with a plastic chair at each one.

As they walked, he could see several other prisoners seated, talking through a phone receiver to people on the other side of the glass. The guard in front of him stopped, and when Giles looked into the empty booth he saw Paige sitting on the other side.

She was wearing jeans and a baggy sweater. Her calf-length gray raincoat was open and he could see large splotches of moisture on it as though it had been raining hard. Her hair looked messy only because he knew how she liked to wear it; it was so short that most people wouldn't have noticed.

But once he'd pulled out the chair and sat down, the less Giles noticed about her superficial appearance. Her eyes were rimmed with red and looked vacant, and her mouth hung open as she breathed. She must know, he thought.

"Don's dead," she said as soon as Giles put the phone to his ear. "They think you killed him." She was staring at him with a look that, had he not known her better, could be constructed as accusatory.

"I know," he said.

"I brought you a pair of shoes and some clean clothes, but they wouldn't let me bring them up."

Giles looked down at his red denim outfit. "Yeah, they've got everything taken care of here."

She didn't even seem to hear him. "You were in bed last night, with me."

"I know, hon', but they also think I did the other murders, Kummer and Boyd."

"What's going on, Giles?"

"It's the stories—they found them in Don's office and now they think I'm responsible."

"So it's true? Those were the same people you saw?"

"I still don't know for sure, but it's beginning to look that way. I haven't seen pictures of them, but I think so."

"Why do they think you killed Don?"

Giles wanted to reach through the glass and take Paige in his arms. "They have a story about Don with my name on it."

She looked shocked. "You wrote a story about Don?"

Giles shook his head. "Of course not. I've never seen it before. I don't know who wrote it, but it wasn't me."

There was only silence in the receiver. On his side of the glass Giles heard a few coughs, someone in the booth next to him hawked and spit, and all around him, it seemed, was a dull throbbing hum. "We need a lawyer," he said finally.

"Marcy came with me. Do you want me to get hers?"

"No. I want you to try and find someone named Janet Raymond. I think she's a lawyer. If not, she can probably find one for me."

Paige gave him a funny look. "Just try," he said. "I know it's Saturday—if you can't reach her, go ahead and get Marcy's lawyer. Somebody has to get me out of here."

Paige put her elbow on the counter in front of her and leaned her head in her hand. "I'm scared."

"Me too, honey. Just get me out of here, okay?"

She nodded.

"I didn't do anything, Paige. Please don't worry."

"Okay. I'll try to take care of this as fast as I can. Are you going to be all right?"

"I'm going to have to be."

She nodded and hung up the phone. Just as quickly she was gone from his sight and the guard was at his elbow waiting to take him back to his cell.

He'd told her he was innocent in an attempt to reassure her. But he couldn't have said whether or not he believed it himself. At this point, Giles wasn't sure of anything.


"How is he?" Marcy asked with genuine concern, but Paige barely heard her. She couldn't get her mind off the stories.

What was going on? Everything she had tried to reassure him against suddenly seemed to have come true. "He has the name of a lawyer he wants me to call. Janet Raymond." She walked past Marcy and ran her fingers through her hair. Paige still couldn't believe that Don was dead.

"Can we have a phone book?" Marcy asked the desk sergeant. "The white pages."

"Sure. No problem."

The officer handed Marcy the book and she flipped through it.

"There's no Janet Raymond listened. Do you want me to call my lawyer?"

"Would you mind?"

"Not at all." Marcy flipped through the book again, asked the officer if she could make a call, and then punched out the numbers on the phone he pushed over to her.

"Hi, John? This is Marcy Miller. I'm sorry to call you at home like this, but a friend of mine has a problem." She listened for a moment and continued. "Before I tell you, I was wondering if you'd ever heard of a Janet Raymond." Marcy looked over at Paige. "Yes, it's criminal." She nodded now. "Bellevue? Sure, I didn't even think of that. Thank you so much, John." Then Marcy laughed. "How about if we have you and Susan over for dinner? . . . Great. Thanks, John. Bye-bye," she said, and hung up the phone.

Marcy looked at Paige and squinted behind her glasses. "He

says she's one of the best criminal defense lawyers in the city, but that she doesn't come cheap."

Paige frowned. "What was that at the end?"

"Oh, he was just saying that he didn't know how much to charge me for a home phone consultation."

"Well, I guess I'd better call her. I don't want Giles to stay in jail any longer than he has to."

Paige dialed the number for information, and breathed a sigh of relief when the recording began to rattle off the number. Marcy handed her a pen from her purse and Paige wrote it down, then she hung up and dialed again.

"Hello?"

The voice sounded like that of a small child, but Paige had never liked the condescending phrase, "Is your mother home?" After all, she didn't know anything about this woman. The tiny voice on the other end could even be her. "Hello, may I speak to Janet Raymond, please?"

The phone on the other end clunked down so hard it made Paige wince. Then she heard the wail of, "Mom! It's for you!"

A minute later a more mature voice answered. "Hello?"

"Hello, I'm so sorry to call you out of the blue like this, but my name's Paige Barrett and my husband's in jail. He gave me your name and wanted me to call you."

"Did he also tell you that I usually require a ten-thousand dollar retainer?"

Paige had eight thousand in her savings. She could probably borrow the rest. "I could write you a check, but it wouldn't clear until I could borrow some money."

"That's okay. I wouldn't deposit it until I decided to take the case. Why don't you tell me about it?"

Paige told her what she knew, a composite of what the detective and Giles had told her, about the stories and Don.

"And you were with him last night?" asked Raymond.

"Yes."

"And the police know this?"

"I told the detective."

There was a pause and finally Raymond said, "This doesn't sound right at all. I'm going to make a few phone calls and then I'll want to come down there and talk to your husband. You're at the King County Jail?"

"The Public Safety Building."

"Same thing. Okay, I'll meet you there in an hour or so."

"How will I know you?"

"Don't worry. I'll find you."

"Thank you, so much."

"Don't thank me yet. I haven't decided to take the case."

"Well, I appreciate your coming down here anyway."

"All right. I'll talk to you in an hour."

When Paige hung up she turned to Marcy, and relief began to flow out in the form of tears. The two women embraced, and Paige said, "I think she's going to do it."


Two hours after Paige had left him, the door to Tank B opened. A guard walked up to the cell Giles was in and yelled out, "Barrett."

Giles stood quickly and walked out of the room alongside the officer. After another pat down he was led to a series of doors next to the visitor's room. The guard opened one of them and let him in. It was similar to the interrogation room he'd been in earlier, but this time there was a woman seated at the table, and no two-way mirror.

"Mr. Barrett," she said, standing up and offering her hand.

"Yes," he said shaking.

"I'm Janet Raymond."

The woman was about five-feet-six, with shoulder-length brown hair. She was thin and dressed casually, in jeans and a blouse, a strand of pearls around her neck and a wedding band on her left hand. She had extremely luminescent blue eyes and didn't appear to be wearing any make-up.

"First off," she said when they were seated, "I'd like to ask you where you got my name."

Giles hesitated, and she seemed to sense this. "Don't worry,

Mr. Barrett. Anything you tell me is confidential, even if I don't take the case."

"Please, call me Giles."

She nodded.

"I got your name from Daniel Lasky."

She smiled this time and with the tension gone from her face, Giles thought she was extremely attractive. "So, you're a friend of Dan's."

"We went to high school together."

"But he's not the arresting officer."

"No. But he is the reason I'm here. That is, it's because he knows about the stories that I was arrested."

"Why don't you tell me about it?"

Giles started at the beginning and spilled everything. Everything, that was, except the trances. All he told her was that the stories had come to him after seeing these people, and then he assured her that he had written no such story about Don.

"Well, they found the story in an envelope." Raymond was standing now, her hands in her pockets as she paced. "The envelope also contained a check, made out to you, and a copy of the magazine with the story under your byline."

"Which magazine?"

She walked over to the table and looked at her notes. "Something called *Dark Imaginings*. There was also a letter stating that the only address they had for you was your agent's. They apologized for any inconvenience this may have caused, and suggested that if you wanted to have future checks mailed to you directly, you should provide them with an address."

Giles wiped the sweat from his forehead with the back of his hand. "I don't know who's responsible for sending them that story, but it's obvious that Don didn't know about it, and Don placed every story I ever wrote."

"So you think someone else wrote the story under your name?"

"Yeah. It's the only thing I can think of, and in a crazy way it kind of makes sense."

"How so?"

"I had pretty much decided to stop writing stories. I was phasing them out and concentrating my energy on a novel. Now, if the same guy who was responsible for the other murders wasn't getting any more material to use, maybe he started writing his own."

"The story didn't use Don Holman's name."

Giles frowned and nodded. That had bothered him, too, "All I can think of is that he didn't know my agent's name when he wrote it, but made a point of finding out when he knew the story was going to be published."

"And somebody could do that? Write a story and put your name on it?"

"Sure. I suppose. I mean, almost all stories are sold by mail. And if he was that obsessed with my writing, maybe he was able to pass off his story as mine. It could be done."

Raymond sat down and began writing on a yellow legal pad while Giles leaned back in his chair, thinking.

He felt infinitely better knowing he had someone to defend him. But the more the fear of being arrested began to abate, the more his grief over losing Don took its place. Their relationship had spanned nearly fifteen years, first as teacher and student, then as partners, and ultimately as friends. It was all too unreal. Then his thoughts wandered to Sharon. Did she know? Was she out in some detective's office now? Did she know that Giles was in here and that they thought he did it?

"Do you know what happened to Don?" Giles asked Raymond.

She stopped writing and looked up at him. "They didn't tell you?"

"No."

"Someone threw him through his office window."

Giles' throat seized up on him and he buried his head in his hands without saying anything. After a few minutes he was able to speak. "Was he already dead?"

Raymond shook her head slowly. "I'm sorry. The police don't think so."

"And it wasn't a suicide?"

"No. There's evidence that someone else was in his office, signs of a struggle."

"Oh, Jesus." Suddenly Giles didn't think he could take one more minute of confinement. "Can you get me out of here?"

Raymond pulled a briefcase up from the floor and opened it, placing the legal pad and pen inside. "I'm afraid I have some bad news for you, Giles. Their evidence stands mostly on the story, and the fact that you don't have an alibi."

"But I was asleep with my wife."

"Yes, I realize that, but in this state a spouse's testimony is not considered substantiation. I'm not worried about that too much, though. Unless the police are holding back evidence that they plan to *discover* over the weekend and present at the arraignment, I think I can get the charges dismissed for lack of evidence.

"I called and talked with the city attorney as soon as I got off the phone with your wife. I tried to persuade him to drop the charges, but I didn't have any luck. For some reason he wants to see how far he can go with this thing. He wants to make a case of it. Maybe he's waiting to charge you with the other murders—I don't know. But from what I've heard, I really don't think they're going to be able to produce any direct evidence linking you to the murders."

"I'm glad you feel that way. What happens now?"

"That's the bad part. We'll have to wait until your arraignment before I can get you released on bail, or the charges dropped."

"And when's that?"

Raymond snapped the locks shut on her briefcase and pulled it off the table to her side. "Arraignment court doesn't meet again until Monday morning."

# Chapter Twelve

Paige sat in the car for nearly fifteen minutes, gripping the steering wheel but not going anywhere. Her emotions drained dry, she didn't cry either, but simply sat there listening to the rain pound on the roof of the car and trying to figure out why all of this had happened.

They had made her wait all day before she was allowed in to see Giles. They wouldn't even let her give him his clothes. The only bright spot was Janet Raymond. She seemed very . . . capable, was the only word Paige could think of. If she could get Giles out it would be worth the whole ten thousand. But that wouldn't be until Monday, an incredibly long weekend away. Eventually, Paige started up the car and drove home in a daze.

The last few months had been good—not great, but within acceptable limits. They had talked, and Giles had confided in her about his visit from Daniel Lasky. There were arguments and much soul-searching, and when all was forgiven and forgotten, a certain calmness extended over their relationship that had been missing all summer. But there was still the drinking.

Giles was putting away two six-packs a week, and even though he was never drunk, it was a constant reminder of how things had degenerated between them. He was working on the novel again, too: another scary proposition, although from what she'd heard about the stories and the murders, she thought it was probably for the best.

Gradually, as the tension eased, Paige had been able to come home from work without feeling drained and, until this morning, she had been ready to believe that the worst was behind them. No such luck.

Paige pulled into the driveway, shut the motor off and sat some more. What was the point of going inside? Giles was in jail, would be until Monday, and all she could do was sit and think about it, endlessly. She left the car outside and climbed the steps into the house. The rainy day perfectly reflected her mood.

The pot of coffee Giles had made that morning was still nearly full. Paige poured herself a mug and put it in the microwave before slumping down in one of the kitchen chairs. She had been awake when the doorbell rang, but she was naked in bed reading and had let Giles get it. When she heard him scream, she'd jumped up and looked out the window, then dressed as fast as she could. The whole thing still seemed like a dream, except for one painful reminder: Giles was gone.

Paige stood up and walked into the bedroom, heard the microwave shut off and ignored it, then looked at the pile of books next to the bed. The last thing she would be able to do this weekend was read. Her concentration was shot to hell. This was her favorite time of the week, the time she spent alone with her husband, and now she just wanted it to be over.

After changing into a long flannel nightshirt, she made her way back out to the living room and sat down on the couch. There was only one way she was going to be able to soak up the next forty-eight hours, and she picked up the remote control to the TV and turned on the time sponge.

Giles' ass was killing him. When he'd come back to his spot on the floor the second time, after meeting with Janet Raymond, he found his bedroll and sheets were missing. The only thing between him and the concrete was his gold blanket.

There were twenty-two other men in his cell, and about the same in each of the other three cells in Tank B. Somehow, the other men seemed to know that Giles was in for murder. The one good effect this had was that they left him alone.

Across from Giles, a Native American man stared intently at him. He was about fifty, with long silver braids, and wearing red like everyone else in the cell. Two white guys who looked like body builders were occupying the space directly in front of the TV. A kid no more than twenty with a wispy black mustache who could have been Latino, Asian or a mixture of both preferred to pace in front of the cell door. And another white guy, Giles' age, with glasses, was leaning against the wall next to the shower. Every other man in the cell was black.

It was not a sociable group. A few of the black guys acted as if they might be pals, but the rest of his cellmates kept to themselves, and that was fine with Giles. He figured that he must have missed lunch during one of his excursions out of the cell. But even though his stomach was rumbling, that wasn't the worst of it. No, boredom was the killer here. The TV was turned to some inane sit-com. Giles would have given anything for a book to read.

There wasn't much to do in the cell except watch TV, which he wasn't interested in, or look at his shoes and think about what had transpired today. The past few weeks had been pretty good. The day he'd told Paige about Daniel coming over, Giles had been scared. He'd lost five hours that day and he had absolutely no idea where they'd gone. It hadn't been like his normal blackouts, either, because he couldn't remember even having it . . . or writing the story.

Yes, things were becoming clear now, painfully clear. In his mind he could still see the DHL delivery van pulling out of the driveway, and he had a pretty good idea why. Its cargo, no doubt, was a story, destination: *Dark Imaginings*. Sure, someone else could have written it, but they didn't. He didn't know why he would have done it, but it was the only thing that made sense.

And if it were true, then he must be responsible for killing Don. The thought of being a murderer was too terrible to even consider, but if he could write a whole story and not remember any of it afterward, what else was he doing? Was he getting out of bed in the middle of the night, without disturbing Paige, and killing people himself? Had he already turned into some kind of sick, twisted psychopath?

Giles spread his blanket out, then laid down on the cold concrete and shut his eyes. If only he could shut off his brain. A half-hour later a guard brought around a trolley of food trays and fed them. When dinner was over he was surprised to find himself escorted yet again to one of the interview rooms where Janet Raymond was waiting for him.

"Hello, Giles," She said as the door shut behind him.

"Ms. Raymond."

"Please, call me Janet."

"Janet."

Giles took a seat across the table from Raymond and she immediately began speaking. "In about ten minutes they want to bring us both into another room and videotape a statement from you. If everything you've told me is the truth—"

"It is."

"—then I think you should do it."

Giles took a deep breath and ran his hands through his hair. "Do you really think it will help?"

"I do, but it's your decision."

He nodded. "Okay, what do you want me to do?"

"Tell me one more time about the stories . . ."

The interrogation room Giles and his lawyer were led to had none of the pretense of the first. A video camera on a tripod was sitting in the middle of the room facing the hot seat. It was a large room, carpeted, with two long tables on each side of the camera. There was one woman in the room and six other men, only one of which Giles recognized: Daniel Lasky.

All of them were standing and one of the men, impeccably dressed in a dark blue suit, walked up to Raymond immediately. "We all set, then?"

"Yes," she said.

"Good. Mr. Barrett, would you take the seat out front please?"

Giles did as instructed and sat down. Daniel nodded at him,

and he nodded back, a silent acknowledgment to the presence of Janet Raymond. There was a uniformed officer manning the video camera, and the snappy dresser signaled him to start before turning his attention to Giles.

"Mr. Barrett, you've been read your rights previously, and your counsel is present. Do you choose to speak with us and answer our questions, and have your statement recorded on videotape?"

Giles looked at Raymond and she nodded.

"Yes."

"Good. Do you understand what it is you've been charged with?"

"You think I killed Don."

"You're being held as a suspect in the murder of Donald C. Holman. Most of our questions will relate to this case but, on prior approval of counsel, we will also be asking questions about two related homicide cases, one Douglas Boyd, and one Gisele Kummer. Are you willing to answer questions about those two cases as well?"

Raymond nodded again and Giles said, "Yes."

"Good, then we can get underway. I'm Detective Dalton, of the West Division, and this is my partner, Detective Haggerty." The natty Dalton motioned to the man next to him, wearing a tweed jacket and clenching an unlit pipe between his teeth.

"We're the detectives in charge of the Holman and Boyd murders," Dalton said of himself and Haggerty. Then he pointed to the young looking black man in jeans and a wool sweater on the other side of him. "This is Kevin Adamson, the city attorney." Adamson wore his hair short, along with wire-frame glasses and a continuous scowl, his hands thrust deep into the front pockets of his jeans. Clearly, he was a man who thought he had something important to do in convicting Giles.

Finally Dalton swept his arm toward the man and woman standing behind him. "And these are Detectives Kimura and Itlis out of the department's North Division, in charge of the Kummer investigation."

Kimura was a slightly built Asian, about five-six with his black hair worn in a brush cut. Iltis, on the other hand, was a big boned woman with blonde hair who stood six inches taller and outweighed her partner by about fifty pounds.

Dalton continued. "Lieutenant Lasky you already know."

Once Raymond and Iltis were seated, the rest of the men followed suit, with the exception of the uniformed officer who stood behind the camera during the entire interrogation.

"Now, Mr. Barrett," Dalton began. "We'd like to begin by asking you how you came to write the story, 'Trick or Treat?'"

Giles took a deep breath and said, "I didn't . . ."

The questioning seemed to go on endlessly, the detectives, especially Dalton, asking the same things over and over again. Daniel was silent through most of it, only talking when Dalton asked for clarification. Adamson and his scowl were silent as well. Two hours into the interrogation the uniform had to stop and change the tape in the camera.

Dalton took the opportunity to stand and stretch his legs, and Haggerty to light his pipe. At that, Iltis and Adamson lit up cigarettes while Giles tried to ward off the fatigue that was rapidly setting in. His muscles were tight and he rubbed his shoulders and the kinks in his neck, but it was little use. He felt tense and his head was beginning to ache. The smoke in the room didn't help.

Once the tape had been changed and the camera was rolling again, Dalton took two photographs from the inside pocket of his suit coat and walked around the far side of the table so as not to obstruct the view of the camera. Then he thrust the pictures in front of Giles.

"Do you recognize these two people, Mr. Barrett?"

It was several moments before Giles could force himself to breath. Then he covered his face with his hands and shook his head. The pipe and cigarette smoke was making his stomach roil and he felt as if he were going to vomit. When he was finally able to look up, everyone in the room was standing and he looked to Raymond. "Please, I can't do this anymore tonight."

"That's it," Raymond said, and was suddenly by Giles' side helping him out of the chair.

Dalton took a step toward her. "But, Janet—"

"No. I said it's over. Your haven't come up with anything that connects him to the crime scene in any of the murders, and frankly, I don't think you're going to."

"He's not going anywhere until Monday, you know."

"Fine. Then you won't need him anymore tonight, will you?"

"Come on, Janet—"

"I said, no."

Giles was led to the other end of the room and out the door. Raymond walked with him as far as the elevator and she left saying that she would call on him in the morning after breakfast. Giles was still in a daze. He said goodbye and walked like a zombie between the corrections officers back to his cell, the images of the two photographs swimming before him.

Doug Boyd, the young man he had seen in downtown Seattle, and Gisele Kummer, the women he had seen on the bus—*they* were the faces in the photographs. They were the people in his stories, and they were the people who had been murdered . . . just the way he'd written it.

The phone rang, and for a moment Paige was disoriented as she came fully awake. She was still on the coach where she had fallen asleep in front of the TV the night before. It could be about Giles, she thought, and pushed herself up a little too quickly, almost tripping over the coffee table. But she was able to rush out to the kitchen and picked it up after the third ring.

"Hello?"

"Dr. Barrett?"

"Yes?"

"This is Janet Raymond."

"Hello. What is it? Is it about Giles?"

"I'm sorry to call so early, but I wanted to know if you'd be able to come down to the jail this morning."

Paige looked at the clock. It was just after nine. "Of course. Is he getting out?"

"Not that I know of. But I will be talking with him this morning, and I wanted to meet with you afterward to discuss everything that's going to happen in the next couple of days. Can you be there at eleven?"

"Certainly. Thank you for calling me."

"You're welcome. I'll see you in a couple of hours then."

"Yes. Goodbye."

Paige hung up the phone. Her mouth tasted awful, and she rubbed the sleep out of her eyes as she walked into the bathroom. She hadn't wanted to stay in the bedroom without Giles the night before, and that's why she'd fallen asleep on the coach. She rubbed the back of her neck as she brushed her teeth, and then climbed into the shower. Paige only had two hours to do what she should have done yesterday.

She toweled off quickly, dressed, and headed out to the garage. The rain had stopped and there was sun coming through the breaks in the clouds. It was still cold, though, and she pulled her raincoat tight around her as she opened the garage door and froze. The car was gone. It took a moment before she remembered that she had left the Peugeot in the driveway. She hit the garage door opener, and after it opened she climbed inside the car started it up. When it was warm, she backed out and drove south down Aurora to Magnolia and into a parking lot next to the Elliott Bay Medical Center.

The building where Paige's dentist office was located housed seven dental specialists and one other general dentistry practice. She parked the car, walked up to the front door and unlocked it. Paige was running on autopilot, trying not to think about Giles.

She sat down at the reception desk and pulled out the appointment book, flipping the pages open to Monday. She had to call her patients and reschedule so that she could be with Giles tomorrow. Instead of turning on the heat, she left her coat on and hoped that the cold would help her work faster. Some coffee would have been welcome, but there wasn't time. So she took a deep breath and waded into her phone calls.

An hour later there was only one patient she hadn't been able to reach. Marcy wouldn't be in on Monday, and though Paige wasn't happy about having Jeanette work on him, she wrote a note asking Jeanette if she could see Mr. Nordlund in the event Connie couldn't reach him that morning. She supposed she should be thankful, though, if she had been in a solo practice she wouldn't have this luxury. She'd just be stuck.

After leaving the office there wasn't enough time to go home before her meeting with Janet Raymond, so she drove downtown to look for someplace to eat breakfast. Not even the thought that she might get to see Giles today buoyed her spirits. All she wanted was for this whole nightmare to be over.

At nine-thirty Sunday morning Giles was led back to the interview room. Janet Raymond was standing at the far end of the room when he walked in.

"They want to talk to you again at ten," she said. "Do you think you're up to it?"

"Sure, but do you think it will do any good?"

Raymond frowned at him. "Listen, Giles, I wouldn't be here if I didn't think it would do any good. Do you really want to spend another night in here?"

"No—"

"Then I suggest you tell them anything and everything you know." Giles looked down at his feet while Raymond continued. "You recognized the pictures, didn't you?"

He nodded. "Should I tell them I don't?"

"Absolutely not. Like I said, if you want to get out of here you'll tell the truth. If they catch you in a lie they won't have any reason to believe anything else you've said."

"You keep talking like I'm getting out of here today. I thought we didn't go to court until tomorrow."

Raymond set her briefcase down and sat at the table. Giles pulled out the other chair and took a seat across from her. The intensity of Raymond's gaze told him how serious this was. He listened.

"You remember Adamson, the guy who looks like he'd just as soon skip the trial and go right to execution?"

Giles managed a smile and nodded.

"Well, he's the city attorney. He's the guy who has to convince the judge on Monday that there's sufficient evidence to hold you for trial. That's why he's been in there listening to the questioning. But what does he really have so far? You've admitted to writing the stories, and today you'll go in there and tell them that the people in the photos were the ones you wrote about.

"But that's nothing, certainly not enough to hold you on, anyway. They have absolutely no physical evidence to put you at the scene of any of the murders, and that's what's going to get you out of this. So what they're looking for is to catch you in a lie—they're looking for a chink in your armor, because that's the only thing that will convince them that they just haven't looked hard enough. They're desperate. And after I tell Adamson what I found out this morning, I seriously doubt whether he's going to want to prosecute."

Giles kept nodding. He wasn't sure what it all meant, but he knew that it didn't matter. He was going to do whatever Raymond told him to. At ten o'clock he was taken to the same interrogation room. Everyone from the evening before was there, including Dalton, Adamson, and Daniel. Giles took the hot seat without being asked, Dalton went through the same spiel again, obtaining Giles' permission to be taped, and then they were underway.

Dalton began where he had left off, with the pictures of Boyd and Kummer. Giles was much more composed this time, and although the detectives were initially captivated by his disclosure, the questions quickly degenerated into a rehash of the ones he had already answered about Don.

Two hours later, when the tape had to be changed, Raymond stood up. "Is that all you have?"

"Look, Janet," said Dalton. "We just want to get the story straight—"

"Well, let me see if *I* have it straight. You have no evidence that puts my client at the scene of a crime, you have nothing to prove he wasn't at home with his wife each of the three nights, and you don't have a motive."

Dalton was on his feet instantly. "Then why can't he explain why he wrote those stories? What about that bullshit call to Lasky? And how did he know exactly how all three murders were committed?"

"He didn't," Raymond said calmly. "But the murderer did. I was on the phone all morning tracking down the editors of the magazines where my client's stories appeared. Without exception, each of the issues in question appeared on the newsstands at least twenty-four hours before the murders took place. Anyone could have read his stories and copied the killings he described. In the case of Boyd and Kummer, it may have been bad judgment for Mr. Barrett to use their real names, but it wasn't murder."

Dalton stormed over to her. "That doesn't prove anything, and you know it."

"I'm glad you recognize that fact, Stan. We don't *have* to prove anything. You do."

"I don't believe this bullsh—"

"Kick him."

The room instantly became silent. The voice had been Adamson's. Dalton whirled back toward the city attorney. "Come on, Kevin. You can't do this to us."

Adamson stood up. He looked at Giles for a moment and then turned his attention back to Dalton. "Do you have anything to put him at the scene?"

"We have fingerprints, hair samples, carpet fibers from—"

Raymond grunted her contempt and the twist on Adamson's mouth was the closest thing to a smile Giles had ever seen on him. "You're pushing, Stan," said Adamson. "You know the guy was his agent. He would have had prior entry. How about the other two?"

When Dalton turned and walked away, Haggerty spoke up. "Nothing."

Adamson looked over at Raymond, "You win, Janet," and then back to Dalton. "Kick him." And with that Adamson turned and left the room.

As the other detectives began to file out after him, Giles could only remain seated in his chair, stunned. Was it really over? Daniel flashed him a smile and shook his head, before standing and following the others out. Raymond walked over to Giles and helped him to his feet.

"Thank you so much." He offered his hand and she shook it.

"You're welcome," she said, as she handed him a check that Paige had apparently written.

"What's this for?"

"It was a retainer, but I'm not going to need anywhere near that much. I'll have a bill sent to you from my office, all right?"

"Sure."

When they reached the door the uniformed officer was waiting to take Giles to be processed and released. Raymond followed them down the entire length of the long hallway in silence.

"Is there someplace I can make a phone call?" Giles asked the officer. "I need to call my wife."

Raymond put her hand on Giles' arm before the officer could answer. "I've already called her. She'll be waiting for you as soon as you get out."

# Chapter Thirteen

"No. Absolutely not." Paige couldn't believe what she was hearing.

"Look," said Giles, "I don't think you understand—"

"I understand why you want to go, and I love you for it, but I think it's foolish."

"I know, I know." Giles dropped his head into his hands and Paige had to fight back her tears.

They were both in the front room amid a forest of beer bottles. Sunday night after they had returned from the police station, Giles had been sullen and unresponsive. He'd drunk all night, and Paige had gone to bed early. Now they were awake Monday morning and had to face each other for an entire day.

"Paige," he finally said, "don't you see how unreal this whole thing is? In some ways, I still don't believe it—"

"But you've already called Sharon and she hung up on you. What else do you need to know? Do you really think she wants you at the funeral?"

"God damn it, Paige. He was my friend."

"He was my friend, too, and so was Sharon. It seems like the least you can do is to respect her wishes."

"What wishes? She hung up on me."

"Don't you think that's pretty clear?"

"It doesn't matter. I'm going."

There wasn't much more to say. "Do you even know when it is?"

Giles nodded. "I called the *P-I*. It's tomorrow at two o'clock in Bainbridge."

Paige reluctantly turned and walked back to the bedroom. There would be no persuading him now. She only hoped that Sharon wouldn't see him there.

She crawled back into bed and began to cry, but there weren't many tears left. Anger was beginning to edge out the rest of her emotions. Giles hadn't told her anything of his stay in jail. He just wouldn't talk about it no matter how hard she pressed. She couldn't read, she couldn't watch TV, so Paige rolled over and, as best she could, tried to sleep the day away.

Giles was scared. No matter how much he drank, he couldn't get Don out of his mind.

Or the story.

He had written a story about Don and mailed it off without remembering any of it. What else could he do without knowing— write one about Paige? He would sooner kill himself, but how would he know? How would he be able to stop himself?

Giles stood up from the couch and began gathering his empties. The afternoon before, when Paige had brought him home from jail, he'd gone downstairs to his computer. The machine was off and he assumed Paige had shut it down. He had completely forgotten about being in the middle of working on the book when he'd been arrested.

After sitting down at the desk, Giles turned on the computer and had to wait a few minutes while it booted up. As soon as he could, he put in the disc that contained his most recent short stories. But when he pulled up the directory there was something else on the disc: a file named TRICK. When he opened the file it turned out to be the story "Trick or Threat." He nodded. It was almost as if he was expecting it. Had the police thought to check his computer he'd still be in jail, and not even Janet Raymond would have been able to get him out of that one.

Calmly, he formatted a new disc and then transferred all of the files from the story disc—with the exception of TRICK—to his hard drive. After that he dumped them back onto the new disc. Putting the old disc back in he typed the command to reformat it and then confirmed for the machine that, yes, he really did want to reformat the disc. He knew that deleting text didn't actually remove it from the disc; it simply allowed new data to be recorded over it. What he didn't know for sure was if there were ways of retrieving text from a reformatted disc.

Giles walked out to the laundry room, found a small screwdriver, and pried off the protective metal slide exposing the floppy disc. Then he jammed the screwdriver into the slot and pried the case apart. Back in his office he took out a pair of scissors and finished the job, cutting the actual disc into as many pieces as possible. He had no idea how long it would be before he would write again. And even though he was fairly certain that since the charges had been dropped and he wouldn't be seeing a cop with a search warrant anytime soon, he wasn't taking any chances.

Afterward, Giles had gone back upstairs, made himself a couple of sandwiches and eaten them along with a beer. The sandwiches were gone in a few minutes, but there had been plenty of beer left and Giles had drunk every bottle in the house. They clanked loudly now as he dumped them on top of each other into the recycling.

Giles began making coffee and wondered what he was going to do about Paige. He didn't dare tell her about his latest possession. She'd probably divorce him, he thought. She certainly had reason enough already. But once she found out that her life was in danger just by living with him, there would be no doubt. He had to find a way of stopping this thing. Unfortunately, short of killing himself, he had no idea how.

And on top of all this uncertainty and fear was the very painful fact of Don's death. Giles couldn't actually attend the funeral, but he would at least attend the graveside service at the cemetery. He had to say goodbye to Don. He owed him that much.

When the coffee had finished brewing, he poured a cup and took it into the bedroom. Paige appeared to be sleeping, so he set it quietly beside her on the nightstand. Then Giles walked into the kitchen, poured his own coffee, and took it down to the library. For now, at least, it wasn't safe for him to be in the same room as his wife.

One thing that Giles hadn't allowed his mind to spend any time focusing on was the possibility that he might have killed those people himself. Despite Janet Raymond's springing him from jail on a lack of evidence, it hadn't been enough to convince him. If he could completely black out and write an entire story and mail it off, why couldn't he have done the same and killed those people himself? But he couldn't dwell on that for long or he knew it would be the end of him. He simply had to go on the assumption that someone else—or even more frightening, some *thing* else—was responsible.

What was compelling him to write these stories? Why was it allowing him to know so much about the people in them? How many other murders had there been that the police didn't know about? And of course, the most important question: why him? These were the questions Giles would have to answer if he was ever going to have peace of mind again. And, if he was going to stay married to Paige.

—————————— ✦✦✦✦✦ ——————————

Rain drizzled down the windshield of Giles' Grand Prix. He didn't bother to turn the wipers on as he waited in line in downtown Seattle for the Bainbridge ferry. He was dressed in his best black suit and had his black raincoat and umbrella in the seat next to him. The radio was off. He had no book. Giles listened only to the rain beating on the vinyl top.

It was some time later before a horn behind him caused him to look up. The ferry had already arrived and unloaded and there were no more vehicles in front of him. He put his car into gear and started forward.

As he approached the gaping maw of the ferry, he could see large trucks and motor homes being directed straight ahead into the tall center section. To each side of this were two car decks. A ferry worker in an orange vest pointed him toward the upper deck on the right-hand side and Giles drove up the ramp and forward until he was only a foot or so behind the light pickup in front of him. Then he turned the engine off.

The weather was making the Sound rough and he could feel the waves as the ferry sat in the dock. Once the boat was full and they were underway it was less noticeable. Giles stayed in his car throughout the trip. He wasn't hungry and there was nothing he hadn't seen before from the observation deck. A half-hour later they arrived on Bainbridge Island.

Giles drove off the boat and headed straight for the cemetery. He didn't know what it was called, but he knew where it was; he'd had to drive by it every time he and Paige had come over to Don and Sharon's place during the summer.

It only took a minute to drive through the few city blocks that constituted the town, and he turned right at the McDonald's on the outskirts. The road wound up a gradual hill and about a mile out he passed the huge, black, wrought iron main gate of the Hill Crest Cemetery. Around the next corner to the right was the back entrance that led up to the funeral home, and Giles parked his car at the bottom of the driveway.

The rain was coming down even harder now and it felt to Giles as if it was beating down his spirit. He began having second thoughts about coming. He checked his watch. It was 3:30, but he could see several cars parked up at the top of the driveway and he knew he was on time. He took a deep breath and picked his coat up off the seat, slipping his arms into the sleeves. Then he took up his umbrella and opened the door.

The rain was heavy, but there was little wind and Giles quickly buttoned up his coat and opened his umbrella. As he walked up the hill he pulled out a pair of leather gloves from the pockets of his coat and put them on. After turning up his collar and pulling down his umbrella, Giles made his way into the cemetery proper.

To Giles' left was a sprawling one-story building. The structure was white with few windows, and he could see a two-car garage attached where the hearses were no doubt parked. Dead ahead loomed an asphalt road running through the middle of the cemetery, but off to the right, around the back of a small copse of trees, Giles saw a paved footpath. That was where he headed now, keeping his eye on the funeral home at all times. He supposed it didn't matter if he was seen, but he certainly didn't want to be recognized, especially by Sharon.

The grass was a bright, chemically induced green that shimmered with raindrops, even under the overcast sky. To his right, as Giles slowly made his way up the footpath, was a tall hedge, delineating the back boundary of the cemetery. To his left, sloping down the hill before him, was the rest of the property and its residents.

Tombstones of every shape and size littered the grass, along with dead flowers and fallen leaves. There were several marble benches along the footpaths, each with its own bank of tiny vaults containing urns. Giles had gone about halfway across the grounds when he stopped at one, brushed off as much water as he could, and sat down.

Past the cemetery were houses lower on the hill, and out further, the gray expanse of Puget Sound. The low clouds and rain made it impossible to see Seattle beyond the choppy water. But even the spectacular view could not distract Giles' eye for long. Eventually his attention was drawn to the large blue and white awning set up down the hill to the right.

His view was partially obscured by a shade tree that had already lost most of its leaves. By leaning forward Giles could see around the trunk to the mourners standing beneath the awning. It was the perfect vantage point from which to stay hidden. The only thing visible as he sat up straight was a large mound of earth covered by a green tarp.

The grave was some fifty yards away, and with the rain beating down around him Giles couldn't hear anything that was being said at the site. That was good. He couldn't have cared less what some minister who didn't even know Don had to say. The real tribute to his friend was the number of Northwest authors who were gathered around Sharon, even those he didn't represent. Among them Giles spotted Don's biggest client, a man who wrote murder mysteries about a crime-solving Seattle dentist.

But it wasn't until Giles saw Don and Sharon's two sons, Ted and Lewis, and their wives, that the first onrush of grief struck him. Giles lowered his head and felt the tears come. There was nothing he could do. There was nothing anyone could do. Don was gone forever and, no matter how hard Giles prayed, he was never coming back.

Giles sobbed freely for several minutes, hunching over beneath his umbrella against the rain. Eventually he reached for his handkerchief to wipe his running nose, and it was as he was replacing it in his pocket that he suddenly noticed a man standing by a tree looking at him.

The man had startled him so much that Giles immediately bolted to his feet. The wet asphalt was slick against the leather soles of his shoes, and Giles nearly fell over backward. His arm shot out instinctively as he braced his body against the bench. By the time he had regained his balance and turned back, the man was gone.

Giles' heart was hammering against his ribs. He had only averted his eyes for a second, and yet there was obviously no one there now. Stepping aside quickly, he could see no one behind the tree or walking back toward the awning; only the silvery veil of rain stood between him and the other mourners.

He couldn't sit back down now, and his eyes busily roamed over the entire cemetery for another glimpse of the man. He had clearly seen a man, dressed in black. Brown hair and light skin were the only features Giles could recall of the image. But was that all it had been—an image, a vision? Could he have just imagined it?

Giles' hands began to shake uncontrollably. The umbrella fell from his grasp and landed on the ground in front of him. Slowly it began to tumble away, carried across the grass by the wind that was starting to pick up. Giles felt powerless to reach for his umbrella and could only watch as it continued to drift further away from him. Rain plastered his hair to his head and washed away the tears on his cheeks.

Finally, he was able to move one of his feet and took a small step backward, then another. All the time the umbrella was making its tortuous, twisted way down the hill. Giles was able to take a few more steps before his body involuntary stopped.

Never had he felt this out of control in his life. Giles was in a panic. His chest felt tight and he reached a hand up beneath the collar of his coat to loosen his tie. Is this what it feels like to lose your mind? he thought. Had reality already slipped away? Would he ever be normal again?

Utter despair began to seep into Giles' spirit. Maybe the best thing to do was kill himself. How could he go on knowing that he was only half there, and not be able to do anything about it? The thought was paralyzing, and Giles stood rooted to the ground, his eyes never leaving the shivering skeleton of the umbrella.

Then a sustained gust of wind battered down on the hillside, whipping Giles' coat around his legs and at the same time dislodging the umbrella. He could only watch in horror as it cartwheeled the rest of the way down the hill, directly toward the gravesite.

The elderly man it hit in the back of the legs started, before turning around to pick it up. Soon, the attention of several more people was drawn to the umbrella, and a moment later Giles saw the old man point to him. With each pair of eyes that turned Giles' way, the hold the earth had on his feet began to loosen.

He took a step backward, then another, and turned just as the scream of a woman knifed through the air and seemingly cut the last hold the ground had on him. His legs shaking, Giles slipped and fell twice as he ran down the driveway. He was barely able to unlock his door, his hands were shaking so badly. Once inside the car he collapsed on the seat and mercifully blacked out.

When Giles came to it was already dark outside. The first thing he noticed was that the rain had stopped. Then he felt the pain in his leg. He sat up carefully and leaned forward against the steering wheel. His head was pounding and he wondered how long he had been out. When he turned on the dashboard light and looked at his watch he saw that the crystal had a deep scratch on it, but it was still working. It was 6:30.

Giles looked down at his knee and saw that his pant leg had torn open and he had been bleeding underneath. The skin was already scabbed over with dried blood and he didn't look at it long. He could clean it up when he got home. That was, if he still had a home. What the hell was he going to tell Paige this time? Nothing again? How long did he think she was going to stand for that?

Gradually, as he looked around the front seat of his car, Giles began to realize that he didn't have his car keys. He went methodically through all his pockets, checked down on the floor and in the ignition, but they were nowhere to be seen. If he had dropped them outside, they would be impossible to find without a flashlight.

Reluctantly, he opened the door, but was rewarded with the sound of jingling. Giles climbed out and found the keys still in the lock. He got back in the car and started up the engine, backed into the driveway, and headed down toward the ferry terminal.

As he drove back, the images of that afternoon began to replay in his mind, especially the vision of the man by the tree. Then the thoughts of suicide returned and he began to imagine how he might do it. Pills, he decided. That was the only way. With Paige's access to prescription drugs, he hoped there would be something in the medicine cabinet that he could take to overdose.

He wouldn't do it in the house, though. He couldn't have Paige find him. It would be hard enough on her without that. Giles didn't have much insurance, but there would be enough to pay off the house if he could make it look like an accident. The bright lights of McDonald's came into view and Giles stopped at the light. When it changed he turned left and drove down to the terminal. He paid for his ticket, pulled into the line, and turned the car off.

He could already see the lights of the ferry as it neared the dock. It wouldn't be long now. Giles leaned his head back and closed his eyes. He just had to keep Paige from falling apart until he could get everything in order. Neither of them was happy now, and he knew it would be for the best. Giles couldn't live with himself like this, and Paige was in constant danger.

Fifteen minutes later, as he was boarding the ferry, Giles felt as if a tremendous burden had been lifted from his shoulders. In just a few days the whole nightmare would be over. The feeling of relief was so intense that, as he sat alone in his car on the trip back to Seattle, Giles actually began to laugh.

Paige was unusually silent that night, which was far from unexpected. Giles supposed that she was trying to cope with the situation as best she could. She was in the front room watching TV, and didn't bother getting up or calling out hello when he came in the kitchen door.

Giles went straight back to the bedroom, shed his damp clothes and walked into the bathroom. After picking the gravel out of his bloodied knee, he stepped into the shower, wincing as the first drops of hot water stung his wound. Then Giles let the heat relax his muscles and wash away the fear he had experienced that afternoon.

When he was through, he wrapped a towel around himself and walked down the hall. Paige was still watching TV, so Giles hurried back into the bathroom and locked the door. He took a quick look through the medicine cabinet but the only thing stronger than aspirin that he could find was a container of Percodan. Though there were still eighteen capsules left, he had no idea whether that would be enough to kill him. It was clear he would have to do some research, and he put the pills back on the chance that Paige might miss them.

When he had dried off and dressed, Giles went out to the kitchen for a beer, but of course he'd drunk the last of it the night before and there was none in the fridge. Afraid to even poke his head in the living room to check on Paige, he descended the stairs empty-handed to compose his suicide note. My final piece of writing, he thought, with grim irony.

It only took Giles about a half-hour at the computer to tell Paige why he was taking his life. He included everything—his possessions, the story about Don, and the blackouts. He told her that he feared for her life and his sanity. Giles didn't expect her to understand, but he did his best to explain everything as well as he could.

When he was through he left the letter on the hard drive. He wouldn't print it until the time came, and then he would leave it on his desk for her to find after it was all over. It might be a chickenshit way to go, but appearances really didn't matter at this point. Giles couldn't trust himself. He wasn't sure what he was capable of when he was out of himself. And that, coupled with the fact that his decision made him feel better than he had in months, was enough to convince him that he was doing the right thing.

All that was left now was to check out the Percodan and make final arrangements for a place to do it. If possible, he would do it tomorrow.

# Chapter Fourteen

"I just don't know what to do anymore."

Paige was slouched down in the chair behind her desk. Marcy Miller was sitting in the chair opposite her. When Marcy had come in right before lunch to express her concern and ask how things had gone after Giles' arrest, Paige had spilled everything.

"What do you *want* to do?"

Paige sighed. "I'd like to get the hell out of that house, for one thing. It's to the point now where I can't even stand to be around him anymore."

"You know you're more than welcome to stay with Butch and me."

"Thanks, but I don't think so. It seems a little drastic—"

"Je-sus Christ."

Paige raised her eyebrows at this, but it was a couple of seconds before Marcy broke into a smile. Marcy had thick curly blonde hair that fell just below her ears. Her face was round with delicate features and a small pinched mouth. At five-ten, she stood a good deal taller than Paige.

"Come on," Marcy said. "What are you waiting for? How much longer are you going to put up with this?"

"I don't know. Maybe I'm hoping that he'll change. Or maybe there's something else I can be doing. I don't really want to leave—I love him."

"Funny, that's what all the women whose husbands beat the shit out of them say."

"Come on Marcy. This is hardly the same thing."

"Isn't it?"

Paige didn't have an answer to that.

"All I know is that you're not happy, and that's not like you. So what if you move out? What's the worst thing that can happen? It's not like you're filing for divorce or anything. There's nothing final about it."

"No, I suppose not."

"And maybe if he's on his own he'll be able to get it out of his system. Or maybe it'll be easier to talk. Or maybe it'll be easier to file for divorce. Whatever. But in the meantime, at least you'll be able to function—he won't be taking it out on you. This is bullshit."

"You said that already."

She grinned. "Well, nothing's changed."

The more Paige thought about it, the more she realized that Marcy was right. Her world had been turned into complete chaos and it was making her miserable. Moving out wouldn't mean the end of their marriage, and just the thought of taking action was beginning to soothe her nerves.

Paige stood and walked around her desk and the two of them hugged.

"I appreciate this, Marcy. I feel a lot better, being able to talk about it."

"I'm glad. I just want to get the old you back."

"Oh, I'm still in here somewhere."

"Good. You want to go out somewhere for lunch?"

"I don't think so. I'm not very hungry."

Marcy pulled open the door. "Okay, but remember, if you need a place to stay for a while, I want you to let me know."

"All right."

"I'll see you later."

Once Marcy had gone, Paige went back to her desk and called home. She needed to speak with Giles, if only briefly, and ask him when they would be able to talk. She needed to reestablish contact with him before dropping a bombshell like moving out. If she was lucky, he hadn't already started drinking and they might be able to come to some sort of an agreement about taking time to talk when she got home. If not, she would have to give serious consideration to just packing up and walking out.

The phone rang three times and the answering machine picked it up. She thought about leaving a message, and then just hung up. I wonder where he is? she thought. He's not writing, that's for sure. Then Paige slumped back in her chair again. She would try calling back later, but for now she had a lot of thinking to do. Either way, once she went to bed tonight she wanted things to be decided.


The second Giles opened his eyes he sucked in a gasp of air and sat upright. He stared across the rumpled covers of the bed at the chair in the corner of the room. His sweats and shoes appeared to be in the same position he had left them in the night before, but he was still a little too groggy with sleep to be certain. He studied them until he heard Paige's car start up in the garage.

The sound of the garage door opening must have been what woke him up. He listened until the door went back down and the Puegeot's engine had faded in the distance before he pushed himself out of bed and walked to his closet. Everything inside— shoes, shirts, slacks, coats, ties, and belts—had been carefully mapped out in his mind the night before. He knew the exact position of each item, and it appeared that nothing had been moved.

Giles finally relaxed. Taking what could easily be considered obsessive measures was the only way he could be absolutely sure that he hadn't left the house in the middle of the night, that he hadn't slipped out of his mind and gone on a murderous writing rampage.

Ironically, he found himself becoming wistful when he looked back at his night in jail. He hadn't slept well, but at least he'd been secure in the knowledge that he couldn't get out. But none of that mattered now. There would be no more future nights. Giles' plan was firmly set in his mind, and he intended to go through with it this afternoon.

The previous night, after Paige had gone to bed, Giles had hunted down an emergency medical hotline in the phone book. He explained to the nurse who answered that he'd had a root canal and the dentist had prescribed Percodan for the pain. Giles said that his tooth still hurt, even though he'd already taken twice the dosage listed on the bottle, and asked if it would be okay to take some more.

In a stern voice she told him that he was already halfway to the overdose limit, and there he had the answer. Eighteen capsules would be more than enough to do the job. Once that had been settled all he needed to decide on was a place. He knew if he just parked his car somewhere there was the possibility of being spotted. A cop or security guard could get suspicious and discover him in time to be resuscitated. Giles definitely didn't want to take a chance of that, so he made the next logical choice: a hotel.

He would check in for one night and take the pills, making sure to get rid of the bottle afterward. When the door was opened with the passkey the next day at checkout time, it would look as if he had simply died in his sleep. Paige would be notified, eventually find the letter on his desk, and life would go on, mercifully, without Giles Barrett to torment.

One thing he wasn't going to do, though, was die in a seedy motel on Aurora. Giles was going to make reservations at the Marriott downtown, the closest major hotel to the morgue at Harborview Medical Center. In the opulent surroundings of the Marriott the whole incident would be treated with respect, and there would only be a few onlookers. His body would be quickly and quietly whisked away to Harborview.

Far from being depressed at the thought, Giles felt surprisingly good. After all, he couldn't write anymore. He couldn't be with his wife. His best friend had died. What the hell else was there to live for? Giles rubbed his face in his hands and walked into the bathroom. He ran a brush through his hair, but didn't take a shower. Instead, he dressed in a pair of worn chinos and a flannel shirt, and headed to the kitchen to make what would be his last pot of coffee.

While the coffee was brewing Giles went downstairs and pulled up his suicide note on the computer. He printed it out, folded it in thirds, and placed it in an envelope with Paige's name on the front. As he leaned back in his chair, for the first time since he had made the decision to kill himself he thought about his folks.

Jon and Becky Barrett still lived in the house that Giles had been raised in. They were, of all things, cranberry farmers, with a mid-sized bog on the outskirts of Hallowell, Washington. They sold their yearly crop to the Ocean Spray facility nearby, and by living a frugal life had been able to raise a son and put him through college. Giles had fond memories of growing up in Hallowell, and usually made it down to visit his parents a couple of times a year.

His mom and dad were nearing sixty now. He didn't know what effect his death would have on them, but he hoped they would outlive him for many years. For a while Giles just sat in his chair, wondering whether he should write to his folks. He supposed that Paige would get together with them after it was over and share the contents of her letter. That was probably enough, he decided. He simply didn't have the energy to write another one.

Giles pushed himself up and began climbing the stairs toward the kitchen. He could already smell the coffee as he reached the landing. Then the phone rang. Giles' momentum was halted as he tried to imagine who it could be. Paige? God, he hoped not. She was the last person he wanted to talk to.

The phone rang a second time and Giles hustled up the stairs to the kitchen. By the time he reached the phone it had rung a third time, and Giles knew that the answering machine would be kicking in any second. At the last moment, he picked it up.

"Hello?"

"Hello. May I speak with Giles Barrett, please?"

It was a male voice, and Giles relaxed slightly. "Speaking."

"Mr. Barrett, this is Mike Bellamy, from the Holman Agency."

Christ. Giles could feel his chest and neck tightening again.

Whatever this was about, he hoped it could be cleared up over the phone. "Sure, what can I do for you?"

"Well, I don't know if you're aware of the situation down here, but Ken Johnston and I have decided for the time being to keep the agency going. Both of us will be handling Don's authors, with the understanding that they are quite free to go elsewhere."

So that's all this is, Giles thought—somebody trying to hustle my business. He was thinking of a way to let the guy down easy, when Bellamy continued.

"As I'm sure you realize, the work Don did for you was quite specialized. I've talked this over with Ken and I'm afraid that we won't be able to provide you with the same service."

Ah—I can't quit, because I've been fired. If it hadn't been so tragic Giles would have laughed. "I understand," he said stoically.

"Great. Then what I'd like to do is have you come down to the office sometime this afternoon. We've taken the liberty of drawing up some papers to dissolve your contract—"

"Is there some way we could do this another time? I'm kind of busy today." The little prick would be rid of him soon enough.

"Uh . . . well, I suppose that would work. But I also have a story manuscript and a check for you to pick up—"

"A check? From where?"

"It's just an agency check. Let me see—I had it right here a minute ago . . . Okay, here it is. It's for thirteen hundred and fifty dollars—payment, less commission, from *Science Fiction Digest*.

Giles couldn't believe it. Don hadn't told him about selling a story to *SFD*. But then Don hadn't told him about receiving the check for "Trick or Threat." Had Don been mad at him about that? Was that why he hadn't given him a call? This thing was getting worse by the minute.

But then Giles' anxiety suddenly launched itself to new heights. "What story is that check for?"

Giles heard paper rustling and then Bellamy said, "'The Unscheduled Stop.'"

Giles had to pull out a chair at the kitchen table and sit down, his legs were shaking so badly. That one was okay; he'd fixed the ending. It wasn't something he'd whipped up and mailed off while in another trance. But it also started him wondering again.

"Trick or Threat" hadn't been written until *after* "The Unscheduled Stop." Was it because he had tampered with "Unscheduled Stop" that his next story had been written completely without his knowledge? Was he being punished for not going along with it? But who the hell would know he'd even changed the names? Certainly not some psychopath reading horror magazines.

The panic was beginning to set in again, and Giles had to do something quickly. "Listen, Mike."

"Yeah?"

"Now that I think about it, why don't I come down there right now and take care of this today? It won't take long, will it?"

"Five minutes, tops."

"Okay, great. I'll be right down."

Giles hung up the phone and looked at the clock. It was still early. He had realized while he was talking with Bellamy that there was one thing he'd forgotten to do for Paige. He needed to transfer all the money from his personal checking account to his and Paige's joint account. He also wanted to cash the check from *SFD* and leave the money in his desk for her to find. He didn't want Paige to have to hassle with lawyers tying up his money before she could get it.

Giles' eyes wandered to the counter and he saw the red light glowing on the coffee machine. Reluctantly, he stood up and turned it off. It looked as if he might not get to drink his last pot of coffee after all. Then he turned and walked into the bedroom to put on some shoes and grab his coat. It was time to take one last look around Don's office.

Giles hadn't realized just how bad the weather was until the garage door opened and he drove outside. The wind was whipping the tops of the trees, and rain was lashing around everywhere. His wipers were barely up to the task and he had to take it slow into town. The sky was dark and most of the cars on the road had their lights on, including Giles'.

Because of the rain he parked in a lot beside the Rainier Tower and walked underground to the elevators. Giles hadn't been to Don's office in weeks, hadn't needed to what with everything that was going on. The garage elevator took him up swiftly to the lobby where he had to get out and enter another that would take him up into the building.

He couldn't remember a time when he'd been up here and Don wasn't. In fact, he'd never even met the other members of Don's agency. The door of the elevator opened and Giles stepped out, suddenly wishing he hadn't agreed to do this. He walked down the carpeted hallway and entered the reception area of the Holman Agency.

Don's secretary, Diana, was at the reception desk and looked up as soon as he walked in. She didn't smile, she didn't say hello, she just said, "Mr. Bellamy is waiting for you."

She hadn't told him whose office he was waiting in, so Giles walked past Don's door to the one with Bellamy's name on it. He knocked and it was immediately opened by a skinny man in a three-piece suit. "Mr. Barrett, nice to meet you. I'm Mike Bellamy."

Giles shook his hand, and then followed him as the man stepped past him. "Why don't we just go down to Don's office? Everything is still in there."

Bellamy was about six feet tall and had on a dark-blue suit. His light brown hair was thinning on top and he wore rimless glasses. He had a fairly high voice and when he smiled Giles noticed an abundance of mismatched dental work.

But when Don's office door was opened for him, Giles couldn't step inside. The first thing he noticed was the large piece of plywood that covered the broken window and it stopped him in his tracks. This had once been one of his favorite places in the world, and what was going on here today began to make him very angry. He'd been friends with Don for so long that it seemed like they'd always known each other. And now he was being given the bum's rush by the agency.

The stern look on Bellamy's face finally convinced him to go in. "All right," Giles said with irritation. "Let's get this over with."

There was a file folder on Don's desk and Bellamy opened it and brought out some papers. "If you'll just sign the last page of this after you've read it over, it will end your contract with the agency."

Giles didn't bother reading, and simply signed. Then, with an exaggerated flourish, Bellamy closed the empty file and held out his hands. "I'm afraid the police took all of the stories you had on file here."

Giles bet he was really broken up over that. "Just give me the check and let me get out of here." Silently, Bellamy handed Giles a small sheaf of papers with a check attached.

Without saying goodbye, Giles took the papers and left. As he reached for the knob and pulled open the door, he noticed that the typeface on one of the bottom sheets was different from that of his printer. Then he stopped, finding three sheets that looked the same way.

It was the manuscript of "The Unscheduled Stop." The last three pages had been retyped, but it wasn't the typeface that bothered him. The new pages contained the old ending of the story. "What the hell is this?"

Bellamy suddenly appeared at the door, his look now one of open hostility. "I think you should leave, Mr. Barrett."

"Not until I find out who the hell did this." Giles held out the pages for Bellamy, but the man wouldn't touch them. "Did the magazine get the story this way?"

"I'm sure I don't know. You'll have to talk to the editors."

Giles was nearly frantic. Someone had restored the original ending of the story where the main character died. He knew now, because of the story about Don, that just giving the character a different name wasn't going to make any difference. "I want to know who authorized these changes," he screamed.

Bellamy's round face was turning red. It looked as if he were about to yell back when a voice from behind Giles stopped him.

"Mr. Holman."

*Eric B. Olsen*

Both of the men turned to see Diana Lund getting up from her chair and walking over to them. She took the pages from Giles and looked them over briefly. Then she nodded and handed them back. "Mr. Holman asked me to make those changes."

# Chapter Fifteen

Giles didn't stop at the bank on the way home. He nearly didn't stop at any traffic lights either. Most of the magazines that he wrote for paid on publication, but he'd never had a story in *Science Fiction Digest* before. If he was lucky, they paid on acceptance and it would still be a few months, or longer, before the story appeared in print. He needed to get on the phone and find out.

But as soon as he walked in the door a thought entered his mind, and the house seemed to close in on Giles as he walked through the kitchen. The air was thick and hard to breath. His tongue felt swollen, too big for his mouth. As he reached the hallway his throat began to constrict and his stomach turned. Giles had just enough time to duck into the hall bathroom and fall down over the toilet.

There was very little in Giles' stomach to throw up. He heaved several times, the thick bile burning the back of his throat and making his eyes water. A thin strand of drool dangled from his lower lip over the cold water in the bowl as his stomach spasmed several more times. Finally he spit, wiped his mouth with toilet paper, and rolled over against the wall.

Sweat dripped down Giles' face. His body felt leadened, as though he might never be able to move again. He closed his eyes and breathed through his mouth for a long time before he was able to pull himself up to the sink and rinse out his mouth. The face in the mirror was pale and stubbled, the eyes sunken and frightened. He didn't even recognize himself.

Coming into the house, Giles had realized the fatal flaw in his logic. The fact that Collette Leavy may or may not be killed had been suddenly overshadowed by the fact of how she would come to be in that position in the first place: a plane crash. Whether or not he changed the names, the plane in the story crash-landed and hundreds of people died. What had he done?

Slowly, Giles moved out of the bathroom, down the hall, and downstairs to his office. He sat down heavily in his chair and took a couple of deep breaths before looking for the phone number of *SFD*. He found it among some old market listings Don had given him. The address he had was in Chicago. He hoped the information was still current as he picked up the receiver and punched out the number.

After four rings a male voice answered. "G.D. Publications."

"Hello. I'd like to speak with Gary Donnelly."

"Okay, can you hold on a minute?"

Giles was put on hold before he had a chance to answer. He automatically pinched the bridge of his nose and ran his hand through his hair. The wait was interminable, but just about the time he thought he had been forgotten someone came back on the line.

"Who are you holding for?"

"Gary Donnelly."

"Okay, just a minute."

He was put on hold again. Gary Donnelly was the managing editor of *Science Fiction Digest*, and the only editor named in the listing Giles had. He hoped that if Donnelly wasn't aware of the story he might be able to put him in touch with someone there who was. Eventually, a voice came on the line again.

"Who are you holding for?"

Unbelievable. Giles took a breath and said the name again. "Gary Donnelly."

"Gary's busy right now. Would you like to leave a message on his voice mail?"

"God, no. Look, this is something of an emergency. I can hold, but I have to talk to Mr. Donnelly."

He was put on hold again without a word, but it wasn't too much later before he was finally connected to Donnelly.

"This is Gary."

"Hello, Mr. Donnelly. My name is Giles Barrett."

"Of course. Sorry for the delay, but I was on the phone with the printer making some last minute changes to the subscription list. The day the magazine comes out is pretty hectic."

"Your magazine is coming out today?"

"Yes. Next month's issue. The one with your story in it. Is that what you called about?"

All the fatigue Giles had been feeling receded as adrenaline began to flood his system. "Listen, I've decided I don't want you to run that story. I'd like you to pull it"

"Are you kidding? What's this all about?"

"I really can't say. I just need you to take my story out of the magazine."

He actually laughed. "No way. I don't mean to be so blunt with you but the plates have already been made. It's already at the printers. In fact, they started the run over an hour ago—"

"Look, I'll pay you whatever it costs, but you can't run that story."

Donnelly was silent for a moment. When he began to speak it was in a soft but stern voice. "Mr. Barrett, I don't know what the problem is, but you should have discussed it with your agent. He signed the contract and sent it back to us months ago. And even if there weren't economic considerations, I'd be hard pressed to remove a story that we've spent so much time building this issue around."

"At least let me make some changes to the—"

"Mr. Barrett, there's really nothing I can do at this point. I'm sorry."

Giles shut his eyes and leaned back. What could he do now? When would it happen? How *could* it happen? Even with all that he'd experienced in the last few days, it was hard to believe that someone could cause an SAS plane to crash land just because he had written a story about it.

". . . Mr. Barrett?"

"Yes. I'm still here."

"If there's nothing else . . ."

"Just one more thing."

"Yes?"

"When does the magazine come out? When will it be on the stands?"

"Tonight, on the East Coast. On the West Coast, not until tomorrow morning."

Giles hung up the phone and pushed himself out of his chair to pace. He had maybe twelve hours before the story would be available to the public, less if he counted the East Coast. It was clear that he had to warn someone. If there was a way to prevent disaster, he had to try.

But who the hell was going to believe him? And why should they? He'd look like a crackpot who was predicting the end of the world. That, or worse. They might think he was planning to sabotage the plane himself. The more Giles thought about it the more he realized who he was going to have to call. He grimaced at the thought, but walked over to his desk anyway.

Giles sat back down and began sifting through the pile of notes he was continually scrawling to himself. Near the bottom he found what he was looking for and picked up the phone again.

"Magnolia Precinct." It was a woman's voice.

"Lieutenant Lasky, please."

"The lieutenant is on an assignment. Can I take a message?"

"Do you know when he'll be back?"

"No, sir. I'm afraid I don't."

"Okay, thank you."

Giles hung up the phone and then bounded up the stairs to the bedroom. He pulled on some shoes and socks, and grabbed his coat on the way out the back door. The wind had begun to kick up, but it wasn't raining as hard as it had been this morning and it only took Giles ten minutes to drive down to Magnolia.

He had to ask a gas station attendant for directions, so it took another five minutes for him to find the police station. Finally, he drove up to the sandy-colored brick building and parked in one of the visitor spots. Once inside the glass doors, Giles walked up to the uniformed police officer behind the front desk and asked for Lasky.

The woman eyed him warily for a moment and said, "Did you just call a few minutes ago?"

Giles nodded.

"That was fast."

"Is he here?"

"Nope."

Giles looked around and pointed to a pair of chairs along the wall. "Do you mind if I wait for him there?"

"Be my guest," she said.

"Thanks."

Now the only problem was trying to think of what he was going to tell Daniel. That is, assuming Daniel came back to the precinct. The only logical explanation for the murders was that a killer was reading and copying the stories. But what about the writing of the stories themselves? Where was that coming from? Giles still didn't have a satisfactory answer for himself. Nothing seemed to fit.

Giles didn't have the opportunity to think it through much further. Fifteen minutes after he'd sat down Daniel Lasky walked in the front door with another man. The two of them were talking intently and, as they neared him, Giles stood up. It was another moment before Daniel made eye contact, but when he did he immediately stopped.

"Giles," he said, hesitating a moment. "What brings you down here?"

"I need to talk to you. It's important."

Daniel looked over at the other man and said, "I'll catch you in a few minutes, Bruce, okay?"

The other man nodded and walked in past the desk sergeant, leaving Giles alone with Daniel. "Could we go into your office?" Giles asked.

Daniel looked Giles over for a moment and finally nodded. "Okay, but I have a meeting in half an hour that I need to be at."

Giles said nothing and Daniel turned and led them through the squad room to a glass enclosed office against the back wall. Daniel closed the door once Giles was inside and then offered him some coffee. It was awful, but Giles hadn't eaten anything all day and it felt good to have something in his stomach.

"So," Daniel began, then he motioned to one of the chairs near the door and sat down behind his desk. "What's so important?"

"Well, first off I wanted to thank you for Janet Raymond. I don't know what I'd have done if you hadn't given me her name."

"I'm still a little pissed that you lied to me."

"I know. I'm really sorry about that, but that's why I'm here now. Something else has happened and you're the only one I can turn to." Giles hesitated, but Daniel was stoic. "A story I wrote several months ago is going to be on the newsstands tomorrow morning, and I think someone else might die."

Daniel shook his head and set down his coffee mug on the desk. "I don't know what kind of publicity racket you're trying to run here, Giles, but I can't be party to it any longer."

"I'm serious."

"I'm sure you are. What do you take me for? You made a laughing stock of me the first time, but I'm not biting on this one."

"Listen to me, Daniel, please. I know what it looked like before, but I wasn't trying to put anything over on you then, and I'm not trying to now. Honestly, I just needed help. I didn't know what was happening before, but this time I think we might be able to stop it from happening."

Daniel shook his head. "Okay, what?"

"I think a plane is going to crash."

Daniel was leaning back in his chair, just looking at Giles. The tension between them was almost palpable. Then, a long moment later, Daniel began to laugh. Giles wasn't quite sure what to make of it when Daniel explained himself.

"Okay, let's just say for the sake of argument that there is an actual psycho-killer out there who's copying your stories. You claim that this time he's going to take down an airplane?"

Giles had to admit to himself that he didn't think so, but at least that would be within Daniel's ability to believe. The point was, they had to do something. "I don't know how he's going to do it, but that's what the story's about."

Daniel laughed again. "This is such incredible bullshit, Giles, even from you. And which flight would this be?"

"SAS to London. The women's name is Collette Leavey."

"What women?"

"The one in the story."

"And she's going to . . . what, hijack the plane and shoot everyone in the cockpit?"

"No, it's just . . . She's not important. I don't know how the plane's going to crash, but at least we can alert the ground crew or the airline or something."

"Hold it right there. *We* aren't going to do anything. And I'm not going to do anything, either. Can't you see that this is tantamount to yelling fire in a crowded theater?"

"Not if I have knowledge—"

"You don't have shit, Giles. What time is the flight?"

"I don't know."

"What day is the flight on?"

"I'm not sure?"

"The flight number?"

Giles just shrugged.

"I'm sorry, but I just don't believe that some psycho's going to be able to take down a plane, period."

"So that's it?"

"Yes."

Giles wanted to scream at him, tell him to his face how stupid he was being, but Daniel had apparently made up his mind. And without his support, anything Giles might try to do would make him look like a lunatic.

"All right, Daniel, I'll go. But I want you to remember that we had this conversation." Giles stood and put his empty cup on

Daniel's desk. Daniel said nothing. "Just remember that I tried to warn you." And with that, Giles turned and walked out of his office.

Paige tried calling Giles again after her last appointment, but either he wasn't home or he wasn't answering the phone. He could also be passed out on the couch, she reminded herself, and then immediately tried to rid her mind of the thought. She needed to get home and talk, and not worry about what she couldn't change. If he was drunk, she would have to find a way to deal with it.

The weather had been bad all day, but now the wind was gusting fiercely, and the rain pounded the windshield of her car as Paige drove north up Aurora toward home. Over the last several blocks, broken branches and garbage were strewn across the roadway, and dead leaves stuck to her wipers.

As she pulled into the driveway Paige felt a surge of apprehension. Far from the dark house she had expected to come home to, it looked as if every light in the place was on. Even within the relative safety of the garage, the wind and rain added an element of fear, lashing against the walls, and Paige hurried into the house.

Inside she yelled once for Giles, but it was clear he wouldn't be able to hear her. The TV was on, and even out in the kitchen it was incredibly loud. She walked into the front room and took a quick look around. There were no bottles anywhere, just the TV blaring.

She could see by the logo in the upper right corner that it was turned to CNN, a live report from somewhere in Montana. The woman on the air was standing in a dark field. Behind her a fire was raging. She was talking about the storm that was moving across the North- and Midwest. Only after listening for another minute did Paige learn that the flaming wreckage behind the woman had been a plane.

The reporter went on to say that the plane had been a Swedish Air Service flight out of Seattle. No one knew what had happened but for the moment they were attributing the crash to the storm.

There were nearly two hundred people onboard and thus far they had found no survivors.

Paige watched in rapt fascination until the broadcast switched back to the studio and she was finally able to walk over and turn off the set. But instead of silence, she heard a loud crash that sounded like it had come from downstairs.

"Giles?" she yelled.

The only answer was another crash. Paige bolted out of the front room and down the stairs. What she saw caused her to scream. Giles was hurling the monitor of his computer across the room.

"Giles, what are you doing?"

He turned to her and she almost screamed again. His face was white and drawn, and his eyes looked sunken and rimmed with black. The two-day growth of beard didn't help matters, either. She almost didn't recognize him.

"Get out of here," he said.

"I will not. What the hell are you doing?"

His eyes had a haunted look she had never seen before. He stared at her but he wouldn't speak. Finally, he picked up the keyboard and slammed it against the corner of the desk, sending white keys flying everywhere.

"Giles," she screamed again, and ran over to him. "Stop it."

Paige took the broken keyboard from his hand as Giles fell heavily into his chair and cradled his head in his hands. She could feel the tears coming in a rush, but she was too scared to worry about fighting them off. She knelt in front of him. "Please, Giles. Will you tell me what's happening?"

Giles looked up and shook his head, and that's when Paige snapped. "Then go to hell," she said and stood up. "I'm not putting up with this anymore, Giles. You tell me what's going on right now or I'm leaving."

He wouldn't even look up this time. "Go ahead."

Paige was incredulous. Ten years of marriage and that was it. No argument, no discussion, just "go ahead?" With tears streaming down her cheeks, Paige walked upstairs to call Marcy.

# Chapter Sixteen

Giles sat in the front room as the sun rose, watching the sky turn first gray and then gradually to a brilliant blue. The power had gone off shortly after Paige had left, just as the worst of the storm hit, and Giles had stayed up all night waiting for it to come back on.

While his breath plumed out in front of his face, the only visible sign of the storm Giles could see outside Thursday morning through the front window was the damage it had done. Part of the neighbors' fence had blown down, lawn furniture and tree limbs were scattered everywhere and, of course, in the pre-dawn darkness there were no streetlights. Listening to a battery-powered radio, Giles had learned that downed power lines had cut off electricity in nearly every county in the entire western half of the state.

Wrapped around him were a sleeping bag and a quilt, and clutched in his fist was the container of Percodan. Though he'd held on to them all night, and certainly had even less to live for with the deaths of hundreds of people on his conscience, he lacked even the motivation to kill himself. He wondered briefly what was on Daniel Lasky's conscience, and then went back to staring out the window and trying to figure out what had happened to his life.

It was hard to believe Paige was gone. But that's what he'd wanted, wasn't it? If he couldn't see her, then there was no chance of his inadvertently writing a story about her. At least that was the theory. The truth was, he really didn't know how he felt about it anymore, and unconsciously he squeezed the container in his hand.

The house was empty without her presence. But then his life seemed empty—was empty—too. And Giles felt he had no other choice but to keep it empty, at least for now. With no computer and no printer, there was little chance of his writing anything. He hadn't been possessed since the story he'd written about Don. And that reminded him of the funeral. Just the thought of it made him shiver, that and the cold house.

He was going to have to think of something to do. Eventually he would have to talk with Paige and tell her . . . He didn't know what. Giles felt immobilized with uncertainty. How was he going to live without Paige? At some point he was going to have to earn a living. But doing what?

It was about an hour later that he saw the gray sedan pull up in front of the house and idle there for several minutes. The windows were tinted and he couldn't see anyone inside. When the exhaust from the tail pipe abruptly stopped, the front doors opened and two men in cheap suits stepped out. The passenger was tall and skinny, six-five, or six-six, bald with a fringe of brown hair hooking over his ears and meeting at the back of his neck.

The driver was a few inches shorter, weighed a little more, and had a full head of black hair. The two of them looked around carefully for a few moments before turning their attention to the house. Giles stood up immediately as they approached the front steps. Just about the time he reached the door, the bell rang. Giles opened the door.

"Hello. We'd like to speak with Giles Barrett," said the black-haired driver.

Not this again. They didn't look like cops, Giles thought, they looked more like—

"FBI." At this both men removed their IDs and flashed them.

Giles could only shake his head. "You boys don't waste any time, do you?"

"Just some routine questions, Mr. Barrett. May we come inside?"

"No, I don't think so. The power's shut off anyway. It's probably warmer out here."

The two looked at each other and then Passenger launched into his questions. "I don't know if you were aware of this, but an SAS airliner went down last night, and we've received information that you may have known about it before hand."

Lasky. The son of a bitch was probably on the phone the second it happened. Well, Giles wasn't going to give them the satisfaction of a confession this time. "No, I didn't realize that. I don't know anything about it."

Passenger narrowed his eyes and then pulled a copy of *Science Fiction Digest* from the breast pocket of his coat.

"Give me a fucking break," said Giles. The whole thing had gotten way out of hand. He'd done what he could. Lasky hadn't believed him until after the fact, and now this. "Look, they've got my fingerprints downtown. I'm sure Lasky must have told you all about it. If you find any that match on the plane, come and see me. But until then, why don't you leave me alone?"

"Take it easy. We just need to talk to you, Mr. Barrett."

"We need some answers," Driver chimed in.

"You want answers, then talk to my lawyer. Her name's Janet Raymond. She's in the book. Works in Bellevue. I'm sure Lasky must have told you about her, too."

"You're not under arrest, Mr. Barrett—"

"Good. Glad to hear it. So why don't you get the fuck off my porch and leave me alone?"

Giles slammed the door and locked it. He waited until he heard them descending the stairs before he ran up to the front room and looked out as they returned to their car. Once inside they started it, then sat there for a few more minutes before taking off.

"Look, can't you guys do this some other time?"

Marcy was pacing Paige's office like a caged animal. When the two men from the FBI first wanted to talk to her, Paige thought she could handle it. Marcy saw them in the hallway and demanded to sit in. But all the questions about Giles proved to be too much too soon and the stress had caused Paige to start crying.

"Just a few more things," said the bald one, but Marcy wasn't having any of it.

"Can't you see what she's going through? I say this is enough."

"Please, Marcy. I'll be okay."

"I just don't see why they can't come back some other time. It's not as if you're going to skip town."

The dark-haired one began to shift uncomfortably in his chair as Marcy stared him down, but the bald one just shook his head and continued. "Do you know where your husband was last night, Dr. Barrett?"

"No. I didn't stay at home last night. I assume that's where he was."

"She already told you that," Marcy shot back.

"All right," said the bald one, and they both stood up. He handed Paige his card and said, "If you feel up to it later on this week, this is the number to our Seattle field office. They'll know how to get in touch with me."

"Thank you," Paige said, and the two men left.

"I don't believe this shit," Marcy said, sitting down in the chair where the bald one had been. "They never did say what this was about, did they?"

"No."

"Do you think it has something to do with the murders Giles was arrested for?"

"I honestly don't know, Marcy. Giles hasn't told me any more about what's going on. It could be anything."

Paige looked at the wad of Kleenex in her hand and dumped it into the wastebasket. She dried her cheeks again with the back of her hand, and then took a deep breath. "God, I hate this."

"He didn't say anything to you last night?"

"Nothing. Just that I should go ahead and leave. Thanks for letting me come over on such short notice."

"Hey, I told you, anytime. If you want to go back tonight and pick up a few things, I'd be glad to go with you."

"No, I think I'd better go myself."

"You think he'll talk tonight?"

"I have to try. I mean, we're going to have to talk about it eventually."

Marcy stood up. "Okay, good luck. We'll be home tonight, so give us a call if you're coming over."

"Okay, thanks."

Paige checked her watch after Marcy left. She still had fifteen minutes before her next patient. She wished she didn't even have that. There were a few cancellations earlier in the morning due to the power outages, but because her office was on the same grid as the hospital the power had been on when they came to work that morning.

She sighed heavily. That was about the only thing that was working. Everything else in her life had been turned upside down. She felt as if she'd been cut loose from her anchor and was adrift on a huge ocean, powerless to help herself. She knew it didn't have to be like that, though. She knew it was because she was still trying to hang on to her marriage.

A more accurate analogy might be that Giles was pulling her underwater, drowning her, and that she only had to cut him free and she would bob back up to the surface. Nice theory, assuming she could do it, which she knew she couldn't. At least not yet. Desperate as things were, she knew she still had some reserve left. She could deal with things a while longer.

Marcy was pushing pretty hard, but she wasn't the one who was going through it. She and Butch were doing fine. And even though Paige appreciated Marcy's support, she felt like she needed to try handling this thing on her own as best she could. If she had to go over to the house every night, then so be it. She and Giles had to talk at some point. He was worth the effort, and the pain.

A soft knock came to Paige's office door.

"Come in," she said, and Connie, the receptionist, stuck her head inside.

"Mr. de Carteret's here."

"Okay, thanks. I'll be right out."

When Connie had shut the door, Paige stood and sighed.

Okay, Giles, she thought. If that's the way you want to play it, then all right. But you'll have to do better than you did last night, because I'm not giving up without a fight.


Giles spent the rest of the morning alternately pacing the house and sitting in the chair looking out the window. The power never came back on. He'd tried calling the power company several times, but the line was always busy. By the time noon rolled around he had to get out of the house and go somewhere, anywhere. The waiting was driving him crazy.

He dressed and walked out to the garage. After opening the door and starting up the car he let it idle for a few minutes, allowing the interior to get plenty warm before he backed out. Giles spotted several uprooted trees along the way, one of which had nearly blocked the road at one point, as he maneuvered his way toward Aurora.

Out along the main thoroughfares it looked as though everything was back to normal. Businesses had their power back, people were flowing in and out of stores, and traffic seemed as heavy as always. Giles decided not to go into town, but drove east to Roosevelt and down into the University District.

He parked on 46th and then walked down to the Ave. Giles bought a *P-I* and decided to read about the plane crash over breakfast at a little Greek diner called the Continental. His waitress was a young dark-haired woman named Jennifer who was ready with an urn of coffee and poured him a cup as he sat down. He pushed the paper aside for the moment and sipped his coffee while watching the people walking past the big picture windows along University Way.

When Jennifer returned he ordered an omelet while she topped off his mug. The hot meal was the first thing Giles had eaten in days, and he took his time with it, savoring every bite. It wasn't until he was finished and sipping his third cup of coffee that Giles finally spread open the paper and began reading.

The crash was being blamed on the storm, pending review of the black box. Giles didn't think there would be any surprises when they listened to it, though. And if two stooges from the FBI were investigating a wild story from a cop in Seattle, it was a good bet there was no bomb, no sabotage, and no psycho-killer. There couldn't be. The only one responsible for the crash was Giles.

As uncanny as it all seemed, it was time to start taking a cold, hard look at the facts instead of trying to dismiss them. First of all, *he* was writing the stories, including the one that had killed Don. And Giles didn't believe for a minute that anyone was combing the newsstand for his stories so that they could frame him.

There was nothing connecting him to the murders *but* the stories, and that tenuous connection had been the only thing that had led to his arrest. It would have been simple enough to plant something of Giles' at the murder scene, or something with Giles' fingerprints on it, but there was nothing. The victims could have all been like Don, people he knew, but they weren't.

No, the explanation lay in his being possessed; Giles knew that instinctively. If all of the natural explanations were ruled out, the only thing that remained was the supernatural. What the hell else could it be? The plane was the clincher. It was just like Daniel said. There was no way for someone to deliberately down a plane with only a few hours' notice. It just couldn't happen.

So how was Giles going to get in touch with this thing inside him that was causing him to write, and if he did find it, did he really want to destroy it? Exactly how much had he written that hadn't been induced by his possession? His novels. Jesus, that was a pathetic thought. Or was it? What if it was the possession that was sabotaging his novels? Maybe if he found a way to exorcise this thing, he might be able to write something significant, be able to resume his marriage, or even get his life back.

When he realized how close he'd come to killing himself Giles began to shudder. He gripped the side of the table to steady himself and closed his eyes. Fatigue was catching up with him, and so was despair. It was all a nice theory, things returning to normal, but he was no closer to figuring out what was possessing him than he had been before. And from the looks of things he might never be.

Giles brought his hands up and rubbed his tired, whiskered face. When he opened his eyes again, he began to feel strange. He looked around, not sure what he expected to see, when he suddenly made eye contact with a man out on the street. The shock of recognition was so great that when his hands hit the table, he knocked his coffee cup onto the floor where it shattered.

Giles stood as quickly as he could, but he'd taken his eyes off the man for just a second, and now he was gone. Jennifer rushed over and began to pick up the broken shards of the mug.

"I'm really sorry about that," Giles said, frantically digging in his pocket for enough money to cover the check.

"That's all right," she said. "Happens all the time."

Though the meal couldn't have been more than five dollars, Giles threw a ten-dollar bill on the table and ran toward the front door.

"Thanks. Bye."

Once out on the street he was confronted by people walking everywhere. Now he realized there was no way to know which way the man had gone. Giles stepped as far out into the street as he dared and looked in both directions, but he couldn't spot the dark suit anywhere.

Perilously, he crossed the street in the middle of the block and looked back across, but it was clear that whoever he'd seen was long gone. Damn it, Giles thought, if only I'd been able to get a good look at him. He'd glimpsed him for just a second, but there could be no mistake. The man outside the window of the Continental was the same individual who had been at Don's funeral. And still, he couldn't quite hold the image in his mind long enough to figure out who it might be.

Giles was sure he knew the man, but something about him was different than what he was trying to remember. Something wasn't right. Finally, he shook his head and began walking back to his car. It wasn't going to come to him.

Now there was something else to add on to his file of facts: someone he knew was following him. Except that it added nothing to his knowledge about what was going on; it only confused things more. Was this person the killer? He thought he'd already ruled out that possibility, and now there was this.

Giles was going to have to go home and write down everything he could think of about what was happening. Maybe if he had it all charted out on paper it would look differently. As he got into his Pontiac and pulled out into traffic, Giles was so preoccupied with the man he had seen that he didn't notice the other car that pulled out at the same time and, from a distance, followed him home.

His heart was racing as he ran to his car and climbed inside. He wasn't sure if he'd been spotted or not when Giles suddenly bolted from his table and ran outside. He'd had to get out of there fast, even at the risk of losing his man. He didn't have long to wait, though. Giles showed up at his car a few minutes later and he was right in position to pick up the tail.

He'd been up all night after the plane crash. He had to know what Giles would do and so he set up an informal stakeout half a block away from Giles' house. His dark suit was rumpled from sitting in the car all night, and he hadn't eaten since the previous morning.

Rena was going to be pissed off when he finally came home. He'd called his wife at work the night before but hadn't been able to reach her, and wound up leaving a note for her on the kitchen counter. It couldn't be helped, though. He had to see what Giles was going to do after the plane crash. He had to know.

As he followed Giles now, he appeared to be heading back the way he had come earlier. That was it? Out to lunch and then home? Sure enough, Giles pulled into his driveway. He pulled his own car to the curb half a block away, stopping where he'd been last night but keeping the engine running. The night had been a total waste, as had the morning.

His face flushed again with shame as he remembered the FBI agents driving up that morning. They hadn't stayed long, and that had surprised him. But maybe it shouldn't have. All Giles had to do was deny it and what could they do? Nothing. He'd done a stupid thing and now he was going to pay for it. And it was all Giles Barrett's fault.

He checked his watch. It was already after one. All he could do now was try to control the damage. If the FBI wanted to continue the case, they could have it. He wasn't going to be involved anymore. And that included seeing Giles. No more visits, no more phone calls. It was over. After one more hateful look at Giles' house, Daniel Lasky turned his car around and headed for home.

# Chapter Seventeen

Apparently it all started after college, with the story about the vampire in the bar. Gradually the "possessions" began to increase in frequency and intensity until there was a certain amount of time left unaccounted for. Multiple personality disorder? It didn't seem likely, but it certainly couldn't be ruled out.

The stories themselves were written about people observed while in something like a fugue state, and several of the very same people were murdered in exactly the same way as written. The exception seemed to be the story about Don. Giles hadn't written that one. At least that's what Janet Raymond had told Paige. She believed that the murders had been committed by by an unimaginative copycat killer who was trying to gain notoriety through Giles' work. Either that, or Giles was killing them himself.

Paige remembered with revulsion the day Giles said, "I think I'm killing people." Was that some other part of him making a confession? Was that why he had destroyed his computer? Was he turning some kind of psychotic killer? And if he was, was there any reason to want to stay together?

She shook the thoughts from her mind. Paige didn't know for sure. It was wrong to make assumptions, and she was going to give Giles the benefit of the doubt until he told her differently. She needed him, and she hoped he still needed her, too. As long as there was a glimmer of hope she wanted to give her marriage a chance to recover. She wasn't going to be a doormat—but she loved her husband.

When Paige pulled into the driveway of the house she stopped for a second and just looked. All the lights appeared to be off, but as her eyes gradually adjusted she could make out a faint glow emanating from somewhere deep within the house. She punched the button for the garage door and nothing happened. She tried again with the same result and finally shut off the car.

Was the power still out here? She'd been so preoccupied that she hadn't noticed the decided lack of street lighting. But once she was out of the car she could see that everything was eerily dark. Paige approached the kitchen door tentatively, and for a second thought about knocking.

"Screw it," she said out loud to herself. "I'm paying the mortgage." Then she unlocked it with her key and walked inside.

"Giles?" She shut the door behind her and walked into the front room. A single candle was burning on the coffee table. The furniture had been rearranged slightly, with the large easy chair pushed up by the window. A couple of blankets were draped over the back.

In the faint light, Paige could see her breath. It was cold in here, and the warmth from being in the car was gradually ebbing away. There was no light coming from the bedrooms, so she yelled downstairs.

"Giles, are you home?"

A second later the flicker of a candle flashed on the walls of the stairway and Giles emerged from below draped in an unzipped sleeping bag.

"Hi," he said. "I was just downstairs in the library trying to do some work. Power's still out."

"So I noticed. I was planning on coming over here and talking with you, but I'm not sure I can stand it in here. If you feel like talking we could go somewhere."

Giles looked at her for a few moments, his brow furrowed. Then he said, "Yeah, that's probably a good idea."

Paige didn't know whether to faint dead away or jump for joy. Instead, she did neither. "We can take my car."

"Okay, just let me throw on some shoes."

Giles walked to the top of the stairs. They were just inches away from each other, and suddenly it was as though nothing had come between them at all. The attraction she had always felt for him was still there, as strong as ever. Giles hesitated slightly, as though he had felt it too, but then turned his head and walked down the hallway toward the bedroom.

Paige stepped back into the kitchen and took several deep breaths. She needed to stay relaxed, and not let the stress of the situation get the better of her. When Giles returned a few minutes later in his heavy coat she was feeling much more in control. He blew out the two candles and they went out to the car.

Giles was silent during the trip, and the few times that Paige looked over at him he seemed to be formulating in his mind what he was going to say and so she decided not to disturb him. She took it as a good sign that he was willing to talk. Good or bad, as least she would have a better idea what to do next.

As unlikely as it seemed for the two of them, they wound up at a Denny's. It was the first place Paige had seen and she wanted to get started before Giles lost his resolve, or decided he didn't want to talk after all. Besides, she wasn't hungry and wasn't planning on eating. Giles would probably just drink coffee, too, if anything.

The place wasn't very busy, and they were seated right away. Giles turned over his coffee cup, as expected, but then he surprised her by ordering a plate of French toast.

"Hungry?" she asked when the waitress had left, and couldn't help grinning.

"Yeah, I guess so. I haven't been eating very regular. You sure you don't want anything?"

"I'm fine. I just want to talk."

Giles smiled at her, and then took a sip of coffee. "I've been trying to think of what I can say to you."

"Why not just tell me what's going on?"

"I'm not sure I understand it myself."

"That's not good enough. Tell me something, anything . . ."

Giles sighed heavily. "I think we should get a divorce."

He didn't even look up from his coffee cup as he said it. Paige closed her eyes for a moment trying to absorb the shock. She probably should have seen it coming. She felt so stupid for hanging on instead of making plans for something like this.

"Damn it, Giles. I thought you were going to talk me." He still didn't look up. "I thought we— I thought you were going to give me a chance."

His eyes raised and locked on hers. Sunken and hollow, they still gave her the creeps. He hadn't shaved in days either, and had the beginnings of a heavy beard. In short, he looked like hell. "I feel like I'm on the verge of understanding what's been happening to me this past year."

"You mean the blackouts?"

He went back to staring in his coffee.

"Giles, please . . ."

"Yes," he said, eyes still lowered. "Whatever you want to call them."

"You can get help."

He smiled again, this time bitterly, and shook his head. "What I need right now is time, and if you can't give that to me then the only alternative I can see is to get divorced."

"So, how long are we talking here?"

In measured tones he said, "I don't know."

"And I'm just supposed to wait around until you feel ready?"

"Like I said, you do have another option."

"Oh, great"

Giles looked with irritation over to the kitchen and then around the rest of the room. Finally a waitress came by, not theirs, and he asked her for a refill of his coffee.

"I'm really sorry about all this, Paige. You have to believe me. But until I know what's happening to me, I just can't be around you anymore."

"Okay, but can't you see how important it is for me to know why? I mean, how am I supposed to be able to make a decision like divorce when I don't know all the facts?"

"I know, I know. But you'll just have to trust me. I can't tell you anything more right now."

Paige hadn't wanted to bring this up, but Giles had clearly told her everything he was going to. "Can you at least tell me why the FBI was in my office questioning me this morning?"

The anger in those sunken eyes was almost frightening as Giles head snapped up. "What did they say to you?"

Paige had to hold back a smile. "I don't think I'm ready to tell you yet."

"Don't play games with me, Paige. What the hell did they ask you?"

"Hey, wait just—"

At that moment the waitress appeared with Giles' French toast and set it in front of him. She asked if there was anything else she could get them and Giles waved her off.

"What did they want to know?"

"No. First you tell me that you think you're killing people, then the police arrest you, and now the FBI. I think I'm entitled to some answers. If you want to know what they asked me then start talking."

His mouth was almost slack with disbelief, but Paige was going to stand firm on this one. The agents hadn't told her what it was about, even though she'd asked. They'd only asked her general questions about Giles' whereabouts and his behavior over the past few months. It wasn't much, and she hated like hell to blackmail Giles, but if that's what it was going to take . . .

Giles pushed his untouched plate away from him, smashing it into his coffee mug, water glass, and silverware. Then he stood abruptly. "I'm leaving. Are you taking me back?"

The lump in Paige's throat rendered her unable to speak. She simply shook her head and watched as Giles stormed out of the restaurant.

She couldn't call Marcy. She needed to be alone. After paying the check, Paige walked in a daze out to her car and fell into the driver's seat. As the first tear rolled down her cheek she made a move to wipe it away, then stopped herself. More tears came and she bent forward resting her head on the steering wheel.

As much as she hated to do it in front of other people, she

wasn't about to cut herself off from her emotions when she was by herself. And besides, right now it felt good to cry.

Giles walked back home with his clenched fists stuffed into the pockets of his overcoat. He couldn't believe it. The FBI hassling him was one thing, but it pissed him off that they were questioning Paige too. The truth was, he was a lot angrier with them than he ever could be with Paige.

He felt shitty about the way he was treating her her, but what else could he do? It was difficult for him just to meet her eyes without thinking about what might happen if he suddenly became possessed. And what if she couldn't even tell? What if it was like some split personality thing where nobody could see the difference in him? Except that another Giles Barrett story would suddenly appear in print and Paige's life would be endangered.

No, it was just too risky. And the hardest part was knowing how much she was trying to help him. He wanted her so badly it hurt. As he was coming up the stairs in the house earlier he had felt it, the connection between them that had always existed. It had taken every bit of his resolve not to take her in his arms right then and apologize. He didn't want a divorce any more than she did. What else could he do, though?

He hadn't lied when he'd told her about being close to understanding what was happening. After coming home from breakfast he'd gone straight down into his office and started writing out everything he knew about his possessions, and he'd made some pretty startling discoveries about his past that he hadn't thought about in connection to this.

Giles had always been an intuitive person. Several women he'd gone out with in high school and college had actually found it kind of spooky. It seemed as if he always knew what they were thinking, what they wanted to do, how they wanted to be touched and kissed. Giles had never given it a second thought, until now.

But that had been years earlier, and was a far cry from looking at a total stranger and knowing everything about him, from his name down to his deepest fears. Still, it was something. And it made sense, in a crazy sort of way, when it was put in the context of another event in his life, a traumatic event that he could only recall bits and pieces of.

The year was 1967. Giles was five years old and his parents had decided to take him to his first movie, a revival of *Bambi* showing at the 7th Street Theater in downtown Hallowell. Giles remembered very little about actually watching the film. It was only afterward, asleep in bed when his subconscious began working overtime, that he could recall in vivid detail. That was when that the real trauma of the Disney film became apparent. He began having bad dreams.

Even some thirty years later the vividness remained in his mind, the flames shooting up all around, the screaming, and finally, death. But it hadn't been the fire in the movie that he was dreaming about; he could tell that much even then. The fire in his dreams had been much more realistic. He had been able to smell the smoke, feel the pain in his lungs and the heat on his skin. When he awoke, he was covered with sweat and positive he could detect the faint odor of burning wood on his pajamas.

Evidently he would scream out in his sleep at some point, because his mother was always there in his room when he woke up. As she was soothing him, his father would invariably poke his head in the door and ask, "Is it that damn movie again?" Then his mother would nod and he would go back to bed.

She always asked him if he could talk about it, but Giles could never bring himself to do it, and would shake his head. After several days, though, his mother asked if he would be able to draw a picture of his dream. Giles thought about it for a second and nodded. His mother went over to his toy box and brought back his crayons and a tablet of paper.

As hard as he tried that night, what Giles came up with couldn't begin to convey the horrifying sensation of his dream: the sensation of burning alive. What he drew looked like a large box with lines on it. In the center, in a smaller box, empty except for the flames, was the small figure of a boy, burning.

His mother looked at it thoughtfully for a moment and said, "Honey, is this you in the middle here?"

Giles looked into her eyes and shook his head.

"Do you know who it is?"

He shook his head again.

"Is this our house?"

And again.

She looked at the drawing for a few more moments and then said, "Giles, honey, would you mind if Mommy kept this dream?"

His forehead had wrinkled with puzzlement until she explained it to him.

"You've been keeping this inside all these nights, but now that it's on this paper, Mommy would like to take it away into her room, and it won't have to wake you up at night anymore. Would you like to try that?"

Giles had nodded enthusiastically. He looked with fascination at the drawing he had made as his mother held it in her hand. She kissed him goodnight, turned out his lamp, and then walked out of his room with the dream. He never had it again. As quickly as his bad dreams had disrupted the household, they were gone.

But that wasn't the end of the incident, not by a long shot. Several months later, during the summer, Giles had gone with his family to visit his grandparents in Port Angeles. When they returned home, Giles' father had stopped the car in town instead of going directly out to the farm. He parked across from Roosevelt Elementary School, and the three of them got out of the car and walked over to the chain link fence surrounding the football field.

The grass field and the track that surrounded it were clearly visible from Roosevelt Avenue. But what had caused his father to stop was the charred wreckage of the large stadium that was on the western edge of the track. Blackened beams and mounds of ash were all that remained of the stadium that the high school football and track team performed in front of. And that Giles and his schoolmates played on during recess.

Later, as his father imparted what he knew about the event to his mother, Giles learned the complete story. A sixteen-year old boy, a runaway, had broken into the storage compartment located underneath the stands in the middle of the structure. The fire department believed that he had been smoking and fallen asleep. Once the fire had started, he couldn't get out and had burned to death inside the locked compartment.

Giles had never told anyone, and over the years had almost forgotten about it himself. But in going over the events of the past six months, and trying to sort out everything in his mind, it had all come back to him. The square structure that he had drawn for his mother had not been a house of any kind. And the lines were more than just lines; they represented the many tiers of seats that ascended to the top of Roosevelt Stadium. The boy who had burned to death every night for a week in Giles' dreams, had burned to death for real.

Only after he'd had time to think about this memory did Giles come to realize that whatever was causing his possession must have been with him all his life. It was frightening, but he also felt relieved in a way. He could stop looking over his shoulder because now he knew that the answer was inside of him. What he was going to do about it, on the other hand, remained to be seen.

Giles turned the last corner toward home and his heart momentarily lifted. The streetlights were on. Thank God. He'd only walked a block when he heard a car rounding the corner behind him and screeching to a halt. When Giles turned around he was surprised by what he saw. There were two cars stopped in the middle of the street. The one in the middle of the intersection had its lights off and it immediately accelerated to the end of the corner and around the block. The other car then proceeded straight ahead past Giles. Was he being followed? It looked like there had been only one person, a driver, in the first car, but even if FBI agents were staking him out they certainly didn't have to be the same ones who had been at the house this morning.

"That's all I need," he muttered to himself, and picked up his pace.

The house was lit up, and while it might not have been warm inside yet, it looked damned inviting. Before he went inside Giles looked around at the other cars on the block. He recognized most of them, but he realized he'd never had a reason to know all of them by sight.

It didn't matter, though. The FBI didn't have anything on him and they weren't going to. An idea that had been germinating in his mind all afternoon was about ready for some serious consideration and, if it became a reality, could put this whole mess behind him. As Giles walked into his house, he finally felt as if he had some control over his life.

Daniel Lasky was pissed. He knew where Giles was going, yet he'd turned the corner too soon and been trapped in the middle of the intersection. He'd left his lights off and drove away as quickly as he could, hoping Giles wouldn't recognize his car from the time Daniel had been out to the house.

He decided to pack it in for the night anyway, and from what he'd seen at the Denny's it was clear that Paige and Giles had decided to do the same thing. Whatever was going on with Giles was affecting their marriage. Lasky hadn't seen her car at the house all day yesterday or today. And then with Giles walking out of the restaurant like that, it didn't take a detective to figure out they were having problems.

Not that Lasky's own marriage was any better. It seemed as if all he and Rena did was fight anymore. That is, on the rare occasions that they actually saw each other. Well, he was going to be home tonight, whether she liked it or not.

He turned his car around and headed back toward the freeway. Whatever Giles was doing, it was clear he wasn't going to just blunder out of his house and do it himself. Maybe he was phoning orders to someone else. That person did the killings so there would be no connection to Giles at the crime scene. It didn't matter. At some point he would make a mistake and then everything would be over.

The day before he had wanted to chuck the whole goddamned

case. He had wanted to hide from his embarrassment, but after thinking it over that morning he realized that he was only running away from the problem. Daniel Lasky was now a man on a mission. And that mission was to put Giles Barrett behind bars.

# Chapter Eighteen

When Giles walked into the house he went straight for the kitchen and made himself a sandwich. He was starving. There was no beer, as he hadn't bought any for some time, but there was a bottle of Chardonnay chilling in the back of the fridge and he promptly uncorked it and poured himself a very large glass. He took a sip and felt himself unwind immediately. Perfect.

After taking a large bite of the sandwich, he descended the stairs into his office. He set his plate down, took another sip of wine, and surveyed the damage. His computer was trashed. Giles shook his head. In retrospect it may have been a stupid thing to do, but if he was in the same position again he couldn't say that he wouldn't do the very same thing. Peace of mind, for someone who thinks he's losing his, is worth any price.

Giles set about cleaning up his mess, putting the broken shell of his monitor in a cardboard box along with the decimated keyboard. Thankfully, he hadn't gotten around to the hard drive or the printer. The monitor and keyboard would be relatively inexpensive to replace. Once he had a space cleared on his desk, he walked out to the laundry room.

There, in the cupboard above the washing machine, was his old IBM Selectric. Ironically, he had bought it after the previous incident in which he had chucked his old typewriter out the window of his Capitol Hill apartment. He lifted it out of the cupboard and carried it to his office, placing it gently on the desk.

Then he plugged it in, heard the old familiar hum, and sat down to write.

Gnawing on his sandwich and sipping his wine, Giles began to formulate what kind of story he would need to write in order to extricate himself from this situation. Simply put, he needed to come up with a story wherein he killed the monster. He realized that he would have to be the one to do battle; he couldn't risk involving anyone else. And if something went wrong—worst-case scenario—then Giles himself would be the only one to die. Either way, the whole thing would be over.

Though he still didn't understand why he was having these possessions, at least he knew that he had been the source of all the murders. He couldn't atone for the people who had already died, but he did have the power to stop any further killing. He was going to have to meet one of the nightmares of his own creation and kill it. And yet, as he sat there at his desk mulling it over, that seemed like the easy part.

Writing on demand, now that was going to be difficult. It had certainly never been Giles' forte, but if he needed any more motivation all he had to do was think of Paige. Just the thought that she might be in danger from his possessions was enough to make him write. He took another bite of sandwich, a slug of wine, and then rolled a clean sheet of paper into his typewriter.

A quarter of the way down in the center of the page he wrote the words, EVEN A MAN, by Giles Barrett. It was going to be a story about a werewolf. The only other story Giles had written on that subject had been about a baby who changed into a wolf. This one would be about two friends, one of whom was a werewolf. The werewolf would ask his friend to kill him, and the friend would refuse. Finally, the werewolf would give his friend a gun with a silver bullet in it, persuading him to meet him in a secluded spot where he could witness the transformation. Once the change occurred, the friend would shoot the werewolf, killing him and ending the curse.

The ending was perfect, because whether Giles was the friend who was cursed and died, or the one who ended the curse and lived, it would finally be over.

The idea, of course, was a total rip-off of a TV show he'd seen several years before, but at this point Giles didn't really give a shit. He was much more predisposed to using a gun to handle the situation than any type of hand-to-hand combat. And besides, with his reputation he would probably be able to palm it off on some small press horror magazine and they wouldn't even know the difference.

*Blood*, he wrote. Then: *Blood everywhere. The animal couldn't get enough . . .*

Paige drove to the hotel in a daze. She had gone to the house with almost no expectations, but when Giles had agreed to talk she had somehow let herself think they had a chance. She wasn't so sure anymore. Had it really come to this, divorce? It was almost unbelievable. Six months ago they were a happily married couple, and now suddenly they weren't.

She pulled into the lot of a Travel Lodge that was about two blocks north of work. As she took her suitcase out of the back seat she realized that she was still going to have to talk with Giles about living arrangements. She couldn't stay in a hotel indefinitely. Correction, she *wouldn't*.

The difficult part was knowing that Giles didn't even have a job. He was a wonderful writer, but he certainly didn't make enough to live on. She hadn't minded supporting him either, not in the slightest. The way Paige figured it, she was going to be a dentist either way. She was going to be doing the same thing whether she was married to Giles or not. And life was infinitely more pleasurable with Giles.

After a deep sigh, she trudged into the office, paid for her room, and then walked up the stairs and down past the railing to her room. It was musty smelling, with a double bed, cheap furniture, and a television set. She immediately opened the windows to air it out before she turned up the heat and changed her clothes.

Paige sat down on the bed and ran her fingers through her hair, massaging her scalp with her fingers. Then she rubbed her eyes and leaned back against the headboard. It was going to be a long night, but then all of her nights seemed longer these days. Marcy would be pissed that she was staying in a hotel, but Paige didn't care. She needed to be alone right now and, in spite of Marcy's denials, she felt like she was imposing.

Paige picked up the remote control off the nightstand next to the bed and turned on the TV. She almost never watched television anymore and didn't recognize the show that was on, but she left the volume up to keep her company. She hadn't realized just how lonely she felt without Giles. It was awful. He was only a few miles away, and yet he had never seemed farther away from her.

It was only the shivering from the cold that moved her from the bed. She shut the windows and thought about turning up the heat a little more, but instead she went to the bathroom and stripped. Paige turned up the hot water in the shower, and stood underneath the numbing spray until it began to cool. When she was finished she wrapped a towel around herself and walked out to call the desk. She left instructions for a wakeup call and then crawled under the covers of her bed.

The last thing Paige wanted was food. Her stomach was churning just thinking about Giles, and the TV mercifully kept her mind off of him for the next few hours. Finally, at eleven thirty, she turned off the lights and cried herself to sleep.

By the time Giles had finished two more sandwiches and polished off the entire bottle of wine—getting pleasantly drunk in the process, then gradually sobering up again—he had completed the story. It was almost three-thirty in the morning. He was pleased with what he'd accomplished.

It had taken a little while to get used to writing on a typewriter again, and he found it liberating in a way. There was always the temptation to tinker with his work on the computer. It was so easy to change things. But on the old IBM, all he could do was push forward. Revision would have to come later. And that was another thing he was looking forward to, sitting down with a pen and doing corrections, reading the story on paper instead of on a screen.

And the story was going to need some corrections, too. It wasn't like being possessed, when it would roll off the printer ready to go, and for once Giles was glad of it. It felt more like something he had created instead of channeled.

The secluded spot he had come up with was a newly erected high-rise on 2nd Avenue. He had driven by it the last time he was downtown. It was still under construction, and the only thing keeping him out was a six-foot chain-link fence along the alley. He had written the story so that he could hop the fence, take the stairs up to the top floor and meet the werewolf there. All he needed was a gun.

A smile crept onto Giles lips. A minute later he leaned back in his chair and laughed out loud. He was tired, yes, but even that couldn't explain the ridiculousness of the situation. Here he was rationally planning to confront a figment of his imagination, with no doubt in his mind that it would be there to meet him. It was ludicrous. But he believed it. With all his heart he believed it.

Maybe it was because he was so exhausted mentally, but he couldn't do anything else but believe. He should have been frightened at the prospect. He should have been questioning his sanity. Then he laughed again. He'd done that already, so much so that his almost childlike faith in the supernatural seemed, at this point, to be the only logical progression.

Giles yawned. He picked up the pages of his story, eighteen of them, straightened the stack and turned it over. He was tempted to read through it right then, but resisted. First things first, he thought. He shut off the typewriter, gathered up his plate and wineglass, and headed upstairs to bed. There would be plenty of time tomorrow and over the weekend to polish up the story. Then, first thing Monday morning, he would try to get it published.

The phone jolted Paige awake Friday morning, and for a few moments she didn't know where she was. She picked up the receiver, was informed that it was six-thirty, and then hung up. It was all coming back to her now. She was in a hotel. It seemed like she hadn't slept in the same bed twice during the last month, though it had only been a few days.

She crawled out of bed and into the shower, and then proceeded to use every drop of hot water again. It may have been cliché, but the one thought that kept running through her mind was, thank God it's Friday. She had to get things with Giles straightened out this weekend or she was going to be worthless to her patients next week.

As she toweled off, Paige chided herself for pussyfooting around. Moving out had been a stupid idea. At the very least, it hadn't helped matters any. In spite of the unexpected results at Denny's the night before, it had felt good to stand up to Giles. She was slowly coming to realize that maybe her desire to make everything in her life orderly wasn't the way to go. Maybe she should take a more active part in making her own happiness instead of trying to manipulate the things and people around her.

Paige looked at herself in the mirror and smiled.

"What do you say," she said to her image. "Don't you think it's about time you got your shit together and did something about your marriage?"

She dressed and felt a new resolve within herself. It was time to stop being the victim and get on with things. If he had to have a divorce then fuck him, she'd give him a divorce. It wasn't as if she hadn't thought about it before. It sucked, to be sure, but it most definitely wasn't the end of the world. And that was really the bottom line.

Paige dressed and checked out. She drove over to Starbucks and picked up a couple of croissants to go with her coffee, and then continued on to work. Leaving the door to her office open, she sat behind her desk and caught up on some paperwork while she waited for Marcy to arrive. It wasn't long before she poked her in the door.

"Well, how'd it go?"

"Awful."

"Ah, shit."

"No, it's not that bad. Come on in."

Marcy walked inside and closed the door behind her.

"He told me he wanted a divorce last night."

Marcy's eyes narrowed and Paige almost laughed. She knew what was coming. "So . . . did you stay at the house last night?"

"No. I stayed at the Travel Lodge up the street."

"Oh, Paige—"

"Don't, Marcy. I'm going to be okay."

Suddenly her eyes widened.

"I mean it. I guess I've just run out of self-pity. At the very least I can say that I tried everything I could—"

"I'll say."

"And if that's not enough, then there's really nothing else to do. If Giles is that set on divorce, then I'm going to have to get used to the idea."

"Wow. You sound great. What happened?"

Paige smiled and began to relate the conversation she and Giles had in Denny's. When she got to the part withholding what the FBI had asked her, Marcy erupted into laughter.

"Did you ever find out what the hell's going on with the FBI?" Marcy asked.

"Nope. That one's still a mystery. Along with practically everything else."

"Well, I've got a early appointment. You want to have lunch together?"

"Sure. That would be nice."

Just as she was opening the door, Marcy turned back. "Where are you staying this weekend?"

"At *my* house."

Marcy grinned. "You'd better watch it, girl. You don't want to turn into a bitch like me."

"I could do a lot worse," Paige replied, and sent Marcy down the hall in another gale of laughter.

Giles awoke to a strange noise. He rubbed the sleep from

his eyes and looked to the clock on his nightstand. He knew he'd slept most of the day and the digital numerals confirmed that it was a few minutes after six p.m. He listened again. The noise was definitely coming from the kitchen. With his heart pounding in his chest he hopped out of bed, slipped on his sweats, and crept out into the hall.

He had almost reached the kitchen when a figure suddenly appeared in front of him. Giles involuntarily screamed and jumped back. The figure did the same. Then he realized it was Paige.

"Jesus," he said, his hand over his bare chest. "You scared the hell out of me. What are you doing here?"

Paige didn't answer right away, and Giles wasn't sure what to expect. Then she took a breath and launched in. "I live here, Giles. This is my house, too, and if you want to talk about it, fine, but until then you'll just have to deal with the fact that I'm staying here."

Giles couldn't keep from smiling and tried to turn away before she saw him.

"What's so funny?" Paige demanded.

"Take it easy. I never asked you to move out in the first place—"

"Don't turn this around on me, Giles."

"I'm not," he said, holding his hands up. "Sorry."

"You wouldn't talk to me. What the hell was I supposed to do?"

"I just need some time, that's all. I'm working things out, really. I just need . . . a little more time."

The fear was still there. Giles knew that he shouldn't be staying in the same house with Paige, but he also knew he wouldn't be able to help himself this time. He tried to rationalize that without the computer whatever was possessing him would have a more difficult time writing, but he knew that wasn't true. There was also the fact that it would have to be published for any harm to come to her, and that made him feel a little better. He just couldn't take his eyes off Paige. All he wanted to do was hold her in his arms again.

"So, why are you still smiling?"

"It's just so good to see you."

"Don't do this to me, Giles. Last night you were talking divorce. You better not be setting me up—"

"What was I supposed to do? You kept pressing me to make some kind of decision and I didn't know what else to say. I don't want to get a divorce, but I can't take that kind of pressure right now. I'm sorry for hurting you, Paige, but I'm so busy trying to deal with all the shit that's going on . . . It's just impossible for me to have any kind of meaningful discussion with you right now."

"At all?"

"I still can't tell you about it. But when it's over, I promise I will."

"And how long is that going to be?"

"With any luck, a month or two at the most."

"And until then?

In answer, Giles stepped forward and took Paige in his arms. Their lips met and Giles felt better than he had in months. He took Paige's face in his hands and kissed her again. She held on to him so tightly that he almost couldn't breath. It was wonderful.

When he pulled back she still wouldn't let go. Giles looked into Paige's eyes, hands still on her cheeks. Tears were nearly brimming over in her eyes.

"Are you all right?"

She smiled and kissed him. "I'm fine. I just love you so much, Giles. I'm so sorry—"

"Don't, don't, Paige. I'm the one who caused all of this. Just give me a couple months and it will all be over. I promise."

The two of them hugged again and Giles dried Paige's eyes. "Let's go take a shower," she said.

"Only if we go to bed right after."

Paige smiled slyly and said, "Oh yeah? What's wrong with the shower?"

# Chapter Nineteen

It was a very pleasant weekend, not quite the same as the old days, but pleasant nonetheless. They had quickly fallen into the rhythm of Giles' working in the morning and the two of them playing the rest of the day. Most of their games this weekend, however, had been confined to the bedroom.

Giles had also managed to get most of his rewrites done. The story wasn't great, but it was passable, and by Monday all he needed to do was to find a magazine to place it in. And that was going to be a problem. After waking up early and making love to Paige before she left for work, Giles had spent the entire morning calling magazines he had previously been published in, but with no success.

Well, that wasn't entirely true. Most of them were happy to tentatively accept the piece for a future issue. When Giles mentioned that he wanted it in the next issue out, however, they had all declined. So, after taking a break for lunch at noon, and calling Paige to say hi, he went back to his market listings and the phone.

Giles concentrated on small press magazines this time, one-man operations that put out an issue at least six times a year. The first two numbers he called only had answering machines and he declined to leave a message. On his third call, to a magazine called *Silent Screams* out of Modesto, California, someone answered.

"Hello?" It was a man's voice.

"Yes, is this Jeff Peters?" That was the name of the editor in the listing.

"In the flesh."

"I'm calling about your magazine."

"Sure, what do you need to know?"

Giles wasn't sure how to begin. He hadn't really thought through what he would say if he wound up talking to someone who didn't know who he was. "My name's Giles Barrett, and I wanted to talk to you about placing a story in your magazine."

"No kidding?" The excitement in Peters voice seemed to indicate that he recognized the name.

"I've been reading some of your back issues," Giles lied, "and I think I have a story that would be right up your alley."

"Oh, man. That would be radically cool."

Giles verified the address in his listing and asked Peters if he should send the story there.

"That would be great. But, uh . . . there's just one thing, Mr. Barrett."

Very nice, Giles thought. He had the upper hand with this kid already. From the sound of his voice and his speech mannerisms, Peters had to be in his twenties.

"What is it, Jeff?"

"I hope you know that I won't be able to pay you anything."

"Yes, I'm aware of that."

"Excellent."

"But in light of that, there is one thing you can do for me."

"You got it."

Giles smiled. This was almost too easy. "I'd like the story to appear in your next issue."

That little request was met with a resounding silence. Inwardly, Giles groaned.

"Uh, the next few issues are actually full, but I can definitely have you in by next summer."

Giles was going to take a chance. He could tell how badly the kid wanted his story. All he needed was a little push. "Not good enough, Jeff. I'm afraid this is a conditional offer. Either you find a way to squeeze it into your next issue, or I'll have to try somewhere else."

He could practically hear wheels turning in the kid's head. "Can I be honest with you, Mr. Barrett?

"Please do."

"If I could have a couple of issues advance on your story, I'd be able to advertise in my magazine and maybe even boost my circulation a little. At the very least I'd be able to sell out the issue with your story in it. But if I put it in the next issue, with no advance, it would almost be a waste of my time."

Giles thought for a moment and said, "Okay, how about this? I'll give you two stories, one goes in the next issue, and the other whenever you want."

"Absolutely."

It was going to have to be a reprint, but since the kid hadn't asked there was no need to tell him right away. "Okay, then. You got yourself a deal."

They made the final arrangements and Giles hung up the phone. He looked over at the story next to his typewriter. Even though it was in its third draft, it still sucked. There was always the possibility that the kid would reject it, but he didn't think so. It was a new story, and since it wasn't going to have any buildup anyway, Giles was betting he'd print it no matter what he thought of it.

Six weeks, that was how long he had. The January issue of *Silent Screams* came out in mid December. Giles would have just that long to find a gun and—this was going to be even tougher—some silver bullets. At least he wasn't in a panic anymore. Having Paige back in the house was exerting a calming influence over him. He felt as if he could think things through rationally again, and that's what he intended to do.

He certainly couldn't count on Daniel Lasky's help, though it would have been nice to confirm that it was the FBI tailing him the other night. Even so, Giles was pretty sure he had taken care of that as well. In the story, a local cop is staking out the main character but the cop falls asleep at the crucial moment and misses seeing the guy leaving the house. It seemed highly unlikely that the FBI would still be watching him in December, but it didn't hurt to be sure.

Giles laughed to himself. All this was assuming, of course, that he actually did have the power to control people simply by writing about them. And yet somehow he knew it was true. He knew it inside of himself. A psychologist would probably have a field day with him for so willingly accepting a supernatural explanation for what was going on. That didn't bother him either. For one thing, he wasn't planning on seeing a psychologist any time soon. But the main reason for his total acceptance was that it finally put him in control.

Ultimately, that was what had allowed him some semblance of sanity. He just might be a raving lunatic, but he sure didn't feel like it anymore. Paige seemed to think he was back to his old self, and that was good enough for Giles. Once he had put an end to his own creation, he knew it would all be over. No more possessions, and no more murders. He would be free one way or another. At least that was the theory.

Giles picked up the phone and dialed DHL. He didn't want Jeff Peters and *Silent Screams* to wait one more day.

Though Paige wouldn't have thought it possible for a person to feel this way, she had been cautiously euphoric all morning. Things were hardly what she would call back to normal, but they were good . . . very good. She had indirectly tried to ask him Saturday night about what he was up to and he had seen right through it. They had talked for a while after that and Giles had been so calm about it that she decided never to bring it up again. She didn't think she ever would.

Even with the secret he was keeping from her, he was so much back to his old self that she sometimes had to remind herself that things still hadn't been settled. It was tempting to slip back into the old routine and pretend that the past seven months hadn't happened. Except that it had happened, and was still happening.

She had to remember that so that if things deteriorated again she would be emotionally prepared.

Instead of being complacent and trying to make sure nothing threatened her happiness, she was now willing to take the responsibility for whatever happened. She had moved out before, but she realized now how it had really been her way of trying to manipulate Giles into doing something he wasn't willing to do. Though she didn't know what she would do when and if Giles had the same problems again, she knew she was going to have to set limits right away. She would tell Giles how she felt—and what she would accept—right up front. Whatever happened after that . . . well, she could deal with it.

Daniel Lasky had been staking out Giles Barrett's home for nearly three weeks when he finally hit the jackpot. Well, it hadn't been a continuous stakeout, but he'd done what he could. Leaving early several afternoons a week, coming in late on others, and sometimes spending a long lunch hour watching the house in Shoreline had finally paid off.

It was just after one o'clock on the Monday before Thanksgiving when Giles pulled out of his driveway and made his way to I-5 southbound. To Lasky's surprise, Giles drove through town and continued south. By the time they had reached Sea-Tac airport, Lasky radioed in that he was checking out for the day. There was no way he was going to lose this tail. Even if it led nowhere, it was the most exciting thing Giles had done in nearly a month.

The two cars continued to make their way south, Lasky a good fifty yards behind, and always in a different lane. They drove for nearly forty minutes, passing by Des Moines to the west, Kent and Auburn to the east, and down into Pierce County. By the time they had reached Fife, Lasky was getting worried. His gas gauge was nearly empty. He hadn't planned on this little excursion. He followed Giles on through Tacoma, past the Tacoma Dome and the Tacoma Mall, and just when Lasky was about to call it quits and head for a gas station, Giles' turn signal began flashing and he made for the Lakewood exit just ahead of them.

But Lasky wasn't quite breathing a sigh of relief. He was still dangerously low on gas as Giles began backtracking through south Tacoma. Then, a few blocks later, it all became worthwhile. Giles turned into the parking lot of a large building that bordered the freeway. The walls of the one-story building were all glass, with black iron bars on every window. Up above, in black letters on a yellow background running across the entire front of the structure, was a sign that read: GUNS.

Not only that, but across the street from the gun shop was a gas station. Lasky pulled up to one of the pumps and got out. He was closely watching Giles the entire time. Giles walked inside as Lasky put the nozzle into his gas tank. There were only a few customers in the shop. Giles walked right up to the counter and began talking to a short, stocky salesman. The man, in turn, began to show Giles what looked like a handgun.

Lasky relaxed now. He paid for his gas and then drove around to the opposite side of the gun shop and parked. Washington State had a three-day waiting period to buy a gun, so Lasky knew Giles wouldn't be leaving with one today. It was perfect. All he had to do was make sure he followed the gun, and he could take Giles Barrett down.

They may not have been able to connect him to any of the other murders, but Lasky was convinced that Giles was involved. And now, here he was buying a gun. The fact that they hadn't nailed him in the first place still galled him. He didn't begrudge the fact that Janet Raymond was defending Giles. It just meant that the evidence this time had to be ironclad. Kevin Adamson had inadvertently done them a favor by refusing to prosecute him on the earlier murders because now they could use all of that evidence in a future trial. A conviction would be child's play. There would be no chance for appeal.

Lasky waited outside the gun shop for twenty minutes before Giles finally emerged, empty handed, and drove away. He decided to stay put, taking a chance that Giles would return to the same place he had left the freeway to get back on. Sure enough, five minutes later, in the northbound lane, Lasky saw Giles' Pontiac heading north back home. Immediately, he climbed out of his car and headed toward the shop. Inside, the place smelled of polished wood and gun oil. It was a familiar smell to Lasky. All around the room were racks of rifles, shotguns, and various and sundry other weapons. Handguns were under glass against the far wall and Lasky walked toward the back after spotting the man he had seen helping Giles. When he reached the counter, Lasky pulled out his badge and flashed it quickly.

"Police," Lasky said. "I'd like to ask you a few questions."

The man behind the counter was about five-six, with greasy black hair plastered to his head. He wore thick, smoked glasses and his teeth, when he smiled, were nearly the same shade of gray. He was wearing a black western shirt, and black jeans with a leather belt and a large brass buckle holding them up.

The curious and helpful response Lasky had expected was not forthcoming. Instead the man just smiled and folded his arms. "Is that right?"

"Yes. That man you were helping a few minutes ago, I need to know what he was looking at."

The smile got wider. "And just why would I want to tell you that?"

"This is a police investigation."

He chuckled this time, and Lasky was beginning to wonder if the guy was all there. "A po-lice investigation, huh?"

"That's right, so why don't you just cooperate and I can let you get back to your business."

"My business is doin' just fine without any cooperation from the police."

Lasky was through playing games. This guy needed to be taken down a peg. "Look, we can do this here, or I can take you down to the station house for questioning. The choice is up to you."

This time the man burst out laughing. Lasky could only stand there, stunned. When the man had finished wiping the tears from his cheeks, he leaned forward on the counter and locked eyes with Lasky. "That's gonna be kind of a long trip, isn't it Lieutenant?"

Lasky couldn't believe it. How could the man have recognized his badge from the brief flash he'd given him. "I'm not sure I understand."

"A Seattle shield don't cut much ice down here. You're kind of a long way from home, ain't you Lieutenant?"

"Look, I'm working on a multi-jurisdictional investigation under Captain Burney of Tacoma Homicide—"

Lasky would have thought he had just told the world's greatest joke by the way the man launched into another fit of laughter.

Lieutenant," the man said after drying his eyes again. "Damn near every cop on the Tacoma force, from the 'cycles and the flatfoots on up to the Chief himself, comes down here to buy guns and use the firing range." The man hitched his thumb over his shoulder and Lasky looked up to see the entrance to, what else, a firing range. The man continued. "But I never heard of any Captain Burney before."

The man reached down below the counter and pulled up a phone, placing it on the counter in front of Lasky. "Why don't you give him a call and he can tell me all about it?"

Lasky hesitated.

"Or you can cut the crap and tell me what this is all about, and then *maybe* I can help you."

Lasky sighed with exasperation and gave the man an abbreviated version of the story. He was tracking a murder suspect who just happened to drive down to Tacoma to look at guns.

The man stroked his wispy mustache and frowned at Lasky. "Well, last I checked, there ain't no law against buying a gun. Murder suspect or no, is there?"

"I'd just like to take a look at the gun, okay?"

The man smiled again, reached under the counter, and set a Smith and Wesson snubbed nosed .38 with a two inch barrel on a piece of black felt. "Model 36," he said. "Look familiar?"

Lasky nodded. It was one of the many revolvers that were used by law enforcement officers all over the country.

"Tried to sell him a Model 38 with a shrouded hammer. It weighs a lot less, but he wasn't in the mood to dicker. Didn't want to spend a lot."

Lasky picked it up. "Is this the one he's buying?"

"Nope, that one's in back with the registration."

"Could I take a look at the registration?"

He was already shaking his head. "Not without a warrant. But I tell you what I can do." He pulled out a business card and scratched out a phone number on it, then pushed it over to Lasky. "This here's the number of Sergeant Hastings of the Tacoma PD. Tell him Walt sent you, and I'm sure he'd be happy to request a copy for you once the gun's been purchased."

Lasky set the gun back down and looked at the card. It was clear he wasn't going to get any more information from this guy. As he was sticking the card in his pocket and preparing to leave, the man laughed again.

"I tell you, though. You two could be a comedy team."

Lasky looked up, but didn't dignify the comment with a verbal response.

"You and your hard-ass cop routine, and that other guy with his werewolves."

"Werewolves?"

"Yeah," he said, and chuckled again. "After I make the sale I start talking to him about ammunition. Well, he lowers his voice and leans over the counter, and you know what he asks me for?"

"What?"

Walt smiled a toothy-gray grin and said, "Silver bullets."

# Chapter Twenty

Getting the silver bullets wasn't going to be the difficult part—it was going to be keeping them, along with the gun, in the house without Paige knowing. The man at the gun shop in Lakewood had steered him to a place that sold ammunition in downtown Tacoma. They weren't pure silver, but they would be close enough. Silver-tipped .38 caliber shells that only came in boxes of fifty, Giles bought a box and stashed them under the passenger seat of his Pontiac.

Before his hand reemerged he knew what he was going to do. He didn't have to take the gun and bullets into the house at all. He could leave them in the car. Paige never drove the Pontiac, and he would just make sure that during the next six weeks they took her car whenever they went anywhere together. All that was left to do now was sit out the waiting period and pick up the .38.

They stepped out of the movie theater at the University district's Metro Cinemas hand in hand. Once they were out on the sidewalk Giles slipped his hand around Paige's waist, pulling her close to him. She rested her head against his shoulder and closed her eyes for a moment as the two of them walked out to her car in a cold November drizzle.

They had just been to see the latest movie based on a Stephen King novel, at Giles' insistence. Giles always dragged her to them on opening night. Well, dragged wasn't really the word. She didn't hate the experience, it just wasn't something she enjoyed watching. In fact, the only horror films that Paige really liked at all were the Universal pictures from the thirties and forties. She went because she liked going out with Giles, and because he didn't insist on seeing every piece of drivel that had the label "horror film" attached to it.

Giles did have his literary heroes and only insisted on going to the adaptations of their work. They'd seen Coppola's *Dracula* and *Frankenstein*, Joe Dante's *Matinee* and Romero's *The Dark Half*, and films based on Anne Rice's *Interview with the Vampire* and H.P. Lovecraft's *The Case of Charles Dexter Ward*, all on opening night within the past few years. But that had been it. Thankfully, she'd been spared the hundreds of mindless slasher films and exploitation trash that had been released during the same period of time.

Paige yawned and when Giles leaned over and kissed her forehead she looked up at him. "Thank you," she said.

"For what?"

"You've been so nice the past few weeks, sometimes I forget that you still have a secret you're hiding from me."

He shook his head and looked up into the sky. "So why should you thank me?"

She'd thought a lot about that herself and there was really only one reason: clearly, there was nothing she could do about it. She'd tried everything short of divorce that she could think of, and that hadn't worked. Paige knew that she could go on resenting him and make both their lives miserable, or . . .

"I just want to be happy, with you, and you're making that possible."

When they reached the Peugeot, Paige unlocked the doors. Once inside, she started the car, turned the heat on, and waited for it to warm up. "I remember what it was like last summer," she said. "You're not like that anymore. Are you sure it's not over yet, that you can't tell me?"

Giles nodded his head slowly and kept his eyes straight ahead of him, staring at the foggy windshield. "I'm sure. It's just that I have a handle on things for the moment." Then he shook his head violently and met her eyes. "I really don't want to talk about it anymore, okay?"

As she'd promised herself, she nodded and said, "Okay." No hurt feelings, no apologies. He said he'd tell her in a few weeks, and she was going to trust him enough to believe he would. Finally, as the cool air from the defroster began to warm and clear the windshield, she pulled out and headed for home.

Jeff Peters read the story again and almost groaned out loud. It wasn't that it was awful; it just wasn't . . . what he'd expected. He'd read nearly all of Giles Barrett's work and this wasn't anywhere near as good. If he hadn't received the call from him, he might have doubted that the same man had written it.

But what the hell was he going to do? Tell the guy to do it over? No fucking way. He remembered reading about an anthology that Harlan Ellison was putting together. Ellison had requested a story from Stephen King and when he got it he told King to do another rewrite. Talk about balls. King never rewrote the story—who could blame him—and Peters was damned if he was going to screw himself out of a two-story deal with Giles Barrett.

He was going to have to do a lot of extra work to squeeze it into the next issue, though. He had already called one of the authors and told him he was going to bump his story back several issues, but he still had to typeset the Barrett story. And that was another thing, didn't this guy have a computer? His manuscript looked like it was done on some piece of shit typewriter, with penciled corrections and everything. What a joke.

Oh, well, he thought, at least there would be another story coming that he could advertise the hell out of. Which reminded him, he had to make up an ad for this issue promoting the later story. The whole thing was a nightmare.

The only saving grace would be if the stories sold more copies of the magazine, and Peters was counting on that. Barrett's name would be displayed prominently on the cover—yet another thing that was going to have to be modified—and with the promise of another story to come he might even pick up a few more subscribers.

Peters sighed heavily and began to retype the story before adding it to the pages ready to be typeset. He only had two more days before the copy had to be at the printers. He hoped it was going to be worth it.


"Okay," Walt said, as he emerged from the back room. "Here she is."

Giles watched as he set the gun on the black felt on top of the glass counter and began ringing up the sale. He was almost afraid to touch it. The only thing that kept him from turning and walking out the front door was the knowledge that he wouldn't be killing a real person, only a manifestation of his imagination.

"I sure hope this works."

"What was that?" Walt yelled over the ringing of the old-fashioned cash register.

"Nothing. How much do I owe you?"

Walt had tried to sell him a bunch of other things for the gun, a carrying case, cleaners, ammunition, targets, but Giles shook him off. He just wanted to get out of the shop with the gun.

"Just one more thing before you leave," Walt said in a conspiratorial tone. "It's none of my business, but I think you should know all the same."

Giles wasn't sure if he did want to hear it 'all the same.' "What's that?"

"The other day when you were in here a Seattle cop came in right after, askin' a bunch of questions. Now if there's any reason the law don't want you having a piece, you might want to arrange a time with me to pick it up . . . outside the shop."

Giles glanced outside instinctively. "Has he been in since then?"

"Nope, just the once."

"What did he look like?"

"'Bout your height, dark hair, brown suit—"

"Looked like he'd slept in it?"

Walt flashed his dark teeth at Giles and nodded. "Yeah, that's the guy."

Daniel Lasky. Jesus, this was unbelievable.

"So, like I was saying. We could meet—"

"No, thanks. I'm fine."

"Okay, but he'll probably be requesting a copy of the registration, and I'll have to give it to him."

"I understand. Thanks again."

"Don't mention it."

Giles kept the gun in his pocket until he reached the car, all the time wondering if he was being watched. Once inside, he deposited it next to the bullets under the passenger seat. The registration he set on top of the seat. As long as he didn't carry the gun on his person, he was okay.

Except for Daniel Lasky. All Giles wanted now, was to get back home.


"All right, let me get this straight. You've been tailing this guy on your own time, and now you want to start an official investigation—on your own—on department time."

"That's about it."

Karl Dahlgren, captain of the Seattle Police Department's Magnolia precinct, was already shaking his head. "I don't like it, Dan."

Lasky had gone straight to the Captain's office after returning from Tacoma when Giles picked up his .38. "I'm telling you, this guy's ready to blow. And now that he's armed, there's no telling what could happen."

"Well, if he really was the one responsible for those murders, why did they kick him downtown?"

"There wasn't enough evidence."

"Okay, but as far as I can see you still don't have any new evidence. Anybody can buy a gun."

Unlike a lot of the senior officers in the department, Dahlgren was one of the few who Lasky didn't consider a hard ass. He would listen, and was usually willing to discuss things. Lasky was doing his best to convince him but it wasn't easy.

"Look, Karl, I don't know . . . call it instinct, but I have a bad feeling about this guy. I think he's responsible for a lot more than just the murders that happened here."

"You're not telling me you still believe that airline crash horseshit?"

"You tell me. A guy comes in and says he thinks a plane is going to crash, and then that night it crashes. I just want a chance, Karl. I want a chance to put the guy away."

Dahlgren folded his arms and leaned forward on his desk. He was looking directly at Lasky with his pale blue eyes. That, along with his white blonde hair and nearly transparent lashes, made him seem like a ghostly figure. Eventually, he pushed himself back off his desk and shook his head decisively. "I can't do it, Dan. But I can make one suggestion, off the record."

"Yeah?"

"If you feel this strongly about the guy, go ahead and keep up your stakeout—"

Lasky stood up and headed for the door.

"Hey, if you still want a job to come back to in the morning, you'd better sit tight and listen to me."

Lasky released his hold on the doorknob and turned back to Dahlgren. "That's why I came to you, Karl, so I wouldn't have to do this on my own time. I feel like I'm so close. I'm so damn scared I'm going to miss him, that I'm not going to be there the one time when he finally does another one."

"I'd like to help you out, Dan. I really would. But the fact is, without any evidence I can't give you the man-hours. Get me something that I can justify putting some more men on, and you've got it."

"And until then?"

"You're going to have to be on your own. But I never heard about it, okay?"

Lasky nodded and walked out of Dahlgren's office, back toward his own. How long would it be before Giles killed again?

There was no way to know. Who would he kill next? Without knowing what magazines he was being published in, there was no way to know that either. If Lasky had the manpower at his disposal there might have been a chance, but for now he was stuck with his periodic stakeout.

"Just do it when I'm there, Giles," he whispered to himself. "That's all I ask. Just do it when I'm there."

Giles sat at the kitchen table holding a mug of coffee and staring blankly out the window. Everything had been planned so perfectly, and then Daniel Lasky had to step in and gum up the works. Was he watching the house right now? Was he tapping the phones? And what about the FBI? Were they still in the mix? There was no way to know.

The only positive thing about the whole mess was there was nothing left to do until the magazine came out, and that wouldn't be for a couple of weeks. Maybe it would lull Daniel and his cohorts into a false sense of security. Or maybe this whole thing was a figment of Giles' imagination. That actually made him laugh out loud.

"Fuck it," he finally said, and took a hit of coffee. He would go through with everything, and if the cops bagged him, so be it. If there was no one waiting for him at the top of the building downtown, so be it. He was going to exorcise this particular demon no matter what it took, and finally get his life back to normal.

Jeff Peters looked at his watch for what felt like the thousandth time, and began another litany of curses in his mind directed at Giles Barrett. He was only an hour away from deadline, and half of that was going to be taken up by driving the copy to the printer. But he was still half a page over.

Barrett's story had taken up more inches than he'd accounted for and now he was going to have to lose something, an ad, no doubt, to make room for the last few paragraphs. If he could have, he would have edited out some of the earlier—and in his opinion, superfluous—paragraphs in the story. But if he did that, there was no telling what Barrett might do. He might even refuse to give him the second story, and Peters couldn't risk that.

It was going to be bad enough losing some of his advertising space to this lame werewolf story, but if he lost Barrett's next story he would be sunk. At the moment, readership of *Silent Screams* was percolating right around a thousand—not bad for a small press horror title. With the Barrett story, he might be able to boost it as high as fifteen hundred. And that was worth every second this pain in the ass rewrite was costing him.

In the end, he decided to bump one of his own promo spots for an upcoming issue in order to squeeze in the end of the story. When he was finished he gathered up the final draft of copy, skipping the envelope, and headed out the door to his car. But as soon as he was outside, he dropped the whole bundle.

"Son of a bitch!" he screamed at the top of his lungs. While he picked up the loose paper he started in again with his mental cursing of Giles Barrett. Then he sat down to go through each page to make sure it was accounted for, and when he was satisfied that they were all there he checked his watch again and headed for the car.


The last time Giles had spoken with Peters, the kid hadn't sounded very happy. Tough shit. Giles was using him, sure, but the kid was using Giles too. It was a wash. The date the magazine came out, that was all that was important. So far, everything was still on schedule. December 13th was the date it would be delivered to the wholesalers, and presumably the following day in the bookstores and newsstands. Well, the few bookstores and newsstands that carried the thing, anyway.

With only a week to go, Giles had everything prepared. He'd dry fired the gun a few times in the garage, and loaded and unloaded it several times. It was strange. After handling it for a while the gun seemed to lose its mystique. He was no longer frightened of it, and that, in turn, helped him become more focused on what he was going to have to do with it.

He'd gone down to the high-rise on 2nd Avenue twice more,

with no sign of Lasky following him either time. But just because he couldn't see him didn't mean he wasn't there. Security had looked about the same. There were lights down the alley, but the small fence was still the only thing keeping him from his appointment with . . . the paranormal or the paranoia? He smiled and shook his head.

It was still so hard to believe that it was actually going to come off like he had planned it. And yet, even with that knowledge, the fact that he had a plan at all had been a calming force in his life that seemed miraculous. He felt in control for the first time in a long time. The gnawing in his stomach as the publication date approached wasn't disconcerting, but comforting. It was all so damned cliché: Giles' date with destiny. Well, so be it. The wait was almost over. And this much was certain: if whatever was menacing him actually showed up at the high-rise, only one of them was going to come back down alive.

# Chapter Twenty-One

It was December 14th but there was no reason for Paige Barrett to know, as she walked in the kitchen door, what was going to happen that evening. It was only a few minutes past one in the afternoon and there was a definite bounce in her step. She turned as soon as she shut the door behind her, breathless, and looked back out the window above the sink. It was still snowing.

It had started about 9:30 that morning, just a few flurries at first, but by ten the big quarter-sized flakes were falling in earnest. And for the next two hours they pushed their way down from the sky in a relentless onslaught of white. Meanwhile, the temperature had dropped twenty degrees and none of the snow was melting. Seattle, caught totally off guard, was virtually brought to a standstill. Nearly all of Paige's patients for that afternoon had called to cancel, as did Marcy's and Jeanette's.

So the three of them closed up shop for the day and sent everyone home. Paige was thankful that she only had a few miles to drive, over relatively well-traveled roads. Even so, it took her nearly an hour to cover those few miles, passing dozens of immobile and abandoned cars. Those that were still moving slipped and slid, and went so slowly that only one or two could make it through an intersection when the light turned green.

But even that had been a breeze compared to Paige's hair-raising experience once she'd turn off of Aurora and attempted to maneuver the last four blocks home. At the first intersection a car appeared on her right and when she tried to stop she began to skid.

The road sloped slightly downhill and, try as she might, the tires would not take hold. She slipped right through the intersection. Luckily, the other car had managed to stop, the two vehicles passing within a few inches of each other. Paige breathed a sigh of relief once she was safely in the garage.

But looking outside from the kitchen, none of that mattered. All that remained was excitement. Paige loved the snow, always had. She hurriedly removed her coat and hung it across the back of one of the kitchen chairs. The coffee pot was still half full and she took a mug out of the cupboard and filled it. Taking a sip she wandered out into the front room. There, standing and looking out of the picture window, was Giles.

They had cleared the usual spot next to the window for the tree, its lights dormant for the moment. With Christmas a little over a week away, the snow couldn't have arrived at a better time. "It's beautiful," she said. "Isn't it?"

When Giles didn't respond immediately she thought he might not have heard her, but as soon as she opened her mouth he spoke. "This sucks. I still can't believe it."

As he turned to her she tried to keep her startled feelings from registering on her face. He was looking decidedly haggard again. "What's wrong, sweetheart?"

"It's tonight."

"What's tonight?"

"The end of it. I have to go out tonight and finish this thing."

Paige looked around for a chair and sat down before her legs decided to collapse beneath her. She didn't want to hear this, especially now. Ever since she'd decided to stay she had been alternately hoping for and dreading this day. She had no idea, not even the slightest clue what it was that he had to do.

And yet, through it all, he had been wonderful. She really did want this whole mess to be over, and at the same time she was more scared at this moment than at any time since it had all begun last summer.

"Does it have to be tonight?" She put on the most concerned

expression she could muster. She didn't want him thinking she was nagging him.

"Unfortunately, yes. There's no way around it." Giles walked over and sat down heavily on the couch.

Paige relaxed a little. At least he was taking her seriously and talking. "Have you heard if the snow is going to stop?"

He shook his head. "It's supposed to go on all night."

She couldn't think of what to say after that, and for a long time they simply sat there in silence, Paige taking an occasional sip of her coffee, and Giles staring off into space thinking of God only knew what. Finally she said, "What time are you going?"

"About midnight."

By four-thirty that afternoon it was already dark, light from the streetlamps reflecting off the falling crystals as they continued to accumulate into ever-deeper drifts. Paige kept a surreptitious watch and breathed a sigh of relief when it stopped snowing at about six o'clock. She fixed dinner for the two of them, and though Giles sat with her he hardly ate a thing.

Giles had been nervous all evening, constantly getting up and doing useless things, arranging and rearranging magazines on the coffee table, bringing up books from the library that he had no intention of reading, flipping through channels of the TV with the sound muted. Paige tried to keep him company but he was driving her crazy. After the dinner dishes had been done she decided to go downstairs and do some laundry, as well as some of the other housework that Giles had neglected.

Paige put a load of clothes in the washing machine and then dragged out the vacuum cleaner. She started in the library and gave it a quick once-over. Next, she moved out into the hall and on into Giles' office. She had almost finished when a tremendous clattering startled her. She shut off the machine immediately and turned it over to see what had been sucked up into the motor. After a little digging and shaking, a large paper clip finally fell out onto the carpet.

Paige stood up, intending to put the errant clip with its brethren, but Giles' desk was so full of clutter that she couldn't see any others. Distractedly, she pulled out drawers, looking for a place to put it. But when she pulled out the middle drawer her distractedness suddenly turned to intense curiosity. There, in the middle of the drawer, was a plain white envelope with her name on it.

"What's the meaning of this?"

The second he heard Paige's voice behind him, Giles' heart jumped up into his throat. He'd been watching TV—well, he'd had it on, though he was barely cognizant of what he was actually watching—and Paige had scared the hell out of him.

"What?" he managed to croak out. Giles stood up and turned to his wife, trying to swallow his heart back down into his chest.

She was standing there holding some sheets of paper. The look on her face was one of pure terror. Giles couldn't begin to imagine what she was so freaked out about.

"Is this what I've been waiting for all this time? If you were really going through with this, then why let me come back here and pretend everything's going to be fine?"

"Paige, I don't know what you're talking about."

"This." She threw the sheets of paper at him. They fell to the floor, and when Giles leaned down to pick them up his blood ran cold. It was the suicide note he'd written.

"Oh, God, Paige, I never meant for you to see this."

Though she was nearly three feet away from him, Giles could feel her breath on his face. The look in her eyes was one of such intense anger and betrayal, he half-thought she was going to come after him with fists flying.

"I'll call the cops before I let you go out of here tonight."

"That's not what tonight is about—"

"God damn you, Giles! You tell me what's going on right now, or so help me I'll call the cops and tell them anything to have you arrested."

He believed it, too. Paige had changed. Some subtle shift in her behavior had happened while he had been preoccupied with his own problems.

He looked down at the letter in his hand. Everything was there. Well, almost everything. "You read all of it?"

Paige nodded.

Giles didn't know what to say next. Tell her about when the note was written? He didn't want to do that, nor did he want to have to explain what he had planned for tonight.

He had called Jeff Peters two days ago and verified that the copies of *Silent Screams* had been delivered to the post office the day before. And now there was this fucking snow. And how long would he have to keep going back to the building on 2nd Avenue if the thing didn't show up tonight?

Finally, Giles sat down on the couch. He tossed the letter on the coffee table and leaned back to talk. "I was afraid something was going to happen to you, something I couldn't control. The only way I had to—"

"You really don't get it, do you?" She was still standing. Giles looked up at her. Maybe he didn't.

"I don't give a God damn *why* you did any of this shit, but I'm pissed as hell that you didn't tell me about it. I don't believe it. How can you keep stuff like this from me? I'm your wife, for Christ's sake."

"Paige, that's what I'm trying to tell you. I was scared."

"All the more reason. I still can't believe this, Giles." She was pacing now, something he'd never seen her do before. "How could you even think of killing yourself?"

"I thought you read this." That stopped her in mid pace.

"You honestly believe that your writing caused those people to die?"

Giles sighed. "Yes, I suppose I do." That was an under–statement.

"And what . . . you were afraid I might be able to convince you that you were wrong?"

"No, I thought I might kill you."

Suddenly the temperature inside the house didn't seem all that different from outside.

"What's wrong with you, Giles?"

"I don't know—that's what's wrong with me. I don't know why any of this is happening."

"So let's get some help."

"That's not going to make it go away."

"What? You keep saying 'it', like there's this *thing* out there that's screwing with your life."

"Well, what else could it be? The cops thought something killed those people. They arrested me, didn't they?"

"But what about you?"

"What do you mean?"

"I mean, what about the possibility that maybe this is all in your head. What about taking responsibility for yourself instead of blaming it on some metaphysical entity? Do you realize how crazy you sound?"

Giles was growing weary of arguing. He'd been over all this in his mind so many times that he didn't feel like rehashing it again with Paige, especially tonight. He looked at his watch. It was almost eight.

"I meant what I said about the cops."

He could only stare as she stood over him. There was no other way. He still had a few hours yet, and if he didn't calm Paige down somehow he wasn't going to get out of here at midnight.

"All right. Sit down, please. There are a few things I need to tell you that weren't in the letter."

Dumbfounded. That was the only word that could adequately describe the way Paige was feeling. She listened as Giles told her about his aborted suicide attempt after Don's funeral—she knew he shouldn't have gone. He told her about the man he'd seen there, and again in the University District.

Then he'd gone on about the airline crash and the FBI agents—something she'd actually been a part of—and his conversations with the police lieutenant he'd gone to high school with. It seemed to her that if anyone was to blame for the way Giles was feeling it was this cop, Lasky. He was the one who had been responsible for having Giles arrested. And if that hadn't happened, he might not have been so quick to believe he was "possessed."

But then, just when she thought she'd heard all she could handle, Giles began to tell her about the latest story he'd written, the gun he'd bought, and about Lasky following him. It was a nightmare. Worse, because Giles was so convinced that this was the only way to deal with it. It was like talking to a crazy person. She didn't want to believe he was crazy because he was her husband, because she loved him. And then the thought occurred: maybe she was just as delusional as he was.

When he was through she just sat there, trying to gather her thoughts. "I still don't want you to go out tonight."

"Don't you see, Paige, I have to."

"Have to what? Go out and shoot somebody?"

"It's not a real person."

"My God, do you hear yourself? What if someone just happens to be in the building? What if that cop shows up again?"

"I told you, I already took care of that in the story."

Paige began to cry. She felt as if he'd finally broken her. Her will to fight was gone. "And what if someone kills you instead?"

He didn't answer.

"I can't do it, Giles. I can't just sit here and wait for you to come back, or wait until the cops call and tell me you're dead."

"I have to go, Paige."

With that Paige stood and began to walk toward the bedroom. She stopped before she reached the hall and turned back. "Giles?"

He looked over at her.

"If you leave here tonight, don't bother coming back."

It was a long four hours until midnight. Four hours for the temperature to get colder, for the snow to harden into ice, and for Giles' resolve to be shaken to its foundation. In the end, however, he knew he had no other choice. Sure, Paige was right that this thing might kill him, but as far as he was concerned he was dead already. All he could do now was hope that she wasn't serious about his not coming back.

Paige hadn't come out of the bedroom all evening. He wouldn't need to go in there, though. The only extra clothing he would be wearing was a heavy jacket and that was out in the hall closet. He wanted to travel light, be mobile, even if it meant freezing his butt off.

He picked up the remote control and flipped through the channels again; even silenced the TV was annoying. Giles was incredibly nervous. He was hungry, but his stomach was churning too much to eat. Gradually the minutes passed and as midnight approached he readied himself. The last thing he expected to see as he took his coat from the closet was Paige.

He heard the bedroom door open and turned as she walked out. She was wearing a long T-shirt, her legs bare, and had her arms crossed beneath her breasts. "I've been doing a lot of thinking, about what you were talking about, and . . ."

For a moment, Giles left the coat hanging. "Yes?"

"And if you leave, I don't want you to come back."

"Come on, Paige. Don't do this—"

"I mean it, Giles. If you don't respect me enough to stay here tonight, then I don't think you ever will."

He walked over to her. "Look, I know all of this sounds crazy, but if I don't go tonight I *will* go crazy. These past few months . . . That's why things have been so good between us, because I've had this plan. I need to do this so we can get on with our life together."

"Don't include me in your delusions."

"All right, *my* life. But I'm telling you, after tonight all of this will be over."

"No, Giles. If you leave tonight the only thing that will be over is our marriage."

"How can you say that?"

"Because it's true." Her expression was stern. She was evidently serious.

"Well, I'm sorry, then. I'd hoped that we could talk some more, but if that's the way you want it then that's the way it has to be, because I'm going."

Giles walked back to the closet and pulled out his coat.

There was nothing else he could do. He had to go through with this tonight. If he didn't, the consequences could be disastrous. Someone else might be unwittingly killed, and he couldn't abide that. With any luck Paige would relent after he returned, and then they could talk and resume their marriage.

But that was all speculation. He looked back over his shoulder and saw that she had gone back into the bedroom. After a quick glance at his watch—twenty minutes to midnight—he headed for the garage.

The conditions were treacherous, no doubt about that, but it wasn't snowing and visibility was good. Giles backed out of the garage slowly, his tires crunching on the snow, and pulled out onto the street at an extremely cautious pace.

He didn't have to wonder long if someone had been watching the house. About a half a block away on Giles' left was a car parked against the curb, tiny clouds of exhaust pluming from the tailpipe. The car was the same one he'd seen when he walked home from Denny's several weeks ago. It was Daniel Lasky's.

Giles hadn't yet reached any significant speed, and slowed easily to a stop directly beside Daniel's Buick. He rolled down his window and looked over at the car. In the story he had written the two cops fell asleep in their car. Daniel's eyes were closed and his head was lolled to one side.

Giles rolled his window up and smiled as he drove on. Then he reached over and patted the gun, now sitting in the passenger seat along with his box of silver-tipped shells and a flashlight. Daniel falling asleep was all the proof he needed. This thing was really going to work.

Giles negotiated the four blocks to Aurora very slowly, even though he never felt the tires slip once. It was almost as if something were making sure he made it to his appointment on time, but he wasn't about to test it. Aurora was well traveled, even with the snow, and the ruts went down to the pavement most of the way into town.

Traffic was understandably light, and the few businesses that were open had equally few customers. The strings of multicolored Christmas lights and holiday decorations seemed strikingly at odds with Giles' mission. But slowly and steadily he drove on, and made his way into downtown Seattle a few minutes later.

He turned right on Denny Way and then left onto First Avenue. Three blocks up he pulled his car into a spot between drifts next to the curb and shut off the car. He could see the skeletal structure of the building and the large crane that loomed above him up on 2nd. Giles took up his gun and loaded each of the chambers with a bullet. Then he put it in the right pocket of his coat, the flashlight in the left, and stepped out of his car.

There was no wind to speak of, but it was still incredibly cold. Giles turned up his collar and headed out across the street and up to the next block. As expected, the streets downtown were nearly deserted and he didn't see anyone on his way to the alley behind the building. The back of the place was awash in bright yellow from the sulfur lights on the construction site, and in the light Giles could see the tiny swirling flakes of snow that had been invisible in the dark. He took a perfunctory glance in both directions, and then quickly scaled the six-foot chain link fence.

Giles was now in the parking garage of the half-finished building. He walked over to what looked like an elevator shaft. It was boarded up, but next to it was an open stairwell. He pulled out his flashlight and shined it around. There was nothing there but clean, gray concrete.

Giles looked at his watch. It was already a few minutes after midnight. Was whatever he was meeting up there already waiting for him? He shut off the flashlight and leaned back against the wall. Until now he had been running on adrenaline, trying not to think about what he was doing.

He reached for the gun in his pocket, fingered it through the fabric of his heavy coat and felt the heft of it. Was he really ready to shoot someone? Even after seeing Daniel Lasky asleep in his car, did he really think that something was actually going to meet him at the top of this empty building? And if it did, would he be able to pull the trigger?

Giles took a deep breath. The cold air felt sharp in his lungs, and the membranes in his nostrils crackled as the moisture within quickly froze and then thawed. He knew the answers to all of his questions, simply because he knew what the alternative was. He rubbed his hands together briskly, then turned on the flashlight and headed up the stairwell.

In the story the two friends meet on the top floor. Halfway up, Giles began to regret that particular artistic choice. The air knifed at his lungs. He began coughing and that only made things worse. Then Giles realized how fast he'd been going. He'd been taking the stairs two at a time. He slowed down the rest of the way up, even taking time on the landings to rest.

There were no doors yet in the stairwell so Giles didn't know what floor he was on, but when he reached the top and saw he could go no further, he walked back down to the last open doorway. The flashlight's beam fell across a mess of construction equipment, piles of sheetrock and metal framing. He shined the light in every direction to make sure he wouldn't be jumped, but there were a million places to hide.

After plotting his course Giles headed for the far wall, against 2nd Avenue. There he would have the light from the streets below behind him, and he would be able to see the entire floor without risking anyone surprising him from behind. He began to feel uneasy as he approached the window: there was no glass in the opening.

Giles shut off the flashlight and turned back toward the elevator. The thin glow emanating from the window behind him cast a diffuse veil of light that reached only a few yards in front of him. The opening to the stairwell was bathed in black, and Giles wondered whether he hadn't made a mistake in choosing this spot. Before he could decide on another, however, he heard footsteps.

They were gradually getting louder, each footfall accompanied by a slight echo. It sounded as if they were coming from the stairwell. Could he have been followed? Giles trained his eyes on the doorway, hoping his improving night vision would give him a glimpse of his opponent. He pulled the gun out of his pocket and readied it in front of him with both hands.

The sound of the footsteps continued to get louder and louder, until finally Giles saw something moving on the other side of the room. A dim shadow stood in the opening of the stairwell. Giles hadn't seen a light. How could he have gone up the stairs in the dark? Seconds later, the figure began to move toward him. Giles lifted the gun in front of him, his hands trembling slightly as he touched the trigger.

But the closer the figure came, the more Giles thought he recognized it. The deliberate walk, the long coat, it had to be . . . It was the man he had seen at Don's funeral, the man he had seen outside the restaurant in the University District. Now he was confused. Was this his imagination, or was this person real? Should he shoot or not? Suddenly his plan had been rendered worthless.

Giles was near panic when the figure stepped from the shadows into the soft glow from the window. Then the man lifted his head and smiled, and Giles' heart nearly stopped.

"Hello, Giles."

It was Don.

# Chapter Twenty-Two

Giles couldn't take his eyes off of the man standing before him. Don? How was that possible? It wasn't until Don spoke again that Giles realized he still had his gun trained on him.

"What are you going to do with that, kill me again?"

Giles let the gun fall to his side. "What do you mean 'again?'"

"They busted you the first time, but I hear you had a good lawyer."

Don flashed Giles his big, toothy grin. His breath puffed out of his mouth in little white clouds. His hands were sheathed in black leather gloves. He looked older, leaner, more weathered since he'd last seen him in September, just a month before his—

"Don? What are you doing here?"

Don chuckled and shook his head. "Is that a rhetorical question? You invited me."

"Jesus Christ, Don. You're supposed to be dead."

"That was your fault, too."

Giles looked at the gun in his hand and, embarrassed, stuck it in his pocket. "What the hell are you talking about? You're supposed to be dead. I was just at your funeral."

"I know. I saw you there. Thanks for coming. It meant a lot to me. You saw me there, too. That wasn't supposed to happen. Sorry about that." Don walked over and sat down on a sawhorse just a few feet away from Giles. He opened his mouth wide and yawned. "Why'd you have to make this meeting so late? I'm missing my beauty sleep."

"What meeting?"

"The story, Giles."

A chill that had nothing to do with the temperature in the building began to seep through Giles body. "What about it?"

"Not one of your best, Pal. I think it could have used a good going over with the blue pencil, you know what I mean? No, actually, now that I think about it, it was pretty much beyond help, a real piece of crap. Is that why you sent it into that shitty little magazine?"

"How do you know about the story?"

"I make it my business to know about your work, Giles. I always have. You know that." Another grin.

"What are you saying?"

"Nothing. It's just that we're such a good team—we always have been—and I don't think you should mess with success, do you? This little venture out on your own certainly proves that. Good God, I never would have let that story out of my office. But the fact that you wanted to get back together with me . . . Well, that was kind of intriguing."

"With you?"

His eyes suddenly went cold. "Cut the innocent act, Giles. You wanted to meet your silent partner, well, here I am."

Giles reeled from this. He stepped back involuntarily. His shoe caught on something on the floor, and before he realized what was happening he'd lost his balance. But when he reached back to brace himself against the wall, all he saw was a big hole where a window that had yet to be installed was to go. He was about to scream when he felt a hand like a vise grab his upper arm and pull him back just before he fell out.

"Careful now." Don was still holding his arm. His face was just inches from Giles' and his breath stunk like rotten meat. It was all he could do to keep from gagging. "I think one of us taking the skyscraper swan dive is plenty, don't you?"

"I have to sit down."

"Good idea."

Don released his grip and Giles walked over to a pile of

sheetrock and sat down. He heard the hiss of a match and looked up to see Don lighting a cigarette. He waved out the flame and tossed the match out the hole in the wall that Giles had nearly fallen through. He took a drag and then turned back.

Giles couldn't believe it. "So, you were the one who killed them?"

Don nodded.

"All of them?"

"I like to think of it as participating in your art, Giles."

"Even the plane?"

"You know, I thought that was going to be a tough little fucker, but it was such a great story that I said, what the hell. It was actually fairly easy. Airport security is for shit."

Giles was speechless. He didn't know whether to feel relieved or horrified, and so he felt both. On the one hand he was no longer a murderer, while on the other his best friend was.

"Jesus Christ, Don. They arrested me because they thought I'd killed you. I went to your funeral. Who the hell is buried over on Bainbridge Island?"

Don began to pace, and the more he walked the more serious his demeanor became. "You know, Giles, I was pretty pissed off at you for a while. It serves you right that you got picked up by the cops."

"Me? What did you have to be pissed off at me about?"

Don stopped and pointed his cigarette at Giles. "You went to the cops. Son of a bitch. Do you know the trouble you almost caused me? I was about ready to kill you myself, and I would have if Davey hadn't come along and bailed me out."

"Davey?"

"David. David Holman, my twin brother."

Giles sat and stared at Don in a stupor of disbelief. The only thing that made any sense was to keep talking, keep on asking questions. "I didn't know you had a brother."

Don smiled. "I know. Beautiful, isn't it? Sharon doesn't even know. That's what made it so perfect. Don't you see? Davey takes the swan dive with my wallet, and presto, I'm the one who's dead."

"Are you telling me you killed your own brother?"

"It was more of a sacrifice, really . . . for my art. Our art, Giles. Besides, he was a real dirtbag. Why do you think I never told anybody about him?"

The cold was starting to get to Giles. His hands were frozen. He rubbed them together and blew into them, but nothing seemed to make a difference. He was saddened and sickened by Don's revelations and he wanted nothing more than to go home and crawl into bed with Paige.

"There's one thing I don't understand," Giles finally said. "That story, 'Trick or Threat' . . ."

"Not a bad piece of Barrett pastiche, if I do say so myself."

"You're saying *you* wrote it?"

"You bet your ass."

"But it was on the computer disc, at my place."

"What the hell. You didn't think I was going to keep it at the office, did you?"

"So how did I wind up with it?"

Don pulled a ring of keys from his pants pocket and jangled them up near his face. "I have a key to your place, remember, for emergencies?"

"Oh, yeah. I forgot." Giles still couldn't believe he was talking to a homicidal maniac. "You realize, don't you," he said, with growing irritation, "that I'm not going to be a part of this anymore."

"Goes without saying, old pal. I figured all along that this little get-together would probably terminate our partnership."

"Just so that it's understood. I don't want anything more to do with you."

Don took a final drag on his cigarette, then dropped the butt onto the floor and crushed it out with the toe of his shoe. "Understood. But I'm afraid you won't be having anything more to do with anybody."

Giles could only watch in stunned disbelief as Don extracted a small cylindrical object from his coat pocket. He held it out in front of him for a second, and with a quiet snick a blade ejected from the end.

"Jesus Christ, Don. What the fuck is that?"

"Come on, Giles. You've seen Hitchcock, haven't you? *The Man Who Knew Too Much*? Can't have a loose cannon like you running around free."

"What are you talking about? If you think I'm going to tell anybody about this, you're crazy."

Don's smile broadened. "The thought has occurred."

Giles stood. "I don't fucking believe this."

"I always thought you had more faith in me than that, Giles."

"Come on. Knock it off, Don. I just want to go home. You do whatever the hell you want, just leave me out of it."

Don shook his head. "No can do, buddy. You're already in it, Giles. But I do plan on relieving you of that responsibility very shortly." Then he began to move forward.

Don was almost on top of him before Giles could react. It was too late to go around the sheetrock he had been sitting on, so he scrambled over the top of it to the other side. On the way over he felt the weight of the gun in his pocket. He'd forgotten about it. Giles pulled out the .38 and looked around for Don, but he was already heading for the doorway.

"Stop, Don! I have a gun!" Giles' voice echoed in the unfinished building, and he immediately wished he hadn't yelled. He was sure that people on the street below had heard, though he knew they couldn't possibly have.

Don didn't stop until he reached the stairs. He was about thirty feet away from Giles, and when he turned around he was laughing.

"That's a good one, Giles. If I really thought you could use that thing I would have killed you as soon as you stuck it in your pocket."

Giles kept the gun pointed at Don. He didn't know whether Don was right or not. He only hoped that it wouldn't come to that. If only Don could somehow be persuaded.

"I just want to go home, Don. I don't want to make any trouble for you. I don't care anymore. I just want this to be over."

"You wrote the ending, my friend—I'm just following the story line. I'm afraid I'm going to have to put you down."

Like an animal. Jesus, Don had gone completely psycho. "Well, it looks like we're at a standoff, then."

"No standoff, buddy. You've got a gun you'll never use, and I've got a knife that's going to see plenty of action." He started moving toward Giles as soon as he finished speaking.

"Please, Don. I don't want to hurt you."

"You won't. Trust me." He kept coming.

"Goddamn it, Don. Stop!"

Don wasn't smiling anymore. He was methodically moving forward, continually gauging the distance between himself and the doorway.

"Don," Giles pleaded. "I don't want to shoot you." But Don kept coming.

Giles decided then and there that he wasn't backing down. As difficult as it would be, he was going to have to shoot Don. And it would be a lot less difficult knowing what he did about his friend.

"Just like in the story, right, Giles?"

"What?"

"You and me, best friends. I thought that was a nice touch."

Giles felt his body begin to sweat, even though the temperature was hovering around zero. It was almost as if Don had read his thoughts. "I didn't plan any of this, Don."

Don was about ten feet away, and Giles slowly began to squeeze the trigger. He would aim for the shoulder and hope for the best. But then Don surprised him and stopped.

"It doesn't matter what any of us plan, Giles. Don't you realize that? Life makes its own demands, and you're either in step or out. And you, my friend, are decidedly out of step."

The gun was cold; Giles' hands were cold. He could barely feel the trigger. Don held the knife comfortably by his side. Their condensed exhalation seemed to hover in the darkened air between them, and beyond the open windows the resumption of the snow had muted the sounds coming from the street. They stood that way for nearly a minute until, without another word, Don lunged.

Giles squeezed the trigger and nothing happened. In the split second that he had to think, he realized that his cold hands weren't responding fully and he was able to try one more time. Don was only inches away from him when the gun finally went off.

The sound was deafening, and the kick nearly took the weapon out of his hand. The shot had hit Don in the left shoulder, he was sure, but the knife had also slashed across Giles' right forearm. And when their bodies collided, they both went sprawling onto the floor.

Giles lost the gun as he let go of it to break his fall. It was too dark to see where it had gone, and he was too frightened of Don to stay where he was. He scrambled across the floor over to the pile of sheetrock, and then stood up behind it, using it as a shield. At first he couldn't see Don, but then a movement over to his right caught his attention.

Don was blocking the opening to the stairwell again, and Giles moved around the sheetrock to put it between them. He didn't want Don to know he'd lost the gun, so he stayed crouched down. The cut on his arm was stinging badly, and blood was soaking the sleeve of his jacket. There was no way to tell how serious it was, but it hurt to touch so he left it alone.

Don was holding his left shoulder. "Well, I'll be damned. Didn't think you had it in you, Giles."

"I'm not going to let you kill me, Don."

"Fair enough. Just means I'll have to adjust my game plan slightly."

"Come on, Don. Why can't you just leave me the fuck alone?"

Don pulled his hand away and looked at the blood on it. "You've never killed a man, Giles. But if by some miracle you wind up killing me tonight, you'll know why I can't leave you alone." Then Don pulled his left arm close in to his stomach, took the knife from his right-hand pocket, and moved forward again.

When Don reached the sheetrock, Giles instinctively backed off, still keeping the pile between them.

"Lost your gun there, buddy?"

Giles didn't answer. He kept his gaze fixed on Don, though he really didn't have any idea what he was going to do if Don made another move. But when Don climbed up on top of the pile, Giles realized he was defenseless. He looked around for something to use as a weapon, and Don chose that moment to leap down.

Giles ran. He ran through the maze of empty framing and the piles of building materials. He turned corners and ducked under wiring. Soon he was on the other side of the stairwell, wondering if he could make it all the way around. But then he felt his knees give way. Don had tackled him and they both slid out onto an open balcony.

The slab of cement they were on was like a sheet of ice. There was only a partial railing on the balcony and almost no light. Giles felt more than saw the knife blade coming down toward him. He deflected the stab with his injured arm and it made him scream in agony. But he was able to grab hold of Don's arm before he could try again. And then the real struggle ensued.

Don rolled them over onto the balcony until they were out of the building completely and Don was on top of Giles. As the blade inched closer to Giles' face, he increased his grip on Don's wrist. But Giles' arm was incredibly painful, and he was losing strength in it fast.

His feet were flailing and Giles felt himself kicking the railing. With the last of his reserves, he braced his foot against it and released his injured arm, pushing Don off of him in the process.

Giles lost all sense of orientation and was horrified to find that the momentum of his push was sending him over the side of the balcony. He reached out in desperation and was just able to get a hold of a piece of the frozen metal balcony railing with his right hand. He screamed again with pain, but held on until he could get his other hand up to relieve some of the stress.

Giles hung for a few moments, unable to pull himself up. What was the point? At any moment he expected Don to peer out over the edge, kick his fingers, and send Giles to the same fate as he had his own brother. But Don never appeared, and Giles finally attempted to hoist himself up. With every bit of strength he had left, he was able to swing his leg up over the edge and keep it there long enough to haul the rest of his body up.

When at last he was safely on the balcony he could only collapse and wait for Don to finish him off. Why was he dragging this out? And then Giles had the terrible thought that Don might have gone over the side. He pushed himself up and grasped the railing firmly in his good hand and looked over the edge. The alley was brightly lit, and empty.

Giles pushed himself up from the frozen concrete and walked back into the building. He couldn't see any movement.

"Fuck you, Don!" he shouted, and started toward the stairs. "If you're going to kill me, just fucking do it."

But it seemed as if Don wasn't there anymore. Either that or he had decided to let Giles go. Whatever the case, Giles proceeded to the stairwell and down the stairs without incident. He had a little trouble negotiating the fence in the alley with his bad arm, but once he reached his car he started shaking uncontrollably from the cold. He climbed in, started the car, and turned the heater on full. Then he locked his doors and nearly passed out.

# Chapter Twenty-Three

When Daniel Lasky's head snapped up he realized that he'd been sleeping.

"Goddamn it."

He looked at his watch. It was after one. A glance at his gas gauge showed he was almost empty.

"Fuck this," he said. "And fuck you, Barrett."

Lasky put his car in gear and pulled out. It was over. All of it. He was going into the captain's office tomorrow and ask for a couple of weeks' vacation. The kids were out of school now and Rena . . . Well, fuck that, too. She could take a couple weeks of impromptu vacation from the real estate office whether she liked it or not. The Lasky family was getting out of Dodge.

In the past three months Lasky's home life had gone to hell. Rena was barely speaking to him, he didn't even see the kids anymore, and the job wasn't much better. Since he'd been devoting so much time to stalking Giles, he'd let his caseload slip to almost nothing. Dahlgren was pissed about it, but at least it would make it easy for him to let Lasky go.

Making his way gingerly along the slippery streets, a smile came to Lasky's face as he wondered where to go. Arizona? California? Screw it—they were going to Hawaii. He'd call a travel agent in the morning.

If Giles Barrett really was murdering people they would eventually get him. One way or another, they would get him.

Because for all his faults there was one thing Daniel Lasky had never lacked: faith in the system.

After a few minutes in the car Giles sat up with a start. The gun. He'd left it up there somewhere. Well, that was just too damn bad, because he wasn't going back. Some construction worker would probably find it, pocket it, and take it home, and that would have been fine with Giles except for the fact that it was registered in his name. If someone were to be killed with it later on, it could be tracked back to him. He'd have to go to the police and report it stolen. But not tomorrow morning, no, there was something else that had to be done first.

Giles looked down at his arm. It was throbbing and it hurt like hell. He gently peeled away the jacket, not sure he actually wanted to see it, and looked at the oozing gash in his skin. For a second he thought he could see bone, and then he quickly closed it back up. He needed to get home.

On the way back to the house Giles drove with his left hand. With almost no traffic, he was able to go as slowly as he wanted. He thought through the events of that night, but it seemed so unreal that it was almost as if it had happened to someone else. Except that the blood on his jacket and the pain in his arm didn't allow for that possibility.

Even with things being so screwed up between him and Paige these past few months, Giles was glad that things turned out as they had. If he hadn't accidently run across those obits, Don might still be killing people and no one would have known about it. No one would be able to stop him. Now, at least, there was a chance. But what had happened to Don up there? That was the one thing that still had Giles puzzled.

If he had really intended to kill me, Giles thought, why hadn't he finished the job? It didn't make any sense. Was he just trying to scare me? It sure as hell didn't seem like it. The cut on Giles' arm was deep enough to make him positive that Don had not been holding back.

Relief surged through Giles as he pulled into the garage. He hauled himself out of the car and into the house. It was dark inside and he switched on the light in the kitchen and stripped off his jacket and shirt. The cut was deep, all right. He walked over to the sink and winced in anticipation as he turned on the water. He only hoped that he wouldn't have to go to the hospital and have it sewn up.

After nearly yelping out loud on his first pass beneath the water, Giles yanked his arm out of the stream and began wiping off the dried blood. Eventually he was able to keep the cut under longer and wash out the threads of stuffing from his coat that had lodged in the wound. That was the white he had seen. The cut was not as deep as he had feared, and after drying it off he was sure it would heal without stitches.

Giles gathered up his clothes, flipped off the light and headed for the bedroom. He walked in quietly and dumped his coat and shirt on the chair, and then made his way in the dark to the bathroom. He shut the door and turned on the light. There was gauze and medical tape underneath the sink and he made himself a tight bandage that held the cut together but wouldn't stop his circulation.

He looked at himself in the mirror. He'd been such a fool. All of that metaphysical crap, his possessions, and his run-ins with Lasky, it was embarrassing. The worst part about it was Paige. He'd put her through the ringer, as it turned out, for nothing. And there was no excuse for it. If he'd been honest with her from the start, their marriage wouldn't be in the precarious position it was in.

With exhaustion catching up to him, Giles turned out the light and walked back into the bedroom. He took off the rest of his clothes and laid them on the chair, then eased himself under the covers of the bed. He lay on his back for a minute, letting his breathing slow, and when he was sure he hadn't awakened Paige, he turned over on his side.

But before he could drift off to sleep, Paige spoke, her voice ringing sonorously in the dark. "I want you out of here by the end of the month."

\*    \*    \*

Paige woke the next morning to the smell of coffee brewing in the kitchen. Normally, something like that would have buoyed her sagging confidence in their relationship. Not today. It was far too late for that.

Last night had been possibly the worst of Paige's life. She had sat up waiting for Giles, with no way to know whether he was actually intent on killing himself. Saying what she did to him last night before he went to sleep was a lousy thing to do, but she still hoped that he'd lost some sleep over it. She certainly hadn't been able to get much herself.

She smiled grimly and shook her head. It was hard to believe it was all over. Not just the crap Giles had been putting her through, but everything. She would listen to him, of course, hear him out, knowing full well that it wouldn't change anything. It couldn't. Inside, she was dead. That's how she knew. She'd used up all of the love she'd had for Giles, and now there was none left, nothing to draw on anymore.

Paige sat up, slipped her legs out of the covers, and set her feet on the floor. She rubbed the sleep out of her eyes and then pushed herself off the bed and walked into the bathroom. After washing her face and pulling on a robe, she was ready to go out and face Giles.

He was already sitting at the kitchen table drinking coffee. She walked over to the pot and poured herself a mug. She would miss times like this—

Stop it, she told herself. You don't need to start making up a list of the things you'll miss about him already. There's going to be plenty of time for that later.

She sat down across from him. Neither of them spoke for a long time. What the hell was there to say? She'd asked him not to go, and he'd gone.

"Listen," he finally said. "About last night . . . Were you serious?"

That wasn't the tack she'd expected. She'd figured on his

doing some heavy-duty wheedling. It was kind of refreshing, actually, to be taken seriously. She nodded and he did likewise.

They both took sips of coffee and then he looked over to her again, a hint of a smile playing on his lips. "Jesus. I really fucked up, didn't I?"

Paige nodded again.

He softly chuckled. "You know, I came out here this morning planning on doing or saying anything I could to convince you to change your mind. And then I started getting this . . . I don't know, this feeling of doom." He looked around absently for a moment and then took another sip. "It's really over, isn't it?"

"I didn't want it this way, Giles. Maybe if you'd stayed last night things could have been different, but—"

"No, I know you were just doing what you had to." He shrugged. "I only wish it could have coincided with what I had to do."

Another lull ensued, both of them comfortable with it. Paige stood up and warmed her coffee. "You want some more?"

"Thanks," Giles said, and she refilled his mug.

Apart from the emotional trauma, she was still quite curious as to what he'd done last night. "Aren't you going to tell me what happened?"

He looked over at her and smiled, then he laughed and shook his head. "You know, I thought a lot about that this morning, too. And the thing is, I'm not sure it would help."

"Help? I wasn't asking you to convince me to stay together—"

"No. What I meant was, I think it might make you even more angry."

"Why?"

"Because there's no way for me to prove what happened last night actually happened."

"And you don't think I'll believe you?"

"I know you won't, Paige. Hell, I was there and I almost can't believe it myself. I'll tell you, though, if you want to know. I'm not trying to keep this from you. Like I said, I just think it might make things harder on you."

It was insulting to have him still trying to protect her from herself, but she knew what he meant. He was like a different person now, someone she'd never known before, certainly not the man she'd married. If things were truly over what point was there in knowing more about this stranger? "You don't think it might help me understand everything that's happened?"

"Listen," he said, as though he were changing topics. "Tell me something, honestly."

"Okay."

"Is there anything I can say, anything at all, that could make you change your mind about us?"

She thought about this. There might be something, but she'd been through all of this before and she wasn't going to do it again. If he flipped out one more time it would probably be the end of her.

Paige looked up into Giles' face and frowned. His expression was one of saddened resignation. She felt her eyes slowly welling up. A tear broke loose and rolled down her cheek. Then she shook her head.

"No."


While Paige was getting ready for work Giles decided to go out to the garage and put the cable chains on the Peugeot. He came in shivering from not wearing a coat just as she was heading out.

"All set," he said.

"Thank you so much. I really appreciate this."

"You're welcome."

"I'm not sure who's going to be coming in today, so I don't know what time I'll be back. It might be early. Will you be here?"

"I don't think so. I have some things to do. It all depends."

"I'd like to have dinner with you tonight."

"Sounds good."

"Okay. I'll see you tonight."

Giles closed the door behind her and then walked into the bedroom. After stripping down he took a long hot shower, holding his wounded arm out of the water, and then dressed in clean clothes. He had another cup of coffee before leaving the house himself.

He was trying to keep busy and keep his mind off Paige.

There was just too much to do right now. There were things that needed to be settled before the two of them could go on. She had obviously decided that it had been too much and, looking back, he couldn't blame her. But the bottom line was that either she would relent and try again or she wouldn't. All Giles could do was finish this business and hope that she might give him one last chance.

From the look of things it hadn't snowed any more since last night. But it was still cold, and even though the sun was out most of the snow on the side roads had been packed into icy sheets. Giles opted to forgo his link chains, and was glad he did once he was out on Aurora. There was plenty of bare pavement along the main thoroughfares.

Giles drove south down Aurora into town, over the Alaskan Way Viaduct and past the Kingdome, and then across the West Seattle Freeway. The address had been in the phone book, but it didn't look as if Giles was going to make it that far. Though he was only a block away the Pontiac couldn't make it up the hill. He tried three times, each attempt making it a little further up, but still slipped back every time. Finally, he parked his car and walked the rest of the way.

The sun and the exertion made Giles warm, and he unzipped his jacket. It was nice. The cold air felt good in his lungs, as opposed to the night before. Things were different today. In spite of almost being killed, Giles found that the relief of not being crazy was almost overwhelming. That was probably the reason he had been able to handle Paige so well this morning.

He rounded the corner and saw the car. So far, so good. Giles made his way up the snow-covered walk to the front door. He took a deep breath, and then knocked. A minute later the door opened. A young girl no more than ten answered the door.

"Hi," Giles said. "Is your father home?"

"Dad!" she yelled, and then ran away down the hall, leaving Giles in the open doorway.

Giles knocked the snow off his shoes and stepped inside, then shut the door and looked up the staircase, waiting. A moment later

Daniel Lasky came down the stairs. He stopped for a second on the landing, glared at Giles, and then continued down to the bottom.

"You've got a lot of nerve coming here, Barrett."

"Look, Daniel, I don't want to take up any more of your time than I have to. I just wanted to apologize."

Daniel looked him over with undisguised loathing. He glanced at his watch impatiently and then waved for Giles to follow him down the hall. Daniel led him to a small den. "Okay, what's this all about?"

Daniel had his arms folded across his chest. If it were possible, he looked almost uncomfortably casual in jeans and a white shirt rolled up to the elbows. There was a black leather couch against the far wall, but Daniel made no attempt to offer Giles a seat.

"I just wanted to apologize for not being straight with you before, when this whole thing started. It was a stupid thing to do, especially since I didn't know everything that was going on. That's all really. I'm just sorry as hell that I dragged you into this mess."

"What mess is that," Daniel said, his face still hardened. "Murder?'

Giles was about to argue the point, but stopped himself short. That wasn't what he had come here for. "Yeah, that's one way to put it. But I want you to know, Daniel, I didn't kill anyone. I know you think I'm responsible—"

"You're God damn right I do."

"—and that's fine. I just wanted to tell you myself. I think I know who's responsible and—"

"You gotta be kidding. You're not going to give me another one of your cock 'n' bull stories are you? Because I've had just about enough."

Giles could sense that Daniel was looking for an opportunity to explode at him but Giles wasn't going to give it to him. "No, I'm not. I did what I came here to do. I just wanted to apologize . . . And to thank you for giving me Janet Raymond's name."

"I wish I hadn't."

"Fair enough."

They stood in silence for a moment, then Daniel looked at his watch again.

"I'll go," Giles said, and began to walk out of the den. But then Daniel spoke up.

"Wait a second."

He stopped and they squared off again.

"This was never personal, Giles."

"I know that. You were just doing your job."

Daniel nodded. "Well, I appreciate your coming down here, but I want you to know I still think you're involved somehow. And if you are, I'm going to do everything in my power to make sure you pay."

"I understand."

Daniel stared at him a few seconds more and then said, "They couldn't get a search warrant, you know."

"What?"

"For your house. They tried, but the judge wouldn't give it to them."

That made sense, Giles thought. "I wondered about that."

Before Daniel could say anything else Giles walked back down the hall to the front door with Daniel trailing him. He reached for the knob but instead of opening the door he said, "Can I ask you something?"

Daniel didn't say yes, but he didn't stop him either.

"If I do get something concrete, not a hunch or whatever, but something I know will prove I didn't do it, can I come to you?"

"Not for the next two weeks."

"Why not?"

"I'm on vacation, as of this very minute."

"Oh."

For the first time that morning Daniel's features softened. "But listen, if you do come up with something, anyone associated with the case can help you. I know that Dalton can come off a little arrogant—"

"Dalton?"

"The guy who questioned you."

"Oh, right."

"But he's a good cop. If you've got something that's legit, he'll listen."

"Okay. Thanks, Daniel."

Giles opened the door and walked out. He turned back once and Daniel was still standing in the doorway watching him leave. But neither of them said anything else. Then Giles squinted into the sun and headed back to his car.

# Chapter Twenty-Four

From Daniel's house, Giles drove back up into town and into a nearly empty ferry terminal. He wasn't certain the ferries would even be running, but there were a couple dozen cars ahead of him and he pulled into the line and let his car idle.

Giles found himself getting nervous at the thought of talking with Sharon. Did she know that the charge against him for Don's murder had been dropped? Would it matter to her even if she did? The signs of struggle in his office suggested murder, and that would certainly be easier to deal with than thinking he had taken his own life. But then Don hadn't taken his own life; he'd taken some two hundred others. How the hell was he going to begin to explain that to Sharon?

As he sat in line, other things began to crowd their way into Giles' mind. For one thing, if Paige was serious, then he was going to have to find a place to live. He had a few hundred in the bank, and there was the check from *Science Fiction Digest*, but that wasn't going to last very long. There was no getting around the fact that he was going to have to find a job.

In time, once Don had been apprehended and his confidence had returned, Giles might be able to support himself with his writing. But that wasn't going to help him any now. What kind of job could he get with a history degree? His prospects were going to be dim, to say the least. It wasn't until that moment that Giles realized how much he'd depended on Paige, and not just financially, either.

The thought of not being with her anymore began to depress him. All of the things they shared, all of the memories they had— he'd been so preoccupied the past few months that he'd forgotten just how much he needed her. There was still tonight, though. She wanted to have dinner together. If they could talk, then there was still a chance despite her assurances to the contrary. There had to be. Giles had to believe it or he wouldn't have been able to go on.

After his meeting with Daniel, he had to admit that he felt much better. Once he had things out with Sharon, he might finally be able to put this whole thing behind him. Paige didn't seem to understand that there were things he needed to do. Part of that was his fault for not making it clear, but he had to make sure he didn't assess any blame tonight. If they could start again with a clean slate, all the better.

Up ahead, with the cold blue sky in the background, appeared the ferry. Once the cars had been unloaded the line began to move forward and the boat refilled again. This time, instead of sitting in the car, Giles went up to the observation deck to wait out the ride. The wind was incredibly cold and Giles hunched against it, but it was just what he needed after the sedative effect of the Pontiac's heater.

Giles laughed inwardly as he watched the bow of the ferry bludgeon its way across Puget Sound. He'd always loved being out on the water, and yet here he was living in one of the boating capitals of the U.S. and he and Paige hadn't even talked about buying a boat. He supposed that he had been waiting for his writing to take off so that some of the financial burden on Paige could be lifted. But, of course, that never happened.

There was nothing traumatic in that now. It was just a fact, like any other. Giles would still have plenty of time to write, with or without Paige. He still had the desire burning in him and he knew it was what he would be doing for the rest of his days. Nothing could disturb the inner peace that brought with it, and Giles walked back inside to wait out the rest of the trip to Bainbridge Island.

Driving through the small downtown, Giles was saddened

further. What had happened to Don to turn him into a monster? He wondered if it was something from his childhood, and if Sharon might know. A few minutes later he was approaching the drive of Don and Sharon's place. He wasn't going to have to wonder much longer.

As he pulled down the dirt and gravel drive, he saw three cars. Two of them he recognized, but the third car was unfamiliar. It was a big, white Cadillac with Oregon plates. Giles parked behind the Caddie and got out. The house had no Christmas lights up, and aside from the snow there were no visible signs that the holiday was fast approaching. Once he'd collected his thoughts, Giles made his way down the walk and up to the door.

Before he rang the bell Giles thought he heard voices. There were noises and then a short burst of laughter. That was interesting. Finally he rang the bell and a minute later an elderly woman with white hair opened the door.

"Hello?" she said.

Giles almost smiled. The woman was old but obviously spry. She had a rosy complexion on her wrinkled skin and something of the Mona Lisa in her mouth that only suggested a grin. But the reason Giles almost smiled is that, although older, the woman was the spitting image of Sharon.

"I was wondering if I might speak with Sharon?"

"Certainly. Come on in."

"Uh," Giles hesitated. "I'm not sure—"

"Nonsense," she said, and what could only be Sharon's mother took Giles by the arm and led him into the foyer. "Can I get you a cup of coffee?"

"Thank you, but I don't know how long I'll be staying."

"That's all right. It's already made." Then Sharon's mother promptly hustled Giles into the kitchen.

There was an older gentleman who must have been Sharon's father seated at the table. He was mostly bald, with a bit of red hair draped over his ears, dressed in baggy slacks and a cardigan, and was looking through reading glasses at a copy of the *Seattle Tribune,* the city's other daily paper.

"Hello there, young man," he said, and folded the paper. He stood up and walked over to Giles. "The name's Frank Erikson. I'm Sharon's father."

He offered his hand and Giles shook it just as Sharon's mother brought over a mug of coffee. "It's nice to meet you, Mr. Erikson."

"Frank."

"Thank you, Mrs.—"

"Eunice."

"Thanks, Eunice—"

"Let the boy sit down and drink his coffee, Frank."

'Young man,' 'boy,' Giles was almost overwhelmed by the whirlwind of hospitality. He'd never met Sharon's folks before. Frank headed back to the table while Eunice went for the oven. From the pungent smells in the kitchen, she was obviously baking something. Giles followed Frank and sat on the opposite end of the small kitchen table.

Frank picked up his own mug of coffee and took a sip, then he pulled off his glasses and tossed them on the folded newspaper. "So, how's the writing game going these days, Giles?"

Giles had been about to take a sip, when he stopped short.

"Uh . . . How . . ."

"Saw you at the funeral."

Giles was stunned. If her father had seen him there, then Sharon knew. And here he was in her house. Suddenly he wanted to run back out to the car and drive away as fast as he could. He felt like an unwanted intruder. More accurately, he felt like a coward. He suddenly didn't want to face Sharon.

"I don't know if I should be telling you this," Frank said, "but—"

"Frank?"

Eunice had turned and was giving her husband a look that Giles couldn't quite read. Anger? Concern? Fear? It was clear that Frank knew what it meant. "Oh, hush," he said. "The boy should know."

Know what? At that moment a shout came from another part of the house. "Who is it, Mother?"

Before Giles even had time to react, Eunice yelled out, "It's Giles Barrett."

Giles stood immediately. He felt cornered, trapped. The last thing he wanted was for Sharon to create a scene in front of her parents. And then, in the next instant, Eunice was standing before him with a covered basket.

"Sit down, Giles. Have some scones. We have strawberry, raspberry and loganberry jam."

"Uh, really, I probably shouldn't be—"

"Giles?"

When he heard his name, Giles turned to see Sharon standing in the kitchen doorway. She was wearing a bathrobe, her brown hair pulled back, and her face looked freshly scrubbed. "Let's go out into the living room."

"Do you want some coffee, Sister?"

"No thank you, Mother."

Sharon had her arms crossed and waited, her face expressionless. As Giles bent to pick up his mug, Sharon's father caught his eye, and when he looked over at him, Frank winked. Giles didn't know what to think, and simply took his mug and followed Sharon out into the living room.

The view was breathtaking. Out of the large picture window it seemed as if Giles could practically see all of Puget Sound from Bellingham to Olympia. He had barely taken his eyes from the view when he suddenly felt Sharon putting her arms around him.

"I'm sorry I hung up on you, Giles. Things were crazy. I meant to call and thank you for coming to the funeral."

Holding his mug in one hand, he hugged her back with his free arm. "You're not angry, then?"

Sharon pulled back from Giles and walked over by the couch. She held out her arm, offering him a seat, and they both sat down together.

"I was devastated," she said. "I don't know if I'd have made it through this if my folks hadn't come up right away."

"Have they been here all this time?"

"No, they only stayed a few weeks. They came back this past

week, though, and I'm following them back down to their place for Christmas."

Giles looked around at the lack of decoration and nodded his head. He took a sip of coffee and looked up into Sharon's face when he felt her hand on his forearm.

"I didn't believe what they said, you know, the police. Not for a minute. But I don't think I realized it until I saw you at the funeral."

"God, I'm sorry about that, Sharon."

"Don't be."

"I just wanted to say goodbye."

"I know. That's when I really knew you hadn't done anything."

Now that the shock had worn off, Giles didn't know what to say. Don was the only one who'd done anything. How was he supposed to explain that to Sharon? He decided then that he would only reveal to her that Don was still alive. The rest could wait.

"How much do you know about Don's family, Sharon?"

She gave him a quizzical look. "Is that why you came here, to ask about Don's family?"

"Anything you can tell me would be helpful."

"Whatever for?"

Giles wasn't going to allow himself to be forced into telling her before he was ready. "Look, Sharon, I know you've been through hell. And I know you've probably done a lot of soul-searching these past few weeks to try and sort out what happened."

Sharon broke off eye contact and looked out the window. Giles continued. "In my own way I'm trying to make sense of this, too. I didn't know that much about Don's past or his family, and I thought maybe you could—"

"This all sounds pretty fishy, Giles." Her eyes were rimmed with red. They looked glassy and heavy with tears.

"Maybe it is, but could you humor me anyway?"

Sharon smiled and put her fingers up to her eyes to dry them. She looked into his own eyes and Giles felt as though she could read his every thought. "What are you up to?" she asked.

"Please."

She took a breath and looked back out the window. "Well, Don never really talked much about his family. I mean, I knew the basics: he was born in Kansas City, the Kansas side—the white side he called it. Went to school there. Did his undergrad work in Colorado. He started teaching there, hated it, and moved up to Bellingham for his graduate work, then got the job in Seattle."

"What about his family? Brothers, sisters?"

"He had one sister, younger. They had some kind of falling out—that was years before I met him—and he never really spoke about her. She wouldn't even come to the funeral."

"You talked to her?"

"Yeah, it was weird."

"Did you ever meet her?"

She nodded her head.

"How about his folks?"

"Let's see, his dad died in '84. We went back to Wichita for the funeral. That was the only time I ever saw Leslie."

"Is she still there?"

"No. Leslie's in San Diego, but as far as I know his mom's still in Wichita."

This next part was going to be tricky. "The night Don died . . . did the police call you to identify him?"

Sharon eyed Giles warily, then she shook her head. "He had his wallet with him," she said. "He was too . . ." Her chest hitched as she breathed, and Giles reached out to grasp her hand. "They said it wouldn't have mattered, that I wouldn't have been able to identify him. Why are you asking me all this, Giles?"

"How about at the funeral home? Did you see him then?"

"No. I think you'd better tell me why you're asking me all this." Sharon had turned almost directly facing Giles. He could see a slow fear creeping into her features and tried to hurry it along.

"One more thing. Did he ever mention having a brother?"

"Brother? I just told you he only had the one sister."

"But did he ever tell you that specifically, that he only had one sibling? Did you ever ask him how many brothers and sisters he had?"

"How would I know—"

"Think about it."

As Sharon turned and leaned back into the couch, Giles could hear the muted sounds of her parents in the kitchen. Silverware tinkled, the refrigerator opened and closed, and Frank's newspaper rustled.

"I honestly can't remember."

Giles stood and walked to the window. The sun was almost directly overhead now. The room was bright with reflected light off the snow and water. He began a slow, easy pace across the hardwood floor and started into his story. "I'd like you to listen to all of what I have to say, Sharon. You might not believe it—I'm not sure I do completely—but I know it happened."

He stopped and looked directly at her. "I saw Don last night."

She barely reacted. Giles supposed she was taking him at his word, so he continued. "I touched him, in the flesh. He's alive as you or me."

When she still didn't speak, Giles launched into the story he'd prepared. In this sanitized version Don had simply come to the house while Paige was at work. They'd talked, Don wouldn't say where he was staying, and then he'd left.

"A twin brother?" she finally asked.

"That's what he told me."

"Do you realize what you're saying, Giles?"

"I had to tell you, Sharon. It didn't feel right keeping it from you."

Sharon leaned forward, elbows on her knees and her hands covering her mouth. One shock at a time. First he had to acclimate her to the fact that Don was still alive, and then he had to verify the fact. It was a shitty thing to do to Sharon, but Giles was left with no options. Don had to be stopped.

What he needed was concrete proof that Don was still alive. Now that Sharon knew, she could help Giles find some evidence of David Holman. Or better yet, maybe she could try and contact

Don. If both of them had seen him, the police would have to believe it was true. They could exhume David's body and check the dental records against Don's.

"How could he have kept that from me all these years, a twin brother?"

Giles walked back to the couch and sat next to Sharon. He reached for his coffee cup, but it was cold. "I don't know. I guess everyone has things that they don't want known about their past."

"But I was his wife."

Giles shrugged.

She looked up and met his gaze. "Are there things you've never told Paige?"

It was all Giles could do to keep from laughing at the irony of that question. "Everyone's different, Sharon. I got the impression that Don thought his brother was an embarrassment. Maybe that's why he never said anything. It wasn't just you. I didn't know anything about him. Maybe Don felt that he had to pretend David didn't exist as far as anyone else was concerned."

"I still don't understand what happened."

"What do you mean?"

"Why would David have Don's wallet?"

That almost made Giles break out in sweat. He hadn't envisioned Sharon going into details. "We never got into that. He was only at the house for a few minutes."

"It all makes perfect sense though, don't you think?"

"What's that?"

"The police said that his office showed signs of a struggle."

"Yeah?"

"So if David was trying to steal Don's wallet, that would explain everything."

"Wait a minute. Sharon. Who said anything about trying to steal a wallet?"

"Don't you see, Giles? That's the only thing that makes sense. Don was alone that night. His long lost brother shows up, and of course Don doesn't want him hanging around, so he tries to buy

251

him off. But when David sees the cash and credit cards, he figures why not go all the way. He could pass for Don.

"When Don refused, they must have fought over the wallet. At some point during the struggle David must have gotten the wallet, and Don must have accidently pushed him through the window. He was probably scared out of his mind that the police wouldn't believe his story and he went into hiding. When they mistook his brother for him, he couldn't reveal himself because it would really look like he was guilty."

Giles could practically see the gears turning in Sharon's head as she spun her tale. It was a nice thought, but unfortunately it had nothing to do with reality. Far from being frightened, her husband was a cold-blooded killer, and the death of David Holman had been no accident.

It was time to inject a little sanity into the proceedings. "Look, Sharon. I don't think we should try to guess what went on that night. You need to talk to Don—"

"He didn't mention anything about the accident to you?"

It was no accident, he wanted to scream at her. "He wasn't there that long."

"Mom, Dad," Sharon suddenly shouted, and she was off of the couch in an instant and running for the kitchen. "Don's alive!"

Giles cringed.

Sharon's folks appeared in the doorway, confused at first, but then genuinely happy for her as she explained her version of the story. Eventually, the four of them wound up talking in the front room—fresh cups of coffee all around, compliments of Eunice.

"Incredible story," Frank was saying. But Giles also noticed that throughout the discussion he would glance over at Sharon as if he wasn't wholly convinced. "Just incredible. And you say this was yesterday?"

Giles nodded meekly. He wanted to cry.

"Do you think he'll try and contact you again, Giles?" Eunice asked. Sharon's mother was harder to read and, despite her question, it was difficult to know what she really thought.

"I hope so," Giles answered honestly.

"Well, I think it goes without saying," Sharon said, "that I need to see him as soon as possible. The police have to know it wasn't his fault. He has to know he doesn't have anything to fear. I just want him back."

At this point it was out of Giles' hands. They were going to find out sooner or later. Granted, it would be a little more difficult for them to take with Sharon's version etched in their minds, but the fact that Don was alive would still remain. They would just have to deal with the consequences when the time came. Giles was tired of being responsible for Don's actions.

"Sharon," he said. "What I really need for you to do is contact Don's mother. Before we go to the police, we have to make sure we have our facts straight."

"But I don't see why that's important. Don can tell them everything himself."

"Look, obviously Don isn't going to walk into the police station cold. We're going to have to prepare them for his coming in. And believe me, I've had enough experience with the cops to know that they're not just going to take our word for it. Besides, what if Don still doesn't want to come in? But if Don's mother can tell them that he had a twin, then maybe they can exhume the body, check the dental records, and then they'll know. They might even help us find him at that point."

The three of them pondered that for a moment, and then Sharon got up and began to look through her desk for the phone number. Giles was getting antsy by now. He wanted to get back home, and finally excused himself.

"I'll let you know as soon as I find the number."

"Thanks, Sharon."

Her eyes teared up and she hugged Giles tightly. "Thank you," she said. "You don't know what this means to me."

"Just remember, Sharon. We don't really know what happened in Don's office that night, okay? We don't know for sure why he's hiding."

"I know. I just can't help the way I feel. He's alive and that's all I can think about."

They hugged again and Giles said goodbye to Sharon and her parents. A few minutes later he was in line for the ferry going back to Seattle. The sun was so hot in the car that he had his window cracked. It was all so close to being over that he whooped out loud. A few people turned their heads to look at him, but Giles could only smile.

# Chapter Twenty-Five

"Giles! I can't believe you didn't tell me this morning."

"I knew you were angry with me for leaving last night. I didn't want to do anything that was going to make it worse."

Paige looked at him across the table but didn't say anything. She picked up her glass of wine and took a sip, then set it down and took another bite of the pasta primavera she'd made. It was already cold but she ate it with gusto. Giles had been telling her of his encounter with Don, of the story he'd written and why, and she'd been so fascinated that she forgot all about the food.

It was still almost incomprehensible that Don could have been murdering people all these years. But he was the only one who had access to Giles' work with enough lead-time to plan it all out. As frightening as it was to consider, it all made sense.

"At least one good thing has come out of this," she said, quickly taking another bite.

"What's that?"

Paige finished chewing and said, "Now you know once and for all that this possession was all in your head."

Giles laughed grimly. "Yeah, but that's not going to mean much if we're not together."

She had another mouthful ready, but Paige set her fork down. "Damn it, Giles. Why the hell couldn't you have just been honest with me up front? Then none of this would have happened."

"I know, I know. I was stupid."

"Yes, you were. And as much as I want to forgive you and

forget about this thing, I'm still pissed off. I meant what I said last night. I don't know if I can ever trust you again."

"After all we've been through?" It was a statement more than a plea.

"That's exactly why. We've been married almost ten years. And the fact that you could pull something like this on me after that long . . . You destroyed something that I took for granted all these years. I don't know if we can ever get that back."

Giles was silent. She felt bad for having to put it to him so bluntly, but it was the truth. And if she started living a lie now, there was no telling what kind of hell it would get her into later. She honestly didn't know what was going to happen over the long haul, but for now she was going to proceed with extreme caution.

Giles set his fork down and sat back in his chair. He wasn't drinking. "So, what, you still want me to move out?"

"Not this minute, no. But I'm not sure how I'm going to feel tomorrow, much less in a few days or next month."

Giles smiled again and shook his head.

"What?"

"Oh, I was just going to say that kind of leaves me in the air emotionally, but—"

"How do you think I felt?"

". . . but I figured you'd probably say something like that."

They both smiled and that made Paige resent him all the more. It also saddened her because she loved him so much. He was funny, good natured, helpful and supportive; they meshed. And yet, in spite of their years together, she couldn't seem to shake the feeling that she had never really known him.

There was something fundamentally unknowable about Giles, she'd decided. It both saddened and relieved her because now she felt as if she had a handle on him. Before, she'd been content to coast. They'd been so good together and had so much fun that she'd never questioned some of the stranger aspects of his personality.

He was back to his old self now, but she was looking at him through different eyes, and that old self suddenly seemed strange to her. Paige was no longer afraid that things might not go her way. Fully confident that she had the power to exert her own will to change the things that confronted her, she felt at peace with herself. Giles, in comparison, seemed weak, as though the slightest thing could devastate him again. Only this time she didn't want to be around when it happened.

"So, if I understand what you're saying, it's not *definitely* over."

Paige frowned. She had to tell the truth. "I guess not. Not definitely."

"Okay, what about tonight, then? Am I sleeping on the couch?"

"You're being awfully accommodating."

He smiled at her, but she resisted returning it.

"Look," he said, leaning his forearms against the table. "I'm not trying to manipulate you into taking me back. Honestly. I'm sorry as hell about what happened, and I'm sorry about lying to you, but I'm not sorry about what I did. I had to do it, and it didn't have anything to do with not loving you or not trusting you. I was scared shitless that something bad was going to happen to you and I did what I thought was best.

"In retrospect, I see where things went wrong in my method, but I can't change that. The only thing I can do right now is to love you. I always have and that won't change either. I might get over you, but I'll never stop loving you. And if I seem a little accommodating, it's because I'm doing what I want to. I want to be here with you. But you're the one with the decision to make, so . . ."

She nodded. "I understand."

Paige pushed her plate forward and picked up her wine glass and drained it. She looked over at the bottle, disappointed that it was already empty. There was no telling what tomorrow would bring, but she knew what she wanted right now. "I think we should proceed for the time being as if everything's the same as it was before."

She saw his eyes widen and could barely keep a straight face. "I think you should sleep in the bedroom and . . . you know, anything else that would occur during the natural course of the evening."

Giles laughed and Paige put the empty glass to her lips to hide her smile.

"Anything else?" he said.

When she finally let herself relax it all seemed so simple. Giles hadn't had a drop of the wine; it was all coursing through her veins. As she stared into his eyes, she ran her tongue over her lips. They felt slightly numb, but the rest of her body felt very much alive and she was going to go with it.

"I'm going to bed," she announced, and pushed herself unsteadily out of the chair. "You coming?"

"Yeah, in a little bit. I was just going to do the dishes."

Paige walked around the table and stumbled into Giles' arms. She kissed him long and hard. "I think the dishes can wait until the morning, don't you?"


Saturday morning the clouds had moved back in and it was snowing intermittently. But the temperature was up, hovering around freezing, and the snow from Thursday that had melted was gradually being replenished. Giles was in the kitchen, and as he made a pot of coffee he tried not to let himself get too optimistic. After all, Paige *had* been drunk last night. Shaking his head and smiling, he sat down at the table while the coffee brewed and thought about what was going to happen next.

He ran his hands through his hair, amused now more than paralyzed, at the thought of getting a job. Jesus, what was he going to put on his resume? Wrote horror stories for the past fifteen years while my wife, the dentist, supported me for the last ten? Prospective employers were going to jump at the chance to land him when they read that. And then there was the writing.

Not much chance of doing anything in that department very soon, what with his computer demolished and his agent turned into a homicidal maniac. And that brought his thoughts back around to Don.

Sharon hadn't called the night before and he wondered how

long it would be before he found out what Don's mother had to say. Not that he wanted to get into that right now. It would be nice to have a few days with Paige before the hunt for Don began, but at least she knew everything there was to know.

The kitchen was still a little cold so Giles stood and poked his head into the dinning room to bump up the heat. He saw the dirty dishes still on the table and sighed. The food had been great; it was just too bad that neither of them had been in the mood to eat. He began gathering the dishes off the table and bringing them into the kitchen. On his third trip in he met Paige.

"You're up early," he said, tossing the empty wine bottle into the recycling.

Paige took a mug from the cupboard and poured herself some coffee. "We went to bed early, remember? Was I as drunk last night as I think?"

"Can I plead the fifth?"

Paige walked over to kiss him, and playfully bit his lower lip. "Just this once." She sat heavily in the chair Giles had vacated. "Do you want me to help?"

"No, I've got it."

"Thanks."

One side of the double sink Giles filled with hot soapy water and let the dishes soak, while he began to wash in the other.

"What are you going to do when you hear from Sharon?" Paige asked.

"What do you think I should do?"

Paige thought for a moment and took a sip of coffee. "I don't know. I hate the idea of you going to the cops again. This whole thing is so screwy. It would be nice if we could just forget about it for a while."

"What about Sharon? She expects me to set up some kind of meeting between her and Don. Christ, I almost feel like calling the cops to get police protection."

Paige didn't respond and Giles immediately regretted saying it. She'd been stony last night when he'd related how he almost died. Thinking about it again made him conscious of the bandage on his arm. He washed the rest of the dishes in silence. A couple times he looked over at her, but she was lost in thought.

"Did you bring in the paper yet?" she asked.

"No, I didn't get a chance."

Paige stood and walked out toward the front door. She was only gone a few seconds when he heard her yell his name. Giles grabbed a towel and dried his hands as he ran out of the kitchen. He met her coming up the stairs.

"There's another goddamn cop here," she said. "What is it now?"

Giles walked out to the living room to have a look. The car was unfamiliar to him, green with gold trim. When he read the shield on the side he didn't know what to think. Giles turned to see Paige coming back down the hall after getting her bathrobe from the bedroom.

"What's going on, Giles?"

"It's a sheriff's car from Bainbridge Island."

"Sharon?"

"I don't know."

"Oh, my God. You don't think Don did anything to Sharon, do you?"

"I hope not."

But in his mind, Giles was thinking exactly that. What if Don had followed him yesterday morning? Would he have killed Sharon? And how about her folks? Giles didn't know what he was going to do if he was somehow tangentially responsible for another blood bath.

A single officer in his late forties—the sheriff Giles presumed—stepped out, hitched his pants up, and began walking toward the steps. He immediately turned up the collar of his black trimmed green jacket against the snow and stuck his hands in the pockets. His round brimmed hat had a clear plastic cover to protect it from the elements and he wore heavy boots that helped him tromp through the wet snow as he walked up the front steps.

Paige followed Giles as he went down the stairs and opened

the door before the sheriff could knock. "Come on in," he said, before the man could speak.

"Thank you." He stamped his feet off before coming in, and then stood on the mat after the door was closed behind him. "Are you Giles Barrett?"

"Yes."

"Does this have something to do with Sharon?" Paige blurted out.

The sheriff removed his hat with one hand. He did not look happy. "Yes, I'm afraid it does," he said, and then he unzipped his jacket.

From the inside pocket he pulled out a sheaf of papers, folded in thirds, and handed it to Giles. "This is a restraining order, Mr. Barrett. You have been ordered by the court not to come within three hundred yards of Mrs. Sharon Holman or a county judge can order your arrest."

The three of them stood there awkwardly in the stairway for what seemed like minutes. Giles stared at the papers in his hand in utter disbelief. "Can you tell me what this is about?"

The sheriff looked both of them over and, probably deciding that it couldn't hurt matters, started to explain. "Are you telling me you don't know why I'm giving you this?"

"Look, Sheriff . . ."

"Morrisette."

"Sheriff Morrisette, I just saw Sharon yesterday and she was fine."

Morrisette looked them over again, and then turned his attention to Giles. "Mr. Barrett, I've known Don and Sharon quite a few years, ever since they moved out to the island. And I've been sheriff on Bainbridge a long time before that. So when Sharon came to me yesterday and said that Don was still alive, well, I was going to give her the benefit of the doubt.

"She said you told her you'd seen Don, and that you requested she call Don's mother to verify that he had a twin brother. Evidently this twin was the one that was really killed. She couldn't find the number for his mother at home, and the number wasn't listed in

Wichita when she called information, which is why she came to me. She asked if I could get in touch with the police back there and see if she was still around. And I did just that.

"But while I was waiting for the call from Kansas, I decided to do a little investigating on my own. I called the medical examiner's office over here in Seattle and talked to the chief himself. You know what he told me? He said that Don's body had been identified by his dental records specifically so that they wouldn't have to make Sharon do it.

"Now in my book that would have been enough, but I kept it to myself. When the call finally came in, I gave Sharon the number and she called Don's mother."

The sheriff put his hat back on and carefully adjusted it, then he zipped up his coat. "Don never had a brother, Mr. Barrett, twin or otherwise. I don't know why you did this to Sharon and I don't much care. The damage has been done. But let me tell you this. Make no mistake, Mr. Barrett, if you so much as step off the ferry in Bainbridge, I'll have your ass in jail so fast you won't remember how it got there."

With that, Sheriff Morrisette opened the door and let himself out.

It didn't make sense. He'd seen Don. Christ, he'd almost been killed by Don. But if the dental records matched . . .

Giles turned and Paige was gone. He bounded up the stairs to look for her so he could try to explain, but as soon as he reached the top the phone rang. Maybe it was Sharon, calling to explain what this whole mess was about.

Giles ran into the kitchen and picked up the receiver. "Hello?"

"Yo, is Giles Barrett there?"

"Speaking."

"Hey, listen, Mr. Barrett, this is Jeff Peters. I know you're probably pissed off right now—I would be, too. But listen, I'm going to make it up to you, swear to God. Just don't pull out on me—"

"Who is this?"

"Jeff Peters."

Giles was confused for a few seconds, and then it hit him. "Oh, right. From the magazine."

"Yeah. Like I was saying, I just can't believe what happened and I want to do whatever it takes to—"

"Hold on, Jeff. What are you talking about?"

"The story."

"The one in your magazine?"

"Yeah. It's about the last page being missing. When I got it back from the printer and saw it was missing I just about shit, but there wasn't enough time to—"

"Are you telling me that the last page of my story wasn't in the magazine?"

"Well . . . yeah."

The floor felt like quicksand beneath Giles' feet. "I'm going to have to call you back later, Jeff," he said, and hung up without waiting for a response.

Giles ran back down the stairs to the landing at the front door. A pile of mail was on the little table there, but the lone Manila envelope was easy to spot. He ripped it open and was at once almost repulsed by the downright amateurishness of the magazine. Still, he turned to his story—set in typeface, underline instead of italics—and flipped through it. Sure enough, the last few paragraphs were missing—the ones where the werewolf was killed.

Giles had to sit down. He dropped the magazine and the envelope to the floor and slid there himself. With his back against the door he could feel a draft seeping in from outside.

The devastation he expected didn't come. He sat in a daze for several minutes, attempting to sort out what had happened over the last two days, but it wasn't working. He needed to talk with Paige. Giles picked up the magazine and pulled himself up from the floor.

He checked the living room and didn't find her there. Then he went down the hallway to the bedroom. The door was shut and he opened it and walked inside. Paige was sitting up, her arms crossed over her knees and her head on her arms.

"I need to talk to you about this."

She lifted her head up and looked at him. There were no tears, only a bitter weariness in her expression that bordered on hatred. "It's too late, Giles, way too late."

"Look, I can explain," he said.

"Don't. It's over, Giles. That's it."

"Are you kidding?"

"No, I'm not. You lied to me, you lied to Sharon, you've lied to everybody. I don't even know you anymore, Giles. But I do know I'll never be able to trust you again, ever."

"I thought you wanted me to come to you with stuff like this. I'm trying to be honest with you."

Her expression was vicious, but somehow she was able to keep the aggression out of her voice. "Do you have a hearing problem? I said it's too late. I don't give a fuck what you're *trying* to be. I just want you to pack up your shit and get out of my house."

Giles almost laughed. "What, today?"

"That sounds like as good a time as any. You can come back to get your stuff later, but you're not spending another night here."

"I don't believe this."

"Believe it. We'll talk about the divorce when I can look at you again without wanting to kill you. Now get out."

Giles walked to his closet and slipped on a pair of jeans and pulled on a heavy sweater. He made sure he had his wallet and checkbook before he left the room. Paige wouldn't meet his eye as he stopped in the doorway, so he just turned and left. Halfway down the hall, he heard the bedroom door slam behind him.

He took his heaviest coat from the hall closet, and slammed the kitchen door on his way out. The Pontiac took forever to warm up. Not that he was in a hurry to get anywhere; Giles had nowhere to go. Finally, he pulled out and closed the garage door, then drove away from the house through the snow.

He fishtailed slightly coming out of the driveway, turned into the skid and the tires caught again. Once he'd crossed Aurora, Giles turned south onto I-5 for no other reason than he though the pavement would be clearer and the traffic moving faster.

His expected emotional collapse never happened. Probably because it was all too confusing. Had the lack of an ending on the story been the cause of his near death or had it been the reason that the entity had disappeared?

There was no doubt in his mind that the thing masquerading as Don was straight out of Giles' story. How could he have been so stupid not to see it? Two men, best friends, it happened just like he'd written it—just like Don said. He'd made a fool of himself, looked like a liar, and everyone he knew thought he was crazy. And then he realized he still was.

Don was still dead, but Giles had brought him back to life. After the night on top of the building he'd tried to pretend that he'd never actually been possessed, that he'd imagined it. But he knew better now. He couldn't have been more wrong.

Giles was possessed by something that caused him to kill people with his writing. It was a part of him. It was real, and there was no escaping it. He'd done it all. It was all his fault. Everything.

Giles smashed his hand on the steering wheel. The car slued slightly on the icy roadway and Giles was able to right it by pulling his foot off the gas and allowing the car to slow considerably. But at that moment a large dump truck, slow coming up the onramp, sped up and crossed two lanes in front of Giles.

Slush buried the windshield, and the weight of it stopped the wipers dead. Trying desperately to make sure he wouldn't rear end the truck, Giles swerved to the right and instantly found himself in the middle of a full on skid. Over the top of the slush on his windshield he could see himself heading for the shoulder.

He turned the wheel in his hand, but the car didn't respond in the slightest, and he careened into the ditch. The force of the impact was softened by the snow and his reduced speed but Giles' head still snapped forward, bloodying itself on the steering wheel.

For a minute everything was silent. It was as though his head was packed in cotton. Gradually, sounds began creeping their way into his consciousness. The motor was off but when Giles turned the key nothing happened. The bleeding lump on his forehead was throbbing with pain. He touched it and then quickly drew his hand away with a wince.

Giles pulled his keys out of the ignition and climbed out of the car. But before he could get his footing he slipped, banging the back of his head on the roof of the car on his way to the ground. He picked himself up out of the wet slush in a fury and slammed the door. Then, for good measure, he kicked the door panel as hard as he could. The large dent it made was addictive, and so Giles kept kicking and kicking.

Cars and trucks roared by through the snow as he pummeled the Pontiac with his foot. "Fuck you!" he screamed after each kick. "Fuck you!"

Then he stopped and turned his head toward the sky as the snow continued to pour down on him. "What do you want from me?"

Giles was panting, out of breath with exhaustion. "Why can't you leave me the fuck alone?" he said, pounding his fists on the hood of the car. "All I ever wanted to do was write!"

Before he realized it was happening, Giles was suddenly wracked with sobs. The tears were streaming down his face and snot was collecting on his upper lip. "Why won't you leave me alone?" he screamed. His chest was heaving and his throat was raw from yelling. "I can't do anything else."

Giles finally slipped to his knees in the wet snow, his head hanging down between his shoulders. His voice was now little more than a croak. "I can't do anything else."

# PART THREE

# The Heart of Darkness

Where there is no imagination
there is no horror.

—Arthur Conan Doyle
*A Study in Scarlet*

# Chapter Twenty-Six

The minute Richard Padovan crossed the city limits into Hallowell he smiled and slowly shook his head. It was hard to believe that both of them had lived here at the same time. While Richard was growing up, going to school, playing the drums in band, and watching movies, he had been here. For a few years, anyway.

And now Richard was back home, too. It had been a long time, and though there were some subtle changes things basically looked the same. It brought on such a wave of nostalgia that he wondered why he'd never come back sooner.

Hallowell was an old logging town situated on the southern side of Grays Harbor between Cosmopolis and Westport. Richard's father had lived there when he was a child and, after marrying his mother and graduating from medical school, he naturally chose Hallowell as the place to set up his practice. Richard had come along a few years later, followed by a brother and two sisters.

Once Richard had guided his rental car through the largely residential east side of town, he crossed over the Hallowell River and drove on into downtown. There he decided to take a detour down to 7th Street. He pulled up and parked next to the bank. On his left across the street was a large grassy square, with glass-covered wooden benches where the Grays Harbor Transit buses came through at regular intervals. Directly in front of him to the right sat a large, gaveled vacant lot dotted with weeds and litter. Of course, it hadn't always been like that. In his mind Richard could still piece together the outline of the huge towering structure that sat on this site some twenty-five years ago: the 7th Street Theater.

He and his brother, and later his friends, had spent so many Saturday nights and Sunday afternoons here it seemed impossible it was gone. As a boy Richard had lived for the movies. Back then he'd collected videocassettes the way some kids collected baseball cards. But all that changed when the 7th Street burned down. Without the theater Richard began to immerse himself in books, much to his parents' delight, and his life had taken a decidedly different turn.

Along with the theater, the fire had destroyed his grandfather's barbershop and two other businesses. His grandfather had taken the opportunity—provided by the insurance money—to retire. But while Richard's grandparents had stayed in Hallowell the rest of their lives, that certainly hadn't been the case with his family.

Halfway down the street from the empty lot across the street to the left, behind a tiny, one-story building that housed a dentist office and an optometrist was a small diner, and beyond that a group of medical buildings where his father had practiced general medicine. His father had died when Richard was only twelve and, fortunately for his family's financial future, a friend of his father's from medical school had been persuaded to buy the practice from Richard's mother.

Since none of her children were in high school yet, his mother had felt no need to stay in Hallowell and moved the family to Seattle a few years later. Richard had been back down fairly regularly after that, but once his grandparents had died there was no more reason to visit. And since he and his wife had moved to New York seven years before, he hadn't been back once.

Richard started up the car and turned around, heading south toward Roosevelt Avenue—Highway 105 through town—and headed west. He reminisced as he passed Roosevelt Elementary and Hallowell Junior High School. And on the edge of town he pulled into Brooke's Beachway service station. He filled up at the pump and then walked into the tiny convenience store, amazed that it was still there after all these years.

Two men were talking across the counter, a man about Richard's age dressed in jeans and a plaid shirt, and an older man who looked an awful lot like Ray Brooke. Richard could remember coming here as a child and buying candy—or ice cream on hot summer days. His family's old house was only a few blocks away.

"How much?" said the old man behind the counter.

"Sixteen twenty-five."

Richard smiled because Ray didn't even bother to crane his neck and squint his eyes to make sure he was telling the truth. He simply punched in sixteen and a quarter in his register and took the twenty that Richard offered. When Ray handed him back four singles Richard actually chuckled. He'd been living in big cities for so long, first Seattle and then New York, that he'd almost forgotten what small town living was like.

As he was putting his change into his wallet he saw Ray giving him more than a cursory glance. "You look familiar, son," Ray finally said. "Do I know you?"

"Richard Padovan."

A huge smile lit up Ray's face. "Sure, Doc Padovan's kid. Your old man and I used to play cribbage together down at the Elks—hardly ever managed to beat the son of a gun. How the hell you been? I haven't seen you since you were in junior high. How's your mom?"

"Fine, fine. She remarried a few years after we moved."

"Good for her." Ray turned to the other man in the store. "This here is Ricky Padovan. Don't think you two know each other, Ricky. Dave went to school up in Aberdeen. Runs an auto repair shop now."

"Dave Walsh," the younger man said and the two of them shook hands.

"How about your brother and sisters?"

"You've got a good memory, Ray."

"Clean living, Ricky. Clean living."

"Well, Brian's still up in Seattle, doing construction work.

He's married. Michelle's in Olympia. She and her husband have two kids. And Tammy is in Spokane. She's a nurse, still single."

"And yourself?"

"I'm married, no kids yet."

"Still in the area?"

"Nope. We live in New York City."

"Wow. What brings you all the way out here, vacation?"

"I guess you could say it's more of a business trip. I'm an editor at a small publishing house back East, and I'm here to see an author."

Dave and Ray looked at each other in bemusement. "In Hallowell?" Ray asked.

"Well, outside of town anyway."

"Who is it?"

"His name is Giles Barrett."

At that Dave burst out laughing. "Old Man Barrett? You've got to be kidding. Are you sure you've got the right guy?"

"What makes you say that?"

"The guy's a recluse. Never comes into town. Never goes anywhere that I know of. I've never even *seen* him before. Just heard stories. Has his groceries brought in, clothes, too." Dave laughed again. "Just seems strange, that's all."

Ray was amused as well. "Giles, huh. Didn't know he had it in him. I've known Giles Barrett a lot of years, Ricky. What makes you think he's a writer?"

"How about enough short stories to fill a book? I'm down here to get his permission to publish a collection of his stories."

Ray scratched his balding head while Dave simply grinned and shook his. Richard let them think about it for a minute and then said, "The last of them was written in 1995."

"Well, that's why," Dave said. "That was over twenty years ago."

Ray nodded. "Just before he moved back down to live with his folks."

Dave seemed to be thinking of 'Old Man Barrett' in a new light now. "Well, what do you know."

Richard had a vague idea about where Barrett's house was—the property was so rural that the GPS couldn't pinpoint a specific location—but he had a feeling he could get something more exact here. "So, how do I get out to his place?"

Ray smiled. He was in his element now. "Well, you just head out the one-oh-five here, toward Westport, until you get to Richards Road."

"I'm not sure I remember where that is."

"Can't miss it. It's the only real intersection on the right between Markham and Ocosta. Road swings up toward the water and then back around to the highway."

That sounded familiar. "Yeah. I think I know where that is."

"It's about three miles down along the water once the road straightens out. The Barrett's have had a cranberry farm out there for as long as I can remember. Sells them to Ocean Spray just down the road."

"All right, then. Thanks, Ray. Nice to meet you, Dave."

Before he left, Richard went to the cooler and was surprised and delighted to find that instead of an array of plastic bottles Ray kept a variety of loose cans there. Like something from his childhood, he reached in and pulled out a can of Coke. He threw one of his singles on the counter, told Ray to keep it, and then headed out the door.

On the way to his car, Richard popped the top on the can and took a long swallow of Coke. He belched contentedly before he got back in the car. It was stuffy inside and he rolled down the window. The sun had been trying to break through the clouds all day and during the last twenty minutes or so it had succeeded. It was unseasonably warm for February.

Richard drove out of Brooke's Beachway Service and headed west toward the ocean. To his right, about a mile away, was Grays Harbor, and twenty miles to the south in the other direction was Willapa Bay. He wished he knew the area better, but Richard had only been fifteen when they'd moved, and he'd rarely been out of Hallowell until then.

His elbow out the window and the can of soda between his

legs, in ten minutes Richard had reached the intersection that Ray had described. He turned right and the road looped down into the marshy lowland right along the water. There were no houses that he could see for the first few miles, then he slowed his car. There were two or three houses clustered together every mile, usually followed by a large stretch of farmland. Everything else was trees.

Finally, Richard came upon a large stretch of land that looked dark green and swampy. Though Richard had never seen a cranberry bog before, he had no doubt that this must be one. He eased the car into the dirt driveway and followed it back behind a screen of trees to a large white two-story house. Parked out front was a blue pickup truck and an impossibly old Pontiac Grand Prix that looked to be in mint condition.

There was no sign anywhere to confirm that this was indeed Barrett's farm, but Richard turned the car off anyway. Even if this wasn't the place, whoever lived here could tell him how to find it.

The first thing he heard was the sound of a car coming up the driveway, and immediately he tensed up. No one was supposed to be here today, and besides, he knew the sound of every vehicle that was allowed on the farm, and what he heard wasn't one of them. When he heard the car motor shut off it forced him up out of his chair. He reached the window just in time to see a kid getting out of his car.

He could tell from the vanity plates that the car was a rental. The guy was in shirtsleeves, tie, leather shoes, and probably in his early thirties. But instead of coming up to the door, he walked over to the Pontiac. He wasn't looking at it critically, though, he appeared to be admiring it. Next, he wandered over and began examining the truck.

Giles didn't like this. He didn't like this one bit.

Giles went to the front door and opened it silently. Then he walked a short ways down the porch and spoke in a loud ringing voice. "What do you want?"

The kid whirled around and Giles had to suppress a grin.

"Oh, man, you scared me." He put a hand to his chest and looked at Giles closely for a moment. "Are you Giles Barrett?"

"Maybe you didn't hear me the first time. What do you want?"

"I'm looking for Giles Barrett."

Giles was silent. As the long minute stretched on, he could see the kid becoming uncomfortable. Then, just before he was about to speak, Giles said, "Go away."

As he turned on his heels and headed for the door, he could hear the kid running after him. "Wait. I need to talk to you, Mr. Barrett."

Giles stopped at the door and turned around. "Listen, kid, if there's another language I can use that you'll understand let me know. I don't want to talk to you."

The amused look that flashed across his face when Giles had called him kid was no doubt the result of his not realizing just how old Giles was. Another reason was that Giles still retained most of the youthful looks he'd had all his life. But while Giles was closing in on sixty, the kid probably hadn't shaken off the fact that he wasn't in his twenties anymore.

"Please, Mr. Barrett. It's important."

That was doubtful in the extreme, but the kid was clearly determined, and it might be the quickest way to get rid of him. "All right, I'll ask it for the third time. What do you want?"

The kid grinned sheepishly and shook his head, but his confidence came back quickly. "My name is Richard Padovan. I'm an editor with Silver Bullet Press in New York. Are you familiar with the kind of books we publish?"

Like a gaff hook through his heart, the mere mention of the publishing industry threatened to pull Giles back into the vortex he'd tried so hard to run away from. Even after he'd regained his composure, he was barely able to speak. "Mr. Padovan, I grow cranberries for a living. Now, I'll ask you for the last time, what do you want?"

"I'm sorry. We'd like to publish a book of your short stories—"

"No. You're not going to publish anything I've written. Now go away."

Eric B. Olsen

Giles pulled open the screen door, but the voice behind him forced him to stop. With his back to the kid, he listened with dread to nothing short of supreme confidence.

"I didn't come here to get your permission, Mr. Barrett. The fact is, Silver Bullet already owns your stories, and I fully intend on publishing this book regardless of your wishes."

Giles turned around and let the screen door slap shut. Would it start again, the murders? Were the stories one-time killers or would they go on gutting and gouging and burning innocent people for all time?

For twenty years he'd managed to evade the questions. For twenty years he'd hid from them, and now they were back. Why now? He didn't want to know. He wanted to run away again, but it was his responsibility and nobody was standing in line to take it from him. So, it was time to see what he was up against.

"All right," Giles said wearily. "Come on in."

"Two years ago our parent company acquired a small publishing house that owned a defunct magazine called *Dark Imaginings*. I'm sure you're familiar with it."

The kid waited as though he expected a response. He was sitting on the couch, across from Giles in his easy chair. But since he hadn't asked a question, Giles simply stared at him.

"Anyway, since our Silver Bullet imprint publishes mostly horror fiction I was given the job of sifting through the back issues to see if there was anything worth reprinting. To be quite honest, I didn't really think there was. Most of it seemed pretty juvenile and predictable, even for the day. But then I came across a story that I actually liked. So I tossed that copy aside and then waded back in.

The next story I came across that I liked, something rang a bell. I compared it to the first story and guess what? Same author: you. After those first couple, I started keeping an eye out for your name. I even went back to look through the issues I'd already read, just to make sure I hadn't missed any others.

"I think they're tremendous, Mr. Barrett. I really admire your work."

276

The kid hesitated again, but Giles was damned if he was going to give him a thank you and a pat on the back.

It was hot and stuffy in the front room where they were sitting. The kid loosened his tie and unbuttoned his collar. Giles had deliberately seated him on the side of the room that caught the afternoon sun. Padovan was perched on the edge of the couch, just barely able to lean his face forward out of the light.

"So there I was, with a handful of stories that I thought were terrific. That got me curious. Some of the brief text on you named other magazines that had published your stories, and all of a sudden I was on this mission to find out more about you and your work. The last thing you'd published was in 1995, and I wanted to know why. Nobody knew if you were dead or alive. It was a real mystery.

"I have to tell you, though, I was blown away when I found out you'd been living here the whole time. I grew up in Hallowell, you know. We lived on Spruce Street. My dad was a physician."

Padovan was obviously fishing for some kind of response, anything, but Giles was content within his stony silence. The kid would eventually get to the point.

"But, back to the stories. When I showed them to my senior editor, she loved them. I knew she would, so it didn't take much to convince her that we should acquire as many of your other stories as we could and publish an anthology.

"Now there's no trouble legally, because we own or purchased the reprint rights to every story I could find. The problem came up when my editor wanted me to write an introduction. I knew next to nothing about you. Like I said before, I didn't even know whether you were dead or alive.

"In one of the other magazines it mentioned that you were born in Hallowell. Just about knocked my socks off. I called the courthouse in Montesano and that's how I found out your folks had died and left their property to you. The deed to the land still has your name on it, but evidentially you don't have a phone so I couldn't call and confirm it.

"When my wife and I came out here on vacation to visit my

brother and his family . . ." he shrugged. "I rented a car and drove down here on a whim."

The kid held out his hands. "I guess I was hoping you'd write a foreword to the book. Maybe get an interview. I think people would be interested to know why you stopped writing, what you've been doing all these—"

"You don't know what the fuck you're doing, do you?" The anger in Giles' voice rocked Padovan back into the couch cushions.

"Excuse me?"

"No, I will not excuse you. You come in here after I say I don't want my work published, and you have the balls to tell me you're going to do it anyway. There is no excuse for that."

The kid pulled his tie down even lower. "I'm sorry, Mr. Barrett, but for some reason I thought you'd be happy about this. This is a chance to give a whole new audience of people the opportunity to discover your work."

Giles was pissed now. "Are you fucking blind? I've been out here in the sticks humping this cranberry bog for the last twenty years. I don't have a phone. Nobody knows who I am. Does it look to you like I want to be *discovered*?"

Padovan sat back and closed his eyes against the sun slanting in through the front window.

Across the room Giles could barely move, the emotions surging in him were so strong. A book of his stories. God, he would have done anything for that to happen twenty years ago. He wanted to say yes to Padovan so badly it hurt. But he'd given up writing for a very good reason, a reason the kid knew nothing about.

That stupid, piece of shit story that he'd published in *Silent Screams*, it had been the confirmation of everything he'd feared. He'd left Paige without an argument, moved in with his folks, and helped them work the farm. He didn't go into town; he didn't see people; he didn't even read. It became harder to keep up his isolation after his folks died, but thus far he'd been successful.

In so many ways he felt as though he'd wasted his life. Hiding from this possession had turned him into a frightened and bitter man. And now, just when he thought he had a handle on his pathetic life, along comes this kid to add a healthy dose of uncertainty to the mix. After all, that was the crux of the situation: would the stories kill again?

"Mr. Padovan?"

The kid squinted at Giles and then slowly sat up. "Yes?"

"During your research, did you ever come across any of my stories that had been reprinted?"

Padovan squinted again, as though he wasn't sure what to make of Giles' question, but he thought for a second and nodded. "Just one. I think it was the last one you wrote."

That intrigued Giles. "Did they restore the last page?"

"I'm not sure what you mean. I only saw the reprint."

Giles settled back into his chair and steepled his fingers. Interesting. It was quite possibly the only way to verify what the situation really was. There was always the chance that he wouldn't look in the right place, but it was a start. First, however, there was a little business to take care of.

"You don't happen to remember the magazine it was in, do you?"

"Actually, it was in an anthology."

Giles sat up. "A published book?"

"Small press."

"When was this?"

"I believe the copyright date was '97. But the introduction said your story had been written in '95. There was nothing about a missing page."

"What was it called?"

"The story?"

"The anthology."

"Oh, uh . . . I think it was just called *Silent Screams*."

Giles shook his head. So, the punk from California managed to self-publish an anthology. Found the missing page, too. Will wonders never cease? "One more question. When did you plan on coming out with this book of yours?"

"Tentative pub date is next spring."

Giles nodded and leaned forward in his seat. The sun was low enough that it wasn't in Padovan's eyes anymore, and Giles locked his with the kid's.

"Before you go, Mr. Padovan, you should know one thing. I plan on bringing every legal means at my disposal to bear against this book being published. I'll take you to court. I'll appeal every decision. I'll tie up this thing for as long as I have to, regardless of whether or not I have any solid grounds. So, you'd better hope that this editor of yours is really behind this thing, because I'm going to make this book the most royal pain in the ass that she's ever tried to publish."

Giles grinned. The kid looked like he'd just been punched in the stomach. "Now, get the fuck out of my house before I have to drag you out myself."

Richard Padovan nearly tripped going down the steps of the front porch. He was still in a daze after visiting with Giles—make that, Old Man—Barrett. He shook his head as he climbed into the car. The old coot even had the nerve to ask him for a business card as he was leaving—so he could spell the name right on the lawsuit, Richard supposed.

Unbelievable. The house, with the sun setting behind it, looked like something from a postcard. He never would have suspected that inside lurked a wild man. The guy's eyes . . . Richard shuddered and thought he would probably have nightmares about them for weeks.

Finally, he shook it off, started his car, and drove off . . . away from the sunset.

# Chapter Twenty-Seven

The next day, as Giles pulled up in front of the Hallowell Public Library, he was surprised to find that the building had been totally renovated. The main, red brick section that he remembered from his youth was still there, but the rear of the building had been expanded, including covered parking. And the giant cement staircase in front had been supplanted by a modern, street-level entrance on the side.

Giles parked the Pontiac on the street in front of the old YMCA—apparently now a church—and walked inside. He barely recognized the place. Instead of the intimating fortress-like front desk he remembered as a kid, an inviting knee-level horseshoe table with computers greeted him. The whole layout was different, too. Where before the children's library had been buried in the basement like a crypt, it now occupied the upper level, bathed in sunlight from the overhead skylights in the new part of the building.

Giles stood awkwardly for a moment, not sure what to do next. An attractive young woman was busy at the desk and he was about to ask her where to go when a small girl appeared in front of him. She was no more than seven, still a little plump with baby fat. The woman looked up immediately when the girl tapped her on the shoulder.

"Did you bring those in?" the girl said, and pointed.

The three of them looked behind the woman to a waist-high credenza with a small pot of purple flowers sitting on it.

The woman smiled. "No, I don't know where those came from."

"Were they out in front of the door when you came in?"

"I'm sorry, sweetheart, Nancy came in before I did today."

"Do you know who left them?"

The woman shook her head.

"Me and Shelly left them for you and Nancy."

The woman stretched out her arms and hugged the girl. "Thank you. That was so nice."

The little girl was positively beaming, and ran off, most likely to tell Shelly. Then the woman looked up at Giles. "I'm sorry, can I help you with something?"

Giles cleared his throat. "Uh, yes. I need to look at some old newspapers."

"Okay." She smiled at him and walked around the desk.

Giles followed her to the other side of the room. Here were the newest periodicals and newspapers, and new book releases. As they walked through Giles marveled again at the transformation.

"When did they renovate the library?"

She gave him a quizzical look and said, "I'm not sure. I've been here five years. And before that . . ." She shrugged. "As long as I can remember."

At the far end of the room, against the back wall, were several cubicles containing computer terminals. She walked up to one of the terminals and pushed the return. The screen came to life.

"That was nice back there," Giles said. "With the girl."

The woman rolled her eyes and smiled. "That's my niece."

They both laughed, and then the woman turned her attention back to the terminal. She opened an Internet browser and clicked a name in a drop-down menu at the top. "The directions are right on the screen," she said, when the website loaded. "You just put in a subject or the article you're looking for and it will call it up. If you have any questions, feel free to ask."

"So, this just calls up the text of the article?"

"Yes. We can access nearly every major newspaper in the

country. The ones that subscribe to this system, anyway. I think there are some foreign newspapers on there, too."

Giles frowned as she began to turn and walk away. "Just a minute," he said. "I don't think this is going to work for me."

Her eyes widened in question, waiting for Giles to explain.

"It's just that . . . I don't know exactly what I'm looking for. What I need is to look through the whole paper. I was thinking it would be on film and I could use one of those magnifying machines."

She was already shaking her head. "We haven't used microfilm for the last fifteen, twenty years."

Giles nodded. "Good. The papers I want to see are from nineteen ninety seven."

"Oh," she said, and thought for a moment. "We might have that. I think all the microfilm is downstairs. Why don't we go down and take a look?"

At the bottom of the stairs she turned right, then took a left at the door to the parking garage and he followed her down a rather dimly-lit hallway. She pulled a set of keys from the pocket of her slacks and began unlocking the door. "Nancy—she's the head librarian—she likes to keep this room locked since it's so far from the front desk."

The woman flipped on the lights in a small room filled with metal file cabinets. "Oh," she said. "I forgot to ask you which paper you needed. We only have a few on film."

"*Seattle Tribune.*"

"Oh, good. I'm sure we have that one."

She walked behind one of the cabinets and ducked down. Then he heard her say, "Okay, what month?"

Giles hesitated. "Uh, the whole year?"

Slowly, her head appeared above the cabinets.

"Sorry," he said. "I'm doing some research. I probably won't be able to finish it all today."

She nodded with amusement. "Probably not. Okay, let's get you started."

She brought over four cartons and set them down next to the viewer. "This should be plenty for now."

The screen was about two feet square and lit up when she turned it on. She dumped the first roll out of the box, threaded it up, and scrolled forward until she was at the January first issue, nineteen ninety seven, of the *Seattle Trib*.

"There you go."

Giles sat down and got the feel of the electronic motor that advanced the film and then thanked the woman.

"You're welcome. I hope you find what you're looking for."

Giles thanked her again, but he wasn't sure he really wanted to find anything.

The work was tedious, though by the second reel of the film he had his system down. Most of the sections he could skip, and eventually he wound up only perusing the front section and the local news. He was looking for anyone who had been killed by falling from a building, preferably one that was under construction.

What that would mean in practical terms is that every time the story appeared in print, someone died. Or in the case of one of his stories, a whole planeload of people. And if *that* was the case he'd have to do everything in his power to stop the publication of the kid's book. The results could be disastrous. Even after twenty years he didn't know what this force was that had killed so many people, and nearly taken his own life. But he'd taken precautions.

Not only didn't he have a computer or a typewriter, but there was nothing to write with in his entire house, or anywhere on the property. He didn't own a pen, a pencil, crayon, felt-tip marker, a piece of chalk, nothing. He took care of his business dealings with Ocean Spray in person and had everything sent to a lawyer in town with power of attorney so he wouldn't have to sign anything. It wasn't like he really had to worry, though. People weren't exactly lining up at his door to publish him. Not until now anyway.

The real question was whether he would chance it even if he didn't find anything in the papers. Did it necessarily have to happen in Seattle? He didn't know. And the temptation of having a book of his works published was incredibly inviting. With any luck, he'd scared off Padovan and he wouldn't have to worry about it anymore.

He was on the last of the four rolls—the last two weeks of February—when there came a knock at the door. The young woman poked her head inside. "Sorry, we're getting ready to close."

"What time is it?"

"Almost nine."

"Have I really been here all afternoon?"

She nodded. "You didn't find what you needed?"

"No, not yet." Giles began unthreading the machine. "Could I come back tomorrow?"

She laughed. "You can come back every day if you like. Just get someone to let you in."

"Great." Giles stood up, stretching the kinks out of his body, and held out the boxes of film. "Where should I put these?"

"Right here," she said, pointing to a wooden tray. "Nancy likes us to put them back in the drawers ourselves. That way nothing gets out of order."

Giles followed her instructions and then walked past her as she locked the door.

"See you tomorrow," he heard her say as he headed out the door to the garage.

Giles raised his hand and after the door shut behind him he walked out to his car. His stomach rumbled as he climbed in behind the wheel. He drove eagerly back home, clearing his weary mind and thinking only about what he was going to make for dinner.

Every night for the rest of the week, Carrie—he'd finally asked the woman her name—would knock on the door at closing time and Giles would shut down his research for the day. He was in surprisingly good spirits which, understandably, continued to buoy with each day that produced no results. By Wednesday he began bringing in a Thermos of coffee and a couple of sandwiches so that he wouldn't have to stop when he got hungry. It was almost like the writing days.

Thursday afternoon Carrie was downstairs putting away the film Giles had used the day before. "Any luck yet?"

"Nope."

A few seconds later she walked up and sat on the counter next to the machine, facing him. "You don't sound too broken up about it."

Giles grinned and leaned back in his chair. "It's a long story. A very long story."

"Hmm. You'll have to tell it to me sometime."

Giles looked up curiously at Carrie and felt as though he'd suddenly been transported across time to a place in his past, a time and place where he actually noticed women. This was very strange. Either that or he was totally misreading the signs. A distinct possibility considering that he hadn't been with a woman since Paige.

"You know how many people have been down here," she said, "since I've worked here?"

Giles shook his head.

"Two. But one of them was a high school kid doing an assignment for English class, so that doesn't count."

"Okay, so who was the other?"

She slowly smiled, and he really noticed her this time. Her mouth was slightly crooked, but her teeth were beautiful. *She* was beautiful.

"You" she finally said.

"What?"

"I think you can tell a lot about people by the way they spend their free time."

Giles laughed now. He rubbed his hand over the salt and pepper growth on his chin. Carrie was what, twenty-five, thirty, tops? And he himself was fifty-six. The mere fact that he was even considering this was ludicrous.

He shook his head. "You don't know anything about me, Carrie."

"You'd be surprised what I know about you, Giles."

At that his eyebrows raised. ". . . Yes?"

"Nancy couldn't wait to give me an earful as soon as she saw you that first day."

He watched her as she swung her legs gently beneath the counter she was sitting on. Her skirt just covered her knees and she wasn't wearing stockings. She was blonde, like Paige, and on her calves he could just detect a soft sprinkling of downy hair.

"Who are you hiding from?"

She was radiant, but now Giles began to doubt her motives. Maybe she was just down here on a mission from Nancy. Get some juicy gossip on the old man to spread around town. "I'm not hiding from anyone."

"Okay, then *what* are you hiding from, out on that farm of yours?"

"Since when did I suddenly become the center of some big mystery?"

"Since you moved down here twenty years ago."

"Nothing mysterious about that. I grew up here. That farm was my folks'."

"And suddenly you heard the call of the cranberries, right?" Her eyes would not leave his. They were blue and bright and there was so much behind them that Giles almost couldn't meet her gaze.

"That's right. Didn't Nancy tell you? I'm just a poor simple cranberry farmer."

Her head was nodding as he spoke. "Uh huh, and I'm Mildred Pierce. You should try my chicken sometime. Glendale's finest."

Giles had absolutely no idea where this was going, but he thought he'd put an end to it. "I'd like that. When did you have in mind?"

Her legs stopped swinging and she looked away now, straight ahead over the tops of the cabinets. He wondered what she must be thinking, probably that he was some kind of lech. Old Man Barrett, all right. All he needed now was the trench coat and a pair of sunglasses. Oh, well, served her right for being coy with him.

"Tomorrow night?" she asked. But she was still staring straight ahead.

"Look, Carrie, I'm flattered, really. But I'm old enough to be your father—"

"And I'm young enough to be your daughter, is that it?" Her eyes were back on his and they were on fire. "I didn't ask you to marry me, Giles. I just want to know whether you'd like to have dinner with me tomorrow night."

Giles could feel his face redden, but he didn't look away. "Sorry. Yes, I'd like that."

"Great," she said, and pushed herself off the counter. In a flash she was around the other side of him and at the door. "I'll give you directions tomorrow."

"To your place?"

She nodded. "You'll be here tomorrow, won't you?"

Giles glanced at the screen. He had only just started in on August. "Yeah, it kind of looks that way."

"Okay."

The door had almost shut behind her when it opened again. "Oh," she said, sticking her head back into the room. "I almost forgot. Nineteen eighty nine."

"Nineteen eighty nine? What's that?"

"The year the library was renovated." Then she waved a hand and disappeared.

Giles shook his head in disbelief. He'd been alone, or with his folks, for so long it was almost inconceivable that something like this was happening. And now, of all times. Or was he getting way ahead of himself? He still didn't know. Okay, so maybe she didn't have romantic designs on him. But he had to admit one thing: it was sure nice to talk to a woman again.

# Chapter Twenty-Eight

As Carrie was taking Giles down to the "morgue" Friday morning she said, "I have an idea. If you're going to stay all day again, why don't you just come home with me?"

Giles tried to look shocked, but he couldn't suppress a grin. "People will talk."

When they reached the door Carrie pulled out her keys, unlocked it, and pushed it open. "If anyone asks," she said dryly, "I'll just tell them you're my father." And with that she headed back down the hall.

Giles had a hard time concentrating all day. The combination of meeting Carrie and going through the old newspapers was bringing all of his regrets out of the woodwork. Maybe there was something else he could have done. Maybe if he'd only talked to someone about this thing he wouldn't have had to go into hiding. Maybe Paige had been right; his secrecy was his own worst enemy.

And now he was going to have dinner with Carrie, and he wasn't going to tell her about it either. If only there was a way to know for sure whether this curse of his had finally left him. What he was doing now, looking through these papers, was guess work at best.

Fifty-six, Giles thought, but I feel like I'm eighty. And the fact that he could even imagine having a relationship with someone thirty years his junior only made him feel older. He felt trapped. Part of him wanted to confide in Carrie; maybe that would be the difference. It could be the thing that changed the pattern. There was even a chance she could help him find what he was looking for in the papers.

Giles shook his head. He didn't even know this woman. He knew in his heart that there was no way he could ever tell her about his past, and that was that. Better to get on with his research, have a nice dinner tonight, then invest his energy in figuring out what to about Richard Padovan.

With his focus restored, Giles was able to work steadily until about one o'clock. He had worked his way through to the end of September by then and still had found nothing. He set the viewed cartons of film in the tray, and after walking over to the cabinets to get more, he remained at the viewer while he ate his lunch. But soon his neck felt tight and his legs began to cramp from so much sitting.

Carrie stopped by around two, ostensibly to put away some of the film, but Giles suspected it was to check up on him. He had to admit; it felt kind of nice. The library closed early on Fridays and a few minutes before five he heard the familiar knock.

"How'd it go today?" She walked up behind him and put a hand on his shoulder.

"I still haven't found what I'm looking for."

"I'll be ready in a few minutes. My car's just out in the lot. I can give you the keys if you want to wait for me there."

"Don't you want me to follow you?"

She shook her head. "I'll drive you back."

"Okay. But I have to go out to my car first anyway, so I'll meet you."

"It's the blue Honda," she said. "See you in a few minutes." Then she breezed back out the door.

Giles took his empty lunch bag and Thermos out to the Pontiac and walked back across the street to the library's covered parking. A dark blue Prelude was one of only four cars still in the lot and he stood next to it to wait for Carrie.

The weather had been clear all week, but that was making for cold nights. It had been one of the mildest Februarys that Giles could remember. He was looking forward to spring. Last fall's harvest had been a good one, and with Giles' frugal lifestyle he would have plenty of money to get him through till September. If he had enough left in the fall, he might even be able to hire a couple of extra field hands. That would be a well-deserved luxury.

A chill wind blew into the lot and Giles hunched against it, wishing he'd worn a heavier jacket. He watched as a woman with two pre-teen boys came out of the building and then drove off in a station wagon. A few seconds later an intense young man in a three-piece suit and carrying a briefcase drove out behind the wheel of a Porsche. The red Bronco must be Nancy's, Giles thought.

Carrie emerged from the building a few minutes later. She was wearing jeans and a flannel shirt beneath her overcoat.

"I went to the store last night," she said, unlocking her door. She climbed in and unlocked the passenger side, and Giles slid in beside her. "So we're all set."

They drove west to "O" Street and then she turned south. Carrie rounded the corner onto Spruce and pulled up in front of a small white house. "This is nice," Giles said as she turned off the motor. "Do you rent?"

"Nope. It's mine."

He followed her up the walk. At the top of the stoop she took her mail from the box and unlocked the door. Inside, she turned on a lamp and walked straight ahead toward the kitchen.

Giles shut the door and looked around the room. The left hand wall of the large front room was lined with bookshelves, and he grinned. He didn't know why that surprised him—after all, she was a librarian—but it did.

"Do you want something to drink?"

He looked over to see her setting the mail on the kitchen table as he pulled off his coat. "Nothing alcoholic."

She opened the refrigerator just as he entered the room. "I have apple juice, grapefruit, ginger ale, and . . ." she held up, "a lone can of Diet Coke."

Giles shook his head. "Ginger ale sounds fine."

As she poured him a glass Giles looked around. The kitchen was fairly small, but beautiful. Blonde cabinets were suspended above clean countertops that were the color of the dull side of aluminum foil. He touched the smooth cold surface and ran his hand along it, feeling the slight texture. She had what looked like a new stove and refrigerator, a double sink, and a large wooden table that matched in color the cabinets, yet looked like an antique.

He thanked her as she handed him the glass. When he heard something creek behind him, Giles turned to see a back door opening, seemingly by itself.

"There she is," Carrie said, and bent down to pick up a large, gray, long-haired cat that had just walked into the room. "Giles, meet Ajanta."

"Ajanta."

"It's an Indian word for mystery, which is a perfect name for this little beast." She set the cat down and it began doing figure eights around her legs. "I turned on the heat. It should warm up in a few minutes."

It was brisk inside the house. Carrie finally took off her coat and walked out of the kitchen. She turned left and disappeared down a hallway. Giles took a sip of soda and then walked back out to the living room.

On the opposite wall from the bookcases was a set of low shelves with a small, flat-screen television on top and cable boxes below. Next to the TV was a small speaker that looked to be an online music device of some kind. Above these shelves and around the rest of the room were various prints by Gauguin, and the hardwood floor beneath his feet had a large oriental rug in the middle and a couch on one end. Opposite the couch were large leafy plants, but the main feature of the room was undeniably the books. And they weren't just on the shelves.

Piles of everything from medieval artwork, to textbooks on physics, to hard-boiled detective novels, were everywhere. Stacked on the floor, leaning against shelves, on the coffee table; it was enthralling. He took another sip of ginger ale, and Carrie emerged from the hallway wearing blue tights and an oversized sweater with the sleeves pushed up to her elbows.

"You doing all right?"

"Great," he said, and followed her back out to the kitchen. "I really like your place."

"Thanks."

They settled into a comfortable conversation as she began hauling things out of the refrigerator. She put three breasts of chicken on a broiler pan and put it in the oven, then began chopping vegetables and preparing what looked like rice, but later turned out to be couscous.

She seemed content to talk about herself and let Giles talk about the present without delving into the past. Totally at ease as she prepared the meal, Giles found her fascinating. She had a maturity that went way beyond her years and attracted him to her even more.

"I've lived in Hallowell all my life," she was saying over dinner. "If I hadn't liked living here, I certainly wouldn't have stayed."

"Don't you ever feel trapped?"

"On the contrary. I think if I'd grown up someplace else, I would have moved here as soon as I discovered it."

"That's wonderful." Giles took another bite of couscous. "And so is this meal. Thank you."

"You're welcome. I'm glad you like it."

"I do. This chicken's great." And then he remembered her reference to *Mildred Pierce*. "You ever thought about opening your own restaurant?"

She smiled as she set down her fork. "I was wondering if you'd read that."

Giles nodded. "I had something of a literary bent when I was younger." He immediately regretted bringing up his past but Carrie didn't pursue it, and he found himself almost embarrassed at his gratefulness to her.

After dinner Giles offered to help with the dishes. Carrie accepted and she washed while Giles dried. When they were done, she poured him another glass of ginger ale and they went out to the front room together.

"What kind of music do you like?" She turned on the box next to the speaker and looked over at him.

He shrugged. "To tell you the truth, I never paid much attention to music after the Beatles broke up."

She laughed. "You *are* old, aren't you?"

"Hey, don't rub it in. Whatever you want is fine."

She pressed a few buttons and before long he could just make out a series of quicksilver notes played on a saxophone as they came tumbling out of the speakers. Giles liked it. "Who is this?"

"John Coltrane," she said and flopped down on the couch next to Giles. She picked up a glass of water she'd brought with her from the kitchen and held it in her hands as she faced him.

For the first time that evening an uncomfortable silence ensued. At least it was uncomfortable for Giles. Carrie seemed fine with it. He set down his soda and leaned forward, standing up.

"I haven't had a chance to look at your books yet. Do you mind?"

"Help yourself."

As Giles stepped away, Ajanta immediately jumped up onto the couch where he'd been sitting, and Carrie began rubbing the cat's stomach. He could hear the purring all the way across the room.

It turned out Carrie's collection of books was every bit as eclectic as those that he'd seen lying about. But what was even more impressive was that, unlike the library he'd had years ago, there seemed to be no junk. Whether they were detective novels or political commentaries, all of the books were classics in their field. Of course, there were plenty of titles he didn't recognize but it was obvious that they belonged together.

He was crouching down, going over the titles of what looked to be every novel by Cornell Woolrich, when he was stunned again. On the next shelf down was the four-volume Arkham House edition of H.P. Lovecraft's work, followed by numerous paperback editions.

Giles turned to her. "You read Lovecraft?"

She smiled and nodded. "Yeah. He was a wonderful writer."

"I know, I know. I just wouldn't have guessed that you were someone who read horror fiction."

"Most of the paperback stuff is in the bedroom. Lovecraft just seemed to belong out here. You know what I mean?"

Giles was already nodding. He moved back to the couch and before long they were having a spirited discussion about horror fiction. With twenty years worth of titles to catch up on, she eagerly brought him up to date on the latest trends. She explained how far the boundaries had been pushed and that the market was currently experiencing a revival of sorts, that modern writers were going back to the styles pioneered in the seventies and early eighties.

That made sense, Giles thought. He'd been trying to maintain that tradition back when he was writing, and that was probably why Padovan had decided to publish the book of his stories now. Of course he didn't tell Carrie this and, as he was becoming increasingly aware, it appeared as though she wasn't going to ask him.

At one point she said she had to go to the bathroom, and stood and walked down the hallway. Giles stretched and looked at his watch. He was amazed to discover that it was almost ten. The five hours since they'd left the library had flown by. He stood up and took the opportunity to go back to Carrie's bookcase and study her horror fiction more closely.

He saw works by King and Straub from the seventies, though nothing newer, as well as some of the more recent authors that she had mentioned. He pulled one of these out and read a couple of sentences, but he was too distracted to concentrate and slipped it back among the others. Then his eyes looked down another row. This shelf held what looked like anthologies. He smiled as he recognized several that he'd had in his own collection.

Then his attention was drawn to the spine of a small hardback. His hand began to tremble as he reached for it. The letters on the spine had been gold at one time but were now mostly worn off.

With the angle of the light he wasn't sure that he'd read it right. He slowly pulled out the black, clothbound book and when he opened it to the title page his heart began to race.

"I see you found that one."

Like something from a dream, Giles heard himself cry out and nearly collapsed.

Carrie, who had come up behind him and spoken, went to her knees to keep him from falling. Giles sat on the floor now, one hand on his chest, the other flat on the cool hardwood, the book splayed spine up next to him.

"Giles, are you all right?"

He reached up to the table and took a drink of her water. "I'm sorry," he said. Giles' heart was still galloping along faster than he thought was good for him.

Carrie looked at him closely for a moment. "Are you sure you're all right?"

Giles picked the book up off of the floor. "Where the hell did you get this?"

"I told you I knew a lot more about you than you thought."

"That's not an answer."

"I thought you didn't want to talk about your past."

"That's still not an answer."

"Okay," she said. Carrie crossed her legs on the floor in front of him. "A friend of mine from school used to get this cheesy horror magazine. He was always talking it up, but I never wanted to read it because, well, you could tell the stories were going to be awful. I think he might have been published in it. I can't remember now.

"Evidently, they finally put out a hardback edition of the best stories—if that's not a contradiction in terms—from the history of the magazine. I think your name was fairly prominent on the dust jacket. Anyway, this guy absolutely insisted that I borrow it. So I did, and after I read the first couple of stories I put it down and then lost the damn thing. I didn't come across it again until I moved into this place."

The look on her face was utterly unreadable, but he had to know. "So . . . You read it, back then?"

She nodded. "And again last Monday night, as soon as Nancy told me who you were. It's the first story in the book."

Giles opened the volume to the title page again. *The Best of Silent Screams, 1992-1996.* He turned to the contents page and there was his name, listed right after the introduction: *Blood Oath*, by Giles Barrett. Inwardly, Giles groaned. If she was feeding him a line of bull, there was one easy way to find out. "What did you think of it?"

Her eyes were looking directly into his. She didn't hesitate. "I didn't think it was very good."

Giles breathed a sigh of relief.

"The way the guy talked you up in the intro to your piece made it sound like you were this monster writer." When she realized what she'd said she added, "So to speak."

Giles closed his eyes and shook his head. "That's one way to put it." She seemed to sense how uncomfortable he was and didn't press him further.

He turned to the copyright page. The date was 1997. No month. And that started him thinking. "When did you say that guy gave this to you?"

"What do you mean?"

"What year?"

"I don't know. When was it published?"

"Ninety seven."

She thought for a second. "Yeah, that's about right."

Giles was confused. "But that doesn't make sense. What were you, all of five years old back then?"

Carrie sat up straight and flashed him another smile. Pulling her knees up in front of her she had a look on her face akin to delight, but something else was there he couldn't quite read. "Is that why you've been so distant?"

"Distant?"

"How old do you think I am?"

Giles could only stare at her.

"Come on," she prompted. "How old?"

"I don't know. Twenty-five . . . thirty?"

She shook her head in disbelief. "I appreciate the compliment, but I was a senior in high school when I was given that book. I'm thirty-eight, Giles."

This time when he looked at her, he really looked at her. In the soft glow of the lamp from across the room, Giles could see the tiny lines in her skin, the maturity in her eyes. In addition to the things like her car and her house, that he should have picked up on right away, he could feel the presence of her experience.

She reached out a hand and gently placed it on his cheek. Her eyes were so deep they seemed to go on forever, and he let her bring his face to hers. Her lips touched his for a moment and as she began to pull back Giles pushed in closer. He didn't want the kiss to end. As he leaned in, Giles brought his hand up to cradle the back of her head, and he felt Carrie's arms wrap around him. Now he could smell the shampoo in her hair and the soap on her skin. It had been such a long time since Giles had reveled in the sensations of a woman. Carrie's every movement, every touch, seemed to reawaken another dormant emotion in Giles. Before long he had to pull away.

When he did, Carrie laid her head against his shoulder. He hugged her, and she embraced him with such force that it seemed to reach inside of him and touch his very core. They both stayed that way on the floor for several minutes, taking it all in.

She took his face in her hands again and gave him another kiss before she stood up. "I need a drink of water," she said, picking up their glasses on the way to the kitchen. "Do you want anything else?"

"No, thank you. I'm fine."

She smiled. "Me, too."

Giles took another look at the book that contained his last story. Talk about going out on a dud. It had served its purpose, though. And if he couldn't find anything in the *Trib*, he might eventually be able to share his other work with Carrie.

It was a miracle, really. Giles had burned every last page of his writing, destroyed all of his computer discs, burned every magazine, and sold nearly everything he owned before moving down to Hallowell to live with his folks. He certainly never expected to be thinking what he was thinking now.

As amazing as it seemed, he suddenly had urge to sit down at a computer and write. He looked up to see what was undoubtedly the reason why: Carrie entering the room.

He shook his head.

"What?"

"Nothing. I was just thinking . . ." He shook his head again.

"Tell me."

"You . . . It sounds corny, but you inspire me." He put a hand behind her head again and pulled her forward to kiss her. Afterward, she reached back to the coffee table to take a drink of water while Giles slipped the book back in place on the shelf.

"You must have an amazing memory," he said.

"Why?"

"Oh, just the fact that you remembered my name from that book. Especially knowing you didn't even like the story."

"I didn't say I didn't like it. I said I didn't think it was very good."

"What's the difference?"

"I don't think I'll ever forget that story for the rest of my life, even if I'd never met you."

Giles waited for her to explain.

"There was this guy at school, Greg Drake. He was a year ahead of me. Anyway, during my senior year—do you remember the old Roosevelt Hotel downtown?"

"Sure."

"Well, the owner had decided to renovate the thing. I think he had some idea about turning it into condos instead of leaving it a flophouse. Greg Drake's dad was hired as the contractor on the job and during his Christmas vacation from college he was working for his father.

"Nobody knows what happened, but Greg stayed late one night after everyone else had gone. When he didn't come home his father went down to the Roosevelt, but he couldn't find him anywhere in the building."

Carrie pulled her knees up tightly to her chest. Giles was too stunned to move.

"The next morning they found him dead in the alley behind the building. He'd fallen off the roof, but the coroner said he actually died from a bullet wound to the chest. They never did find out who shot him. But when I read your story in that book, I couldn't help thinking about Greg. It was eerie. I guess that's why it always stuck in my mind."

Stupid. So fucking stupid. Giles had been looking at the goddamn Seattle papers. It didn't have anything to do with a place, it was *him*. The thing had followed him to Hallowell.

Giles' arm jerked suddenly and he realized that Carrie had just touched him.

"Did I say something wrong?" she asked.

He stood up to get away from her. She stood as well but didn't move toward him. Giles walked to the other end of the room and paced while Carrie stared at him.

"I need to get to the library."

"Tonight?"

"Right now."

"I can get fired for being in there after hours."

"Fine," he said a little too quickly.

"Giles." The tone of her voice stopped his pacing.

He looked over at her. Her look was stern. His head was so full of conflicting thoughts that he could barely think straight.

She sighed. "How long would we be in there?"

"Ten, fifteen minutes."

"Get your coat."

Giles retrieved his jacket from the rack by the door and shrugged it on. He took Carrie's coat and when she came out of the bedroom with her shoes on, helped her into in. She locked up and they walked out to the car.

They drove in silence. A block from the library Carrie pulled the car over. Giles could see the taillights of two cars in the next block. After they had turned left onto Simpson, Carrie turned off her headlights and inched up to the intersection. There were no cars coming from either direction and she drove straight across the street and pulled into the covered area of the library parking lot.

"Stay in here," she said after the engine had died. Then she flipped a switch on the dome light. "I need to get the alarms turned off. I'll signal you from the basement door, okay?"

Giles nodded. She opened the door—the dome light stayed dark—then she quietly left the car and headed for the side entrance.

He smashed his fists against the dash. He'd been a fool to think it was over. For twenty years he'd done the right thing, and then along comes this woman and it's as though no time had passed at all. Another death.

When he saw the door open he stepped out of the car and ran up to it. He closed it behind him and before he could even tell her what he needed, Carrie was unlocking the door to the newspaper archive. There were no lights on in the hall, but a thin gauze of illumination from the streetlamps had worked its way through the front windows and he could just make out Carrie's silhouette.

The door opened and he followed her inside. He heard it close and the light inside temporarily blinded him when Carrie flipped the switch.

"Okay," she said. "What do you need?"

"*The Washingtonian*," Hallowell's daily newspaper. "December 15th, 1997."

Seconds later she handed him the box. Giles turned on the machine and threaded up the film. The spool began on the first and he ran it forward without stopping until he was near the end. When he stopped it was on the thirteenth, then he slowly ran through the next day and stopped it on the fifteenth.

The banner headline read: Hallowell youth dies in fall from building.

"How did you know what day that happened?"

Giles ignored the question. "How can I get a copy of this?"

"You just . . ." Carrie reached over his shoulder and when he flinched she said, "Why don't you let me get in there and do that?"

Giles stood and paced while Carrie adjusted the photocopier that was attached to the viewer. A minute later he heard the machine come to life, and then she was handing him a copy of the front page.

"Anything else?"

"No. Thank you."

"Okay. Let's get out of here, then."

Once she had turned off the machines they walked to the door. The lights went off, and Giles had to feel his way out into the hallway. As she locked up, his eyes adjusted and he walked over to the garage door.

"I have to leave by the front door," she said.

"My car's just across the street."

Carrie took hold of his arm as he was leaving. "Am I going to see you again?"

Giles was thankful he couldn't see into her eyes. He didn't think he would be able to say what he had to if he could.

"No," he said, and pulled away from her. He heard the soft click of the door behind him and then he ran across the street to his Pontiac. He warmed it up for several minutes, but he never saw Carrie come out of the building. Finally he pulled away from the curb and headed for home.

# Chapter Twenty-Nine

As soon as Carrie Mueller had closed and locked the door to the garage, she let herself back into the morgue. She flipped on the light, fired up the viewer, and made herself a copy of the article about Greg Drake. Before she read it she tried to make some sense of what had happened with Giles.

Her first thought, back at home, had been an instinctive reaction: that Giles must have killed her schoolmate. But she didn't believe that was the case now. The turning point in his behavior had been her telling him about Greg's death. He didn't try to hide his reaction at all. It was almost as though Giles hadn't known about the murder. If so, what difference could it make now, after twenty years?

Carrie looked down at the article and began to read. It was vaguely familiar to her, having read it several times back in high school. A nuts and bolts account, really, the five w's and little else. It was basically what she had told Giles. She knew there were follow-up articles in subsequent editions, but if Giles didn't need them, neither did she.

And then she laughed to herself. What she needed was Giles Barrett. Old Man Barrett. Nancy hadn't really known anything about him, and Carrie wasn't about to tell her that she knew he was a writer. The few people in town who even knew of his existence were only aware that he'd moved to Hallowell in ninety-five and had kept a low profile ever since. No one really cared why he'd moved back, and that seemed to keep speculation to a minimum.

Nancy had mentioned something about a divorce, but so what? That was hardly a scandal.

She folded up the article and stuck it in her pocket and then she locked everything up so she could leave. After engaging the alarm, she left by the side entrance and walked back toward the lot. His red Pontiac was already gone.

Back at her house on Spruce, Ajanta met Carrie at the door as she let herself in. She took off her coat and hung it by the door, and then picked up the cat.

"What do you think, girl? Is he coming back?"

She flopped down on the couch and closed her eyes. With her head leaning back she slowly stroked Ajanta's long fur. She smiled. He thought she was twenty-five. Now *that* was funny.

She supposed it was understandable, though; Giles certainly didn't look fifty-six. His skin was creased and weathered from working on the bog for twenty years, but his face was youthful and his eyes were bright and extremely penetrating. It was as though he could look right through her. She liked that, she decided, that and the way he made her feel.

Carrie yawned fiercely and sat up. She could think about what to do in the morning. Right now she needed to get some sleep.

"Looks like it's just you and me tonight, girl." Then Ajanta hopped off her lap as Carrie stood and headed for the bedroom.

Saturday morning was wet and gray. Clouds had moved in overnight and a light, intermittent rain had been falling ever since. As a result, the temperature had warmed up considerably. All of this was good for the cranberry vines, but Giles paid little attention to the thought as he paced in his front room.

He had barely slept the night before, dozing in fits and starts on the couch before giving up and wandering through the house. At five-thirty he made a pot of coffee. There was nothing else to do until eight. But come the morning, he already knew what needed to be done.

Since learning about Greg Drake, Giles felt as if his life were somehow careening toward a predestined end. And if he was going to have any say in what that end was to be, he was going to have to take some decisive action. He'd been acting like a victim of this thing for far too long.

His only regret now was Carrie. He would never be able to see her again. Thankfully, things hadn't gone any further than they did. But he couldn't allow himself to dwell on her or he might risk doing something stupid. Giles needed to keep a clear head, especially during the next couple of days.

The dawn seemed interminable, but finally eight o'clock rolled around and he headed outside to the truck. Ten minutes later, at the edge of town, Giles pulled into the side lot of Brooke's Beachway Service.

Ron was behind the register as he walked in and the two of them nodded in greeting. "Is your dad up yet?" Giles asked.

"Yeah, go on back."

In the back of the store was a door that connected to a house on the adjacent lot behind the building. Giles knocked twice, and a few seconds later a husky woman in a pink bathrobe opened the door. She had curly gray hair that rode close to her scalp and a round pleasant face. She smiled at him.

"Hello, Giles. You looking for Ray?"

"Yeah."

"Come on in."

Ray's wife stepped aside and Giles walked across the threshold into a medium sized living room. The TV was turned to a news program and one of the Brooke's granddaughters was eating a bowl of cereal on the floor in front of it.

"Ray's out in the kitchen having breakfast. Can I make you something?"

"No thanks, Jeannie."

"How about a cup of coffee?"

"That would be fine."

"Well, go on back."

Giles took the familiar path to the kitchen with Jeannie following. Ray was at a table in a small windowed nook. He was eating bacon and eggs and reading the newspaper through half-glasses perched on the end of his nose. Giles sat across from him and Jeannie instantly set a mug of steaming coffee in front of him.

Ray glanced up briefly over his glasses before returning to his paper. Giles was content to sip his coffee and look out the windows into the backyard. A few minutes later Ray folded the paper and set it to one side. He dabbed up the last of the egg yolk on his plate with a crust of toast and ate it, then pushed the plate aside. Once Jeannie had picked it up and poured him some more coffee, Ray took off his glasses and leaned back in his chair.

"What can I do for you, Giles?"

"I need a typewriter."

Ray broke out into a big grin. "That young guy from New York that was here the other day, he said you were a writer."

"I was, when I lived up in Seattle."

"How come we never heard about you?"

"I didn't publish any books. I wrote mostly short stories, and most of those were published in small magazines. I had a good-sized following, but it wasn't like I was famous or anything."

"Interesting."

Ray took a sip of coffee and contemplated this. Across the room, Jeannie watched as she leaned against the kitchen counter, arms crossed beneath her ample bosom, one hand holding her own mug.

For the past seven years Ray Brooke and his family had been helping Giles. The arrangement was mutually beneficial. Ray profited from Giles' business, and Giles was able to maintain his reclusive lifestyle. Once a week either Ray or his son Ron would bring Giles the groceries he needed. If he needed anything else, like clothes or building materials, he would drive in and give Ray a list.

For a man who had managed to raise a family by running a gas station and convenience store, Giles' business was greatly appreciated. Often they would invite him for dinner, and most of the time Giles accepted. The fact that he could trust Ray implicitly, as he had with his conversation this morning, was invaluable. Giles knew that if he stayed away from people, whatever possessed him would not be able to write anything about them. Because of Ray, that was possible.

"What did he want?" Ray finally asked.

Giles smiled and shook his head. "He wants to publish a book of my short stories."

Ray and Jeannie looked at each other. Then, while Jeannie turned to the sink and began washing dishes, Denise came in from the front room and poured herself another bowl of cereal and returned.

"He gonna make you famous in spite of yourself?"

Giles shook his head. "I doubt that."

Giles had never told Ray why he lived the way he did, though that didn't keep him from asking at first. But it had only taken Giles' explanation that it was something he couldn't talk about for Ray to honor his wishes. Ray was inquisitive, though, and if he wanted to know something, he asked. When Giles could tell him, he did, and Ray never seemed to feel rebuffed by a refusal.

"You'll have to give us a copy when it comes out."

"Don't worry. I'll make sure you get an autographed first edition."

Catching the facetious tone in Giles voice, Ray shook his head. "All right. But a typewriter's a tall order these days. What kind do you need?"

"Anything. Electric would be preferred. I just need it for a little while."

Ray thought for a second, and then Jeannie chimed in. "I think there's one in the garage, isn't there?"

"That's right," Ray said. "I think it used to belong to my folks. I used it to type out statements back in the day—"

"You mean *I* use it to type out statements," came Jeannie's response from across the room.

Ray dismissed her cheerfully with a wave of his hand. Jeannie winked at Giles, and he couldn't help but smile back. "Anyway, you sure you don't want me to get you a laptop or something?"

"No. I don't want to have to mess with a printer or computer discs."

"Thumb drives"

"Whatever. The typewriter sounds perfect. I'll need a ream of paper, too."

"Take a look out in the store. If you don't see what you need I'll have Ron pick up something for you at the drugstore."

They both stood, and Giles reached into his pocket and took out his money clip.

"Put that away," Ray said sternly. "You can pay for the paper on your way out. Typewriter rental's free."

They walked back to Ray's garage, where he dug out a dusty machine from a storage closet. Giles grinned. It was an IBM Selectric, much like the one he used to own. Ray draped the cord over the top and said, "There you go."

Giles hefted the machine under his arm and followed Ray back out to the front room.

"I really appreciated this, Ray."

"No problem, Giles. Take care. I'll see you Monday."

"Okay."

Ray opened the door for him and Giles walked out through the store.

"You need a hand with that, Mr. Barrett?"

"No thanks, Ron. But could you see if you have any typing paper around?"

"You bet."

Giles put the typewriter in the car and when he came back inside Ron had a package of low-grade filler paper on the counter. It wasn't the optimal choice, but it would be fine.

"I also need to make a phone call, Ron."

Ron reached back to pick up the cordless phone and set it on the counter in front of Giles.

"Do you have a piece of paper and a pen?"

"Sure."

Ron pushed them across the counter and Giles took out the card that was in his jacket pocket. He copied down the number and said, "Give this to your dad. It's a long distance call. Tell him to let me know what the charge is so I can pay him."

Ron smiled. "Good luck."

Giles shrugged. "Give it a try, anyway."

"All right."

Giles dialed the number. As he had hoped, a voice messaging service answered. He left a brief message and then he hung up. After thanking Ron, he paid for the paper, ran back out through the drizzle and drove home. It was time to write another story.

Giles' entire body was tingling as he came in the front door with the typewriter. He set it down on the dining room table and quickly stripped off his jacket. The idea for the story had been subconsciously forming in his mind for the past two decades. He knew it was there; he just hadn't acknowledged its existence until now. Somewhere deep inside of him, though, he knew the day would come when he would have to write it.

Giles felt the comforting vibration and the quiet hum of the motor as he switched on the machine. It was old and battered, marked up and dirty, but somehow that seemed to make it just right. He rolled two sheets around the capstan and centered the carriage, then he realized he needed to make a fresh pot of coffee.

While he was in the kitchen grinding the beans he suddenly stopped what he was doing and ran out to the table. He typed the words, "Burial at Sea, by Giles Barrett," and then stood to look at his work. Giles laughed out loud and then went back to the kitchen to finish brewing.

With a steaming mug of coffee at his elbow, Giles was now ready to work. Part of him was surprised at how easily the words began to flow out of him, and yet he had almost expected nothing less. After all, this was going to be his masterpiece, the crowning achievement of a decidedly mediocre career.

He worked long into the afternoon, steadily turning out pages. Each of them was meticulous and unhurried, possibly the finest work he'd ever done. By the time he finished the fourteenth page he was beginning to tire. Giles pulled the sheets from the typewriter, shut down the machine, and headed for the couch.

When he awoke it was dark. Giles turned on a lamp and headed for the kitchen to make more coffee. He worked that way all weekend, writing until he tired, then sleeping. Saturday turned into Sunday, and as that second day ended Giles felt himself nearing the end of his tale. By the time the gray light of Monday morning seeped in through the windows Giles rolled page 83 out of the typewriter, set it on the pile next to him, and shut off the machine.

He was suddenly exhausted. Giles pushed himself up from the table and slowly made his way into the bedroom. After barely managing to get his clothes off, he climbed in between the sheets. Sleep did not come right away, but when it did, it was fast and deep.


"Is it really necessary to do that now? We're supposed to be on vacation, you know."

"Yes, I realize that, but if it's something important I need to make sure somebody can take care of it while I'm gone."

Karen Padovan wasn't buying it, but he also knew from experience that she didn't like to argue. "All right, but remember, Brian and Lisa are taking us to brunch this morning, business or no business."

"I know. I won't be long."

It was obvious from the look on her face that she didn't believe him.

"I promise."

Richard's wife left him alone in the guest bedroom of his brother's house, and went downstairs. Richard took out his briefcase and snapped it open on the bed, then he pulled out his cell phone and called his office in New York.

No one would be there on a Saturday, of course, he was simply calling his messaging service. He hadn't been in touch since before he'd driven to Hallowell and, as he'd suspected, there were a dozen messages. Ten of them were nuisance calls that he rerouted to his secretary's desk one by one. She could take care of them on Monday.

Amid these was one legitimate concern that he was going to have to handle himself, but that was nearly forgotten as he began to listen to the last message on the tape. It had been left only an hour ago. A distinctive voice said, "Hello, this is Giles Barrett."

Richard had been busily writing down the instructions he needed to give his secretary, but he let the pen fall on the pad. Then he sat up straight and leaned back on the pillows against the headboard to listen.

"Mr. Padovan, I've decided to reconsider your offer. What I needed to contact you about are some provisions of mine. Assuming those are met, I won't stand in the way of your publishing the book." Barrett then gave a number where a message could be left for him and signed off.

This was unexpected to say the least. Richard had already written off the book. There was no way in hell he was going to get permission to publish it if the author wasn't even behind it. Had it been some exploitative exposé where the publishing house could make more than enough in sales to offset the legal cost, it might be worth it. But a book of short stories by an obscure horror writer? No way. Deborah would kill the project dead as soon as she heard about his refusal.

But now . . . The thing to do was immediately drive back down to Hallowell and see what Barrett wanted. That made Richard grimace. Karen would kill him. She had things planned for the entire weekend. But Richard had spent his adolescence in the Seattle area and he was already bored—and they still had another week to go. Oh well, he thought, Giles Barrett won't be going anywhere. He could wait until Monday to drive back down and see what the old man wanted.

# Chapter Thirty

Giles wasn't sure what had caused him to wake him up until he heard it again. After another knock on the door he threw off the covers, slipped into a pair of sweats and a shirt, and went to answer it.

"Late night?" Ray said as he walked past Giles toward the kitchen.

"Late weekend. What time is it, anyway?"

Ray had a bag of groceries in each arm and deposited them on the counter. "One."

Giles shook his head and yawned. "You want some coffee?"

"Yeah, but I can't stay. Credit slip's in the bag."

Giles nodded. Ray simply charged whatever Giles purchased on his debit cart, and the bank transferred the funds. The paperless system that was just beginning to be used when Giles had moved back to Hallowell was now the rule rather than the exception. Checkbooks had become obsolete.

"How's the writing comin'?" Ray had wandered out to the dining room. Giles watched him from the doorway.

"Good. I'm almost finished. I should have the typewriter back to you next week."

Ray was unabashedly taking in the papers on the table. "No hurry."

"Did you want to read some of it, Ray?"

"No, no . . ." Ray looked up at Giles—arms folded over his

chest as he leaned on the door jam—realized he was being baited, and said, "I'll wait till the book comes out."

"All right. I'm going to put this stuff away. I'll see you later."

"See you, Giles."

Ray let himself out while Giles began to unload the sacks of groceries. He was just sticking a head of lettuce and a pint of half & half in the fridge when there was a knock on the door. Ray must have forgotten something, he thought.

"Come in!" he yelled.

Two tomatoes went onto the counter next to a loaf of bread, and he was frowning at the sorry state of the bell pepper Ray had delivered when a voice he didn't recognize came from the doorway. "Mr. Barrett?"

Giles turned to see Richard Padovan. "Well, I'll be damned. You fly out here from New York again?"

"Never left. I'm up in Seattle on vacation. I decided to drive down and see what you wanted."

"Well, that's even better. What I want, is for you to read what's out on the table there."

"Next to the typewriter?"

The two of them eyed each other momentarily and then Giles nodded. "Why don't you have a seat and get started. Can I get you a cup of coffee?"

Padovan hesitated.

"I'm making some anyway."

"Sure," he said, and then turned back toward the dining room table.

When Giles was finished with the groceries he brewed up a pot of coffee, filled two mugs, and brought them out to the living room. He set one of them on the table next to Padovan, who was so engrossed in the story that he barely mumbled a thanks. Giles sat across from him. Both of them were in the same position as last time, but with the overcast weather Padovan looked considerably more comfortable.

Giles sipped his coffee, content to watch Padovan read. He was taking his time, Giles noted with pleasure, each page gently removed from the front when it was finished and carefully placed in back. A little over two hours later, with Padovan's mug still untouched, he turned the last page.

Padovan didn't look at him right away. It was as though he were trying to assimilate what he had just read. His head was moving back and forth ever so slightly. With the story still in his lap, he reached over for the mug.

"Don't," Giles said, standing up. "Let me warm that up for you."

Giles poured the cold coffee into the sink and brought Padovan out a fresh cup. He was just about to speak when Giles cut him off. "What do you think?"

Richard Padovan contemplated the question for a moment, took a sip of coffee and then gathered his thoughts. "Well, I'm not sure I know what I think of it, but I can tell you how I feel."

Barrett nodded for him to continue.

"I've read a lot of your work, and I've truly enjoyed most of it. But this . . . It's unlike anything I've ever read, by anybody. I mean, the struggle in the plot is nothing compared to the struggle inherent in the language itself. It's as though . . .

"I want to say it's overwritten, but it seems to me that the extensive characterization is what makes the power of the ending possible. I mean, there are pages of stuff that really have no bearing on the plot whatsoever, and yet, if it wasn't there . . . It's what gives the story life. I think it's tremendous."

What he really wanted to say was to hell with putting this in the anthology, which is what he assumed Barrett wanted. Richard wanted to publish it as a novel.

"Has this been published before?"

"Nope."

He didn't think so. A story like this wouldn't have languished in an obscure magazine for long. Besides, sitting next to the typewriter the way it was, Richard figured Barrett had been working on it for some time. "When was it written?"

"This weekend."

"You're kidding me." Richard had assumed it was simply a revision, or the completion of something Barrett had started a while ago.

Barrett didn't respond. He just sat in his chair sipping coffee while Richard sank back into the couch. It was all he could do to keep from going crazy. When Deborah saw this, he might even be able to offer Barrett a contract for a novel. Jesus, that would be spectacular. This guy wasn't just a neo-classicist; he was the genuine article.

It was clear, however, that Barrett had his own agenda, and he planned on hearing him out.

"Does your publishing house own any magazines?" Barrett asked.

Richard felt his heart sink. He nodded warily. "About half-a-dozen, I think. But it's all done online now."

"Any that publish fiction?"

Richard set the story on the table next to him and pushed himself up to the edge of the couch leaning forward. "Yes."

"This is what I want. I want you to get in touch with one of the editors of those magazines and have him publish that story."

Richard frowned. "I'm not an agent, Mr. Barrett."

"Don't patronize me, Padovan—"

"Please, call me Rick."

Suddenly the conversation was at a standstill. Richard wasn't about to put up with anymore of Barrett's indignant artistic bullshit. If he couldn't handle that, too bad. Richard figured he might as well scrap the idea of a book deal. If he went back to Seattle now, all he would be out was the car rental and a little gas money.

And then Barrett chuckled. He was a crafty old man. He was probably willing to deal with Richard as an equal, but it didn't look as though he was going to give any ground.

"Okay, Rick. But don't get the wrong idea about why I showed you that story. This isn't a negotiation. Either you give me what I want or no deal."

Barrett held up a hand just as Richard was about to protest. "I know you can talk to one of your editors and cut a deal. I've been out of the business for a long time, but I know that part of it hasn't changed. Maybe you can publish an anthology for him, whatever, I don't care. What I need is for that story to be published in the next few months, and then you're free to do the book."

Richard sighed with frustration. "To be honest, Mr. Barrett, my first instinct is to publish this story as a novel."

Barrett laughed long and slow, then shook his head. "Under different circumstances, Rick, I would be delighted. But the timing is all wrong."

"The timing?"

"I can't wait a year or more to see that in print. It either needs to be published in the next few months . . . or I burn it."

"No," he responded a little too quickly. Suddenly the thought flickered in Richard's mind that he would take the story and kidnap it before he let Barrett put a match to it.

"You do this for me, and you can write your own ticket as far as I'm concerned."

Richard chewed on his lower lip, thinking. "Could I put this in the anthology afterword?"

"Absolutely."

"If I did that, I'd like to leave out 'Blood Oath.'"

Barrett laughed again. "Nothing would make me happier."

Richard pointed to the story. "I'll need to take this with me, to New York."

"I figured as much."

"I assume there's no digital copy," he said, looking over at the typewriter.

"I trust you, Rick."

Richard rubbed his fingers across his forehead. He was stalling for time, but there was really nothing else to think about. He'd already made the decision. "Okay, Mr. Barrett. You've got yourself a deal."

After walking Padovan to the door with the story and shaking his hand, Giles sent him on his way, with the proviso that he mail out a copy of the story as soon as he reached New York. Giles was definitely going to need it if everything was to come off as planned.

Padovan had been very perceptive about the piece. Though Giles had written it alone, without the possession, it had been a struggle. The fact that he had succeeded was testament to the empowerment he was now beginning to feel over this thing. The struggle that Padovan had seen on the paper was real. Giles had wrestled with the possession, not letting it in, not letting it take control of the writing process.

He looked at the typewriter as he was bringing the mugs out to the kitchen. Once he had deposited the cups in the sink, he went back out to the dining room and unplugged the machine. After wrapping up the cord he hefted the whole thing out to the living room and set it by the door. Then he went back into the kitchen and brought back a pair of scissors.

Giles opened them up and stuck one of the loops of the power cord in between the blades. With a little effort and three attempts, he was able to see-saw the blades until he cut it in two. The ball of type came out of the carriage with only a couple of tugs, and he tossed it up and down in his hand on the way back to the kitchen to return the scissors.

Next, Giles walked to the back door and out onto the back porch. It had begun raining again and water was dribbling off the roof, already pooling down at the foot of the steps. Giles closed his eyes and, throwing side armed and slightly underhand, pitched the ball out into the bog. He listened to the slightly louder splash of it over the rain, then opened his eyes and headed back in the house.

He washed his hands in the kitchen sink, secure in the knowledge that he wouldn't be getting up in the middle of the night to write any other stories. He might have a handle on this thing, but there was no way he was going to trust it. Giles was taking no chances. He'd already planned on buying the Brooke's a new computer and a printer. He would have his lawyer purchase it online and have it delivered directly to the house so that Ray couldn't refuse it until it was too late.

After he dried his hands, Giles walked into the living room and lit a fire. Then he turned on the TV. Snow appeared on the screen and he powered up the VCR. You couldn't get reception out on the coast unless you had cable or a dish, which Giles didn't. He had no way of knowing whether the possession would kill somebody he'd only seen on television, but he wasn't taking any chances on that, either.

Against one wall of the room was a cabinet containing about five hundred video cassettes and DVDs. Movies, all of them, none had been filmed after nineteen sixty. He wanted to be sure all of the actors he watched in his free time were already dead. He was finally able to get a set of Hammer's Dracula films after Ray had mentioned in passing that Christopher Lee had died.

The films had been purchased online for him over the years, first by his parents and later by Ray. With a mischievous grin he plucked *The Lost Weekend* off the shelf and fed it into the machine. While the credits rolled, he went to the kitchen and poured himself a tall glass of tomato juice before settling into his chair to enjoy the film.

But he didn't really enjoy it. It was as entertaining as always, but because of what had transpired during the past week it suddenly wasn't enough. Giles had virtually stopped reading when he'd moved down to Hallowell. Not being able to write, reading had gone from being a pleasure to a torment. Films had always been his haven. But now, he wanted nothing more than to sit down in front of the fire with a good book.

When the movie was over he got up and replaced it with *The Sea Hawk*, one of the few Errol Flynn movies he owned, as Olivia de Havilland was still very much alive. Then he put another log on the fire and went to the kitchen to make supper. Giles reached into the fridge and took out two salmon steaks he had put in to thaw the day before. Whenever Ray went out to Westport he would usually bring back some seafood for Giles' freezer.

He was just putting water on to boil for the rice when there was a knock on the front door. Jesus, he thought, I've had more visitors in the last five hours than I've had in the last five years.

When he went out to see who it was, somehow he wasn't surprised to find Carrie Mueller standing on the porch, her hooded raincoat dripping with water.

"I know I shouldn't have come by like this," she said as he opened the door. "I'm sorry. If you want me to turn around and leave, that's fine."

Giles didn't say anything right away.

"I just want to talk."

As much as he wanted her to leave, Giles wanted Carrie to stay even more. "Come on in."

He helped her off with the raincoat and she stripped off her boots and left them by the door. "Taking this in for repairs?" she said, in reference to the typewriter.

"Something like that." He was actually planning on taking it to the dump.

"Are you hungry? I was just starting dinner."

"Starved," she said, and headed straight for the fire.

"I hope salmon's okay."

"Are you kidding?"

"Just checking."

Carrie rubbed her arms by the fire and took in the room, her gaze eventually falling on the TV set. She frowned for a moment. "*The Sea Hawk*, right?"

Giles nodded.

"Michael Curtiz was amazing."

"What? Don't tell me you're a film buff, too."

She shrugged. "I'm a librarian. I know a little bit about an awful lot. Can I help with dinner?"

While Carrie set the table Giles began boiling the rice and put the steaks on a broiler pan. Carrie turned a dining room chair around to talk with him while he cooked. His pleasure at simply having her around was immense. She talked about work and he listened. When the rice was almost done, he slipped the salmon into the oven and steamed some spinach.

"You're pretty good at that."

"I should be. I've been doing it long enough."

"When did your parents die? If you don't mind my asking."

"No, that's okay. My mom died six years ago, my dad, two years before that."

"Was it hard for you?"

Giles was busy dishing up the plates, but eventually he got around to answering her question. "They didn't seem that old, at least not to me, but Dad had lung cancer—smoked all his life— and it took him pretty fast. Mom never recovered after that."

"I'm sorry," she said.

"You know, sometimes I think it's harder for me now than it was right after it happened. I'll be walking around the house and see a picture of them, and that's when it really hits me that I'll never see them again."

Giles brought the two steaming plates of food into the dining room and set them on the table. "Do you want something to drink?"

"I'll get it," she said, and came back with two glasses of water.

As they sat down and began eating, their conversation turned to more academic topics and Giles was pleased that he was able to contribute equally.

"Should I make some coffee?" he asked over their empty plates. She shook her head, and then he knew it was coming.

"We have to . . . I need to talk about Friday night, Giles."

He nodded. "All right."

Carrie took a drink of water first. "It's just that things seemed to be heading in a certain direction . . . and then suddenly they weren't. I know that I could rationalize what happened by saying that I misjudged what was going on, but it didn't feel like I did."

Giles had thought about how he was going to handle this, and there really seemed to be only one way out. "Listen, Carrie, you're a terrific woman and I'm glad we've become friends, but the age difference is just too much for it to be any more than—"

"Bullshit."

The comment was so understated that Giles laughed in spite of himself. "You're calling me a liar?"

"If the shoe fits . . . You're forgetting something, Giles. I was there. I mean, if you'd have called me up the next morning—or better yet, rolled over next to me in bed—and fed me that line, you'd have had a lot better chance of pulling it off.

"But that's not what happened. We were talking about that story you wrote, then I told you about Greg Drake, and *that's* when you decided to get cold feet. Now, I've been wracking my brain all weekend to figure out how all of that connects with you ditching me, but I haven't been able to come up with anything. I was hoping if I came out here that you'd be straight with me."

Giles rubbed his face and marveled again at her. "You don't beat around the bush, do you?"

"What good would that do me? But I guess if it's going to get me another chance with you, I'll consider it."

"No, please . . ." The frustration must have been evident in his face, because Carrie waited for him. "Could you accept it if I said it's just something I can't talk about right now?"

"This isn't about what I can or can't accept, Giles. This is about the truth, and if that's the truth then say it and stop trying to figure out what's going to placate me."

Giles found himself getting embarrassed, and angered at what he was doing to Carrie. She deserved better than that.

"All right, Carrie, I'm going to be straight with you. What happened Friday . . . My feelings toward you in that regard haven't changed. You're intelligent and beautiful and I enjoy your company more than I probably wanted to admit to myself. But the fact of the matter is that I can't continue to see you, as much as I'd like to. It has to do with my past."

"In Seattle."

He nodded. "No one really knows what happened to me up there, and I plan on making sure that no one ever does."

She frowned. "Do you think that's healthy, keeping everything inside like that?"

"It's a moot point, because I'll never tell anybody, ever."

Carrie looked at him for a long time across the table, her brow wrinkled with concern. Finally she leaned back. "I'm sorry to hear that. I was looking forward to seeing you again. You're a fascinating man, Giles."

With nothing else to say, Giles stood and began clearing the table. Carrie helped him and when they were in the kitchen he asked her again if she would like some coffee.

"No thanks, I'd better get going,"

He didn't disagree and they walked together to the door. Giles helped her on with her raincoat and braced her while she slipped into her boots. Before he could open the door, however, she put a hand on his arm and turned him.

"I've only known you for a short time, Giles, but I'm going to miss you. If you ever change your mind, promise you'll call me, okay?"

"I promise."

He opened the door and Carrie stepped out onto the porch. Then she turned to him, lifted her face to his and kissed him full on the lips. Before he could even say goodbye, she turned and ran down the steps into the rainy night.

"What the hell happened to the typewriter?"

Giles took one of the bags from Ray and headed back toward the kitchen. He set the bag on the counter and said, "I was taking it out to the car and I dropped it. I'm sorry, Ray, but I didn't think you'd be able to get it repaired, much less find parts."

"So what makes you think you owe me a computer?"

"I owe you a lot more than a computer." Giles reached out and took the other bag from Ray. "And I'm not going to hear any arguments otherwise."

"Okay, Giles. Thanks." Ray snorted a laugh and shook his head. "I thought Jeannie was going to wet her pants, she was so excited."

That broke up both of them.

"Well, if you need anything else, you let me know."

"Sure thing. Oh, that reminds me, you got a call this morning."

"Who was it?"

Ray grinned. "That guy from New York. Wants you to call him. Today, if possible, he says. Before four, his time."

Giles checked his watch. He was going to have to hurry to reach Padovan in time. "You heading back to the house?"

"No, but Jeannie is there. I'd ask you to help her set up that computer, but she already had the damn thing up and running before I left."

Giles put away his groceries as fast as he could and then drove into town. It was two weeks to the day after he'd last met with Padovan. He wondered if the call was good news or bad. One of Ray's day employees was at the counter in the store, so Giles pulled around to the front of the house.

He knocked on the door and a minute later when Jeannie answered she almost knocked him over trying to hug him. Then she grabbed him by the hand and dragged him into the den to show off her new toy. Giles was barely able to break away and get to the phone before one o'clock.

After going through the secretary, Padovan picked up on the second ring. "Hello?"

"Rick, this is Giles Barrett."

"Mr. Barrett, you just caught me."

"Please, call me Giles."

"Giles it is. I've got some good news. Your story is going to be in the summer issue of *Strange Stories*. It's a quarterly."

"Wasn't that the name of an old pulp magazine?"

"Yeah. It's a revival, like the new *Weird Tales.* We acquired the rights several years ago and it's done fairly well."

"Sounds good. That was pretty fast."

"Well, I called the editor last week and he said if the story was good it wouldn't be a problem, so I scanned it into my computer and sent it over. Needless to say, he loved it. I got a call from him this morning giving me the go ahead. Of course, I practically owe him my firstborn son now. I sure hope this is worth it."

"What do *you* think?"

After a moment's hesitation Padovan said, "Yeah, I guess it

is. Anyway, he wants the contract signed right away, and that's why I needed to talk to you. Considering your situation out there, what I thought we could do is have you sell the story to us first, for the book. I can date a contract for today and mail it out to you tomorrow. That will give me the power to sign the contract with the magazine myself. We don't have to do it that way, it's no big deal, but it will expedite matters."

"As long as it comes out in the magazine first."

"Oh, yes. I'll be selling the first serial rights to them."

"What about editing?"

Padovan laughed. "I talked to him about that and he felt the same way I did. He thought it was overly long, but couldn't come up with a way to cut it that makes any sense. Like I said, the magazine only appears online so there's no issue with room."

"What's the release date?"

"Oh, right. You wanted to know when it was going to be available. Let's see . . . I had it right here. Here it is, May 22nd."

"That's great, Rick. I really appreciate this."

"There's just one other thing."

"Yes?"

"I'd like to send you the contract for the anthology, and get that out of the way, too. I'll include a list of stories, and a royalty schedule, advance money—"

"No advance, okay?"

"Are you sure?"

"Positive."

"Okay. If there are any other changes you want once you see it, let me know and I'll shoot you a new contract. You can just throw the old one away."

"All right."

"Well, I guess that about does it. If you have any other questions, just give me a call."

"Thanks, Rick."

"Thank you, Giles. I'll be talking to you soon."

With that Giles hung up the phone. He looked over at Jeannie, hunched over her computer, and smiled. So far, so good.

Everything was falling into place. Now he just had to make the final preparations.

"Giles." Jeannie said his name with obvious frustration. "Can you tell me what this means?"

"Sure." Giles didn't know how much help he was going to be, but he pushed himself up off the arm of the couch and headed over to the desk.

His mind was still on the phone call from Padovan. It was February twenty-fourth today. In three months it would all be over.

# Chapter Thirty-One

Sun streaming in through her bedroom window woke up Carrie Mueller well before her alarm had a chance. She looked sleepily over at the clock. It was still an hour before she had to get up, but she decided that because of the weather she would get up early and walk to work.

Ajanta was at the foot of the bed, but as soon as Carrie sat up, she jumped down and ran for the kitchen. Breakfast, oh joy. She went to the bathroom first, and then into the kitchen to feed the cat.

After putting a scoop of food in Ajanta's bowl and giving her some fresh water, Carrie poured some water in a kettle for herself. She turned on the burner under it and then took out a mug and put in a bag of herbal tea. Out of the fridge came some apple butter for her toast, and then she peeled a banana and broke off a chunk and popped it into her mouth.

When her plate was full she sat at the kitchen table and ate lazily as she looked out the back window. All of her trees had now bloomed, the apple blossoms the last to arrive. She had several rhododendrons, a cherry tree, an apple tree and two pear trees. The fruit was small, when it produced fruit at all, but the flowers were gorgeous.

Her backyard was flooded with pink and red and white. With any luck she could get some time in her garden after work. Now that the weather was warmer and it was lighter in the evenings she took advantage of every minute she could to be outdoors.

When Carrie was finished with breakfast she put her dishes in the sink. Then she showered and dressed, and fixed herself a sandwich for lunch. She put it in her backpack—along with an apple and a couple bags of tea—said goodbye to Ajanta, and started out for work. She met a few kids walking the other way, toward school, but otherwise she had the residential streets to herself. The neighborhood was as familiar to her as the inside of her own house, and with the sun on her face and the smell of a new morning all around her she found herself at work far too soon.

The morning had gone by uneventfully until about eleven. Nancy answered the phone, and then told Carrie she had a call.

An unfamiliar male voice spoke when she answered. "Is this Carrie Mueller?"

"Yes?"

"Ms. Mueller, my name is Charles Elsdon. I'm an attorney here in town."

"Yes, I've seen your office."

"Good. I was wondering if there was a time today I could meet with you, informally? It would only take a few minutes."

Carrie's immediate reaction was dread. "What's this about?"

"I really can't say over the phone. That's why I'd very much like to see you in person. Would that be possible today?"

"Well . . . The only time I can really get away is during lunch."

"Would you like to meet somewhere for lunch?"

"I brought mine."

"Perfect. I'll have my secretary get something from the Hub and we can eat together in my office. What do you say?"

Carrie had planned on eating outside in the park, but from the sounds of things this was important. "All right. Is noon okay?"

"Perfect. I'll see you then."

After the call from Elsdon, Carrie's concentration was shot for the rest of the morning. She realized her worries were irrational but that did nothing to stop them, and it seemed like an eternity before the hour passed. Finally, just before noon, she picked up her backpack and headed out for the entrance.

"See you in a half hour," she called to Nancy.

"Have a nice lunch."

She told Nancy she would, but at this point she had no idea what it was going to be like.

Elsdon's office was only a block away and in a couple of minutes she was pushing open the front door of Stottlemeyer, Bikar, and Elsdon. The faint smell of fried food, corn beef, and onions assaulted her as soon as she stepped inside. A harried woman in her forties, wisps of hair escaping her bun, smiled bravely at Carrie. She remembered seeing the woman in the grocery store but she didn't know her name.

"Ms. Mueller?"

Carrie nodded, noting that the nameplate on her desk read, "Judy."

"Mr. Elsdon is expecting you. Go right in."

She followed the smell of French fries and grilled bread down the hall. The door to Elsdon's office was ajar and she pushed it open. He was just biting into a huge sandwich. Mayonnaise and melted cheese dripped out the opposite end onto a foil wrapper spread out on his desk. Next to it was an oil-spotted bag of French fries and a large red and white swirled cup of Coke, heavily beaded with condensation.

"Mmpf, mmpf," Eldson grunted, waving her inside with a greasy hand. While he chewed he set down the sandwich and wiped his hands with a paper napkin. The smell was so claustrophobic, in spite of the relative spaciousness of the office, that Carrie thought she might get sick. It certainly put her in no mood to eat.

Elsdon finally swallowed and said, "Sit down, please."

Carrie sat and waited while Elsdon took a long pull on the straw of his Coke and then muffled a burp. "I'm so glad you could make it."

Other than the food the office was tasteful, decorated in earth tones, an Elton Bennett on one wall and pictures of his family on the otherwise Spartan desk.

"What's this about, Mr. Elsdon?"

"Just call me Chas, everyone does."

She nodded, but wasn't about to use that name. Elsdon was

about her age, a few gray hairs, okay-looking, tall from the looks of it, even sitting at his desk. Wedding band prominent on his left hand, he was wearing a blue pinstripe suit—jacket over the back of his chair—solid blue tie, and a white shirt that looked as if the collar were too tight. His face looked freshly shaved and she could just make out the alcohol scent of his aftershave even beneath the cloying odors of his lunch.

"The reason I asked you here," he said, wiping his mouth, "is highly confidential. In fact, I shouldn't even be telling you, but . . ." He frowned. "I don't know. Can you promise me that this meeting stays just between us?"

Carrie nodded intently. "Of course. What is it?"

"Are you acquainted with a man named Giles Barrett?"

The sound of his name ran through her like electricity. Though she'd tried not to think of him during the past three months, he usually wound up worming his way into her thoughts several times a week.

"I met him a few months ago. Why?"

"Then you *have* met him?"

She nodded. "Please, Mr. Elsdon, if you could just come to the point and fill me in afterward. I'm nervous enough as it is."

Elsdon frowned, clearly disappointed at having his big show undermined. "All right. Yesterday, out of the blue, Mr. Barrett called me on the phone. Evidently he usually deals with Les Stottlemeyer but he didn't know Les was out of town this month. Well, he wasn't very happy about that but he decided I would have to do. Lucky me.

"So, I get a call from him last night saying that he wants to see me, that night, at his place. Can you believe it? He says if I don't come out he'll raise holy hell with Les, which is the last thing I need, so I say okay. You know what he wanted? I get out there and he says he wants me to draw up his will.

"Had to be done that night, he says. So I say, fine. Well, I've heard about Barrett for years, mostly from my partners but from other people as well, only this was the first time I'd ever seen him. Have you ever been out to that place of his?"

Carrie nodded.

"Well, then you know what I'm talking about."

"What does this have to do with me?"

Elsdon regarded her across the desk for several long seconds. "You really don't know, do you?"

Exasperated and queasy, Carrie said, "Know what?"

"He left everything to you. The way Les talks, the guy's loaded, too. Of course, the way the will is made out there are no specific dollar amounts. The property, the house, the cars, you get everything, except for twenty-thousand dollars, which goes to Ray and Jeannie Brooke."

"The people who own the gas station?"

"Yeah, which makes sense in a weird sort of way, I mean, the guy has to eat and Brooke's right on the edge of town."

It took a minute for what Elsdon was saying to sink in. "Giles didn't die, did he?"

"Not that I know of. Like I said, just saw him last night."

"Then why are you telling me this?"

The frown returned. "I'm sorry to get you involved in my little breach of ethics, Carrie, but I didn't know what else to do."

Elsdon pushed his sandwich aside, popped a couple fries in his mouth and washed them down with Coke. "The thing is, people don't come in to have a will drawn up unless they have a good reason. I know that sounds stupid, somebody should be able to come in and have their will drawn up just because they want to, or just because it's the right thing to do, but that's not the way it plays out in real life.

"What really happens is somebody gets cancer, or someone in their family gets in a car wreck and dies, or someone they see on the news goes into a coma, or maybe their wife just nags them until they finally do it, whatever, but they *always* have a reason. And the thing about reasons is, it's no good having one unless you can tell somebody, and the somebody they always tell, without exception, is me."

Carrie still wasn't sure where all of this was going. Evidently

Charles Elsdon—make that Chas—wasn't used to getting to the point. "Did Giles tell you what his reason was?"

"No. I mean, I'm sitting there taking notes and finally I can't stand it any longer and I come right out and ask him. Know what he says?" Elsdon laughed, apparently at the memory. "None of your fucking business. Sorry, that's a direct quote. So you can see the dilemma I was in."

Carrie didn't, but if she let Elsdon ramble on long enough she assumed he would get to it eventually.

"I just figured that if you were already in his will anyway, then it wouldn't look like you were trying to ingratiate yourself. I'd do it myself, but he made it pretty clear that he doesn't like me very—"

"Do what?"

Elsdon looked at her with the most serious expression he must have had. "Find out why he thinks he's going to die."

"My God."

"Something strange is going on, Carrie. He's out there all alone. Nobody ever sees him, and now . . . He must be in bad shape to want to make out a will. Or he thinks it's bad, anyway. I'd just feel a lot better if somebody else knew, if somebody could check up on him. Maybe it's cancer, or AIDS, or God knows what, but whatever it is he shouldn't have to go through it alone. Do you think you could see your way clear to stop in and talk to him?"

"Yes, of course. I appreciate your telling me."

"And I'd appreciate your *not* telling anyone about this conversation, especially Mr. Barrett."

"No, of course not."

"That's great. I didn't get more than an hour's sleep last night trying to figure out what I was going to do about this. I feel a lot better now, though."

Carrie couldn't suppress a grin. "You're going to give your profession a bad name."

He shook his head. "I wouldn't worry about that. What I just told you constitutes a major ethics violation. I think that alone will keep me a member in good standing."

Carrie glanced at the clock on the wall behind Elsdon. Her lunch was almost over. "I'm sorry but I'm going to have to get back to work."

"Sure. Look, if you could let me know what's going on with him, nothing specific, I mean, just to let me know that things are okay, I'd appreciate that, too."

"Of course."

Elsdon stood and offered his hand across the desk. Carrie shook it and excused herself.

Back out into the spring sunshine Carrie breathed deeply. What was she going to do? She hadn't seen Giles since he'd kicked her out of his life. So why on earth had he put her in his will? Could she really just show up on his door and not look suspicious?

Carrie's stomach grumbled. She looked at her watch and decided she would have just enough time to eat her sandwich on the way back. Now that her nostrils were clear she was hungry again. As she sat outside the library and ate, she decided that she would have to drive out there tonight. What would happen at that point was anybody's guess. She would just have to improvise.

Carrie Mueller knew one thing for certain, though, and as she folded up the empty piece of wax paper and placed it in her backpack she articulated that thought in her mind. She didn't want Giles Barrett to die.

The drive out Highway 105 to Westport was as pleasant as Giles had ever seen it. He could smell the cool salt air coming in off the harbor and feel the heat of the morning sun as it streamed in through the open windows of the Pontiac. Traffic was light and he pushed the speed limit, taking the corners of the winding road as fast as safety would allow.

Giles had expected to be nervous when the day arrived, but he wasn't. The waiting had actually been the most difficult part. He wanted this thing to be over, and as he drove his mind went over the story that had appeared on computers and smart phones all over the country this morning. It was perfect.

He realized after the debacle with Don—make that, the

entity that looked like Don—how he had fucked up. Giles had left nothing to chance this time, not to mention the fact that he had also managed to write a pretty good story. But now it was show time and, butterflies or not, it was time to mount the stage. One way or another, after today, it was all going to be over.

He must have been on the phone at Ray's half a dozen times in the past week, talking to the marina out in Westport, checking in with Padovan, and getting his affairs in order. Last night he had completed the final task and had slept like a baby.

The highway made a ninety-degree right before heading into downtown Westport and he had to pass through the center of town, restaurants, fishing and tackle stores, the outdoor market, before the road finally swung left toward the marina. Giles pulled into the marina parking lot alongside an ancient blue Geo Metro, out of which stepped a grinning Ron Brooke. From the passenger side emerged Ron's wife Gale, and the two of them waited with their arms around each other.

Giles pulled a duffel bag off of the passenger seat, and after getting out of the Pontiac he threw his keys to Ron. He caught them deftly with one hand and released Gale to come up and talk with Giles.

"You going to make it back to the store in time?" Giles asked.

"Driving that baby? I'll have time to spare. I don't know how soon Gale's going to make it back, though."

Giles watched her glare at Ron's back while she climbed behind the wheel of the Geo. "Thanks for helping me out, Ron. You remember what to do?"

"Drive the car back to your place, lock it up, and leave the keys in the mailbox. No problem."

Giles nodded and pulled out his money clip. He peeled off two one-hundred dollar bills and handed them to Ron. Ron's eyes widened as he accepted them. "You told me fifty bucks, Mr. Barrett."

"Yeah, well, this is how much it's worth to me, as long as you promise me you won't tell your dad."

Ron laughed. "You got it."

"Take your wife out to a nice restaurant." He clapped Ron on the back and watched as the two of them pulled out in their separate cars and headed south back toward Hallowell. Then Giles turned and walked up to the boathouse of the marina.

A bell tinkled over the door as Giles entered and a bearded man in a plaid shirt and a stocking cap looked up from his morning paper. He squinted at Giles and said, "Barrett, right?"

"Yeah, that's right."

"Rusty Stasiek," he said, offering a thin but heavily calloused hand which Giles shook. "I was the one you talked to on the phone."

Stasiek was five-eight, thin and wiry and looked like he was no more than twenty-five. Which, with Giles' uncanny ability to guess age, meant that he could be anywhere from fifteen to forty.

"Is the boat ready?"

"Fifty-foot trawler, gassed up and ready to go. You sure you can handle that thing by yourself? I can send someone out there with you, no problem. Wouldn't cost you extra, either."

"No thanks. I'll be fine."

"All right. If I can just get you to sign a couple of things you can have the keys and get started. It's too early for salmon, but I guess you know that. Should be some good bottom fishing, though."

Giles took a cursory glance through the contract and, satisfied that Rusty would be fully compensated for the loss of the boat should anything happen, put his name to it. Then Giles took out his money clip and laid out twelve one-hundred dollar bills on the counter, six hundred a day.

"Okay then," said Stasiek, "That about covers it. Come on back with me."

Giles picked up his duffel bag and walked out the rear door of the boathouse. Stasiek pointed down the dock. "There she is, the *Shaw*," he said, and they walked toward it together.

Seagulls flew lazily around the marina, and the smell of fish and saltwater was thick in Giles' nostrils. There was only a mild breeze and the swells were gentle. A frothy brine clung to the sides of the boats as the two of them walked the silvery wooden length of the dock until the *Shaw* came fully into view.

It was perfect—gray and weather-beaten, it sported a jutting bow that tailed off into a flat stern. In between was a raised helm with fishing poles surrounding it like naked ribs. Giles walked across the gangplank ahead of Stasiek and then waited while he climbed up to the helm. Stasiek started up the motor and let it run while he showed Giles around the rest of the boat.

Down below in the cabin Stasiek pointed out the radio. "If you get into trouble just flip this thing on and start squawkin'. It's set to the frequency in the boathouse. I keep the radio up there on all the time so you don't have to worry."

Then he looked at Giles and scratched at the sparse strands of hair that constituted his beard. "You really gonna spend the night out there?"

"Sure. Cuts down on travel time. That way I don't spend half a day going back and forth."

Stasiek nodded. "I guess. Only reason I ask is that you didn't bring a sleeping bag."

Shit. Not that it was any of his business, but Giles didn't plan on doing any sleeping on this trip. He looked around and then pointed to an orange life jacket. "No need. I just put one of those under my head and I can sleep anywhere."

"Okay, it's your ass. Long as you don't mind freezin' it off I guess I don't either. Well, that's it, then. You want me to throw the bow lines for you?"

"Yes. Thank you."

"You bet."

Giles stowed his duffel ban in the cabin and then climbed up to the helm as Stasiek pushed the gangplank onto the *Shaw* and untied the bow and the stern lines from the cleats on the dock. "See you in a couple of days," Stasiek shouted over the rumble of the engine.

Giles waved back and then pushed the throttle forward, easing the *Shaw* out into the gray rolling waves of the Pacific Ocean.

# Chapter Thirty-Two

What had begun as a near-perfect day had become a disaster by the time five o'clock rolled around. Not only did she have Giles on her mind but Carrie had to walk all the way home before she could do anything about him. As pleasant as the walk to work had been that morning, that's how bad it was coming home. Too many dogs, too much sun, and not enough time.

After her meeting with Elsdon she wanted nothing more than to drive out to see Giles, but she still had another four hours of work. Carrie was thankful for one thing, though: she had the morning shift this week. If not, she wouldn't have been able to see him until well after nine. As it was, she was nervous and distracted all afternoon.

When she finally reached her doorstep and let herself inside, Carrie began peeling off the layers of sweaty clothing she was wearing and dropped them to the floor on her way to the kitchen. Clad only in her underpants, she fed Ajanta and then hurried to the shower. The cold spray revived her—enough to where she could bear to climb back out again—and she hurriedly dressed and drove out to Giles' place.

The late afternoon sun slanted heavily into the drive as she turned down the path to his house. The Pontiac was parked out in front of the garage and the truck over to the side. She pulled up behind Giles' car and turned off the engine. He was probably looking out the window at her right now, wondering what the hell she wanted. She wished she knew.

Carrie still had no idea what she was going to say to him. While she was rushing to get there it hadn't much mattered, but now that she was here the whole thing seemed stupid. What was she supposed to say? Pardon me, Giles, I woke up this morning with a strange premonition that you're about to die. Any truth to the rumor?

She cursed inwardly and got out of the car. She would ask him how he was doing, tell him she'd been thinking of him—which was true—and if he kicked her out, so be it. She'd worry about the rest when the time came. If the time came.

Stepping up to the front door she knocked twice and waited. When no one answered she knocked again, loudly this time. No answer. Carrie walked down the porch and looked in through the windows into the dining room. He'd tidied up, that much was apparent, but she couldn't see him. She went back to the front door and banged on in this time—there was no bell—before walking down the porch in the other direction. The curtains were closed across the living room but she could just make out shapes through the sheer material. No Giles, though.

Carrie walked out to the stoop and was heading back to her car when she froze. Both the car and the truck were here. So where was Giles? The guy never went any—

And then the thought of the will began to creep up the back of her spine and into her brain. What if he was dying, right now, in his bedroom or something, maybe passed out on the kitchen floor. She ran back to the door and began banging it in earnest.

"Giles!" she yelled. "Are you in there, Giles? Open up. It's me, Carrie."

Still no answer. She ran down off the porch and around the house, but because of the marshy terrain of the bog, the house was built up so high that she couldn't see in the windows. Grabbing a rock on the way back around, this time when she reached the front door she broke out one of the panes of glass and let herself inside.

It was like a hotbox inside in the house. All of the windows were closed up tight and the air was barely breathable. She left the front door open and yelled again. "Giles, are you in here?" Still no answer. She checked the kitchen, and when he wasn't there she began to explore the rest of the house. Downstairs was his bedroom, empty. Upstairs there were a couple of empty rooms with boxes stored in them, a guest bedroom and a small bathroom. He wasn't there.

But far from feeling foolish, Carrie began to get angry. Where the hell was he if his vehicles were right outside? She supposed he could be tromping around the bog, but it seemed too late for that. It wasn't as if he wasn't allowed to be somewhere else, but to hear the townspeople talk the guy barely left his house. So why the library, and why the dinner at her place? It was that damned story.

She was sure that if she could figure out why it had upset him so much she could get a handle on the man himself. And, just maybe, they might have a chance to let what was obviously a shared attraction take hold.

Back downstairs, she went to the kitchen and hunted down a broom and a dustpan to sweep up the glass. But on her way to the front door she saw the neat pile of paper on the dining room table. Glancing at it she could see that it was a photocopy of a typewritten manuscript. Quickly she picked up the glass and swept the shards into the dustpan. After depositing them into the trash she went back to the story.

The first few pages went like wildfire. It was obviously fiction . . . and yet it wasn't. She continued to read, fascinated, hoping he would walk through the door at any moment, and at the same time hoping she could finish it first. Halfway through, she stood and walked to the kitchen. She poured herself some juice and walked back to the table.

It was written in first person, a journal, or log, of someone at sea. The narrator was a thinly disguised version of Giles. She could see that at once, even having known him for only a short time. Fascinated, she read on. The plot was disturbing, and when she finally finished she had to sit still for a while and digest what she had just read.

The sun was no longer streaming into the house, and the open door had cooled things off considerably. Carrie shivered. After getting up to shut the door she walked out back to find something to cover the broken window. All the while, thoughts were sifting through her head.

After locating his stash of paper bags, she folded one down to the proper size and taped it over the hole in the window. Yet she still couldn't escape the feeling that Giles wasn't coming back. But why not?

The answer had to be in the story about Greg Drake. Giles had written it before he'd moved back to Hallowell, and apparently hadn't been aware of Greg's murder until she'd told him. It was obvious from Giles' reaction that he hadn't been the killer, but what if he felt responsible for his death somehow because the name he happened to pick out of thin air was the same as her schoolmate?

In a weird way it began to look as though Giles intended to commit suicide. First he withdraws from her, then makes out a will, then apparently disappears. Carrie looked at the story on the table and couldn't help smiling. It was brilliant, *The Old Man and the Sea* in first person, only instead of a fish the old man duels with a demon. But in light of her recent thoughts, the pages on the table began to look less like a story and more like a suicide note.

Carrie stood, not quite panicked, but needing to take action. There was only one other person that she thought would have any idea where Giles was and she immediately headed out the door. Ten minutes later she was pulling into the parking lot of Brooke's Beachway Service.

After squinting into the sun for most of the day, Giles was almost relieved to see the bank of clouds that were rolling across the sky from the west. He hadn't prepared for rain, though, and he knew he'd regret it later. It also meant that he was going to have to get the boat ready tonight instead of waiting until the morning.

The long rolling swells of the ocean and the salt tang of the sea air, combined with the rumble of the engine and the diesel fumes had put Giles in a particularly good mood. A confident mood, he thought with some amusement. He could use it. He'd been charting a course due west all day long and he still had the night to go. Of course there was always the possibility of alternation to his finely tuned plan, but for some reason the thought didn't bother him.

It was strange. Though Giles knew much about this power that was inside of him, there was still so much he didn't know. The missing page in "Blood Oath," for instance. Would he really have been able to kill him—the Don-thing—if the last page had been published? His protagonist had certainly been able to kill Greg Drake, but that hadn't been until two years later, to a kid with the unfortunate luck of having the same name as the werewolf in his story.

The real question was whether Don would have been able to kill him instead. The one time he'd tried to manipulate this power had been a failure. And here he was trying his hand at it again. But there was one big difference this time, a difference that was bound to guarantee success. Regardless of what happened tonight or tomorrow morning, Giles would not be coming back alive.

Carrie walked into the tiny convenience store and looked behind the counter to her left. A tall, balding man in his late fifties was giving change to a teenager, and a woman was waiting behind the boy. Carrie wandered around the store for a few minutes until the woman left. Then she walked up to the counter.

"Something I can help you with, Miss?"

"Are you Ray Brooke?"

His face lit up as he nodded. "That, I am. I've seen you down to the library, haven't I?"

"Yes. My name's Carrie Mueller."

"You wouldn't be Kent Mueller's girl would you?"

Carrie's eyebrows raised. "That's right."

"So, where'd your folks end up after they moved away?"

"California," she muttered, still taken aback.

Brooke nodded as if mentally filing away the information, while Carrie took a breath and plunge ahead.

"You're friends with Giles Barrett, aren't you?"

Now Brooke's expression changed, and he suddenly became guarded and suspicious. "Where'd you ever get an idea like that?"

Carrie appreciated Brooke's response, but there was no time for fencing. "From Giles," she said.

"From Giles," he repeated. "You know Giles?"

She nodded, somehow embarrassed by the admission. "Yes. And now I'm worried that something has happened to him. He's not out at his place. His car is still there, but he's gone."

"What about the truck?"

"It's there too."

Brooke's mouth hung open in delighted surprise as he looked at her, then he shook his head grinned. "Well, I'll be damned. What do you know about that?"

It was obvious what he was thinking, but she didn't have time to formulate a denial. "Like I said, I'm pretty worried."

Brooke was already shaking his head. "No need to be. I know exactly where he is."

Relief flooded through her like a drug. "Could you tell me where? I'd really like to get in touch with him and make sure he's all right."

"Giles didn't tell you where he was going?"

She shook her head.

"Well, I don't know all the details—Giles isn't exactly forthcoming with his plans—but I'm sure you know that."

Carrie couldn't help returning his smile.

"The reason I know," he continued, "is that my boy, Ron, met him out there this morning."

Carrie frowned. "Out where?"

"Westport."

"Oh, no." Carrie's heart began to race. "Oh, shit." She looked at her watch and saw that it was nearly eight. "I've got to get out there. Where did he go?"

"Now hold on. Giles just went fishing, that's all."

"He's on a fishing boat, all right," she practically yelled, "but he's not fishing. He's heading for Japan and if I don't stop him he's going to die out there."

Ray wasn't smiling anymore. He eyed her for a few seconds before he worked up his mouth again. "Now, just what makes you say that?"

"Ray, I wish I had time to explain but I don't. I have every reason to believe he's not coming back on that boat. I don't care if I make a fool out of myself. If I get out there and he's tossing back a Bud and dangling a line over the side, great."

"Giles doesn't drink."

She shook her head. "Whatever. I may be wrong, but if I'm right and I don't do anything . . . Ray, please tell me where he went."

Ray licked his lips nervously, and she wasn't sure he was going to tell her.

"Please . . ."

He looked around as if he were afraid someone might overhear. "Ron met him out to the marina and drove his car back. I think he chartered a boat. Someone must be out there with him, though."

"No. He's alone. If you want to call the marina and check, fine. But I'm going out to rent a boat of my own and find him."

Ray reached a hand across the counter and grabbed her forearm. She looked up at him, about to demand her release, but the look on his face said something else and she waited.

"No," he said. "I've got a better idea."

A few minutes later the two of them were driving west in Ray's Buick Riviera. Ray was driving. They couldn't take her Honda because Ray didn't like to ride shotgun—his words.

"Are you sure about this, Ray?"

"Listen, I know this guy. If anyone can find Giles out there in the ocean, it's Marc."

They'd only gone a couple of blocks when Ray turned right and headed north of town. A minute later, past the empty saw mills and lumberyards, the road wound down along the water of the harbor and out to Bowers Field.

When Ray told her how much easier it would be to find Giles in a plane, she realized how stupid she'd been to think she could find him in another boat. Ray parked along the fence that guarded the single runway, and the two of them raced toward the small building that was the Bowers Field Terminal.

There were half a dozen people inside, and for some reason that surprised Carrie. She'd expected the place to be deserted. Ray obviously knew who he was looking for, and she followed him. Ray stopped in front of a desk and said, "Hi, Marc."

"Hey there, Ray. What brings you out here?"

Ray turned to Carrie and introduced her. "Marc Fontaine, this is Carrie Mueller, and she would like to procure your services for the evening."

The man behind the desk leaned forward. He had a full head of silver hair and a beard to match. Fontaine was probably in his mid-forties and had a thick muscular build. His high-pitched voice was incongruous with his appearance, but it was pleasant. "So, you want to get up for a little moonlight flight, huh?"

"Marc flew in the Iraq War," Ray interjected. "He knows his stuff."

Fontaine seemed irritated by Ray's disclosure, but stood up and walked around the desk. He stuck his hands in the pockets of his flight jacket and smiled at Carrie. "Well, I am free tonight, as it so happens, but there's not much daylight left. If you want to do some sightseeing it might be better tomorrow—"

"No, I need to go tonight. I need to find someone."

Fontaine looked from Carrie to Ray. "What is this, some kind of search and rescue mission?"

Carrie looked at Ray. Of all times to be mute, he chose now. "Exactly," she said.

"What's the story?"

"He's in a fishing boat and we think he might be in trouble."

"In the harbor?"

"No," Carrie said. "In the ocean, out at Westport."

Fontaine broke out in a high-pitched laugh. "Are you serious? It's going to be dark in a few minutes. What do you think you're going to see?"

Carrie's jaw clenched. "Money's no object."

Fontaine sobered up in a hurry. "Look, lady—"

"Carrie."

He rubbed his bearded chin and started again. "Look, Carrie. There's no way in hell to find whoever you're looking for in the middle of the ocean at night. And even if there was, I'm not going out over the ocean on this particular night."

"Why not?"

"Because, there's a storm headed right this way." Then he held out his hands, palms up. "And I don't do storms at night. I don't care how much you pay me."

Carrie turned from the two men and took a couple of steps away.

"Did you notify the coast guard?" she heard Fontaine ask Ray.

"No," she said angrily, turning back to him. "What are they going to do? He just left this morning."

"Has anyone tried to reach him by radio?"

She hadn't thought of that. "No."

"Look," Fontaine walked over to her. "Let's try to get in touch with him tonight by radio. If we can't, then I'll take you up tomorrow morning."

There was nothing else she could do. She felt helpless. It would be another seven or eight hours hours before they could even begin to look for him. She knew he wouldn't answer his radio, but there was no way she could explain that to these two men, both of whom were trying the best way they could to help her.

"What time is sunrise?" she asked.

"Five thirty-eight," Fontaine told her. "I usually get here around five thirty, if you want to leave then."

She nodded. "I'll be here at five."

Fontaine walked around to the other side of his desk and sat down. Then he picked up the phone. "Westport Marina?" he asked Ray. Ray nodded. "Then we'll call the Coast Guard after this. Maybe there's something they can do between now and then." Looking over at Carrie he said, "*I'll* be here at five-thirty," and began to dial.

# Chapter Thirty-Three

The choppy waves made it hard for Giles to keep his balance. Add to that the darkness he was working in, and he would be lucky to get any work done at all. The storm wasn't particularly severe, and had he been at home in front of the fire he would have hardly noticed it. But out here on the Pacific, the weather made itself known.

Giles' course had changed, too, with the onset of the storm. The waves were coming from the southwest, and it was either head into them or run back toward land. Giles had chosen the former and was now on a southerly course. So be it. He had far more important matters to tend to.

Down in the cabin he dug out his duffel bag and emptied the contents onto the small wooden bench. The rocking boat forced him to work one-handed so that he could hold on to the storage bay above his head. It was either that or fall down every time a wave struck the bow, lifting the *Shaw* on its crest and then slamming it down again.

On the bench were five bundles of dynamite, four sticks in each bundle, and a roll of duct tape. The two jerry cans of diesel were inside, and the door was doing an effective job of keeping out the rain and the seawater that was crashing over the sides. A leaky cabin would have made things much more difficult.

Giles looked around and when he spotted the radio he grinned. He hadn't so much as turned it on the entire trip. And he wasn't about to, not even to falsely reassure Stasiek. Rusty would find out soon enough, and right now there was work to do.

First, Giles taped one of the bundles of dynamite above his head, fuses hanging down. The next went up by the window, and the last on a support beam along the left well of the cabin. He probably should have put one of the charges below the waterline, but there was no way he could manage that with the storm. Besides, even if the boat didn't sink he was pretty sure he'd be killed in the blast. When he was finished he wired up each of the individual fuses to a long roll of cable and set the spool next to the detonator on the bench.

The dynamite had been a long shot, an extremely long shot. Giles hadn't even thought about it when he'd written the story, but then the story took place over a long two weeks and Giles didn't have that kind of time. He supposed he could have found a way to steal some or bribe a construction worker at a blast sight, but thankfully he hadn't needed to. One call had done the trick. It was to a gun shop in Tacoma.

The man who'd sold him a gun quite a few years back was still there. Giles had forgotten his name, but when he heard him say the name Walt over the phone he knew it was the same guy. The miracle was that Walt had remembered Giles too and, ironically, Daniel Lasky was the reason why.

Without going into details, Giles explained to Walt what he wanted to do. He didn't ask for an answer and they didn't even discuss price. Giles simply gave Walt his debit card number and told him that if he accepted, to take out his fee and deliver the merchandise to his garage in Hallowell. Then he left the door unlocked and waited.

A week later he heard a car pull into the driveway. Glancing sidelong between the curtains he saw the familiar form of Walt—now twenty years older—hoist himself out of a new Cadillac and deposit a duffle bag in the garage. Without even seeing anyone Walt gave a salute to the house as he got back in his car, and then he drove away. Checking his bank balance at Ray's a few days later, Giles found out his account had dropped by exactly one thousand dollars.

There had been a piece of notebook paper with a hand-drawn diagram inside the duffel bag and Giles was looking at it now as he connected wires in the center of the spool to the detonator. He was so absorbed in his work that he wasn't paying attention when the next wave picked up the *Shaw*. Suddenly the bow tipped down and Giles was thrown forward against the bulkhead.

Pain erupted inside his head as it slammed against the polished wood. Giles was on the floor rolling with the waves beneath the boat. His eyes wouldn't focus. He reached up to feel his head and his hand came away bloody. If there had been anything in his stomach he would have thrown it up. As it was, his stomach clenched several times, but he was able to keep from retching.

Then one of the jerry cans fell over and Giles pushed himself up to grab it. But as soon as he was on his knees he lost his equilibrium. His eyelids fluttered for a moment, and then he passed out.


"You gonna be all right?" Ray asked as they drove back to the gas station.

Carrie nodded but she couldn't look him in the eye. She didn't really know.

"Marc's a good man. If Giles is out there, Marc'll find him."

Carrie continued to look out the window. That was the real question, wasn't it? Was Giles actually out there, or was this all some hysterical hallucination that would amount to nothing? My God, she hoped so, but it sure didn't feel that way.

Ray pulled his car in beside hers and shut off the motor. "Well . . . I guess I'd better get inside."

Carrie looked over at him and saw how uncomfortable her introspection had made him. Ray opened his door and Carrie stopped him with a hand on his arm. "Ray?"

When he looked at her, she could see in his eyes how worried he was. It was silly of her not to understand that earlier. "Thank you, Ray . . . For believing me."

"Ah, hell, he's probably kicked back in his easy chair, drinking a beer and watching a movie."

Carrie smiled for what seemed like the first time all day. "Giles doesn't drink, remember?"

He smiled. "Oh, yeah."

"We'll find him, Ray. I promise."

He nodded and they both got out of the car. "You call me tomorrow," Ray said. "Either way, I've got to know."

She said she would and they said an awkward goodbye before Ray walked around front and into the store. Then Carrie climbed into her own car, but instead of driving home she headed straight out to Giles' place. She was praying the whole way that he would be there, that she was being stupid and silly about this whole thing. But when she turned into the driveway her heart sank: the house was dark.

It was then that she realized she hadn't even left a note about the broken window. Carrie parked behind the Pontiac again and got out. The note didn't matter. She knew in her heart that he was out on the ocean. There was no way he was coming back. But still, she was going to stay here anyway.

She had locked the door as she left and had to push out the brown paper that covered the windowpane and let herself back in. Despite the warm day, Carrie felt a sudden chill as she walked inside. No sooner had she started a fire than she began to hear raindrops on the roof. Sparse at first, they were soon coming down hard and fast.

She called out to Giles again, and then made another search of the house before she gave in to the grim reality. At least what she thought was the grim reality. The fire was warming the house fast, but when Carrie spotted the story on the table as she left the kitchen she felt even colder.

What could be inside a man to make him write something like that? She'd read horror stories all her life, but nothing like this. The fear inherent in the prose was almost palpable. She would have liked to read it again, but she couldn't. It was too disturbing.

He was in a boat out on the ocean that very moment, in a storm, and there wasn't a goddamn thing she could do about it.

Carrie was exhausted. It was only nine-thirty but it felt like two in the morning. And as tired as she was, she knew she still wouldn't be able to sleep. Her stomach was churning with emotion. She couldn't eat; she couldn't sleep; she was going to be a total wreck in the morning.

And that made her chuckle. She was a total wreck now. But she made herself rest. She pulled a quilt off of Giles' bed and sat in his easy chair as she watched the fire die down. Between the pops of burning wood she could hear the whistling of the wind around the house.

The warmth tired her quickly, and just before she nodded off she had one final thought. If Giles did die, she only hoped it was because the boat was never recovered. If they came upon the boat tomorrow and it was too late, she didn't think she could live with herself.

# Chapter Thirty-Four

Carrie woke with a start. The room was aglow with light and at first she didn't know where she was. When it finally came to her it was all at once. She was in Giles' house, and he hadn't come home. The light was coming from a lamp in the dining room. The windows were still dark. She looked at her watch: it was quarter to five.

The fire was cold and the quilt was pooled on her lap. Carrie pushed it aside and went to the kitchen to make some coffee. While it brewed she wandered the house, looking at the pictures of Giles and his parents. The place was modestly furnished, but there was something strange about it. It wasn't until she uncovered his video collection that the simultaneous discoveries hit her.

There was nothing to read. Giles didn't have any books or magazines anywhere that she could see. The film collection was an enigma as well. Everything was old, and not necessarily classics, either. *The Return of Dr.X? Dark Eyes of London?* Among the films like *Casablanca* and *Double Indemnity* were a lot of titles she'd never heard of. But there wasn't any more time to ponder that.

Carrie went out to the kitchen and, after rooting around, came up with a Thermos. She filled it with coffee, drank a quick cup herself, and about five minutes after five, headed for the airport. Outside, the rain had stopped but the wind was still gusting hard. Several times, even with the windbreak of trees along the road, the car shimmied and she had to fight to keep it under control.

Brooke's Beachway Service was probably open and Carrie thought about stopping in to talk to Ray, but decided she didn't have the time. She also didn't have the heart. First things first. Find Giles, and there would be time for everything else later. And then she moaned out loud. She'd forgotten about work. She would have to call the library and leave a message for Nancy that she wouldn't be in today.

As she pulled in next to the fence Carrie saw a light on in the terminal, so she got out and went inside. There was only one other person inside: Marc Fontaine, bent over his desk.

"I thought you said you didn't get here until five-thirty." It was only twenty after.

He looked up and flashed her a sheepish grin. "I said I'd *be* here at five-thirty." He looked up at the clock on the wall. "And I will be, in ten minutes. We can't leave for a half-hour and I didn't want you around here climbing the walls while I gassed up and drew up my flight plan."

Carrie had walked over to him. She stopped and nodded.

"Are you okay?" he asked her.

Instead of answering she held up the thermos. "I brought coffee."

"Hey, thanks a lot, but I don't think I'd better."

Carrie set the Thermos on the desk. "I thought all pilots drank coffee."

Fontaine laughed. "Sure, on the big commercial planes. But unless you brought along a catheter, I wouldn't recommend it."

"Oh." She hadn't thought about that. "Uh, now that you mention it—"

"Down the hall, there," he pointed. "On your left."

Their eyes met and he shrugged. Carrie turned and walked down the hall and into the restroom. After she was done and she'd washed her face and run her fingers through her hair, she called the library on her cell phone and left a message for Nancy. Then she went back out into the terminal.

"Well, I think we're all set," said Fontaine.

"Are you going to have trouble with the wind?"

"Yeah, I suppose. Not major trouble, or anything. It just means I'm going to have to pay closer attention to what I'm doing. Which means you'll probably have to do most of the spotting. I've got a couple different pairs of binoculars in the plane so you can take your pick."

"Okay." Carrie sat down across the desk from Fontaine, waiting for him to say it was time to go. "I know I probably should have asked this last night," she said. "But do you know how much this might cost me?"

Fontaine's brow furrowed as he rubbed his beard. "Well, seeing as how you're a friend of Ray's, and this is something of a mercy mission, I figure if you kick in for the fuel and Donny's time we'll be square."

"Who's Donny?"

"Today's my day to run the tower. Donny takes over on the days I'm off."

"And what about *your* time?"

"I wouldn't be doing this if I didn't want to."

She thought about that for a moment. "Ray said you flew in the Iraq War."

He turned away from her and his gaze wandered to the ceiling. He nodded.

"And after that?"

"After that I got out of the killing business."

"I'm sorry, I didn't mean to—"

"No, that's all right. It's just . . . I don't talk about it much."

She nodded. "Did you ever fly commercial jets?"

"Nah. I've got a wife, kids. I run the airport, do some charter flights out of here, and I can get in plenty of pleasure flying. I'm happy here."

"That's nice."

They were silent for a few moments more before Fontaine said, "So, how do you know Old Man Barrett?"

Carrie wasn't sure how to respond. "We're friends," was all she said.

He nodded. "And you think he's headed due west out of Westport?"

"Positive."

"All right. Well, here's what I have planned." He centered a map of the coast in front of her. "The currents, after you get about twenty miles out, are generally southerly. What I'd like to do is take a course west-southwest from Westport. We head out about a hundred miles—I don't think he could have gone more than seventy five—then turn due north for about ten miles. After that we can come back heading east-northeast.

"I'd say that's our best shot at finding him. If we don't, you'll have to decide what to do once we come back to refuel. We can head out due west, turn north a ways, but he'd have to be heading north to be up that way . . . To be honest with you, it's a crap shoot after that."

"I understand."

"Last night after you left I made another call to the guy who owns the marina out at Westport. He tried to get Barrett on the radio again, but there was no answer. This morning when I called him back he told me that he'd tried all night. He thinks Barrett's radio is off."

"Or underwater?"

"He didn't say that."

"Did he have to?"

Fontaine didn't respond but they were saved from an awkward silence by the sound of the wind coming in the door. Behind her Carrie heard the door open and she turned to see a clean-shaven man about her age walk in the door.

"She's all gassed up and ready to go."

"Hey, Donny," Fontaine called to him. "Thanks again for coming in."

"No problem. You expecting much traffic today?"

"Nope. Should be painless."

"When are you coming back in?"

"No way to know. Could be out all day. Can you cover that?"

"No problem."

"All right, then." Fontaine turned back to Carrie. "You ready?"

Carrie nodded.

He held the door for her as the two of them braced the wind and walked out onto the tarmac. As she buckled herself into the tiny cockpit of the twin-engine Cessna, Carrie felt as if the plane might break loose from its tentative hold on the earth and blow away. The wind came in whips and swirls and impossibly long gusts. Fontaine started up the plane and then began conversing in aeronautic jargon over the radio with Donny.

Meanwhile, Carrie picked up the two pairs of binoculars and tried them out. The largest pair, black with ten-inch scopes and rubber eye cushions, were the obvious choice. But she could feel that they would get heavy over the course of the day. Next she took out a smaller brown pair. It only took one glance through them at the milky grayness of the dawn to know they were the ones she would use.

Fontaine turned to her, gave her the thumbs up, and began taxiing out onto the runway. He was working furiously to keep the plane under control while they were on the ground. When he reached the end of the runway they sat for a long time not moving. She suspected that he was waiting for a favorable wind. Finally, just as the glow of the sun became perceptible above the covering of dark clouds, Fontaine began his takeoff.

The plane shook violently, so much so that Carrie felt endangered and gripped tightly to the handhold above the door, but as soon as the wheels left the ground, the ride smoothed out. Carrie had never been afraid of flying, but then she had always flown on commercial jets before. This was a whole new experience. Earlier, she thought she might have trouble staying awake, but it was clearly evident as the plane banked from its easterly takeoff around to the west that falling asleep would not be a concern.

The dark and fast moving cloud cover was like a low ceiling, and they hit several patches of rain as they flew above the white-capped water of Grays Harbor. Ten minutes later Fontaine tapped her on the shoulder and pointed down. Then he banked the plane so she could get a better look at Westport.

Here they were at last. There was nothing more to do but look and pray. "Please," she said out loud, unable to hear the sound of her own voice over the drone of the engines. "Let me find him."

# Chapter Thirty-Five

Giles regained consciousness to find himself coughing up seawater. His stomach muscles burned from exertion and his head throbbed so heavily with pain that he couldn't open his eyes immediately. He had only just realized that his clothes were soaking wet when he found himself buried by a wave of icy water.

He jerked up to a sitting position, his head flaring in pain. Giles spit out more seawater and raised his eyelids enough to see. The door to the cabin was swinging open, and eight inches of water was ebbing and flowing in the cabin, mirroring the movement of the boat. But worse than that, it was already daylight.

One of the compartments above him had opened and there was stuff everywhere. Both of the jerry cans had tipped over, but thankfully had stayed closed. The detonator was rolling around in the water, and though it was crucial to his plan Giles wasn't sure he had the energy to pick it up. Not only did his strength feel sapped, it was as though his will to proceed had abandoned him. That was immediately followed, from somewhere deep inside of him, by the comforting thought that if he just sat here long enough someone would eventually find him and take him home.

Entropy, it seemed, had paralyzed him. Pain shot through his head again and he pressed the heels of his hands against his eyes. The rocking of the boat suddenly made him lean over and retch. Giles continued to heave and heave until he began to lose consciousness again. By using every ounce of strength he had left, he was able to stop himself.

Then he noticed that the engine wasn't running. Down deep he found an extra reserve of energy and pulled himself up to a standing position. With one hand he hauled up the detonator, then fished for the spool of wire and set them both on the bench. The door to the cabin must have opened fairly recently, because while the floor was awash in water everything else seemed relatively dry.

Wedged between the wall of the cabin and the bench was the last bundle of dynamite, and Giles reached out to pick it up. He'd been planning on seeing if there was some way he could get it below deck, but now that the detonator was in doubt he would have to think of something else to do with it. He put the bundle inside his shirt and made his way out to the helm.

Wind nearly whipped the door from his hand as he left the cabin. Giles waited until the boat had tilted most of the water out and then slammed the door tight and latched it. The wind chill made him instantly colder, but it also helped to heighten his senses. He climbed the ladder to the helm, the salt spray stinging his eyes, and looked down at the console.

The wheel was still locked in position, but both the ignition and the autopilot were off—*turned* off from the looks of it. He had planned on running the *Shaw* until it was out of gas, so far out to sea that he couldn't get back in even if he'd wanted to. A glance at the fuel gauge told him that the engine must have been off most of the night. But that wasn't possible either.

Giles looked out over the ocean. With the gusting winds, the waves were small and choppy and the swell was three or four feet at most. Last night's eight foot swells surely would have upended the *Shaw* if it hadn't been running. And then he saw it. He squinted and rubbed his eyes but the apparition was still there: a distant strip of darkness on the horizon. He was in sight of land. How was this possible? It was almost as if someone had been onboard last night running the boat in the opposite direction.

A chill ran through him as he realized what must have happened. Giles raced down the ladder and into the cabin. He began to dump out one of the jerry cans but was too impatient and threw it to the floor half empty. Then he picked up the detonator and without a second thought, twisted the handle.

Nothing.

"Fuck," he yelled, and twisted it again. After two more unsuccessful attempts he threw it down in the five inches of diesel and water floating on the floor.

How was he going to detonate the goddamn dynamite? And then it came to him: flares. Giles began tearing through the compartments in the cabin, flinging away things as fast as he could grab them. Then he came upon a blue plastic case and pried it open. Inside was a gun and three flares. To his dismay Giles realized he'd been thinking of the wrong type of flares. The diesel was going to be tough to ignite; a road flare was what he needed.

The fumes from the fuel were making him sick. He was done with the cabin anyway, and he grabbed the duct tape and headed out to the aft deck. It took a few seconds to catch his balance with nothing to hang on to. Slowly, Giles made his way to the watertight compartments along the side of the boat and began systematically working his way through all of them until he hit the jackpot. In a plastic zip-lock bag were half a dozen road flares.

Quickly, Giles extracted a flare. He pulled out the bundle of dynamite from his shirt and began taping them together. He only hoped that it would detonate the rest of the dynamite before it blew the cabin apart.

"What do you think you're doing?"

Giles whirled around so fast that he fell to the deck and almost dropped the dynamite overboard. Though he knew someone else—correction, some *thing* else—must have been onboard last night, it still surprised him. Another surprise was the form it had chosen. Giles pushed himself up to a standing position. Across the deck of the ship he was looking at an absolute duplicate of himself, right down to the wet clothes and two-day beard.

"I'm killing you once and for all," Giles said, in answer to his double's question. "What the fuck does it look like?"

Giles expected the thing to burst out into a hideous laugh, but the look on his clone's face was one of incredulity. This thing was serious. "No," it said, its head shaking resolutely. "That's not going to happen."

Giles understood everything now. While he had spent the night unconscious in the cabin, the entity that lived inside of him had been stepping out. It had made up almost all of the distance Giles had gone the day before. And now it wasn't even going to let him die.

Once again, he'd screwed up. In the story he'd written the demon had been inside of him all right, but it had been a psychological demon. Whether the reader thought the entity was real or not depended on his interpretation as the protagonist slowly lost consciousness. If the reader thought the narrator was mad, it was obviously all in his mind. Naturally, Giles had written it from a literal viewpoint, but the subjectivity inherent in the story had been his mistake. In the story, the narrator starves to death. In real life, Giles had hoped to accelerate the process with TNT. But it didn't look like he was going to get the chance.

"What the fuck do you want with me?" Giles screamed at his image.

"What I've always wanted, Giles. For us to write stories together."

It was eerily like his episode with the Don-thing. Teamwork like this he could do without.

"Fuck you," Giles said wearily, and he reached up to pop the top off of the flare. "I'm breaking up the act."

The thing flew at him with such speed that Giles didn't even have time to blink. He thought he was going to be bowled over, but instead the thing seemed to meld right into him. As soon as the thing had assimilated into his body Giles fell to the deck.

The pain that he had felt when he awoke in the cabin was like a dull probe in comparison to the ice pick that stabbed his brain now. The wind was building, whipping across the stern as Giles writhed on the rocking deck. Soon he was screaming with abandon and flailing about, thoughts of the dynamite long forgotten.

The boat began slamming into the wave troughs as the swells

became bigger. Giles screamed again in agony, helpless as he watched the horror that his body had become. First, his clothing began to tear. Then, beneath the shreds of cloth that had been his pants, blood began to flow from every rent in the fabric. The realization why, nearly drove him mad.

His skin and muscle were splitting apart. Giles screamed as the pain worked its way up his body, and continued screaming even as the tendons in his neck popped and snapped. His eyes felt as if they were bursting and yet he could still see the grisly carnage of his open chest before him.

With his shirt and jacket in shreds, he could see the skin split down the middle and hear his ribs cracking. Whatever was inside of him was coming out. Soon, his bowels were spilling out of his abdomen onto the deck and suddenly, with a final jolt of electric pain, Giles was free.

It was several long minutes before the pain had subsided enough to where Giles could open his eyes. His clothing was still intact. He wasn't bleeding. He seemed to be fine but for one thing: he couldn't move.

It was as though he were in a catatonic state. Giles could feel the wind and hear the ocean, but could make no voluntary movements. And then he found himself laughing. His whole body shook with the effort. Tears streamed down his face. He could actually feel its absence. The thing that had been inside him, like a parasite all his life, was gone. Giles was finally free.

"Laugh all you want, because it won't last for long."

The voice was one of such chilling intensity that it nearly pushed Giles over the knife-edge from laughter to tears. He looked up to see the thing standing above him now. It looked as solid as the deck Giles was lying on. He'd touched the Don-thing, so he knew this was no ghost.

It towered over him, how tall he couldn't say. From his vantage point on the deck it looked perhaps eight or nine feet tall. But it wasn't any one shape, its body was constantly in motion, changing its shape many times a second. What it looked like more than anything was an undulating mass of human tissue. The only time he could really get a fix on it was when he recognized the flashes.

He saw Don, and what must have been Pam Dugan, the Golem, Christian Leavey, and even himself. And there were other characters from stories he'd forgotten he'd even written.

Since he'd just been laughing, Giles knew he could speak. "What do you want from me?"

"Only your ability to write."

"Fuck you—"

An arm whipped down and plucked Giles' limp body from the deck. Suddenly the catatonia was gone, and he could feel strength in his limbs again. But the thing held him like a rag doll, face to face, a foot above the deck. "Why me?" Giles breathed.

Something like a smile spread across the shifting mouths of the thing. Giles caught glimpses of rotted teeth and braces and fangs and pincers as each image shifted seamlessly into the next, almost faster than his eye could comprehend. "You were chosen because you were receptive."

"I didn't ask for this."

"Your wishes had nothing to do with it. You are weak, and therefore receptive."

The thing lowered him to the deck, and though Giles was standing on his own, he was unsure how much strength he really had. Out of the corner of his eye he could see the bundle of dynamite on the deck.

"You will go back and write," said the thing. "Or you will suffer."

"I believe you."

With the shape changing it was almost impossible to detect any kind of facial expression on the thing, but Giles would have sworn that he saw satisfaction in its multi-faces.

"But I'm going to have to decline."

Giles leapt across the deck and in the instant before the thing was on top of him, he hit the deck on his belly and was just able to pop the flare. The flame froze the thing for another partial second, and with what Giles figured was his last breath of life he skidded the bundle across the deck toward the open door of the cabin.

He grinned as he heard the whomp of the diesel igniting. And then something totally unexpected happened: the thing went after the dynamite. It was actually trying to save him, Giles realized, and he almost burst out laughing. Without Giles the thing would have to find somebody else. Or maybe there was nobody else.

Whatever the case, there was no time to think. Giles sucked in a lungful of air and dove over the side. He hadn't been in the water a second when he felt the concussion of the blast.

His body was numb from the cold, his eardrums could hear only silence after the explosion, and his eyes could make out nothing but the frothy blackness of the water that enveloped him. Giles had expected to die, but the one thing he hadn't expected was that he would die free. And with an almost joyous serenity, Giles slipped once again into the black void of unconsciousness.

# Chapter Thirty-Six

Carrie hadn't realized just how difficult it was going to be to spot Giles until they were actually out over the ocean. The few boats she'd seen on the way out had seemed tiny, even through the binoculars. From the plane, the Pacific was a vast tract of nothingness. The heavy cloud cover made things worse; it turned everything into a massive expanse of gray.

After only a few minutes Carrie began to worry that she might not be looking in the right direction, that perhaps they would fly right over the top of him while she was looking off into the distance. Fontaine had taken the slightly southern tack, she was sure, to afford her the best possible vantage point. The air was turbulent, and the sudden shuddering of the plane and abrupt losses of altitude were nerve wracking.

Not ten minutes into the flight she found herself pointing the binoculars over Fontaine's shoulder every few minutes just to make sure she wasn't missing anything on his side. She was suddenly extremely paranoid and sure that they had already missed him. And yet, realistically, he must be miles further out to sea. Carrie couldn't remember a time in her life when she'd been more frustrated.

Then, on one of her glances over Fontaine's shoulder she thought she saw something. It was difficult to pick out amid all the gray, but it looked like a tiny plume of smoke. She nudged Fontaine and pointed. He squinted in that direction, then turned back and shook his head. Carrie handed him the binoculars and he took another look.

Fontaine stripped off his headphones and shouted, "Looks like a fire. If I didn't know better I'd say it was an oil rig burn off."

"It's not?"

"No drilling off the Washington coast."

"I want to take a look," she yelled back.

A bemused look came over his face. "I thought you said he was heading out to sea? We're not even twenty miles out yet."

She shrugged. "I want to check it out."

Fontaine nodded and banked the plane a hard left. It took them ten more minutes before they reached the source of the smoke. As they approached the area it became clear what had caused the fire. In fact, they almost lost sight of it as the smoke began to dissipate.

When Fontaine had lowered the plane and it was close enough to view with the naked eye, they could see the flotsam of a destroyed vessel. It had been a fairly small ship, from the looks of the empty life vests and debris that were strewn across the water. Carrie felt her heart jump up to her throat as she looked over to Fontaine, but he was already busy talking on the radio.

They made two more passes, but Carrie saw no sign of life. She squeezed her eyes shut and still the tears came. This has to be it, she thought. She knew that this had been the boat Giles had chartered. She was too late.

# Chapter Thirty-Seven

At four o'clock Richard Padovan was clearing his desk and preparing to leave for the day when the Manila envelope caught his eye. It contained the original, typewritten manuscript of the latest Barrett story. In his anthology it was going to be in the leadoff position, and he sort of hoped the old man would forget that he had it. Over the last three months Richard had managed to do the layout for the book and one proofreading. The new story had been a real coup.

The old man still wouldn't consent to any biographical information, so Richard had to limit his introduction to a discussion of the works themselves. As it turned out, there had been plenty to write about. It was a nice piece, and he was proud to have written it for what he considered to be an important book.

On a whim, he decided to call Barrett's message phone and tell him he could expect a galley copy in the next couple of days. The phone rang for a long time and Richard looked at his watch. It was only one o'clock out west. He was about to hang up when someone answered. A woman's voice said hello.

"Hello. I'm calling from New York. I'm trying to reach Giles Barrett."

He waited for an answer, but there was only silence on the other end of the phone.

"I said I was calling for—"

"I heard you," the woman said. "You'd better talk to my husband."

Richard sat up at his desk wondering what was going on. A few seconds later a man answered. "Who is this?"

"My name is Richard Padovan, from New York. I'm calling for Giles Barrett."

"Jesus, Ricky, you gave us kind of a start."

"Who am I speaking with?"

"This is Ray Brooke."

Richard's eyes widened. He'd never talked to Ray when he'd called this number before. Besides, most of his business with Giles had been conducted by mail. He thought back to his first visit to Hallowell and wondered how well Ray actually knew Giles.

"I just wanted to leave a message for Giles, Ray. He gave me this number—"

"I'm afraid I have some bad news for you, Ricky." Ray waited a few beats and then continued. "Giles died yesterday."

"Oh, no."

"Yeah, it came as quite a shock to everyone around here, too."

"What happened?"

"A boating accident."

Richard's thoughts went immediately to the story. "Are you serious?"

He was about to ask Ray if Giles had died of starvation out in the middle of the Pacific when Ray answered his question.

"It was a fire. He was just a few miles offshore when the damn thing blew. They never found his body."

"What the hell was he doing out on a boat?"

Ray waited just long enough for Richard to become embarrassed that he'd asked, and then said, "Fishin', I suppose. I'm pretty sure he wasn't water skiing."

"Is there going to be a service?"

"Nothin' to bury. Wasn't many people who knew him around here, anyways. They'll probably just put an obit in the *Washingtonian* and call it good."

Richard didn't know what else to say. He thanked Ray and then hung up.

For a long time he sat at his desk trying to make some sense of what he'd just been told. In spite of everything that had happened, Richard was glad he had met Giles Barrett, but now the book had suddenly taken on a whole new relevance. A lump formed in his throat, and he knew that his work on the book still wasn't finished.

Richard turned on his computer and then took a glance at the calendar on his desk. Giles Barrett's passing was going to be commemorated by more than a tiny obituary in the *Washingtonian*. And with that, Richard Padovan began to write a new introduction.

*On May 23rd of this year, one of the most distinctive voices in horror fiction died. That voice belonged to Giles Barrett . . .*

# PART
# FOUR

# Out of the Darkness
# and Into the Light

I am certain of nothing but the holiness of the
heart's affections, and the truth of the imagination.

—John Keats
*Selected Letters*

# Chapter Thirty-Eight

The old man sat at a small outdoor table surrounded by palm trees and lush tropical vegetation. Off in the distance he could hear the murmur of waves and the sound of birds in the trees. The breeze coming in off the ocean was warm and humid.

The old man sat bare-chested and barefoot at the table, a pair of khaki shorts his only clothing. A long mane of silver hair cascaded down his back, and his face, freshly shaven, glistened in the late morning sun.

On the table sat an old manual typewriter and a ream of paper. A sheet of paper was rolled into the machine and he leaned forward and typed a couple of sentences. Then he sat back and read them. At his elbow was a glass of fresh mango juice, beaded with condensation. He picked it up and took a sip, then wrote another sentence and admired it.

From his left the old man heard the sound of children laughing. The sound came closer until he could hear the accompanying footsteps. He leaned back in his chair and waited until the two boys emerged from the greenery around him.

"Dad, you have to come and see this!"

The oldest boy's name was Kent; he was ten years old. His brother Kurt, at eight years old, stood beside him. Both of them had grins that threatened to reach around to the backs of their heads. Though each of them stood in a single spot they were in constant motion, one foot to the other, arms squirming beside their lithe little bodies.

The old man chuckled and pushed himself up from his chair. "What is it?"

"We don't know," said Kurt. "That's why you have to come and see it."

Kent's head bobbed in agreement.

The old man's body was thin and wiry, but still strong. His skin was dark, bronzed by years in the tropical sun, and he marveled again at how much the two boys looked like miniature versions of himself. Then he followed them into the foliage.

A few minutes later, after he had explained to the boys that the sea of lizards sunning themselves were called geckos, the old man was back at his typewriter. Then a door to his right slid open and the boy's mother, his wife, emerged from the rear of a small house.

"Can you take a break?" she asked.

"Sure."

Her blonde hair was tied back exposing her smooth, tanned face and bright blue eyes. She was wearing a flowered sleeveless dress and was carrying a book.

"The mail just came. I thought you'd like to see this."

She handed him the book and he smiled as he saw the cover. *The Dark Woods*, the title read, *A Mystery by Donald C. Holman.*

When he saw the look on her face he said, "They didn't send us a boxful again."

She nodded. "Twenty-five copies."

"I can't believe it. What are we going to do with twenty-five copies?"

She laughed and then leaned over to kiss him. "Should I send them over to that bookstore on Maui again?"

He nodded.

"Are the boys still out playing?"

"Yeah."

"Well, tell them it's almost time for lunch. You too, or are you going to eat out here?"

He thought for a second. "No, I'll come inside."

"Okay. Don't forget to tell the boys." She had turned to walk away and then suddenly stopped. "Oh, I almost forgot. Do you know what day this is?"

He grinned at her and nodded. "How could I forget," he said. "It's my birthday. May twenty-third."

Her eyes told him all he needed to know, and then Giles watched as Carrie walked back into the house.

It had become a tradition in the Barrett household to celebrate the day that Giles had been freed from his curse.

When he'd regained consciousness that day he never expected to be alive, much less see a plane circling overhead. He had held on to a life vest and what floating debris he could find, until twenty minutes later a boat manned by Ray Brooke and Rusty Stasiek picked him up out of the water.

There was no rational explanation for what he did next, but while he was recovering from the effects of mild hypothermia on the way back Giles decided to complete the metamorphosis that he felt he'd undergone. He wanted to end everything that was even remotely connected to his old life, and with Carrie and Ray's help he was able to do it.

Once the will had gone through probate and all of Giles' assets had been liquidated and placed in Carrie's name, the last vestige of his former life had finally been erased.

The thought of writing again hadn't even entered his mind until five years ago. The idea for a hard-boiled noir series set in nineteen-thirties Seattle had entered his mind fully blown. He'd picked up an old typewriter at a second hand store and begun to write in a deliberately slow and methodical way that pleased him so much it became addictive.

When Carrie finally convinced him to try and publish the first book, he decided to pay tribute to his friend and use Don's name as a pseudonym. He never expected the book to be published, much less for it to become as popular as it had. He was already working on the third book in the series. The fact that the reclusive "Donald Holman" never appeared in public only added to the series' appeal. It was also the lifestyle Giles preferred.

From the outside it may have looked as though he had

everything he could wish for. But the reality was, Giles felt as if his life was only ten years old. He had never really lived during his first tortured fifty-five years on the planet. He deserved every bit of happiness he could get from the years he had left, and he was going to take it.

He stood up and yelled. "Boys. Lunchtime."

A few seconds later the two of them burst out of the trees, breathless. Then, with an arm around the shoulder of each of his sons, Giles Barrett walked inside his home to share a meal with his family.

E.B.O. / May 24, 1991, Issaquah, WA
/ January 27, 1993, Bellevue, WA

# About the Author

Eric B. Olsen is the author of six works of fiction in three different genres. He has written a medical thriller entitled *Death's Head*, as well as the horror novel *Dark Imaginings*. He is also the author of three mystery novels, *Proximal to Murder* and *Death in the Dentist's Chair* featuring amateur sleuth Steve Raymond, D.D.S., and *The Seattle Changes* featuring private detective Ray Neslowe. In addition, he is the author of *If I Should Wake Before I Die*, a book of short horror fiction.

Today Mr. Olsen writes primarily non-fiction. His books include *The Death of Education*, an exposé of the public school system in America, *The Films of Jon Garcia: 2009-2013,* an analysis of the work of the acclaimed Portland independent filmmaker, and a collection of essays entitled *The Intellectual American*. Mr. Olsen lives in the Pacific Northwest with his wife.

Please visit the author's web site at https://sites.google.com/ericbolsenauthor/home or contact by email at neslowepublishing@gmail.com.

Printed in the United States
By Bookmasters